BABYLON BY THE SEA

The magnificent, multi-generational saga of dynasties driven—through the technicolor montage of motion picture, television, and rock music history—to the heights of fame . . . and the depths of oblivion.

Sucked irresistibly into the dark whirlpool of decadence, two influential Hollywood families are consumed by power, greed, and passion . . . and their compulsive desire to succeed—at any price.

Other Pinnacle Books by Pamela Wallace:

The Fires of Beltane
Caresse

WRITE FOR OUR FREE CATALOG

If there is a Pinnacle Book you want—and you cannot find it locally—it is available from us simply by sending the title and price plus 50¢ per order and 10¢ per copy to cover mailing and handling costs to:

Pinnacle Books, Inc.
Reader Service Department
2029 Century Park East
Los Angeles, California 90067

Please allow 4 weeks for delivery. New York State and California residents add applicable sales tax.

_____Check here if you want to receive our catalog regularly.

MALIBU COLONY

a novel by
Pamela Wallace

PINNACLE BOOKS   LOS ANGELES

This is a work of fiction. All the characters and events portrayed in this book are fictional, and any resemblance to real people or incidents is purely coincidental.

MALIBU COLONY

Copyright © 1980 by Pamela Wallace

All rights reserved, including the right to reproduce this book or portions thereof in any form.

An original Pinnacle Books edition, published for the first time anywhere.

First printing, September 1980

ISBN: 0-523-40873-0

Cover illustration by Norm Eastman

Printed in the United States of America

PINNACLE BOOKS, INC.
2029 Century Park East
Los Angeles, California 90067

Contents

1. Maggie—*Passion*, 1922–1936 — 5

2. Michael and Brendan—
   Love and Hate, 1953–1954 — 129

3. Shannon—*Survival*, 1976–1979 — 213

PROLOGUE

Maggie Jones lay awake in her loft bedroom, listening to the cock crowing in her mother's henyard. The Calaveras Street rooming house in Fresno was silent around her, except for the gaunt, hollow-cheeked Texas revivalist with the withered leg in the room below relentlessly pacing off some intimate horror visible only in his obsessed mind's eye. The rhythmic thump of his booted step, followed by the scrape of the trailing, twisted foot on the wooden floor, had begun in the deep of the night and continued unabated: Maggie was conscious of the sound but had long since shut it out. After eighteen years in the rooming house she'd become very good at shutting certain things out.

Through the tiny, hexagonal window near her bed, looking out beneath the crown of the roof, she could now see dawn coloring the eastern sky, silhouetting the craggy peaks of the Sierras, and could hear the distant whistle of the milk train coming up from the south of the county on schedule. It was time to go. She was fully dressed and had been for hours, waiting only for early daylight. The rooming house was not located in a neighborhood that was safe for a young woman alone and afoot in the dark. She arose quickly, grabbed the small suitcase and crossed to the door. There she paused for a last look around the tiny room and her few things, especially the books that had sustained her. She waited for a feeling to come, knowing that with any luck she would never set eyes on this place again. But nothing happened; the room had nothing to say to her. In a moment she closed the door on it.

In fact, she found, tiptoeing down the stairs of the sleeping house, none of it had anything to say to her. Maggie despised the rooming house, from the filthy spittoons on the landings to the cracked and yellow-stained porcelain in the communal bathrooms. But it was a mark of her that while she despised the house, she did not hate it. The distinction was important: it maintained her apartness, fortified her desperate conviction that she was in some fundamental way superior to these surroundings. Her life thus far had been spent entirely in the rooming house, cooking and cleaning up after a staggering cargo of broken human spirits: down-on-their-luck salesmen, over-the-hill show people, drifters, con men, an occasional prostitute . . . a gallery of characters, despair haunting their eyes. As she became older, and after she discovered the movies, Maggie thought of herself as a spectator in a nightmarish movie house, except the movie was incoherent, beginning nowhere and ending in the same place. But in her heart she knew it was no fantasy, and she also knew how easily it could swallow her up. She was determined not to let that happen.

The door to her mother's room on the second floor was ajar, and Maggie could see Sam Draper's trousers slung over the bedpost and hear his snoring. She slipped silently into the room and began to rifle the pockets of the trousers, shutting out the sour sleep smell emanating from the sheet-covered couple. Finally she found what she was looking for: Sam's money clip. It felt satisfyingly thick. He called it his "gamble," his stake for the nightly game in the little room in the back of the Southern Pacific station across the tracks.

Sam was the main reason she was leaving. For some weeks now she'd been conscious of his eyes following the movements of her body under her thin summer dresses. Then, the night before, coming in late from his game, he'd found her alone in the kitchen. He trapped her against the sink and drove his hand urgently under her skirt. They struggled silently, his breath hot on her cheek with the smell of mint and liquor, and his fingers prying insistently between her clenched thighs. She could have cried out for help, but she wouldn't do that. It would be an admission that she needed something from her mother and this place that caged her. He tried to place her hand on his trousers and desperately she spun away, her hand falling on the handle of a paring knife in the sink. Sam was reaching for her again when she slashed out, laying open the back of his hand from the base of his thumb to the pudgy knuckle of his ring finger. He froze, staring at the blood beginning to well from the cut, and his face drained of color. Suddenly he lashed out with his good hand, slapping her almost senseless. When her eyes swam back into focus, he was gone. She stared after him, her cheek red and stinging. It was not the first time a boarder had tried to have his way with her, but it was, she promised herself, the last time.

Dim, early morning light was pouring in the window as Maggie closed the door of her mother's room. She only regretted that she wouldn't be there to see Sam's face when he discovered his gamble was gone. With that she put Sam Draper out of her mind.

Her mother was not so easily dismissed, although she was almost equally responsible for Maggie's going. Maggie could forgive her mother all the transient faces she'd allowed into her bed. Maggie understood loneliness. But she could not forgive the other thing. Most of her brief life Maggie had been trying to win her mother's love. But lately she'd begun to realize that the love she sought was not there for her mother to give. And when she realized that she also realized there was no point in waiting around for a miracle.

But despite all of this Maggie clung to a guarded optimism. She knew she was bright and had the great good fortune of being quite beautiful. Besides that she was a realist, and possessed a realist's natural dignity and courage; she would not waste either on inconsequential matters. With Sam Draper's poker money in her purse, she felt well armed for her adventure.

As Maggie turned from her mother's room, she was startled to discover the ravaged eyes of the Texas revivalist fixed on her through the partially open door of his room. Feeling suddenly light, she abruptly squared her shoulders saucily and gave the haunted face a wink and a frank smile. Paranoiac alarm flashed in the eyes and the door closed quickly, leaving her alone in the hallway. Maggie ran softly down the remaining flight of stairs, smiling wryly. A lifetime in the rooming house had also forced her to develop a sense of humor.

At the Southern Pacific depot the stationmaster sold her

the ticket she asked for, lifting his eyebrows at the size of the roll of bills she produced from her purse, but saying nothing. Maggie stepped out onto the platform to await the 6:40 Daylight Limited south. The pinkening dawn promised to bring another scorching day, typical of the San Joaquin Valley in late summer. But this was her eighteenth birthday and Maggie would not be there to suffer through it.

She was going to Hollywood.

PART I

Maggie—Passion

1922-1936

CHAPTER 1

Maggie Jones stood in front of the Garden of Paradise Apartments, clutching her worn suitcase and a copy of the Los Angeles *Times*, and feeling frightened and utterly alone for the first time in her life. The buoyant confidence with which she'd left home that morning had suddenly abandoned her. A hot Santa Ana wind was blowing, its gusts bringing a stale, acrid smell of smoke and cinder; the night before a brushfire had swept over the hills above Laurel Canyon and from where she stood Maggie could see a few blackened crests, some still smouldering. For years afterwards, whenever that strange, soul-troubling wind sprang up, it would bring with it for Maggie a troubled image of herself standing timidly before the absurd, lemon-yellow, tile-roofed towers and cupolas of the Garden of Paradise on her first morning in Hollywood.

That morning was September 5, 1922, and Maggie was among the first wave of thousands of young women who in those years flocked to Hollywood, the slumbering little outstation surrounded by palm gardens and citrus groves.

A small group of East Coast tradesmen, immigrants and sons of immigrants, who knew a good thing in the nickelodeon when they saw it, were turning Hollywood into a vital, exuberant center of movie-making. Most of these young women, for all their dreaming and striving and sinning, would be used and discarded like so much waste paper; the stamp of Babylon was already firmly affixed on the infant industry. But Maggie, even as she stood on the hot, palm-fringed Sunset Boulevard sidewalk, was different from all those others: not because of her beauty, which was fresh and innocent with a special luminous quality, or even her talent, which was not so much a gift for drama as a product of her spirit and independence and all the other positive qualities of her personality, which the movie camera would one day single out, heighten, and intimately befriend. No, she was different from all those other girls whose chances of realizing their dreams were next to hopeless because, in Maggie's case, the events of the next twenty-four hours would make it almost impossible for her *not* to succeed, even beyond her own wildest fantasies.

But of course Maggie knew nothing of this as she stood on the sidewalk and frowned again at the *Times* ad, which read simply, "Actress will share bungalow, $5 per week." Maggie considered. The money was probably more than she could afford, but Sam's roll had counted out to $86 after train fare, a small fortune. Recalling Sam Draper refueled her resolution, and abruptly, with a firm step, she crossed the street toward the apartments. Walking through the Garden of Paradise courtyard she took in the low-slung, Spanish-style main building surrounded by smaller bungalows. Across the large pool a Mexican houseboy was lazily sweeping the sunny deck, and her eye fell on an overturned gin bottle and empty glasses, some of them lipstick-smeared, on a patio table.

Loud jazz music from a phonograph was coming through the open windows of Bungalow Nine and Maggie had to knock loudly twice before the phonograph was abruptly shut off. A moment later the door opened. A young woman stood there staring curiously at Maggie, blinking against the bright sunshine. In that first moment Maggie could see almost every thing there was to know about Lyla Moran.

Lyla was a pretty platinum blonde with round blue eyes and a cupid's bow of a mouth. Petite, barely five feet tall, but with a stunning figure, she looked attractive, not overly intelligent but generous and friendly.

"I guess you're here about the ad," Lyla began easily.

"Yes, I . . . that is, I just got into town, and . . ." Maggie stammered.

Lyla looked her up and down with a wry smile. "You just got into town? No kidding."

Maggie was suddenly very conscious of her cheap, cotton print dress and the cracks in her cardboard suitcase. She felt a surge of stubborn pride. "I have money."

Suddenly Lyla's half-mocking smile became warm, as though Maggie had passed some kind of mental inspection. "Hey, don't get your back up in such a hurry." She opened the door wider and stepped aside. "Come on in and look around."

The bungalow consisted of a small living room, a smaller kitchen with barely enough room for a tiny table, and two small bedrooms with a conecting bath. It was cramped, but Lyla had hung bright curtains and flower prints on the dingy walls in an effort to cheer up the place, and it worked.

"It's very nice," Maggie said politely.

"Actually it's a dump." Crossing to the kitchenette, Lyla moaned audibly, "Lord, am I hung over this morning."

"Did you go to a party?"

"Didn't have to. There's always a party going on around here somewhere." Lyla laughed. "You don't have any idea what kind of people hang out around this place. They're all in the business and they're all lushes, if not worse. And usually worse."

Maggie frowned. "What about Prohibition?"

Lyla spooned some baking soda into a glass of water. "I don't think anybody's heard about Prohibition out here yet. And they don't quit partying long enough for somebody to come along and break the news."

She cracked a raw egg into the milky brew. "Don't watch," Lyla cautioned, then closed her eyes and downed the concoction. Maggie stared at her. Lyla caught her look and forced a weak grin. "I know. And it tastes as awful as it looks. Still, it does work wonders."

Visibly freshened, Lyla dropped onto a chaise and waved vaguely in Maggie's direction. "Go ahead. Take a look around. See what you think."

Maggie, somewhat self-consciously, began to do so. As she inspected the apartment Lyla rambled on, "You should have been here last night. You missed all the excitement."

"What do you mean?"

"The *fire*. You heard about the big fire, didn't you? For heaven's sake, you can still smell it. Well, last night you could see it from the pool. The whole sky was all red and smoky and we could see the flames leaping across the canyons. Naturally everybody in this zoo was outside watching it, yelling and screaming and getting blinder by the hour ... it was better than the last reel of any Griffith movie you've ever seen." Lyla suddenly frowned. "It was crazy, if you want the truth. You'd think everybody wanted the whole town to burn down. Well, maybe we did."

Lyla shook off the somber thought. "Anyway, when the fire started down the hill, here come the cops—they wanted to evacuate the apartments." She laughed again. "But by then everybody was too drunk to evacuate anything. So we all took off our clothes and jumped into the pool and watched the rest of it from there."

Maggie couldn't help showing her shock. Lyla glanced at her and chuckled, "That's the kind of place this is, hon. Better you should know it early."

"But what happened?"

"Nothing." She glanced toward the bedroom. "In the pool, anyway."

"No, I meant about the fire."

Lyla shrugged. "The wind changed. That's Hollywood for you. Nothing but happy endings."

She gave Maggie a look. "Well, are you going to move in with me?"

Maggie hesitated only a moment. The Garden of Paradise wasn't quite what she'd expected but it was a considerably more cheerful prospect than the alternative, a dormitory at the YWCA. The rampant sexuality of the residents surprised her, but it was only a more open form of the things that went on in her mother's boarding house. Or the things that went on in her mother's own bed, for that matter. And besides, beneath Lyla's hard edge of cynicism and amorality there was an appealing humor and optimism— and a vulnerability—that appealed to Maggie. She smiled. "If you'll have me."

Lyla watched Maggie unpack the few things she'd thrown in her suitcase, which was actually one of Sam's old sample cases. Sam traveled in a line of home dental hygiene products and the case had a residual antiseptic smell about it, the same smell Sam had. It brought back a sharp memory of his mint breath on her neck and his hand searching insistently under her dress as he pinned her against the kitchen sink.

Lyla frowned, then crossed to open a window. "I was

fourteen when I came out here to get famous in the movies. How old are you?"

Maggie smiled, more sure of herself now. "How old do I look?"

Lyla arched her eyebrows. "Old enough. And then some."

"Good. I'm eighteen."

"I don't mean to butt in where it's not my business, but what happened at home? Family problems?"

Maggie wasn't eager to talk about it, but there was something guileless about Lyla that invited confidences. "My mother . . . she has a friend. A toothpaste salesman. He thought it would be fun if he could be my friend too."

Lyla nodded knowingly. "Oh, I get it. Why didn't you tell your mom to throw him out?"

"It wouldn't have done any good." Maggie forced a smile. "Anyway, at least his breath didn't smell."

Lyla laughed, looking at her with new regard. "You don't look tough. But you are, aren't you? I think you're going to do just fine."

Maggie shook her head. "What if I told you I don't have any idea where to start?"

"So what? Neither did I."

Maggie glanced at her. "But you *are* an actress, aren't you? You said so in the ad."

Lyla glanced up brightly. "You bet, kiddo. I've been in dozens of movies. Actually had a line to say in the last one. It was one of Sennett's comedies, and I said, 'Officer, arrest that man' just before somebody threw a pie in my face."

They both laughed easily, already feeling comfortable with each other. Maggie showed her the advertisement she'd circled in the *Times*. "I thought I'd begin by taking acting lessons—I mean after I get a job."

Lyla shook her head. "Forget the lessons. I couldn't tell you what they're looking for out there anymore than anyone else can. But acting ability comes somewhere between clean fingernails and good table manners."

Maggie frowned. "But you had to get started somehow. What did you do?"

Lyla shrugged. "What I usually do. I met a guy . . ." She caught Maggie's look, then changed the direction of the thought. "Look, you don't understand. Here you are. You just got off the train. What you don't know is how they put up all kinds of barriers. So you have to get around them somehow. So it's not like what you think. Not *just* like that, anyway. So—" Lyla stammered to a perplexed halt. Maggie suspected that "it" was indeed just exactly what she thought. Lyla gave up trying to explain. "Listen, Maggie, you're a smart girl and your mind's made up. I'm not going to try to argue with you because I know you wouldn't pay any attention. You're going to have to see for yourself."

Maggie glanced at her, disturbed not so much by what Lyla was saying as the tone it was said in. "See what for myself?"

"The way it is. The way it changes you. The way it changed Anna . . ."

"Anna? Who is Anna?"

"She was my roommate until last month. She got in trouble." Maggie frowned but Lyla shook her head. "Not pregnant. She got in trouble with opium."

Opium. The word rang with exotic familiarity in Maggie's mind. The traveling men who wandered through her mother's Fresno rooming house told her stories about opium, and she remembered the vial of belladonna in her mother's medicine cabinet, the concoction that made her mother's fleshy, pale skin seem to take on a glow and become almost translucent.

"What happened to Anna?"

Lyla shook her head. "She's dead. The police found her body under the pier in Santa Monica. There was a party at the beach and somehow she'd wandered down there. I guess she was in a fog. Towards the end she was in a fog most of the time."

"I'm sorry." Maggie glanced around the room where Anna had lived. Suddenly she felt very awkward, like an interloper.

Lyla shook off the memory. "I'll tell you, since that happened I haven't touched the stuff." Maggie gave Lyla a surprised look, but the older girl was already planning ahead. "Like I said, you'll just have to see for yourself. So for the next few days I want you to stick with me. I'll show you the town, help you meet some people. I won't promise you're going to thank me for it, but at least you won't have to ask how to get started in the movies."

That evening, as Maggie and Lyla were sitting down to plates of warmed-over spaghetti, Jimmy Knowland entered

Maggie's life, dressed in a powder-blue blazer, white ducks and deck shoes. A jaunty young man with pale blond hair and a boyish grin, he was almost a walking parody of idealized American youth. But his bright blue eyes were already beginning to show telltale signs of dissipation. He had been an actor, a talent scout, a writer, a producer, but always that marginal yet somehow agreeable kind of person whom those in power find useful. He and Lyla knew each other from an earlier picture; for a while they'd been lovers, but that had burnt out quickly, leaving in its place the sibling affection of two functional innocents who needed each other's support.

Jimmy eyed Maggie appreciatively as Lyla introduced them.

"Tell me, are you an actress or merely a stunningly beautiful common laborer?"

Maggie smiled. She recognized the tragically harmless, unprotected quality in Jimmy, yet could not help but like him. "Neither one. I'm unemployed."

He grinned. "Me too. Since we have so much in common, let's get married."

Lyla waved him to an unoccupied chair. "Why should she marry *you*? You're nobody. I'm going to see if I can get Goldwyn interested. I might even get a finder's fee for her. Have some spaghetti and keep your hands to yourself."

Jimmy eyed the food distastefully. "Spaghetti? Are you kidding? Do you have any idea what I have in my pocket?" He produced a heavy white envelope from a breast pocket and twirled it around in front of them. "This very expensively engaged piece of white paper is going to get all of us in to an evening of free eats, unlimited liquor, and sin according to individual taste."

Lyla snatched the envelope, then glanced up in surprise. "Wally Gordon's place? I don't believe it. What'd you have to do to get this?"

Jimmy grinned. "Don't ask. You're not old enough to know."

Maggie glanced back and forth between them. "Wally Gordon? You mean we're really going to Wally Gordon's house?"

She was immensely impressed and excited. Gordon was one of the biggest stars in Hollywood, the handsomest and most popular member of a group known as "daredevils" because their films featured daring stunts.

"We're not going to Wally Gordon's *house*, Maggie my dear," Lyla corrected her, excitement glittering in her eyes. "We're going to Wally Gordon's fabulously fabulous *estate*, which is where, if I'm not mistaken, everybody who is anybody will also be going tonight. This is what I was talking about. This is where you start getting started."

"But . . . but how?"

Lyla laughed. "By just *being* there. By just being *seen* there. Never mind. You'll see."

Jimmy checked his watch. "Hurry up, kids. The way those freeloaders eat up there, nothing'll be left but scraps."

Suddenly the evening was charged with excitement; Lyla was alive with reckless anticipation and Maggie found it contagious. Lyla propelled Maggie into her bedroom and began rummaging around in her closet.

"I've got just the thing for you to wear." She pulled out a long white evening gown studded with shimmering silver sequins and held it up for inspection. "It was a gift from a . . . uh . . . friend. He got my size wrong, though, and it's too long for me, but it should be just right for you. I think he bought it for his wife and it accidentally got sent to me." She laughed. "I always wondered what she ended up getting instead."

Lyla also took command of Maggie's face and hair; under her hands, and with a liberal application of shadow and rouge, Maggie saw herself rapidly transformed into a creature who approached in appearance the smouldering vamp currently the vogue in the magazines and movies. Lyla stepped back to study her handiwork with a judicious frown. "Well, at least we got the Fresno rubbed off. What do you think?"

Maggie stared in the mirror, completely startled, and said honestly, "I don't know."

Lyla grabbed a sequined purse. "Well, I do. That's The Look, and if a girl's going to get a break she'd better have it." She turned to the door. "Come on, Cinderella, before you turn back into a pumpkin."

Minutes later they were careening over the crest of the Hollywood Hills on Mulholland Drive, the three of them wedged into an expensive two-seater Bugatti that Jimmy had somehow managed to borrow for the evening. The road was little more than a treacherous lane snaking from hilltop to hilltop, and Jimmy hurled the little car into the dangerous curves with a gleeful abandon that had Maggie's heart pounding with excitement. An ocean breeze, cool and fresh smelling, had turned back the Santa Ana winds and settled the cinder dust from the fire of the previous evening; below them, spread out across the darkened plain stretching to the sea, outposts of twinkling lights marked the infant communities of the Los Angeles basin. Jimmy and Lyla were passing a bottle of gin between them; Maggie, caught up in the abandon, had taken the bottle when it was offered, but she was unaccustomed to the raw liquor and it burned like fire. Nevertheless she felt pleasantly flushed from the warmth spreading through her, heightening her anticipation of the events to come. She thought to herself, *On a night like this, anything can happen.*

The Bugatti's headlights cut the angle of a corner to reveal a massive iron gate set between stone battlements. A uniformed guard inspected the invitation Jimmy offered, then passed them on through. Beyond the gate a wide, curving brick drive carried them up to the portico of a three-story stone mansion, its windows ablaze with light. There was something almost medieval about the massive building and the spectacle took Maggie's breath away. Lyla nudged her with an elbow, prompting her to take the arm of the attendant who had opened the door for her. Another attendant slipped behind the wheel and whipped the Bugatti away to join a line of elegantly gleaming limousines and town cars parked further along the drive, many with uniformed chauffeurs idling nearby. As they walked up to the massive oaken doors they could hear a loud orchestra at work and raucous laughter from within. Jimmy winked at Maggie conspiratorially and whispered, "Abandon hope, all ye who enter here."

The doors opened, and it was as if they did indeed enter onto a netherworld built of Maggie's wildest fantasies. The first floor of interconnecting rooms was packed with glamourous people, spilling out of the high-ceilinged ballroom beyond the foyer. Maggie instantly recognized some of the most famous names in the film community: the childlike Mabel Normand, a cigarette waggling nervously between her fingers, chatting with almost manic intensity in a group which included Mack Sennett, the gravelly-voiced king of comedy, once Mabel's fiancé but now merely her director since she caught him in bed with her best friend; the matched set of Rudolph Valentino and the rumored lesbian, Natacha Rambova, both looking sleek and remote; Charlie Chaplin with the *very* young actress, Lita Grey; Gloria Swanson, looking like a queen in a three-thousand-dollar Parisian beaded gown . . . and on and on. Maggie felt like a child in a candy shop, looking excitedly from one treat to the next.

Jimmy steered the girls through the crowd toward a bar set up near the ballroom entry. "You girls get started. I've got to make a delivery." He disappeared in the crowd.

Maggie turned to Lyla. "A delivery? What was he talking about?"

Putting a drink in Maggie's hand, Lyla glanced about and then confided, "Wally, I'd guess. He's feeding an awful habit. Everybody says it's bound to kill him." Maggie frowned, still uncomprehending. Lyla sighed. "I mean *heroin*. Now forget I said anything about it. After all, we are Wally's guests."

But her eye had already fastened on a lean, intense young man in a tweed jacket who seemed to be lecturing a group of admirers near a blazing fireplace. "Look, there's Tod Browning. He's a director under contract to Bill Fox." She gave Maggie's arm an encouraging squeeze. "You're going to have to take care of yourself for a while. I'm going to work."

Maggie watched as Lyla gregariously joined the group at the fireplace, her eyes offering a frank invitation to the young director. In almost no time she whisked him off in the direction of the ballroom.

With Lyla gone the party swirled around Maggie. Suddenly the exhilaration was gone and she felt confused and alien among these glamourous people. The champagne she was sipping, on top of the gin she'd had in the car, was making her dizzy. She found herself backed into a corner next to a grand piano which was topped by a small golden casket. The music hammered wantonly in her ears; a few feet away a young woman, quite drunk, abruptly threw aside her blouse to shimmy bare-breasted and with complete abandon. The girl was hardly noticed by the throng. Maggie watched as a sleek woman in a scarlet dress slashed to her midriff casually lifted the lid of the gilded box atop the piano and dipped her fingers into the contents. A handsome young man of about Jimmy's age was the next to visit the piano. He spotted Maggie and smiled. "Care to join me?"

Maggie, encouraged, smiled back. "What is it?"

He chuckled. "What is it? It's opium, my dear. And the finest Benares blend, if I know Wally Gordon."

Maggie shook her head. "No thank you."

He shrugged. "Suit yourself."

She watched, fascinated, as the young man helped himself to a pinch of the contents. "What's your name?" He was looking at her out of the corner of his eye as he inhaled deeply.

"Maggie Jones."

He exhaled sharply and blinked as the narcotic registered a sudden effect. "Are you new in town?"

"Yes, just this morning." Suddenly she felt laughter welling up inside of her.

The young man frowned. "What's so funny?"

But she couldn't explain the sense of absurdity that had seized her; there she was, only one day away from a Fresno rooming house, standing in a Hollywood star's mansion trying to look like Clara Bow and exchanging civilities with a young man over a keg of opium.

"It's nothing," she managed to stammer. "I'm sorry."

But he was put off, obviously assuming that for whatever reason she was laughing at him. He drifted away, his feelings clearly ruffled. Lyla reappeared at Maggie's side, glancing after the young man.

"What'd you say to scare *him* off? That's Bill Haines—everybody says he's going to be the next Doug Fairbanks."

But Maggie was still trying to control her laughter. "I'm sorry. I didn't recognize him."

Lyla shook her head, puzzled, "Well, I'm glad you're having a good time. Listen, I'm going for a drive with Tod. Tell Jimmy I'll find my own way home."

The news sobered Maggie. "But—"

Lyla reassured her. "Don't worry, you'll be fine. And if I play my cards right this could be a big break for me." She started to go, then turned back. "And another thing, don't breathe a word of what I said about Wally, okay? Tod told me the studio has private detectives out tonight and Wally's got something up his sleeve that's going to make a big stink."

With that Lyla was gone, leaving Maggie puzzled and more than a little bit alarmed at the prospect of coping on

17

her own. She was glancing about for Jimmy Knowland a few minutes later when suddenly the lights went down, the orchestra sent up a fanfare and Wally Gordon, a surprisingly slight man dressed in an ochre smoking jacket and cravat, appeared in a pool of light on the second floor landing above the ballroom. A murmur of anticipation swept the crowd and there was a general surge in Gordon's direction. Maggie, pressed against a glass-doored cupboard which displayed a collection of antique snuffboxes, could make out the actor's chiseled features clearly, familiar from dozens of afternoons and evenings spent in the balcony of the Crest Palace in Fresno. Although Gordon seemed pale, with an almost glazed look in his eyes, his voice was firm and clear. It was the articulate voice of an intellignet, sensitive man, yet it was sharpened to a cruel edge of sarcasm. There was almost derision in the look he cast down over his assembled guests. He began, "Welcome, all of you, to my home."

A voice from below cracked, "Where'd you get that outfit, Wally? Left over from your last picture?"

There was a ripple of laughter. Smiling, Gordon continued, "Now we come to the reason I asked all of you here tonight. As you are well aware it was one year ago today that Roscoe Arbuckle, better known as Fatty to the filmgoing multitudes, overwhelmed by a heroic passion, carried one Miss Virginia Rappe off to his boudoir with the intent of having carnal knowledge of her."

At the mention of Arbuckle's name the crowd had grown deathly silent and Maggie felt alarm building all around her; this was what Lyla had meant when she said Gordon had something up his sleeve. She knew the Fatty Arbuckle story. Everyone did. It had been front-page news for months. The one-time funny man, known affectionately to his public as "The Prince of Whales," had not had a film publicly screened or distributed since the brutal death in San Francisco. But Maggie did not understand the connection of that incident with this party and these people. Suddenly Jimmy Knowland materialized beside her. He looked shaken. "Jimmy, what's going on?"

Jimmy shook his head. "Wally's committing suicide, that's all."

Gordon had paused for theatrical effect. Now he continued, "As scurrilous rumor has it, Fatty accomplished his amorous intent with the aid of a Coke bottle."

Now there were uncomfortable mutterings in the audience. But Gordon was obviously only beginning to enjoy himself.

"And, as you are all aware, the public stink raised by Miss Rappe's death summoned preachers to every pulpit and propelled the purity leagues into the streets. Suddenly the whole country realized that Hollywood is nothing less than a crawling nest of degenerate hedonists hellbent for whoopee. 'This must stop!' the cry went up. 'People out there are having a good time!' "

Maggie saw Gordon falter, wet his lips and then continue.

"And in face of that cry Messrs. Zukor, Laemmle, Fox, Selznick and the rest suddenly contracted mogul-panic, and we were given Master Censor Will Hays and the dread Doom Book."

The mention of the studio chiefs, whose names were familiar even to Maggie, sent a jolt of electricity through the audience. Now some of the guests tried to shout Gordon down. A general exodus began. Maggie gave Jimmy a look. "Are we going?"

He shook his head, exasperated. "I can't. He still owes me for . . ." he glanced at Maggie, ". . . for what I brought him. And after this stunt, if I don't get the money tonight I may not get it at all."

Gordon pressed on. "Yes, my friends, all of this sudden concern for morality in films we owe to one man. And in that spirit of appreciation I am going to have a small token of our respect and admiration delivered to Will Hays and his friends at the offices of the Motion Pictures Producers and Distributors of America."

He nodded to the orchestra and another fanfare went up. There was a gasp from what remained of the audience as another spotlight hit a large serving trolley which was being wheeled into the center of the ballroom by a team of waiters. Slowly revolving on a turntable atop the trolley was a giant Coca-Cola bottle, at least ten feet tall, carved of some sort of shimmering material. But instead of the familiar trademark, written in the familiar script were the words, "I love you, Virginia."

Suddenly there was a commotion in the foyer. Gordon frowned in that direction as abruptly the house lights were ignited and chandeliers blazed over Maggie's head. She turned with the others to stare at the entry where a man dressed in elegant evening clothes was standing silently and alone. He seemed to tower over everyone else because of the aura of strength and power that infused him.

Maggie realized immediately, *He isn't one of them.* But exactly what he was, she wasn't sure. Whatever, his presence sent a bolt of awe and fear through the company.

Gordon smiled wryly. "Hello, Ben. Glad you could drop by."

But the man's brilliant blue eyes were fixed on the serving trolley. He said quietly, "Get that thing out of here."

CHAPTER 2

In the silence that fell with the man's entry the waiters handling the trolley shot an inquiring look up at Gordon on the second floor landing. He nodded, and they obediently wheeled the grotesque display back toward the kitchen. All eyes, including Maggie's, followed the man as he crossed grimly to the staircase and started up to join Gordon. He took the actor by the arm and ushered him into an upstairs room without a backward glance, seemingly oblivious of the attention focused on him from below. The door closed behind them.

Maggie turned to Jimmy. "Who was that?"

Jimmy expelled a deep breath. "That's Ben Montgomery. And it's a good thing he showed up and not Sam Lendt." He put a reassuring hand on her shoulder. "Listen, I've still got some business with Wally once Montgomery finishes reading him off. I won't be long." He gave her a wink and added, "I hope."

Maggie stopped him, finally giving in to her feeling of helplessness. "Do you have to? I don't know how to talk to anybody."

He grinned. "Don't worry. In a minute there won't be anybody to talk to. This place is going to empty out like there was a fire upstairs. Which there may be by the time Montgomery finishes with Wally."

He left her standing there. Maggie glanced around to discover that Jimmy was right; the remaining guests were making haste to reach the door. Maggie, noticing a waiter giving her an odd look, and for want of anywhere else to go, made her way outside through the big French doors to a broad veranda overlooking an enormous pool ringed by a heavy Roman colonnade gleaming whitely in the moonlight. At the far end of the pool a man and a woman were engaged in loud conversation. Maggie frowned. They seemed to be arguing, although at that distance their voices reached her only in muffled snatches. The woman saw Maggie, and in a moment they disappeared into a darkened poolside cabana. Maggie waited for a light to come on, but none did. Perhaps the couple wasn't fighting after all.

The damp ocean breeze was invigorating after the almost claustrophobic tension of the events within the big house. A broad flight of marble steps led her down to the pool and as she dropped, suddenly exhausted, into a deck chair she wondered what words were being exchanged between Gordon and the strangely compelling man who had invaded his party and sent his guests scurrying. Although she didn't understand the nature of what had happened, she knew instinctively that she had witnessed a perilous sequence of events, which somehow was at the heart of all the wealth and glamour that had flaunted itself at the gathering. She sensed the desperation lurking beneath the glittering surface, familiar from the fabric of her own life. That particular terror had its own tangible scent whether you found it in a Fresno rooming house or a Hollywood mansion. But the man who was now closeted with Gordon represented something else: power, and the ability to manipulate power. Although she could not as yet define it, she knew that of all the people at the party she and that man had something in common that none of the others could remotely imagine.

Suddenly her thoughts were shattered by the sound of a shot, followed almost simultaneously by the sound of breaking glass. Maggie leaped to her feet as, at the opposite end of the pool, the man she'd seen earlier talking to the woman broke from the cabana. He rushed straight toward Maggie, wild-eyed and stumbling, a pistol dangling from one hand. In that instant, with time standing still, she saw him clearly: a young man, hardly older than herself, with dark circles under his eyes and madness burning within. Abruptly he stopped to stare at her, aware that she had seen him. The blazing eyes wavered with confusion, attempting to weigh her presence. For a moment she thought he was going to move on. But then his eyes locked with hers and she knew he had made a decision. He began to raise the pistol. He was going to kill her. Maggie started to scream, but her voice constricted in her throat.

"Jack!" The voice came from behind her and seemed to lash the boy like a whip. He froze, and Maggie turned to find the man, Montgomery, standing at the top of the steps, the lights of the big house in the background throwing his figure into silhouette. His face was impenetrable, but cold humor sounded in his voice. "Just how many of us are you willing to shoot, Jack?"

A harsh laugh, savaged by hysteria, seemed to erupt from the boy. "Maybe I'll get to you, Montgomery. How do you think my ol' man'd like that?"

Montgomery moved easily down the steps. "I imagine he'd like that just fine. But that's hardly the point, is it?" He stopped only inches in front of the wavering muzzle of the pistol. Maggie held her breath as Montgomery calmly looked the boy over, and then said with utter confidence, "Don't shoot me, Jack. Because I'm the only one left in this world who can help you now. And I think you know that."

Jack managed to keep the pistol level for a moment longer as the words penetrated; then the burning eyes dampened and the face went slack. Montgomery reached out and took the pistol as it was dropping from the boy's fingers. "Good."

There was a sudden commotion of voices from the veranda and figures appeared at the top of the steps. Montgomery turned and snapped, "Stay back, all of you! Wally, don't let anyone leave until we talk."

Gordon's sobered voice reached them. "All right, Ben."

Montgomery turned back to the suddenly hollow figure of the boy. "Now, Jack, I want you to show me what you've done this time."

The boy nodded numbly and started back toward the cabana. Then, for the first time, Montgomery seemed to notice Maggie. He looked at her curiously, as though she were a component that did not fit the equation he was forming in his mind. "I think maybe you'd better come, too." She followed him without thinking, as if her legs were instruments of his will.

The shot had sent the woman crashing out through the window of the cabana. She lay sprawled across the sill, her head thrown back, exposing her slim, pale throat, her dead eyes staring sightlessly into the moonlight. Maggie could see locks of her blonde hair tangled in the unpruned vines of a climbing rose outside the window. Even in death there was a hardness in the woman's features; it was the face of a cruel, selfish woman who would prey on weakness wherever she found it. It was also a face that would be etched in Maggie's memory for the rest of her life, to come swimming up from the depths of her subconscious at random moments: in dreams, as she strolled down a sidewalk, and most terrifying of all, superimposed over her own face as she sat in darkened screening rooms viewing her own performances.

Maggie held back as Montgomery knelt next to the girl to feel for a pulse, a wave of dizziness suddenly turning her knees to jelly. It was not just the dead girl; it was the whole sequence of fantastic events which had brought her in one short day to this moment. But she refused to show weakness in front of Montgomery. By the time he rose from the dead girl's side, Maggie was herself again.

He turned to the boy, rubbing his fingers together absently as though the touch of the lifeless flesh had left something there he was trying to erase. "Ellie Wade."

Jack nodded. He was staring at the body with a chilling fixedness. Maggie couldn't begin to imagine his thoughts.

Then Montgomery turned his attention to Maggie. "Did you have any part in this?"

Maggie shook her head, as yet unable to speak. Montgomery nodded. "Good. Now, did you see the shooting?"

She found her voice. "No. I heard the gun go off. And then he came running toward me. And that's when you came."

Montgomery frowned thoughtfully, turning back to the body. Finally he sighed, "All right. It's manageable."

Maggie stared at him in disbelief. The reasoned judgment that a violent murder was "manageable" staggered her. She started to protest, but Wally Gordon suddenly pushed past her, only to rock back on his heels when he sighted the body. "My God," he gasped. He looked from the boy to Montgomery. "Jack?"

Montgomery nodded. "That's right."

Gordon was obviously shaken to his foundations. "What are you going to do, Ben?"

Maggie couldn't keep herself from blurting out, "What

are you talking about? There's been a murder! You've got to call the police!"

Gordon shot a frightened look at her, but Montgomery gently took her by the arm. "Don't worry, the police will have their turn. I want you to come up to the house with me while I make some phone calls."

He started to take her back to the house, then turned to Gordon with a distasteful motion toward the dead girl. "Wally, make sure no one else sees that. And make sure Jack stays right here with you until I get back."

A pair of burly waiters were blocking the steps leading down to the pool and keeping the few remaining guests confined to the veranda; there they speculated excitedly among themselves in hushed tones. They fell silent as Montgomery and Maggie came onto the veranda, and Maggie saw Jimmy Knowland staring at her in disbelief. A voice called out, "What happened down there? Somebody said they heard a shot."

Montgomery paused, smiling easily. "There was no shot. *If* any one of you heard something, it was a backfire."

There was a chorus of protest but Montgomery silenced it with a sharp look. "The party is over as of now. I want you all to go home."

It was something Maggie noticed for the first time just then: Montgomery almost invariably spoke in terms of "I want," and what he wanted almost invariably came about.

As the guests hurriedly left the veranda, Montgomery turned to her. "Who brought you here?"

She identified Jimmy and Montgomery summoned him to his side. Jimmy swallowed, not knowing quite what to expect. "Yes sir, Mr. Montgomery."

He was obviously familiar with Jimmy. "Jimmy, I'm going to see this young lady home." Then, as an afterthought, "That is, if it's all right with you."

"Sure. Whatever you say, Mr. Montgomery," Jimmy managed to stammer.

"Drop by and see me next week, Jimmy. I might have something for you. Come by any time."

Maggie saw Jimmy's face light up like a candle. "You bet, Mr. Montgomery. I'll be there." They left him standing alone on the veranda.

Maggie glanced up at Montgomery as he showed her into the house; his face was completely composed. He seemed hardly aware of her but she sensed his mind was working at a furious pace. She would always remember that night with some degree of awe, the way he moved through the crisis casually, confidently tying off one loose end after another, always completely in control, letting not a single detail escape him.

He took her to a study off the drawing room where a log fire was blazing in the fireplace, throwing rich reflections onto the thick carpet and cherry wall panels. There was someone in the room waiting for them, sitting comfortably in the big swivel chair behind the desk. He was a slight, rather fastidious-looking middle-aged man with red, narrow eyes. His evening clothes were of an ill-fitting cut and a bit frayed at the cuffs. He smiled. "Hello, Ben."

Montgomery didn't seem surprised. Surveying the man coldly, he responded "Hello Gerrard. If we rented that tuxedo for you try to get one that fits next time. I like the help to look organized."

Gerrard snapped, "I report to Mr. Lendt."

"And I get copies of those reports, except, of course, the ones about me. I suppose you've been here all evening?"

Gerrard smiled. "Sure have. And I'll tell you something, between all the joy powder floating around this place and Wally's little speech from the balcony about the bosses I figure I've got enough on him to guarantee nobody will ever put his face in front of a camera again." He laughed nasally. "But I've got to admit, that Coke bottle was something. A real topper, all right."

Montgomery eyed him mildly. "Yes, wasn't it."

Suddenly Gerrard sobered. "Okay. Now why don't you tell me what happened down by the pool."

Montgomery smiled. "I intend to, Gerrard. Because since you're here and have a certain sleazy kind of expertise, I intend to use you."

At this Gerrard frowned; Maggie sensed that Montgomery had caught him off guard. Grimly satisfied with Gerrard's reaction, Montgomery continued, "And I'll tell you something else, Gerrard, you might as well destroy everything you've got on Wally Gordon because after Sam and I have a little talk tomorrow all your dedicated work is never going to see the light of day."

The little man seemed to recoil in the chair. "What are you talking about, Montgomery?"

Montgomery, leading Maggie through the study into a

little anteroom, said over his shoulder, "I'll get to it in a minute. Don't go away."

As Montgomery closed the door on Gerrard, Maggie turned to him. "You still haven't called the police."

Montgomery frowned, but ignored her protest. He summoned a servant and ordered hot tea and croissants brought in. Once the servant had hastened off he turned back to give her an appraising scrutiny. She tried to meet his eye, but never in her life had she felt so self-conscious. And what he said next did little to erase that feeling. "Who on earth put you in that Gibson girl-cum-flapper getup?"

The question caught her completely by surprise; with everything that had happened he wanted to know about her appearance!

"A . . . a friend of mine." That sounded lame so she added, "She said it was The Look."

He smiled wryly, "Let me tell you something, The Look is a nickel a gross these days." Crossing to her he tilted her chin up for a closer assessment. "There might be something under all this garbage. There's a bathroom over there. Why don't you see what you can do about it while I take care of a few things. And when you're done, and I can see just who it is I'm talking to, I'll answer all your questions."

He turned back to the study, but paused to glance back at her. "What's your name?"

"Maggie Jones."

He nodded thoughtfully. "Well, one other thing, Maggie Jones. I want you to know you're in no danger. I promise you that."

He closed the door behind him. She found the bathroom without any trouble and spent the next half hour scrubbing furiously at her face and redoing her hair. The bathroom was oversized with gilded cherubs and laurel clusters for fixtures, and an enormous mirror. Remembering the stained and seamy bathrooms of the old rooming house, Maggie promised herself that one day she would own a bathroom like this, even if there wasn't another room in her house. When she finished, the girl staring back at her from the mirror looked like her old self. She breathed a deep sigh of relief. That will have to do, she thought. Long afterward she would realize that Montgomery had handled her as easily as he had Jimmy Knowland: he'd wanted to keep her mind occupied and had accomplished that simply by commenting on her appearance. But it was obvious that

Montgomery, when he returned, was startled by what Maggie's half-hour in the bathroom had accomplished.

He stopped in the doorway, staring at her. "You're a very lovely young woman."

A flood of relief washed over her at his approval. She attempted a smile. "Thank you."

He glanced at the still outtakes of Gordon's movies mounted on the wall. "I've just about had enough of this place for one night."

His tone suddenly and unpretentiously revealed for the first time the strain that events of the evening had placed on him. And that tiniest hint of human vulnerability completely won Maggie over. From the moment earlier in the evening when she realized Montgomery wasn't going to call the police, that he was going to use the girl's death to achieve some goal of his own in a remote power struggle that Maggie couldn't even imagine, she had been torn between his relentless magnetism and her conventional sense of right and wrong. But now that he had opened himself up to her, however slightly, she only hoped that whatever his plan was for evading the police and covering up the murder it would succeed as he desired. If, in this bizarre and sinister world into which she'd suddenly been thrust, people did not play by the old rules, then she knew without a doubt that she wanted to be on Montgomery's side. If she'd been more experienced, she'd have realized that she was falling in love.

But Montgomery was all business when Wally Gordon joined them on the portico; at his command an attendant jogged off to fetch his car. Gordon, looking haggard, listened as Montgomery gave him specific instructions.

"In the morning you'll take Jack to the Wallingford Sanitarium. I've talked to them and they know what to do. Wallingford is already drawing up commitment papers. Then you'll come back here and wait for my call."

"Yes, I understand."

A gleaming, cream-colored Rolls roadster glided to a halt in the drive and the attendant hastened to hold the door for Maggie. The rich leather upholstery seemed to enfold her as she settled into it. She should have been exhausted, but the night air, suddenly chill, was still charged with anticipation. She glanced up at Montgomery, who lingered on the portico with Gordon. He was studying the actor's face as though he were trying to penetrate a tedious riddle. Maggie sensed a special bond between them, but she wasn't at all sure it was friendship. She could barely make out Montgomery's words.

"Tell me something, Wally. What on earth did you hope to accomplish tonight?"

Gordon smiled bleakly. "Accomplish? Nothing, I suppose. But it did seem to me about time somebody said something. Rather well past time, in fact."

"For God's sake, next time write a letter to the newspaper."

Gordon frowned. "They're all such petty little men, Ben. Such dwarfs. They all ought to be exterminated." Then, glancing at Montgomery, "You could do something about them, you know. You have the power."

Montgomery shook his head. "I don't, Wally. Not that kind of power. And if I did, I'm not sure I'd use it."

"Yes, you are part of the establishment after all, aren't you, Janus-faced bastard that you are."

Montgomery shrugged. "My business is making films. I try to stick to it."

The actor shook his head. "I suppose so. Anyway, I do appreciate everything you've done." He chuckled. "If it's any consolation, there are certain painfully lucid mornings when I wonder why you put up with me."

Montgomery smiled. "If it's any consolation, I have those same mornings."

They parted. Montgomery set the big car in motion, rocking smoothly through the gears as they seemed to float out along the drive. Maggie looked back to see the figure of the famous movie actor, Wally Gordon, watching after them from the portico, hopelessly dwarfed by the brilliantly lit mansion where her life had just begun.

Montgomery drove in silence, absently negotiating the harrowing Mulholland twists. It seemed an eternity since Maggie's rollicking ride up this same road. After a moment she turned to him. "Why is Wally Gordon so unhappy?"

He glanced at her and Maggie sensed that he approved of her question.

"After that whole macabre circus back there you want to know why he is unhappy? What made you ask?"

She didn't quite know how to respond. "You seem to care about him." It was the truth.

He frowned. "I do. He's brilliant. And I suppose that's why he's unhappy. Beyond that I can't say. I've tried to understand him, but . . ."

Montgomery shook off the thought. "Don't you want to know about the girl?"

She frowned. "I don't know."

He glanced at her again, then his voice resumed its efficient tone. "Well, you're going to need to. Her name was Ellie Wade. She was a prostitute, with certain specialties—homosexuality, sado-masochism . . ." Maggie wasn't quite sure what he was talking about but she didn't interrupt. The sense of it was clear. "Rumor has it that she operated a sideline, blackmailing her clients. She was well overdue for what happened tonight. She won't be missed. And, as it turned out, something useful might come of it."

She stared at him. "I'm sorry . . . I couldn't think of it that way."

He nodded. "I know. But I want to finish. Jack Lendt, the boy who shot her, is one of the sons of Samuel Lendt, who happens to be my partner at American Universal Pictures. Jack has a history of violent, psychotic behavior, particularly with young women, but there's never been any deaths before that I know of. And up until tonight his father has been able to buy the police out of it. Anyway, the kinds of things Ellie traded in were just up Jack's alley. I suppose you might say they were meant for each other."

She was puzzled. "But . . . it all has something to do with Wally Gordon, doesn't it?"

Montgomery nodded grimly. "It will. Tomorrow. You see, Sam Lendt is afraid of Wally. He's afraid of what it would cost him in prestige if some of Wally's personal habits made the headlines. Also, he hates Wally because he knows that I like him. Maybe that's most important of all. Ideally he'd like to find a reason to disown Wally before anything embarrassing can happen. That's why he sent a private detective to the party tonight."

Maggie realized he was talking about the little man, Gerrard. "But that won't happen now?"

Montgomery shook his head. "No. Because I can put his son on trial for murder if he makes a move against Wally. And he knows I'd do it." Montgomery shook his head. "What's incredible is that Sam is forgetting how much money AUP, meaning he and myself, have tied up in Wally Gordon right now."

Maggie was disappointed. "And that's why you're doing all of this? For the money?"

He snapped angrily, "No!" Then, his voice softening thoughtfully, "Yes. Certainly the money. But that's not the important reason. I'm doing it because I don't want to see Sam Lendt destroy Wally. He'll take care of that soon enough on his own."

Maggie considered what he had told her; unless she was mistaken all of these people were locked in a struggle from which there could emerge no real victors.

"That's very sad," she said.

He frowned, barely acknowledging her words. After a moment he glanced at her again. "What about you? How did you get tied up with Jimmy Knowland?"

Nettled, she gave him a sharp look. "I like him. Is there any reason I shouldn't?"

Montgomery shrugged. "Of course not." His response left countless observations about Jimmy unsaid, and Maggie knew what most of them were.

"I'm not mixed up with him. My roommate thought it would be fun if we went to the party with him. I just got in town this morning."

"You did? What do you want here?" he asked bluntly.

Suddenly she was more than a little confused about what exactly she did want from Hollywood. "I want . . . I wanted to be in the movies."

He looked at her with wry amusement. "Oh? Surely nothing's happened to change your mind?"

She smiled in spite of herself.

In the dusky, far reach of the headlights a coyote loped onto the pavement, then paused, his yellow eyes staring insolently over his shoulder toward them. Ghostlike, he melted into the brush on the opposite side of the road. Montgomery nodded. "Bad business, coyotes. They turn up rabid as often as not." Maggie frowned. He seemed to have put her out of his mind.

But he hadn't. After a moment he said, "Well, Maggie, if what you really want is to be in the movies, then I want to show you something."

They rode on in silence. The big roadster seemed to float effortlessly, almost silently, on a cushion of power and craftsmanship. It was almost as if they were descending on a cloud down through the misty, moonlit night toward the bunched cluster of lights nestled against the base of the hills. The spell was broken when Montgomery turned off the road onto a rutted trail and drove on for a few hundred feet. In the moment before he stopped the headlights swept an abruptly unreal landscape of gargantuan pillars, crumbling statuary, and towering, Mediterranean arches. Startled, Maggie glanced at Montgomery uncertainly. She half expected him to take her in his arms, and she wasn't quite sure how she would respond. But he only reached across to open her door. "Come with me. Maybe you'll find this interesting. I always do."

Maggie stepped out of the car and, as her eyes adjusted, what she found confronting her took her breath away. In the luminescent moonlight it appeared that they had come upon an enormous courtyard, its battlements vaulting six and seven stories overhead. Great-tusked ceremonial elephants, each of them rearing forty feet or more, topped enormous columns planted on pedestals as large as small bungalows. In the ghostly light Maggie could make out strange, sphinx-like figures carved on the pedestals and bizarre etchings of winged gods on the great altar that was the centerpiece of the courtyard. Everything about the place was scaled to dwarf mere mortals and stagger human imagination. It was a place clearly designed for pagan excess.

"Where are we?" Maggie's voice was little more than a whisper.

"Babylon." Montgomery surveyed the surroundings without dismay. "At least Griffith's notion of what Babylon might have been. I don't imagine the reality would have lived up to his expectations." He nudged a fallen timber with his foot. "It's a movie set, Maggie. And it looks like it's finally about ready to tumble down. After seven years I'd say it's just about time."

Maggie looked closer. Decay had indeed set in. Whole sections of the courtyard were overgrown and plaster rubble was underfoot everywhere. A gust of breeze whistled softly through the slats and chicken wire substructures where large sections of plaster had fallen away from statues and columns, and a fire had blackened the base of the great altar.

Maggie was stunned. "You mean somebody built all this for the movies?"

Montgomery smiled. "For *one* movie. *Intolerance*. Griffith did it on the heels of *Birth of a Nation*, which was an enormous success." He waved grandly around the courtyard. "This, however, was an enormous flop."

"How could it be? It's . . ." Words failed her. "I've never seen anything like it."

"Neither had the accountants at Fine Arts. D.W. almost put the studio under with this one. They say it cost two million before he was finished. It never made back a quarter of that." He shook his head. "I never would have allowed something like that to happen."

She turned to look at him. "Why do you come here?"

He leaned against a pedestal, eyeing the towering battlements. "Every so often I like to remind myself what the business is about." He frowned. "Don't get me wrong. I'll spend two million at the drop of a hat if I find a story that interests me and demands the set. Griffith went at it backwards. He built this monster and then shot the film from notes he stuffed in his trousers the night before."

She watched him, realizing that the tension that had charged his whole being from the moment she first saw him was draining away. There was something about these bizarre surroundings that made him feel at home here. She wanted to encourage him. "You seem to know a lot about it. That movie, I mean."

Montgomery nodded. "I do. I was an extra on the picture. I hit town on a freight from Albuquerque. I was broke and half starved and they paid us two dollars a day and threw in a box lunch." He chuckled. "I was an Assyrian soldier, one of the first to go when Cyrus charged the gate in his chariots." Now Montgomery was completely relaxed, intrigued by the recollection. "That was my first taste of the movies and even then I knew something was out of control on the picture. I think I realized it when Griffith decided he had to charge a chariot along the top of that wall up there and his set designer told him it would bring the whole thing down on top of him. I figured that was no way to run a railroad."

Maggie was caught up in the story. "What happened?"

He laughed. "What happened was the arrogant bastard put his damned chariot up there anyway, horses and all, a hundred and fifty feet above the ground. Then he shot the scene three times with that whole wall rocking and creaking like there was an earthquake and scaring everybody half to death. And when he finished, the film looked great."

He gazed musingly at the high wall, reliving the scene in

his mind, then abruptly frowned. "But the thing I have to keep reminding myself is that a big statement doesn't necessarily make an important film. You can't buy it with money. Good film is saying simple things clearly, and the simpler the better." He smiled at her. "That's the movies for you, Maggie. Child's play. Do you still want to be in them?"

What Maggie wanted suddenly and above all else was to be with Montgomery, whether he was making movies or riding a freight train from Albuquerque. She smiled. "Why not?"

He nodded. "Then that's settled. You will be."

Maggie stared at him; not for a moment did she doubt that he was telling the truth. She should have been exhilarated, bursting with a thousand questions. But something else tugged at her. She turned slowly to let her eyes scan the crumbling grandeur of Griffith's vision of destruction bred of pagan lusts and excess. Troubled, she turned back to Montgomery. "I think I'd like to leave now."

They walked back to the car. It was after midnight. Montgomery located a thickly woven woolen lap rug folded in the trunk of the car and Maggie nestled into it. He started the engine and then turned to her. "Shall I take you home?"

She looked at him without guile. "No. I don't think so."

He nodded, eased the car into gear, and set it in motion along the rutted trail that led away from Babylon.

Some time later the car topped a hill and began a descent toward the narrow highway that ran along the coast. For the first time in her life Maggie saw the ocean, glistening silver and deep blue in the moonlight, the waves brilliant white as they crashed, foaming, on the broad white beach. Something about the scene struck a deep chord in Maggie, igniting emotions that had lain deeply buried. She was moved, excited, made almost breathless by the vision of the ocean stretching into infinity. The brooding sense of disaster which had seized her at the old movie set was swept away by a feeling of freedom and release. Here in this place there were no boundaries, no restrictions, no agonies wrought by dark currents of human endeavor . . . there was only unlimited freedom.

Montgomery drove in silence. She watched him, trying to fathom his thoughts. His hands, protected by expensive leather driving gloves, gripped the wheel; images of those hands, free of the gloves and exploring her body, assaulted her. She knew that if he had stopped at the side of the road and proceeded to take her right there she would have gone passionately to him. But as yet he had not touched her. And the drive seemed endless.

They came to a broad gate that straddled the highway. On either side of the road was a tall fence. On the ocean side the fence stretched along the beach, on the landward side it stretched as far as Maggie could see. In the glare of the headlights she could see two armed men posted at the gate, with horses tethered nearby. One of them cautiously approached the car, cradling a rifle warily. But when he recognized Montgomery he grinned, his eyes lingering appreciatively on Maggie. "Evening, Mr. Montgomery."

They exchanged a few words and then the guard ordered his companion to open the gate. It occurred to Maggie, with a mild flush of resentment, that she was not the first girl Montgomery had brought this way. But the thought did nothing to dispel the other feelings building in her body and, as they passed through the gate, she made no protest.

The road was rough and unpaved now, a track carved along the shoulder between the ocean and the mountains that rose abruptly from the beach. All was silent except for the muted rush of the waves breaking on the beach. Shortly they crossed a rickety wooden bridge that spanned a narrow inlet, and she could see waterfowl bobbing on the silvery, moonlit waters of the lagoon. The beach widened and Montgomery pulled off the road. "Here," he said.

She stepped obediently from the car, folding the lap rug over her arm. They walked along the beach, neither speaking for several minutes. Suddenly Montgomery stopped and gently took her in his arms. She could feel him responding to her warmth, and the knowledge set her on fire. He held her there for an interminable moment. "How old are you, Maggie?"

"Eighteen."

She felt him tense. "My God, I never would have guessed."

His grip on her relaxed, and with sudden fear Maggie realized the moment was about to be destroyed. Abruptly she reached up with both hands, letting the lap rug fall to the sand, and pulled him into an instinctively passionate kiss. It was like no kiss she'd ever experienced before. The whole world exploded, all reason was lost, and only the immediate physical sensation of his mouth upon hers mattered.

Distantly she realized his arms had surrounded her again, strong and confident. As he lowered her gently to the sand only one exultant thought filled her mind, *I've won . . .*

Slowly he began to unbutton her dress as his mouth explored her face and neck. The dress slipped away and his hands, so strong and yet so gentle, were moving expertly from her high, firm breasts to her long, slender thighs.

As she opened herself to him, shuddering with both pleasure and delicious fear, her last thought was that she did not know where he was taking her, but it didn't matter. She would go with him, wherever it was.

The sun rose early that late summer morning. Maggie awoke before Montgomery, and found herself covered with his overcoat. Though there was a slight breeze from the ocean, she wasn't cold. She felt bathed in a warm glow as she lay still for a moment, savoring the sense of happiness and contentment that filled her.

Rising slightly, she looked around. Last night she had been able to make out very little of her surroundings, but now she could see it all. A broad white beach, the center of a long curving bay, stretched to gently sloping green mountains. Behind them more mountains rose, ending in a flat-topped peninsula. The colors were sharp and clear: the deep blue of the ocean, the green of the chaparral-covered hills, and the white sand. *It's the most beautiful place I've ever seen*, she thought peacefully. *And right here, right now, I'm happier than I've ever been.*

Montgomery had pulled a corner of the lap rug over him. Otherwise he was naked, and she stared, fascinated, at his body. He was a big man, tall and broad-shouldered. Everything about him seemed to be perfect, not a plane or an angle out of place, except for a scar that ran white and puckered beneath his ribs for a few inches across his muscled belly.

He stirred, slowly opening his eyes. Maggie saw once more how brilliantly blue they were.

"Good morning," she said with sudden shyness. Then, "Where is this place?"

"It's called Malibu," he answered tiredly, his voice full of sleep.

Malibu. Maggie looked around her once more. *I'll come back here someday. I'll own a piece of this place and I'll never forget how happy I was here.*

CHAPTER 3

Maggie sat on the rear seat of a Mercedes limousine, feeling small and ill-suited to the luxurious appointments of the car. The slick, black vehicle was sweeping her along palm-lined Pico Boulevard toward American Universal Studios and a confrontation with an unknown man named Sam Lendt, which would, of necessity, be nothing short of terrifying. Trying to ignore the icy knot of fear in her stomach, she concentrated on the back of the driver's head beyond the glass panel between the seats. He was an older man, his hair greying beneath his chauffeur's cap. She wondered if he was curious why he'd been dispatched to fetch a nondescript girl from a second-rate motel. Her resentment built unreasonably upon itself, until she noticed the driver's eyes crinkling as he studied her in the rear view mirror. His voice filtered through an intercom. "Steady, miss. I won't let them eat you alive." She was wrong. His voice was kind, and just what she needed. "Thank you." She smiled and immediately relaxed.

The arrival of the limousine in front of the Garden of Paradise had created something of a stir. The residents turned out in force, those who were up at mid-morning, to stare covetously at the car and resentfully at Maggie. Lyla accompanied her as far as the curb, eyeing her with a mixture of envy and awe. Her eyes took in the limousine and driver and she shook her head in despair. "Five years I've spent turning over every rock in this town so that someday a studio would send a car like that to pick me up, and here the little girl from Fresno pulls the trick off in twenty-four hours." She turned to Maggie with a wry smile. "Tell me, what am I doing wrong?"

Then, sensing Maggie's anxiety, Lyla gave her a comforting hug and whispered, "Listen, I don't know what's going on, but you be careful, you hear? Sometimes they can play awfully rough." Suddenly it seemed Maggie had known Lyla all her life, and she would never forget the older girl's genuine concern for her as she set off that morning.

Of course she told Lyla nothing of the murder that had occurred the night before, partly because Montgomery asked her to keep silent, but more because her instincts warned her that whatever Lyla's good intentions the story would not be safe with her. For that matter the whirlwind events hardly seemed real to Maggie herself; her recollections were a chaos, half nightmare, half romantic dream.

Maggie frowned; the drive back from the beach that morning had been disturbing, despite the fresh sunshine that set the frothy ocean sparkling. Montgomery, preoccupied, spoke little, leaving Maggie feeling not quite sure what was expected of her. There was a shadow of a beard on his face and his jaw was set in a firm line. She desperately wanted some reassurance from him, but all he said as he let her off in front of the Garden of Paradise was, "I'll want you at the studio around eleven. I'll have a car sent for you." He left her standing on the sidewalk staring after the big roadster, fighting back the empty feeling that threatened to overwhelm her.

The limousine barely slowed as it was cleared past a guardhouse between high, dun-colored stucco walls. Within, Maggie was disappointed to find only row upon row of rather unremarkable wooden bungalows and huge, forbidding blockhouses. But the place was teeming with activity; studio messengers pedaled furiously back and forth, and trucks loaded with lumber, lighting equipment and racks of costumes crowded the narrow lanes between the stages. But only an occasional, gaudily dressed bit player or extra going about his or her business even hinted at the fantasy world Maggie had expected to discover within the walls. Her surprise must have shown in her expression. The driver's filtered voice chuckled, "That's right, Miss. It's a factory, pure and simple."

The only variance from the drab, utilitarian atmosphere was a modern building of white stone, rising four stories, even higher than the stages that dominated the lot.

"They call it the Ivory Tower," the driver explained through the intercom, as he stopped the car.

A severely dressed, middle-aged secretary was waiting out front, eyeing her watch impatiently. The driver delivered Maggie into her hands.

"Miss Jones? Mr. Montgomery wants to see you right away in Mr. Lendt's office." Before Maggie could respond, the woman was striding purposefully into the building. Maggie glanced back over her shoulder, but the limousine was already pulling away. She had no choice but to follow.

As they rode up the four flights in the elevator, the older woman's eyes seemed to be drawn to Maggie in spite of herself. Finally she hazarded, "Something big must be happening. Mr. Montgomery almost *never* asks to see Mr. Lendt."

Maggie said nothing, and the woman, swallowing her curiosity, stared grimly ahead.

Maggie was shown into an ornately furnished suite of offices where a rank of four secretaries were busily hammering at their Smith-Coronas and fielding telephone calls. Maggie's escort spoke to one of them; the girl glanced up to give Maggie a cool appraisal, then spoke into her intercom. A moment later Maggie was shown into Samuel Lendt's inner office.

Montgomery was standing at a tall, draped window overlooking the lot. The bright sunlight falling over him seemed to cast a halo around his silhouette, presenting him, like a strange and remote deity, to Maggie's eyes. It seemed impossible that only hours earlier his body had been joined with hers.

Montgomery turned as the door closed behind Maggie, and she was left standing alone in the middle of the thickly carpeted office, which would have occupied a whole floor of her mother's rooming house. There was a massive stone fireplace built into one wall, and near it an exceptionally wide sofa and love seat arrangement. Plaques, photographs, and mounted posters advertising AUP releases covered the paneled walls. Without preliminaries Montgomery said, "Maggie, I want you to tell Mr. Lendt what happened at Wally Gordon's last night. Tell him *exactly* what you saw."

Now, for the first time, Maggie forced herself to look at

the man who was sitting behind the desk at the far end of the room. He was not a large man, and his face had the narrow, cruel cast that she remembered in the face of the young man who had committed murder the night before. But she sensed a dangerous shrewdness in the elder Lendt, and an unyielding, arbitrary will.

Maggie would learn much of Lendt in coming years. He was among those tough-minded individualists, including Fox and Laemmle, who had accomplished the almost impossible feat of breaking the "trust" of production companies that controlled the motion picture industry from its earliest days. She would also learn that he had a deserved reputation as an alley fighter who never forgave a grudge. But at the moment all Maggie saw in Samuel Lendt was a small man with a pencil-thin moustache, almost dwarfed by his desk and high-backed swivel chair, who was watching her with calculating eyes.

She found her voice. "I . . . I don't think I know where to start."

Montgomery turned back to the window. Lendt gave a vague, deprecating wave of his hand. "This seems to be your big scene, my dear. Start where you want." His voice was rasping, as if the smoke from the thick cigar he held between his thumb and two fingers made his throat raw. "Go on," he commanded.

So Maggie told him, slowly but clearly, what she knew about his son and the events of the night before. And as she did so she saw his face drain of color and his body shrink even further into the big chair. The calculating focus of his eyes gave way to the dilated terror of a cornered animal and for the moment, Maggie realized, she had nothing to fear from Samuel Lendt.

Montgomery said nothing until she finished. Then he turned to Lendt. "I arranged for Jack to be taken to a private sanitarium where he'll be watched and receive treatment. The commitment papers should be ready for you to sign this afternoon. The hospital fees will be charged to your personal account here at the studio under household expenses and the money washed through Sy Abrams in the legal department. You can trust him. There's no need for anyone to know any more about it than that. I expect you to leave Jack in the hospital, Sam, for his own sake if for no one else's."

Lendt was still staring at Maggie, but his voice had no

bite in it when he made the accusation she'd been half expecting. "What'd he promise you to get you to say those things about my boy?"

She held herself firmly. "He didn't have to promise me anything. It's the truth."

Montgomery eyed Lendt levelly. "But you might as well know it now, Sam, I'm going to give her a test."

Lendt laughed harshly. "That's more like it. For a moment there she almost had me fooled."

"Don't be stupid," Montgomery snapped. "Look at her."

Lendt frowned. Suddenly his eyes were traveling over Maggie's face and body, making some kind of cold, impersonal analysis that, incredibly, detached itself from the matters concerning his son. Finally he nodded. "Yeah. Okay."

With that he seemed to put Maggie out of his mind. He turned to face Montgomery. "So what'd you do with the bimbo?"

"Gerrard handled it. Don't worry."

Lendt nodded grimly. "Gerrard better have handled it."

Montgomery frowned. "I shouldn't have to say it, but I will for the record. Don't give me any more trouble about Wally Gordon." Lendt hesitated, then nodded, and Montgomery seemed satisfied. He glanced at his watch. "I think that's all we have to talk about."

Lendt stared at him, and some of the gristle returned to his voice. "You're some kind of bastard, Ben, you know that?" He laughed harshly. "And I'm the one with the reputation around here."

Montgomery shrugged. "You earned it." Taking Maggie's arm, he started to show her out.

Suddenly Lendt seemed to go slack again, and a flicker of helplessness haunted his eyes for a moment. "Ben, I've got to tell Ruth something. How long is he—how long will my son have to stay in that place?"

Maggie was startled. *He cares,* she thought. *He cares about the boy.*

But Montgomery said coldly, "Unless they can work miracles out there, which I doubt, then I imagine for the rest of his life."

Maggie was still shaken when Montgomery brought her into his office and formally introduced her to his secretary, Charlotte, the woman who had escorted her to Lendt's office. She saw the older woman frown with concern as she took her hand, but Montgomery was issuing rapid-fire instructions. "I want to set up a test for Miss Jones. I don't want just anybody. Call Billy Reiter—he's good with women and he owes me a favor."

Charlotte was jotting notes on a pad. "What about costume?"

"Whatever Billy likes. I'll leave it to him. I want to see the footage first thing in the morning. And call Murnau, tell him to hold an ingenue walk-on in that desert picture he's starting next week. I'll get back to him later to let him know for sure. And get hold of accounting. Tell them to start Miss Jones at a hundred a week, to increase by fifty a week until further notice."

Maggie watched Montgomery order her future in a daze. It was all happening, just as he had said it would. But Lendt's last words still echoed in her mind. *"How long will my son have to stay in that place?"* Until this moment Maggie had been convinced that everything Montgomery had done was right; however dark and sinister the events that had made him set all this in motion, she was sure he had been guided by some principle that justified it all. *"How long will my son have to stay in that place?"* Now she realized there was no principle at all, only Montgomery's unalterable will. Maggie did not doubt that Jack Lendt was in a place where he belonged, or that his father was capable of capriciously and viciously destroying Wally Gordon. But for Montgomery to have made such a judgment . . . She stared at him, hopelessly in love yet torn by her sudden realization. And suddenly she became frightened for him, as she thought, *he reaches too far* . . .

Charlotte glanced up brightly from her pad. "Will there be anything else?"

"The San Francisco trip. Is everything arranged?"

She smiled. "I have your tickets and the Fairmont has confirmed."

Montgomery took Maggie into his office and sat her in a thickly cushioned leather chair. His office was not nearly so large as Lendt's, and more spartanly furnished. In fact, it was little more than functional. Lendt's office was personalized with pictures of his family and mementos of the accomplishments of his career. There was none of that here; it was as though the occupant of this office could not risk putting down telltale roots. He glanced down at her with some concern. "How are you feeling? I know that was quite an ordeal, but you were perfect. It was important that you be absolutely convincing and that's exactly what you were."

"I'm fine," she snapped. He frowned, surprised at her tone. But she could not hold his eyes. "But I've changed my mind."

His frown deepened and he crossed to his desk and sat down. With that adjustment the atmosphere in the room abruptly chilled, throwing Maggie off balance. "You've changed your mind about what?"

For a moment she felt intimidated. Then suddenly her pride and her sense of outrage at the way he was manipulating the conversation welled up in her. She glared at him, determined not to let him put this distance between them. "I wish I'd never met you. I wish I'd never made love to you."

The words were lies, but they had the desired effect. She noted with satisfaction the uncertainty flickering in his expression. "Are you going to tell me why?"

She ignored his question. "I don't want a screen test. I don't want to be on your payroll. I want to go home."

Now the uncertainty was gone; he rose from behind his desk and took the chair opposite her, obviously intrigued. "Fine. As soon as you tell me why."

Remembering the way Lendt's eyes assessed her after Montgomery told him she was going to have a test, Maggie's anger took control. "Because I feel like I'm being bought and sold. The way you men looked at me—I didn't come here for that. I came here because you asked me to and because I thought you needed my help."

He frowned. "All right. I understand. You're wrong, but I'll get to that later. There's something else. What is it?"

So she would not get off so easily. He knew. She forced herself to meet his eyes as the anger drained out of her and the dread feeling replaced it. "I believe what you did last night was evil."

He regarded her thoughtfully. "You didn't say so at the time."

"I didn't understand until this morning."

He nodded. "Fair enough, Maggie." He rose and crossed to the desk. Through the intercom he ordered a car brought around. "Miss Jones will be returning home, Charlotte." She watched him, fighting back hot tears. He was letting her go after all.

But he wasn't through with her. Frowning, he crossed to a window that looked out over the high walls of the lot on a drab landscape of city streets. "I want you to understand that I didn't make you that offer because I thought I owed you anything, Maggie. The truth is, I think you have a special quality. I think the camera will worship you. I saw it last night at Wally's after you cleaned yourself up, and that's when I decided you ought to be working for me." He turned to face her again. "And for what it's worth, Sam saw it too. The cagey bastard saw it despite the fact that he would have liked nothing better than to come across that desk and rip your heart out for what we were doing to him."

He expelled a deep breath. "I still want you to work for American Universal, Maggie. If you have any sense you won't let what you think of me stand in the way of that. I want you to think about it some more. Will you do that?"

His penetrating blue eyes were boring into her and she felt her resolution crumbling. She knew that ultimately she would not refuse him. But she would not give him the satisfaction of knowing just now. Besides, there was another question gnawing at her.

"Won't it ever bother you?"

His eyes wavered, then firmly locked with hers again. "I make decisions, Maggie. I don't carry them around with me."

After a moment she rose abruptly to her feet and hurried from the office. In the elevator she gave in to the stinging rush of tears.

The next morning her screen test went off with remarkable ease. The director, Billy Reiter, proved to be an explosive, powerfully built man in his mid-forties with a twinkle in his eye. He was as voluble as Maggie was reserved, and in the first fifteen minutes she learned that he'd been married and divorced twice, had reported the Mexican Revolution for the New York *Sun*, and had boxed semi-professionally before hiring out to Biograph in 1914 as a camera grip. He took Maggie under his wing and in short order dispelled her panic at the prospect of facing the camera for the first time.

"My dear," he counseled her with theatrical resonance, "the movies are one of the great frauds of the twentieth century. They masquerade as art, but never forget that the motion picture camera concerns itself only with surfaces, the thinnest skin of reality. And because *my* eye is the camera's eye, you must put yourself entirely in my hands. Your job is to imagine yourself as an envelope with nothing inside, and I will take it from there."

He ferried her through wardrobe where, at his direction, a cigarette-puffing matron put her in a simple linen shift which barely covered her knees and clung to the full line of her breasts. Then a hairdresser put her hair in curls and brought them down around her shoulders. A makeup man added a touch of color to her cheeks and lips but, obviously under orders from higher up, added little more.

Billy was sitting in a straight-backed chair with his kneeboots propped up on a cutting table when Maggie, feeling half-naked, was delivered to him. He leered appreciatively. "Now that's what I call an envelope." He waved off her protests. "You're supposed to be a woodland nymph driving hairy-chested woodcutters into beastly excesses of lechery with the innocent flaunting of your tender flesh. You're supposed to feel half-naked."

The set was a forest glade, left over from a Pola Negri picture that had just finished shooting. Maggie felt enormously self-conscious and thoroughly ridiculous as she tiptoed barefoot through the papier-mâché woods under the hot lights with men busily at work only a few yards away hauling off properties for use on another stage. But take turned into re-take, and then re-take upon re-take as Reiter, barking at the technicians and coaxing a range of emotional responses from Maggie, searched for something only he could imagine. She began to understand that the actual work of filmmaking involved much boredom, occasionally punctuated by sharp directorial outbursts of frustration.

Finally Reiter rose, stretched, and announced, "All right, gang, that's a wrap," and the test was finished.

On the way back to wardrobe Maggie was burdened by a feeling of anticlimax. She turned to Reiter. "What am I supposed to do now?"

"Now, my dear Maggie, you will wait until a decision about your future filters down from that white rockpile." He smiled. "And while you're waiting, why don't we have dinner together tonight?"

Maggie was surprised; the difference in their ages was almost thirty years. Then she remembered that she wasn't in Fresno any more. And besides, Billy had been very kind to her. She wavered, but suddenly memories of Montgomery intruded. She smiled. "I don't think so."

Billy took the rejection in high good humor. "In that case I'm going to pump Montgomery for another five thousand on my next picture. Somebody owes me something for this humiliation."

She gave him a look. "You *are* kidding, aren't you?"

"About the money?" He laughed. "Certainly not. Maggie my love, money is the one compensation the movie business pays for all the indignities it heaps on people. Don't forget that."

In all her years in Hollywood, Maggie never would.

Two mornings later Maggie was frying eggs while Lyla sat drinking coffee and reading the newpspaer. There had been no call from Montgomery. Suddenly Lyla rattled the paper. "Hey, listen to this. They fished Ellie Wade's body out of the ocean down by Newport Beach."

Maggie stiffened, then continued basting the eggs. But the hard lines of the dead girl's face swam in her vision. Lyla hadn't noticed her reaction. "You wouldn't know Ellie but I'll tell you something, I wouldn't be surprised if it was murder. Ellie wasn't exactly Little Bo Peep."

Maggie frowned. "Doesn't it say?"

Lyla shrugged. "It says she was swimming with friends and a rip tide carried her out to sea."

But she was shot! Maggie's mind protested. *How could they say she drowned?*

Lyla glanced up, sniffing. "Hey, you're burning my breakfast!"

Maggie ignored her, grabbing the newspaper out of her hands. It was true; there was no mention of a bullet wound in the girl's body. There was a photo accompanying the story, obviously taken just after the body was recovered. The face was white, bloodless, the hair matted, tangled, lifeless. Otherwise it looked exactly like the face Maggie had seen two nights before at Wally Gordon's mansion.

Lyla was staring at her in some surprise. "What is it Maggie?"

Maggie put the paper down, shaking her head numbly, and fighting off a nameless terror that threatened to engulf her. *What kind of power do these people have?*

Lyla frowned, then dropped the skillet into the sink and

began scanning the newspaper again. In a moment she glanced up, stricken. "Oh," she said softly. "I get it."

Maggie turned with a frown. "What are you talking about?"

Lyla smiled weakly. "Listen, Maggie, try to put him out of your mind. I can give you lessons. I've had plenty of experience."

There was something terribly wrong. Maggie snatched the paper back again. Beneath the story on Ellie Wade there was a headline that read, "Sheila Moreno Weds Studio Chief." She read on slowly, each word sinking into her like a lead weight. "Last night the beautiful and popular Mexican actress Sheila Moreno, who recently starred opposite John Gilbert in the highly successful motion picture *Betrayed,* eloped with Benjamin Montgomery, creative chief of American Universal Pictures."

That afternoon Charlotte, Montgomery's secretary, called to tell Maggie that she had been assigned to an F.W. Murnau picture, as yet untitled, which would begin shooting in a week's time. She said Montgomery regretted that he was unable to congratulate her personally, but that he was out of town for an extended vacation.

Two weeks later Maggie ran into Billy Reiter on the AUP lot where he was preparing a picture. That evening they drove out Wilshire and ate spicy bouillabaisse in a secluded booth at the rear of a small Italian restaurant at the foot of the pier in Santa Monica. Maggie had a lot to drink of the fruity, chilled white wine, and Billy seemed pleased that she was having such a good time.

CHAPTER 4

In early summer of 1926 Wally Gordon was found sprawled dead on the floor of a Beverly Hills hotel room. His plummet had been as rapid as his ascent. In the year following Maggie's arrival in Hollywood the public stayed away from his pictures in masses. It was a phenomenon that struck terror in the hearts of the biggest of names, the unaccountable drowning of some spark that had previously ignited audiences. Although in Wally's case it was not so inexplicable. Will Hays's censors, riding high with the studio chiefs' blessings, and aware of Gordon's hostility toward them, singled out his films for special attention. They put an unshakable curse on his career. Also, the years of dissipation finally began to take their toll, draining the surface vitality that the movie cameras had exploited successfully so many times. In 1924 Gordon appeared in only one film, an AUP production, as the second male lead. The film did badly and thereafter, despite Montgomery's efforts, Gordon could find no work at all.

The coroner accounted the death to natural causes, but the working film community knew the truth: Gordon had died of a massive overdose of heroin. Maggie, alone of that community, would never accept either explanation. She would believe always that Wally Gordon's sudden eclipse was the work of nameless forces set in motion that glittering night in 1922 when a young woman was murdered and a handful of people set about manipulating her death for their own ends.

In that same year of 1926 Maggie Jones, now known as Margaret Marshall, was named "Most Popular Female Star" in an Associated Press poll, and her face appeared on the cover of *Vogue* magazine. Gordon's funeral at a grim little Toluca Lake mortuary was not well attended, except by a rather ghoulish lot of sensation-seekers who remembered Wally's name from his heyday, so that Maggie's appearance there created a greater commotion than the service. A couple of rather seedy freelance photographers, who had shown up on the off chance of catching someone like Maggie, clamored after her, and the mourners, forgetting about Wally, swarmed out of the chapel pews with clawing hands as if touching her would put life into their empty eyes. Billy Reiter, who had agreed with a notable absence of enthusiasm to escort her to the funeral, managed to ward them off and return her safely to her car. Maggie, sickened by the spectacle, hurried back to her rambling wood-frame house on the beach at Malibu. The funeral had turned into a debacle, and naturally pictures of the whole business were splashed across the front page of the next morning's paper.

Maggie's house was in the cluster starting to be called "The Colony," because of the elite group of film personalities who had built there. Maggie had begun the exodus to the beach two years earlier. Money for that first home of her own had come from her first starring role, an AUP release entitled *Awakening*, which had borne out Montgomery's predictions by instantly vaulting her into the front ranks of Hollywood's leading women.

In the rush of events following Montgomery's marriage and her own bitter disappointment, Maggie had thrust from her mind her secret promise to preserve for herself the place where she and Montgomery had lain together and where she'd known such total—if fleeting—contentment. But as time passed and the tempo of her new life became more frenzied, she began to feel a need for the sense of peace and freedom offered by Malibu's endless horizons and gently folding green mountains. And having gone there first, now she felt a surge of resentment toward those who followed. These days, on any given weekend, when actors drove out from their big houses in town, their rollicking drunken caravans sending up clouds of dust along the beach trail, some of the screen's biggest idols could be found frolicking nude on the sand or partying with total abandon until dawn, plundering the solitude Maggie cherished.

As Reiter drove across the wooden bridge over the inlet on the way back from the funeral, Maggie sighed. Workmen were unloading building materials from a truck and a bulldozer was clanking out onto the strand.

"More neighbors," Billy observed wryly. "You'll have to send over a pie when they move in."

Billy was the one person to whom she'd confided the whole story of what had happened at Wally Gordon's mansion the night Ellie Wade was killed. It happened the first night in Maggie's new home. Billy had spent the afternoon helping her to move in, and later they were sharing a bottle of wine before a blazing fireplace. Outside a big surf from an offshore storm was pounding the beach as a rain squall pelted the windows.

Maggie had planned an evening of celebration and candlelit romance, but the elemental forces at work in the night disturbed her, summoning troubled images to the surface of her memory. Suddenly seized by irrational fear, she realized that unless she could banish those images she would never be able to live alone in this place. Finally, unable to hold back any longer, she began to talk about Montgomery and the events of the one night they had shared together four years earlier. Billy listened thoughtfully without interrupting.

When Maggie finished, he frowned into the fire. "I knew you were holding something in. I had no idea . . ."

He held her closer, under a protective arm. She yielded gratefully, and then in her mind his proportions began to change; he became larger and the familiar lines of care and concern on his face became lines of superior wisdom and strength. She surrendered to her feelings, which were not those of passion, in a way she had never done before, even with Montgomery. Outside her windows the wild night screamed, but she felt safe and sheltered. Maggie spoke softly into the woolen, masculine-smelling folds of his sweater. "Then you don't hate me?"

She knew the question sounded childlike but, for one of the few times in her life, that was how she felt.

He said gently, "No, I don't hate you, Maggie. I don't

think you're capable of doing anything that would make me hate you."

His words were an absolution, washing away years of guilt and self-incrimination. In the flickering firelight the demons that she had battled in loneliness for so long were dissolving into wisps of harmless smoke. It was then that she began to cry, sobbing deeply into his shoulder, and Billy held her that way long into the night.

The next morning he insisted on driving back to town. As she was seeing him off under a freshly-washed sky, with a crisp breeze whipping at her hair and stinging her cheeks, Maggie felt light and free as a feather. Billy smiled, running his finger along her cheek and allowing his eyes to linger on her face. "You look fresh and new as a colt this morning and I feel as old as Solomon. It's a hell of a note, Maggie."

His voice troubled her and she hugged him tightly. "You're not old. You're wonderful. And if you are old, you're a wonderful old man."

He nodded. "I am wonderful, true. But not quite wonderful enough to turn the world around."

She smiled up at him. "Why would you want to do that?"

"Because I'd have given you a father."

She stared at him, sensing his pain, and understanding for the first time what had evolved the night before. And with sudden, complete clarity, she knew he was right.

Billy forced a smile. "It's all right, Maggie. You were bound to elect somebody."

Maggie's relationship with Billy Reiter, which had never been marked by consuming passion, mellowed after that night. But they remained close. His career had reached a plateau while at the same time, Maggie could sense, he felt age tugging at him. She understood why he valued her youth and vitality, and they shared a natural integrity. For her part Maggie needed in her life the steadying influence that Billy offered. He was a talented and knowledgeable Hollywood survivor with much to teach a willing pupil in matters of craft and commerce, and it was to his direction and advice that she owed much of her success. But years afterward she would wonder bleakly how she could have supposed that the web of murder and vengeance in which she was caught up could fail to entangle one for whom she cared so deeply.

The next afternoon Lyla drove out to the beach in a shiny red Packard convertible with a copy of the morning paper, which carried an account of the near riot at the mortuary. Maggie refused to look at it and Lyla, shrugging, dropped the newspaper into the trash. "It's sad, isn't it," she mused. "Your showing up there was the only way Wally's funeral ever would have made the front page."

The friendship between Maggie and Lyla had endured through the years. As Maggie's career began to skyrocket she found herself in a position to secure work for Lyla, usually cast as her brassy and faithless romantic rival. After a few of these roles Lyla began to joke that if she had a nickel for evey guy who dropped her for love of Margaret Marshall she'd never have to work again. But Lyla's affection for Maggie never wavered, and if it became obvious quickly that Lyla's screen presence would never seize the public fancy as Maggie had, her disappointment never surfaced. Then one bright Sunday afternoon a year or so earlier Lyla's life had changed dramatically.

Maggie had invited Lyla for a weekend at the beach house. An eighty-foot motor cruiser, crisp white with bright pennants fluttering in the breeze, had anchored in the blue-green water off the strand the day before. Lyla, who was forever fascinated by the gossip potential of the Colony, quickly learned that the yacht belonged to millionaire publisher Anson Wilkening, who was the guest of director Rex Ingram. Lyla was bubbling with excitement. "And he's throwing a big buffet on board tonight. Everybody on the beach is invited!"

The prospect of a party did not entice Maggie, but Lyla was determined to go. And since it would have been awkward for her to attend alone, Maggie agreed to go with her.

That night, as Maggie and Lyla were ferried out from the beach in a dinghy, phonograph music drifted out across the water from the brightly lit yacht. The vessel was strung from bow to stern with Japanese lanterns, and the teakwood decks were lit by Polynesian torches, the smoking flames reflected in the spotless, polished brass fittings. Crewmembers in starched white uniforms served drinks and caviar hors d'oeuvres, and tables were laden with every conceivable delicacy, from pheasant to an exotic Chinese dish of marinated raw fish.

Anson Wilkening presided over all of this, a small, wiry man with piercing black eyes and rough, prospector's hands. Maggie knew little of Wilkening, except that he had amassed a fortune in copper in the nineties, and of late had branched out into publishing as a forum for some rather militant political views. Striking out as a young man across the trackless wastes of Utah and Arizona, with no more in assets than a sturdy pack mule and his two hands, he had wrenched millions from the scorched, rocky earth. Now, it was rumored, his interest had shifted to films and he was poised to finance an Ingram biography of his own early years prospecting in the desert.

Wilkening greeted Maggie and Lyla as they came aboard, looking somewhat uncomfortable in an immaculately tailored blazer and open-collared silk shirt. Maggie received the impression of a mistrustful, tightly contained personality concealed behind the sinewy exterior. She smiled to herself as they exchanged cordialities. *He feels as out of place here as I do.*

But if he was awkward with Maggie, his weathered eyes suddenly fired and began to devour Lyla, who gave Maggie an alarmed look as Wilkening swept her away toward the stern where couples were dancing to a rather dated Jolson recording of "Time and Again." Betty Bronson, under contract to Louis Mayer and a neighbor of Maggie's, joined her to watch Lyla and Wilkening dancing. She observed wryly, "I don't know much about that man, but I'd say he knows what he wants when he spots it." Within the hour Lyla and Wilkening had disappeared.

The party had a stiff feeling about it, as though Wilkening had gone through the motions of catering to what he imagined was Hollywood decadence. In fact, once the strangely reserved man had departed the party livened up. But Maggie was not in the mood for such an evening; she nibbled at a seafood salad, finished her glass of wine, and asked the rather aloof first officer if she could be taken back to the beach.

As the sailor rowed her back she contemplated the brightly lit yacht and wondered what it was in Lyla that had triggered Wilkening's sudden interest. As the sailor's oars lapped the water, her mind drifted back over the years with a vaguely disturbing insistence to that first party in the Hollywood Hills that she had gone to with Lyla.

That night Maggie's sleep was troubled, and when she awoke the next morning Wilkening's yacht had lifted anchor and was gone, and Lyla with it.

* * *

It was almost a month before Lyla returned, driving out along the beach trail in a new, shiny yellow Packard convertible, the first of an endless line of such cars that Wilkening would buy her as soon as the paint dulled on the last one. She waved merrily as Maggie came out on the porch to greet her with an exasperated shake of her head. "You could at least have dropped me a postcard, you know."

Lyla jumped out of the car and gave her a hug. "Don't be mad. They don't have postcards in the places we went, and the mail travels by mules anyway."

Wilkening had taken her to the Gulf of California, to explore wild, lonely coasts and tiny fishing villages. Lyla was ecstatic. "It's wonderful. I know he seems . . . different. But he comes alive in places like that, where there aren't any people for miles and miles. And I did too. I never imagined I could be so happy sleeping on a beach with God knows what sorts of creatures prowling around in the night. I don't know whether you can believe it or not, but I didn't ever want to come back."

Maggie smiled. "Sounds lovely."

Lyla sobered, troubled for the moment. "I mean it. I really didn't. It's not good for him. He bottles himself up when he comes back to civilization." Her frown deepened. "I think it's dangerous for him."

Maggie sensed that something about Wilkening disturbed Lyla, something that she refused to face squarely. But whatever the drawbacks, Lyla was happier than Maggie had ever known her to be, and that was enough. And this animated response to the primitive, however surprising, was obviously what Wilkening had sensed in her that first night on his yacht.

In weeks and months to come Maggie would begin to understand what it was about Wilkening that troubled Lyla. Beneath his uncomplicated and complete love for her he was fiercely possessive. Maggie would discover that Wilkening had never come to terms with the world of cities and crowded masses of people; it was as though he had banished that part of himself in order to survive his years of wandering the desert in solitude. He would forever be an outsider, except in the sealed world he forged for himself and Lyla. Despite his shrewd business acumen, the world of bright lights and laughter held much terror for him, and he lived in fear that lesser men who operated freely in that world might one day take Lyla from him.

But for the moment Maggie was content that Lyla was happy, as yet unaware that Wilkening's fears would be realized eventually, destroying lives and fortunes—and that when they were, Maggie's whole world would be destroyed as well.

Maggie and Lyla were having lunch on the deck when the phone rang. During her first years at the beach Maggie had been completely and blissfully cut off from the world. But as other film personalities and executives began their migration to her haven, a phone line quickly followed. Sometimes it seemed to Maggie that without telephones the whole movie industry would collapse. It was exasperating, but once the phones were there Maggie decided that she might as well have one.

Lyla jumped up. "I'll get it. It's probably Anson."

But it wasn't. Lyla listened for a moment, then turned blankly to Maggie, covering the mouthpiece. "It's Ben Montgomery."

If it had been President Coolidge it would have caused no more surprise. For a moment Maggie's legs felt weak, then she rose abruptly to take the phone from Lyla.

It was not that Maggie and Montgomery had had no contact over the years. She was after all the foremost in his stable of leading women, but their dealings had been professional and perfunctory. Charlotte, his secretary, would send the customary flowers to her dressing room at the beginning of a new picture, and at major openings they would embrace and offer surface smiles for the photographers and newsreel cameramen. Apart from the studio they almost never ran into each other since neither of them was part of the Hollywood social scene and some twenty miles separated Maggie's beach house and Montgomery's brooding, Spanish-Gothic Beverly Hills mansion. And in the four years since signing her to her first contract with A.U.P., Montgomery had never called her at home.

Lyla winked. "Why don't I take me for a walk?"

"Hello," Maggie said into the receiver, hoping her voice did not betray the turmoil of her emotions.

His voice was impersonal, businesslike, but Maggie thought she detected a strained effort to keep it that way,

"I saw the morning paper. I wanted to say I'm glad you thought about Wally. I'm sorry about what happened."

Maggie's shoulders sagged with disappointment. It was a courtesy call, then. "I suppose it was foolish to go. I thought I might not be recognized."

"Yes, I suppose so. At least you weren't hurt."

"No."

There was a hesitation, and then he abruptly changed the subject. "There's something else. I want to talk to you. It's something I want to explain personally."

She frowned. "We could talk at the studio."

His voice became impatient. "We could. I'd prefer it if you came into town." There was a trace of weary resignation in his voice. "This has to do with a personal situation."

It was rare that Montgomery asked Maggie for anything other than her signature on a contract, and he paid for that. Dearly. Maggie had no idea what he wanted, but she intended to enjoy the moment. "I was planning on spending the weekend out here. But if you'd like to drive out I have the whole evening free."

"Yes, I understand.. I'd like to do that but there are reasons why I can't." There was a new strain in his voice, as though some governor on his emotions was dangerously close to snapping. She hesitated. "You want me to come to your house?"

He became impatient again. "Certainly, to my house. Do you know how to find it?"

"Yes. On Doheny, isn't it?"

"Will eight o'clock give you enough time?"

She sighed; he had made an infuriating leap from asking her to come to assuming she would. But she put her irritation aside. Now she was curious and, despite herself, concerned for him. "Yes. Eight o'clock."

Maggie wandered back out onto the deck; the ocean, far out beyond the mild, frothy surf, was darkening under a front of dark clouds rolling in over the point a couple of miles to the northwest. At first, after she put down the receiver, she'd been seized by alarm, fearing that somehow the secret that she and Montgomery shared between them had finally come to light and all who had been part of it would now be called to account. She knew Samuel Lendt, whose son was still locked away in a madhouse, had not forgotten and would never forgive. During the intervening years Lendt had behaved as though Maggie didn't exist, not even participating in her salary negotiations except to rubber-stamp whatever numbers Montgomery forwarded to him. At first she'd been surprised that Lendt could apparently with equanimity pocket the hundreds of thousands of dollars that her films earned him. But she grew to accept Billy Reiter's verdict: "My dear, Moses himself would tremble to stand between a studio chief and a trip to the bank."

The breeze freshened in advance of the turbulence and Maggie turned her face into it. No, Montgomery had said his summons had to do with a personal situation. It must be urgent. She knew him well enough to realize he would as soon cut off his arm as invite anyone into his personal life. Thoughts of Sheila Moreno, his wife, forced their way into her mind.

Sheila's career had peaked at about the time of her marriage to Montgomery. By the second year there were those who said Sheila's fiery personality had mellowed with her marriage and she was content in her new role as homemaker. Then again, less kind sources had it that Montgomery's demanding personality had crushed her spirit. Whatever the truth of the matter the marriage had been childless, and in recent months dark stories had reached Maggie of screaming tantrums in the Doheny mansion, and it was rumored that Montgomery often slept at the studio.

Lyla came up from the beach to join Maggie on the deck, giving her a sly look. "You don't have to tell me if you don't want to. But on the other hand, if you don't I won't tell you what I found out."

Maggie smiled. "You don't have to blackmail me. He wants me to come to his house tonight for a talk."

Lyla arched her eyebrows. "Well now. That should be cozy. Just you and Ben and Sheila."

Maggie shook her head. "He wouldn't do that. Whatever he wants, Sheila has nothing to do with it. That much I'm sure about."

"Whatever you say," Lyla shrugged. "Then you're going?"

"I said I would." Then she laughed, remembering. "No, I didn't say it. But I am." She glanced at Lyla. "Okay, I told you. Now what's your big secret?"

Lyla studied her fingernails. "I just happen to have found out who's building the new place up the beach by the bridge."

Maggie stared at her with a sense of foreboding; suddenly she knew the answer, even before she asked. "Who, then?"

Lyla glanced up. "Him," she said. "Ben Montgomery."

Montgomery's sprawling, tile-roofed home occupied two-and-a-half acres behind a high and forbidding stucco wall. Maggie pulled to a halt in the drive and announced herself to a microphone hidden somewhere in the recesses of a large buttress, and the heavy wrought-iron gaites swung silently open before her on oiled hinges. Beyond the gates the house loomed dark and cheerless, a single lamp burning in the high, arched windows on the ground floor beyond the portico.

A heavy, broad-faced Mexican woman admitted her into a large, tile-floored foyer and from there showed her into a darkened sitting room at the top of a short flight of brick steps. In passing Maggie glanced into the formal living room, where the single lamp burned forlornly; it was immense, the walls climbing to darkened recesses above huge, carved beams, while a massive, cold fireplace anchored the opposite end of the cavern. The maid switched on a light in the sitting room and, motioning Maggie to a chair with a timid smile, shuffled out.

Maggie knew that Montgomery had bought the big house as a wedding present for his new wife, and while there had been no children she realized the chilling, pervasive emptimess of the place had nothing to do with the number of people who lived there.

She heard a muffled exchange of voices from upstairs, and then a door slam. Soon Montgomery came into the room. "I appreciate your coming tonight. Can I make you a drink?"

"No, thank you." Maggie was surprised and somewhat alarmed at his appearance. He was dressed casually in a rumpled polo shirt, a size too large, and faded trousers. Somehow the casual clothing seemed out of place on him, an almost pathetic attempt to fit the picture of a film executive relaxing at home. There were tired lines in his face while his eyes were restless, searching here and there with a futile, abstracted urgency.

"No? Fine. Then I won't either."

She watched him carefully. "Ben, what is it you wanted?"

He paced the sitting room. She never could have imagined him this way. "This is a bit awkward," he began. "But I just found out today and it seemed to me that I'd better talk to you so there wouldn't be any misunderstandings."

"Misunderstandings about what?"

"The house. The house my wife is building out there where you live."

Maggie frowned. "Your wife?"

"Yes. I was against it but she went ahead anyway." His voice was becoming ragged. "You see, Sheila seems to think a change of location might help her . . . us . . . with some problems that have come up recently. But I didn't want you to think that I was intruding . . ." He trailed off inconclusively as the maid passed outside the door, climbing up the stairs.

With sudden anger she began to understand. He wanted to disassociate himself from any proximity to her. She rose abruptly to leave.

"If that's all you asked me here for then I think I'll go now," she said coldly.

He stopped pacing to stare at her helplessly. "Don't go yet. Please." He searched for words. "I'm sorry if I put it badly. Listen, I'll have some coffee brought in." With some dismay she realized that he needed someone to talk to and had no idea in the world how to go about asking for that kind of help. Possibly he didn't even realize just why he had summoned her.

Suddenly a scream pierced the air, a long, high wail originating from the bedroom suite upstairs, echoing through the empty house to freeze Maggie and Montgomery where they stood in the sitting room. In that chiseled moment Maggie saw him undergo a transfiguration she would never witness again. The cry of terror seemed to pierce him to the soul: his face drained of color and, with clenched fists, he raised his eyes as though trying to see into the rooms upstairs. *"No!"* The cry was torn from the depths of him, as though by willing it he could erase whatever horror awaited him.

Maggie rushed to him. "Ben!" But he was completely rigid, his eyes staring remotely, as the wailing scream from upstairs continued.

Maggie stumbled frantically up the unfamiliar stairs, following the sound into the master bedroom wher she found the maid standing in the dressing room doorway, her hands covering her face, wailing hysterically. Maggie thrust the woman aside, plunging through the dressing room to pull up short in the bathroom entry. Sheila Moreno's pale nude body lay slumped in the sunken tub, the bathwater crimson beneath the pink-tinted white suds that floated on the surface. A straight razor lay nearby.

Maggie fought off the wave of panic that threatened to overwhelm her. She rushed to the bath, her sandals slipping on the bloodstained tiles, and began desperately trying to pull the woman's slippery, unconscious body from the tub. But Sheila's weight was too much for her and the hot, sweet smell given off by the bathwater sickened her. She sobbed, gasping, and hauled at the body again, this time succeeding in pulling Sheila halfway out of the bath, and exposing the ugly, sliced flesh of her wrists, which were welling terrifying rivers of blood over the limp, whitened hands.

Vertigo seized her; the bloodspattered bathroom was receding in her consciousness, as though seen through a reversed glass. Then suddenly Montgomery was there, in command of himself again, unalarmed and methodical, his voice reassuring. He turned Maggie away from the bath and firmly propelled her toward the door. "Go into the bedroom and call emergency. Tell them we'll be there within ten minutes."

Maggie, collecting herself, did as she was told. By the time she finished the call Montgomery was emerging from the dressing room with Sheila in his arms. He had knotted thick towels around the wounds on her wrists and thrown a dressing gown over her body. "Let's go. I'm afraid you'll have to drive." The maid, huddled in one corner of the enormous bedroom, watched with terrified eyes as they rushed out.

The hospital waiting room was almost empty; the few people there eyed the bloodstains on Maggie's dress with some interest but none of them, to her great relief, recognized her as Margaret Marshall. It was an hour later when Montgomery rejoined her, looking drawn and exhausted. At her inquiring look, he nodded. Apparently they'd delivered Sheila to the doctors in time.

In the parking lot Maggie started to put the car in gear but Montgomery stopped her. "Not yet. I don't think I want to go back there tonight." Maggie felt a desperate need to change out of her soiled clothes, but waited patiently for him to speak. He stared out the open window at the lighted floors of the hospital, breathing in the cool night air. "You saved Sheila's life, you know," he said musingly after a moment. "I would have let her die."

Maggie shook her head. "I don't believe that."

Then he told her about his marriage. Despite her tempestuous Irish-Mexican beauty and blazing screen presence, Montgomery had discovered his new wife to be an astonishingly insecure personality, suffocating him with her desperate need for reassurance. Maggie could almost be amused at the puzzled disappointment in his voice. She marvelled at the naïveté of someone in Montgomery's position who could not comprehend that the Sheila Moreno the screen presented was not necessarily the same woman a husband would find waiting in his bed. And with some pity she began to realize that Montgomery was possibly the worst man in the world for Sheila to have married. He would never understand Sheila's vulnerabilities, except as abstract dramatic elements to be manipulated as screen stories demanded.

But Montgomery had resolved with awesome determination that the marriage would not fail. That resolution had made his life a living hell for four years as Sheila's personality began to disintegrate before his eyes. Alcohol and cocaine had taken a toll too. But they could not blunt the paranoia that was responsible for her withdrawal from first her career and then the world at large.

There had also been earlier suicide attempts, and Montgomery had arranged for round-the-clock attendant care for his wife. This evening had been an attendant's night off, which was why he had insisted Maggie come to his house.

Of late, Sheila's obsessiveness had focused on escaping Montgomery's Spanish-Gothic mansion. Since the luminaries of the film world were migrating to Malibu, that' where she determined that she should live, whether Montgomery chose to accompany her or not. He'd opposed her but somehow she'd managed to move ahead on her own, buying a lot and hiring an architect. That afternoon, when Montgomery discovered what was happening behind his back, they fought violently.

Maggie knew the rest. He was tired now from the years of maintaining for the world's benefit that his private life was as well ordered as his studio, and his piercing blue eye were no longer able to conceal the pain within. Maggie's heart yielded. "We'll go to my house."

He looked at her for a long moment, then nodded.

At the beach the weather front had passed, unveiling a full moon. Maggie led Montgomery inside and then to her bed. He held her close for a long time, as though drinking peace from their coming together. Then she began to unbutton his shirt. When he was undressed, she left him to slip into the bathroom where she hurriedly discarded the bloodied dress. Naked, she returned to the bed and lay down next to him. They fell asleep almost immediately in each other's arms, her soft, slender body pressed against his hard, strong one.

At some point in the night he awoke and made love to her, urgently, without tenderness, and yet not cruelly, as if he needed to prove to them both as quickly as possible that she was his again. She shuddered with pleasure and pain as he took her violently, his passion hammering at her.

In the morning he seemed renewed. They made love again, slowly, savoring each sensation, and he was more gentle with her than she had dreamed a man could be, his large, strong hands caressing her as tenderly as if she were a fragile porcelain doll. She allowed herself the exquisite pleasure of exploring every inch of his body, her hands and mouth lingering on the special places that made him swell with desire. And all the while she whispered, "My love, my love . . ."

But later in the morning, as Maggie was making breakfast, he wandered off alone along the strand. She watched his figure disappear behind a shelf of beach, knowing his mind was troubled by thoughts of his wife and memories of the night before. Her own thoughts were troubled as well, but if she was not content, she was not alarmed. She knew that whatever happened now, she would never let him go.

CHAPTER 5

In the summer of 1926 Jimmy Knowland vacationed in Paris, and when he came back a dark shadow followed him. The change in him frightened Maggie.

Montgomery, as good as his word, had brought Jimmy into AUP as one of his stable of line producers. Since either Montgomery or Lendt had a finger on virtually every stage of every production, Jimmy had very little to do. But even at that he failed miserably. He lacked judgment and was completely incapable of imposing his will on headstrong directors and vain, demanding actors. Although he was well liked, the truth of the matter was that Jimmy could never be at home anywhere except on the ragged periphery of events. But success had been draped firmly over his shoulders by a quirk of fate and, sadly for Jimmy Knowland, no amount of shrugging could dislodge it.

Once Jimmy had conclusively demonstrated his incompetence, Montgomery had shunted him aside. Then, as his wife's disintegration became more pronounced, he somehow concluded that Jimmy would make a useful companion for her, providing Sheila with a reassuring link to the world of film production. Besides, he knew he could count on Jimmy's silence. So Jimmy was assigned to "develop" projects with Sheila in which she would star and he would produce, hopefully keeping both of them occupied and out of Montgomery's way. But it was a cruel charade, deceiving no one, and although Jimmy was extraordinarily well paid for his services, the story conferences he and Sheila convened more and more often were fueled by fifths of Remy Martin.

Under such circumstances it was almost inevitable that Jimmy and Sheila would become either violent enemies or passionate lovers, forging a conspiracy against their common oppressor, Montgomery. Since Jimmy was by nature incapable of establishing himself as anyone's enemy, it was not long before Sheila took him into her arms. Montgomery, of course, was completely unaware of the affair.

During this period Maggie saw little of Jimmy, and when she did run into him he seemed distant and uncommunicative. Lunching on the set one day she told Lyla she was worried about him. "He looks so . . . frantic." At the time she knew only that he had been assigned to work closely with Sheila Moreno. "Maybe there's something we ought to do."

"Stay out of it, that's what we can do," Lyla said shortly, and changed the subject.

Later Maggie would learn that Lyla, in whom Jimmy had confided, had told him to quit AUP and put as much distance between himself and Montgomery's wife as he could. But Jimmy was incapable of surrendering his caricature of success, and his relationship with Lyla had become strained.

Only much later did Lyla break her pledge of secrecy to Jimmy and reveal the whole story to Maggie. And when Maggie knew it all she was stupefied that Montgomery did not anticipate the disaster of which he had been the chief architect. But she well knew that as far as intimate human affairs were concerned Montgomery was cursed with a blind spot. Until the very end, as long as she remained by his side, she would have to guard him from himself where matters of the heart were concerned.

On his return from Europe Jimmy drove out from town one morning for lunch with Maggie and Lyla at the beach house. They were surprised to discover him suddenly endowed with a rather precious fatalism as well as a fine contempt for the craft of movie-making.

"Look, ladies, Griffith himself said we couldn't call movies art until something comes along to equal Shakespeare or Ibsen." They were at a table outside, watching flights of pelicans diving for small fish just beyond the mild, sparkling surf. Lunch was cold chicken, cheese, and hearts of romaine, with a chilled bottle of French Chablis. Jimmy eyed Maggie directly. "You have to admit, even Ben Montgomery wouldn't know Ibsen from one of his own continuity writers."

Maggie laughed; she was forever bored by "film as art" tirades, but she was amused by Jimmy's new pretentiousness. Lyla, however, quickly became exasperated. "Oh? And you would? Listen, my boy, when I first bumped into you, you were stirring your coffee with your soup spoon."

Jimmy grinned. "When I could borrow a nickel for a cup of coffee in the first place." Maggie was pleased that some of Jimmy's old humor had returned. But as lunch progressed and he almost single-handedly disposed of the bottle of Chablis, a new and disturbing side of him began to surface. He began to talk about death. "It's the most important event of your life. Don't you ever think about it?"

He'd directed the question to Maggie, but Lyla abruptly rose and began clearing the dishes. "If he's going to get morbid on top of everything else, I'm going in and listen to Bessie Smith."

When they were alone Maggie tried to change the subject, but Jimmy persisted. "Maggie, what if I told you I met some people over there who taught me how to conquer my fear of death?"

She smiled indulgently. "I'd be surprised you didn't find pleasanter ways to spend your time in Paris."

"I'm serious, Maggie." He frowned. "You should listen. You see, you never think about death and that's how you run away from it. But death must be embraced. You should approach it as you would an ideal lover. It should be a perfect climax."

He was serious, Maggie realized. And although he was dishing out thoughts he'd pick up secondhand somewhere, Jimmy's brooding intensity cast a shadow over the bright, seaside noontime. Bessie Smith's rich voice came drifting from the house to be snatched away by the breeze as Lyla started the Victrola.

Suddenly Maggie's common sense rebelled at the gloom Jimmy was spreading over the day. "Listen, if you expect me to sit here and smile like a little moron while you try to glamourize suicide, you've come to the wrong house. Suicide is . . . dirty."

Jimmy's eyes fired. "No, you're wrong. 'Suicide' is a dirty-sounding word. But death is beautiful. Harry Crosby helped me to understand that."

For the first time Maggie sensed the depth of the change in him, and that realization brought with it a vague, dreadful premonition. But she set her fears aside and firmly directed the conversation to other matters.

Later Jimmy found a sunny spot on the deck and fell asleep on a chaise. The breeze freathered wisps of his pale hair, which Maggie noticed had begun to thin. But his features were relaxed and boyish in sleep.

In that moment he seemed to her incredibly vulnerable to the stresses of time and human strife, and she was overwhelmed by a profound feeling of pity for him.

Much later, in the wake of the tragedy at Malibu, Montgomery had dispatched Gerrard to discover what he could about Jimmy's stay in Paris. According to the detective's report Jimmy had passed himself off as a young film maker and operated on the fringes of the expatriate artist community. As well as such names as Gertrude Stein, Ernest Hemingway and F. Scott Fitzgerald, this group also included the author of *Red Skeletins*, Harry Crosby, the black sheep heir of a Boston financial empire who held court in Byzantine decadence in a Left Bank flat he rented from a Rumanian princess. Crosby was the prince-patron of a morbid and, some said, diseased court of *culturati*, worshipers of Huysmans, Wilde, and Poe. Rumors that they conducted demonic rites abounded.

With his own compass points abandoned or lost, Jimmy was apparently completely seduced by Crosby's bleak vision and headlong rush toward oblivion. All of which, Gerrard's report suggested, was costumed in riotous sexual anarchy, blasé world-weariness, and literary despair.

Maggie could understand how Jimmy, aware that events in his life had catapulted completely beyond his control, must have been particularly susceptible. Reading between the lines of Gerrard's report, she realized that at some point during his strange summer's sojourn, with Harry Crosby serving as his guide, Jimmy opened the door on a rushing vortex in his own soul which held a hypnotic fascination for him, and into which he would shortly plunge, pulling Sheila Moreno with him.

* * *

The fall and winter months of that year were among the happiest of Maggie's life. With Sheila undergoing treatment in a Vermont clinic, far from Hollywood's prying eyes and ears, she had Montgomery almost entirely to herself.

Maggie tried not to think about Sheila. But her sense of right and wrong was too strong for her to forget for very long that Montgomery had a wife. Her self-judgment was inevitably harsh. But if she was a harsh moralist, she was also a harshly analytical realist. Sheila and Montgomery meant destruction for each other. Any life they attempted together would be a continuing nightmare. And if fate had dictated that Sheila could not have Montgomery, then Maggie intended to.

Montgomery finished the bungalow his wife had begun, a pleasant little villa with low white walls and a bright red tile roof, which anchored the strand where the soft green bluffs dropped abruptly off to meet the sea. As the villa neared completion, he asked Maggie to decorate it for him. They were standing in the spacious, parquet-floored living room; in the next room carpenters were putting the finishing touches on the cabinetwork amid smells of sawdust, fresh wood, and new paint. Maggie frowned. "I don't think so." Making a home, it seemed to her, was a wife's work.

Montgomery merely shrugged. "Okay. I don't blame you. I'll have Tommy Everson send some things out."

Everson was Montgomery's chief set decorator at AUP and Maggie could imagine what kind of furnishings he would dispatch to the beach. She laughed. "All right, you win. But you're going to regret it."

She started by demanding that he take the following day off for a furniture-buying expedition. He grumbled, but finally went along with her. And, despite the fact it ended up costing him a small fortune, he seemed to enjoy himself on the outing. As Maggie shopped he interrogated sales clerks and store managers about their movie-going tastes, all the while cheerfully scribbling checks as the purchases mounted.

By early afternoon, in a Santa Monica antique shop, she'd had enough. Exasperated by his total detachment from what was supposed to have been a joint project, she singled out a garish love seat upholstered in ermine-trimmed zebra, which carried a twelve-hundred-dollar price tag. Montgomery, who was just then defending Ramon Novarro's recently released *Ben Hur* to a skeptical sales clerk, hardly glanced at the monstrosity as he reached for his checkbook. Maggie put her foot down.

"Listen," she said, taking him aside. "We're supposed to be furnishing your home, not conducting an audience reaction survey. You might at least *look* at what I'm spending your money on."

He stared at her in some surprise, his eyes lighting with amusement. "I think it's all fine. If I didn't think so I would have said something."

It didn't happen that day, but finally Maggie would come to accept the fact that Montgomery cared next to nothing about his surroundings. He expected comfort commensurate with his wealth, of course, but he would have been as happy living out of a good hotel as a home of his own. The cozy touches Maggie added to his beach bungalow usually passed him entirely by. And when they were pointedly indicated to him they generally inspired little more than perfunctory praise and a perplexed glance or two at the bright curtains or flower arrangement or whatever the item in question was.

That evening found them prowling the import shops in the vicinity of the harbor, and they stopped at a little dockside Armenian restaurant for supper. Maggie was delighted; familiar from her childhood with the exotic sounding dishes on the menu, she ordered kufta—spicy meats wrapped in grape leaves—and cracker bread and shishkebab. The owner, recognizing her as Margaret Marshall, sent over a bottle of red wine that carried his own label. His name was Kazanjian. He was a big, good-natured man with a booming voice and a thick brush of a moustache. He had lived as a boy in Fresno and his family still operated a winery there where his label had its origins.

He joined them for coffee after dinner and was delighted to learn that he and Maggie had common roots. He began talking about his sons and daughters, who apparently numbered in the dozens. He seemed immensely proud of the whole clan, with one notable exception.

"My second oldest boy didn't like to work in the restaurant so he ran off to sea. Never even wrote his mother a letter. If he ever comes back I'm going to take him by the scruff of the neck and send him on his knees to beg her forgiveness."

Kazanjian was equally outraged when he learned that Maggie had never gone back home. "What about your poor mother? Maybe she's dead. Did you ever think about that?"

Maggie smiled. "I doubt it." *If he knew my mother,* she thought, *he wouldn't be quite so worried.*

Kazanjian shook his big head sadly. "You youngsters these days. Look at you . . . a big movie star. You have everything. Big cars, swimming pools—"

"I don't have a swimming pool," Maggie pointed out with some amusement.

"Never mind. You know what I mean. Once you have the whole world at your fingertips, in no time at all you forget where you came from and the people who brought you into the world."

Suddenly Montgomery pushed back his chair. "It's time we were getting back." His eyes had clouded over and Maggie could see that something was troubling him.

On the drive back to Malibu Montgomery seemed preoccupied. Finally he frowned impatiently. "Don't you ever wonder who I am?"

The question puzzled her. "I know who you are."

"I mean where I came from. My family. The kinds of things Kazanjian was talking about back there."

The truth was that she had often been curious about his past. But, fearing to intrude on his fierce sense of privacy, she'd never felt comfortable in asking. "It never seemed important. Is there something I should know?"

So he told her about himself. Born to a strict Episcopalian bishop and his retiring wife, Montgomery's Vermont upbringing had been rigid and barren of love. His father, an elitist by nature, expected Montgomery to follow him into the High Church ministry and spared no effort to protect his willful son from worldly influences.

When Montgomery's remarkable drive quickly established him as a leader among his classmates, the bishop withdrew him from public school and hired private tutors to provide for his education. From then on Montgomery's almost nonexistent social life had the church for its focus. And, as training for future responsibilities, he was required to sit in on the weekly councils of the church elders.

"So there I was in my knickers with my hair slicked down, barely able to see over the top of the table, while the old coots kicked around whichever poor bastard it was that week they suspected wasn't tithing up to his full ten percent. My God, I would have been bored even if I had known what they were talking about."

In that way, Maggie learned, were Montgomery's natural energies smothered. It was inevitable that he would make his escape.

"When I was fifteen the bishop put me on a train for the seminary. He gave me a ten dollar bill. It was the first spending money I ever had. And off I went. The train stopped in Boston and I got off long enough to mail his ten dollars back to him and caught the next freight out of town. And I've never heard from him since."

He paused thoughtfully. "You know, sometimes I can still feel him watching me and hear him quoting Proverbs: *A foolish son is a grief to his father, and bitterness to her that bore him.*" He smiled. "Now there's a verse Kazanjian could sink his teeth into."

Finally Maggie began to understand why Montgomery seemed so isolated within himself; he'd had to become that way to endure the solitude of his childhood. But there was more.

Reckless years on the road followed Montgomery's escape; if the world at large had been shut out of his boyhood, he now plunged into it with a vengeance. He was swallowed up by the shifting legions of dispossessed immigrants, misfits, and vagabonds who crisscrossed the country aimlessly in those days, following the harvests or working at whatever odd jobs came to hand. Montgomery learned about sex in a fifty-cent Toledo brothel, and a rusty can opener left the jagged scar under his ribs during a fight over a can of stewed apricots in a Great Falls hobo jungle.

His mind was too active and, as an ironic result of the bishop's rearing, too disciplined to remain idle while his body learned the techniques of brute survival. He read whatever came to hand voraciously: newspapers, discarded magazines, whatever books came his way. Ideas intrigued him and, sickened by the wretchedness around him, at seventeen he had a fling with the International Workers of the World. He was there that bitter winter of 1913 when Kelly's Army of fifteen hundred jobless farmworkers marched on Sacramento, to be greeted by eight hundred special deputies armed with warrants, ax handles, and guns. After that experience he drifted in other directions. The Wobblies, he concluded, generally marched out with high élan, got their heads kicked in, and then the wretchedness went on as before, except usually worse.

Besides, while ideas intrigued him, stories seized his imagination, human stories about ordinary dreams, romances, and failures. As he came across such anecdotes in his aimless odyssey he tried to write them down. But reading them over he realized that some spark was missing; that his function, whatever it was, was not that of the storyteller. However, he catalogued hundreds of such stories in his mind during his time on the road, many of which he planted successfully with filmwriters in later years.

Following the winter wheat harvest through Denver in 1912 he saw his first movie, Sidney Olcott's *From the Manger to the Cross*. He was unmoved. The harsh lighting and stilted performances had little to do with reality. And for Montgomery, a good story had to be firmly rooted in reality.

He discarded the movies as a novelty until he landed in Hollywood three years later and found day work on Griffith's *Babylon* as an extra. He discovered a film industry that was casting about, experimenting, beginning to find itself. It was chaos, but at the bottom the business was story-telling; a remarkably intricate business requiring men of enormous drive and persuasion to bring all of the disparate pieces together. And when he understood the nature of the movie business, Montgomery knew that he had finally found his function in the world of fantasy.

That night they went to bed on Maggie's screened-in sleeping porch. The surf was gentle beyond the slope of the beach, tumbling luminescent in the moonlight, reminding her of that first night he'd brought her to this place. Stirred, she allowed her hand to drift along his belly, and felt his immediate response to her touch. She owned all of him now, his past and his future. As though emblematic of that new sense of possession, she held him firmly as she raised herself atop him and guided his sex into her own. Afterwards he went to sleep quickly. It was a while before she followed, and at one point she heard him protest sharply in his dreams. She wondered if he'd felt his father's eyes on him again.

In January of 1927 Sheila Moreno returned home from her treatments, officially ending Maggie's idyll with Ben Montgomery. But for all practical purposes it had ended a week earlier, when Maggie first realized that she was pregnant.

She was standing under hot lights on the set of her latest film, a Civil War epic under the direction of George Fitzmaurice, for which she'd been costumed in heavy crinolines, when suddenly she fainted. She came to in her dressing room with Fitzmaurice hovering over her. She was sure that she was carrying Ben Montgomery's child. It was all she could do to fend off the panic that threatened to engulf her.

A call had been put through to Montgomery and he was there in minutes, his presence emptying the dressing room instantly.

"What on earth happened?" he demanded once they were alone.

She watched him carefully as she lied. "I fainted." She hoped her smile was convincing. "As a frail magnolia blossom of the plantations I have a right to do that every so often. Particularly after the seventh take under three kliegs."

Instantly she regretted having chosen that excuse. Montgomery would no doubt take some hide off Fitzmaurice, who was a nice and a talented man, and some lighting grips might well find themselves out of work by wrap time. But at least he seemed to believe her.

He nodded. "Okay. As long as you're sure there's nothing wrong. I'll shut down the picture until you're ready to come back."

She protested, but not energetically. She desperately needed time to think.

Montgomery ordered a limousine to take her back to the beach. During the drive Maggie tried to think things through rationally.

She and Montgomery had talked of marriage. But it was clear to both of them that Sheila would have to be well again before he could risk asking her for a divorce. Maggie did not doubt his commitment, and was prepared to wait patiently for the time when he could safely leave his wife.

But the child . . .

My child will have a name, whatever the cost.

She knew Mexican divorces could be had quickly, but it would depend on Sheila's condition when she returned. Montgomery said that her doctors had told him that her progress had been excellent. *It might just be possible*, Maggie thought. But she would have to see for herself.

And she knew that if it was not possible, there was only one person to whom she could turn.

It was a week after Sheila's return that Maggie arranged a visit. She did so through Jimmy Knowland, who had resumed his duties as Sheila's companion, and without Montgomery's knowledge.

Sheila had come back to live at the Beverly Hills house, apparently determined to renovate it from top to bottom. Montgomery had given her a free hand, assuming it would be therapeutic. He told Maggie that Sheila hadn't mentioned the Malibu house and he'd been happy not to raise the subject.

She and Jimmy arrived at the sprawling, Spanish-Gothic mansion on an afternoon of blustering rain which had flooded surface streets and turned the hillside gutters into torrents of mud. If Jimmy was curious about her mission, he kept it to himself. But his attitude troubled Maggie. Since his return from Europe he had behaved as though he were carrying with him a secret knowledge which, by its possession, made the doings of less aware mortals pale to insignificance. But, preoccupied with her own problems, she dismissed his attitude as mere pretentiousness. He was almost cheerful as they approached Montgomery's house. "Sheila's really coming along. Her weight's back up and she hasn't touched a drop since she got back. You would have to have seen her before she went away. It was pretty rocky there for a while."

Maggie, of course, had seen Shila before she went away but she preferred not to think about it. She smiled. "I'm glad for her. Do you think she'll ever be able to go back to work?"

Jimmy shrugged. "If Montgomery will let her. But he probably won't. That's how he controls her, you know. He saps her confidence. In fact, he tries that little trick with everybody."

She looked at him. "Do you really believe that?"

He nodded. "Sure. There are people like that. Spirits, I should say. Incubi." Jimmy drove on blandly. "They're really very easy to spot, once you know what you're looking for. And once you recognize them, then you have nothing to fear from them."

Maggie stared at him, not quite sure whether he was making a joke. He wasn't. And then, for the first time, Maggie realized that he was no longer rational.

Her heart sank again when Sheila made an appearance. Battalions of carpenters and painters had invaded the house and plaster dust hung in the air amid sounds of hammering and sawing. Montgomery's wife swept in to greet them wearing a scarlet day gown with long sleeves that covered her wrists.

She embraced Jimmy affectionately, all the while keeping her eyes warily on Maggie. Maggie realized instantly that Sheila and Jimmy were lovers. It was also perfectly clear to her that Sheila's sanity was stretched as tight as a drumhead.

Maggie forced a smile. "I hope I'm not intruding. I had some things to talk over with Jimmy and so I came along for the ride."

A frown flickered uncertainly in Sheila's eyes, but Jimmy's innocent, reassuring smile erased it. She smiled and embraced Maggie. To Maggie her body felt tense as a coiled spring. "Of course not. In fact I've been dying to show somebody what I'm doing to the house." But her enthusiasm rang hollow, as though the energy source for her once combustible personality had dampened, and she was carrying a dead weight in its place.

So they toured the house. Sheila chattered away at a manic pace, constantly seeking reassurances from Jimmy and ignoring Maggie almost completely. Maggie watched them with a growing sense of dread. At one point she paused in a doorway; Jimmy and Sheila moved on as though they had forgotten Maggie existed. They stood at the window on the far side of the drawing room, heads tilted toward each other as they spoke in low tones, etched against the cold, rain-spattered day outside like two children trapped indoors by the storm.

Maggie's vague sense of dread coalesced into awful, certain knowledge. Sheila and Jimmy were even more than lovers; somehow, under Montgomery's eyes and in his own home, they had managed to create a world of their own. Suddenly Maggie was terrified, remembering Jimmy's obsession with death, and the bloody scene she'd come upon in Sheila's bath five months earlier.

She swallowed her panic, then walked across the room to join them. "Jimmy, maybe we ought to go now."

Sheila frowned at the intrusion, quickly turning to take Jimmy's arm. "You can't go now. We have to work on the script. I promised Ben."

Jimmy turned to Maggie. "I should stay. I really should."

Sheila jumped into the opening. "Let me call you a taxi, Maggie. It will be here in no time."

Maggie started to protest, then silenced herself. Whatever was going on between Jimmy and Sheila, she wouldn't be able to undo in one afternoon. Sheila, obviously relieved, hurried off to make the call. Jimmy stared after her.

"We're not going to work on the script. I quit kidding myself about that a long time ago." He turned to face Maggie. "But she can't live without me. She really can't, because I'm the only one who understands about him."

Maggie felt she had to reach him in the few moments that were left between them. She knew that once she left this place her concerns would be for others than Jimmy Knowland and Sheila Moreno. "Jimmy, you're wrong. Please believe me."

He smiled condescendingly. "I'm not wrong. You just don't understand. Remember what I said in the car about Montgomery? He almost destroyed her. But now, because of me, Sheila has nothing to fear from him."

"The taxi will be here in ten minutes." It was Sheila, standing in the doorway. She was looking at Maggie and Jimmy, pouting like a little girl who has not been included in a secret.

As the taxi rolled away from the house, its windows pelted by cold rain, Maggie huddled in the back seat, wrapping her arms tightly about herself to ward off the cold fear that beset her. She realized that instead of finding a cure, Sheila had merely exchanged one form of madness for another. And if Sheila were to be saved, then Montgomery would have to be told. He would have to deal with the problem directly.

But that, Maggie knew, would take time. Much time, as the poison Jimmy represented was expelled from Sheila's mind. If that could be accomplished.

What would happen to them all? Sheila, Jimmy, Ben Montgomery, whom she would never have for her own after all—even herself? With chilling determination she forced all such considerations from her mind and her heart. Only one thought obsessed her: *my baby comes first.*

Once away from Montgomery's house she ordered the driver to take her to Pasadena, to the familiar address in the steep hills overlooking the San Gabriel Valley and the Santa Anita racecourse. She knocked at the door with a trembling hand, suddenly frightened that he would turn her away. It was unspeakably arrogant of her to assume that she could hurl herself back into a man's life this way.

The door opened and Billy Reiter stood in the doorway, obviously startled by her appearance. "My God, Maggie . . ."

She tried to speak, but suddenly she was weeping incoherently. She clung to him desperately when he took her in his arms. He spoke soft, reassuring words to her, and then took her into his house.

Billy knew about her affair with Montgomery. He had, in fact, stepped gracefully out of the picture when he saw that there was room in Maggie life for only one lover. She had broken the news to him the day following Sheila's attempted suicide as they were lunching in the studio commissary.

He seemed more concerned for her than surprised at the turn of events. "I can see why he needs someone like you, Maggie," he said thoughtfully. "Inside Ben Montgomery's mind must be the loneliest place in the world. But what is it he's going to give you?"

The question surprised Maggie; she'd never thought of her relationship with Montgomery in that way. She knew that Montgomery would never be able to open his heart to her in the way she would like. And she knew also that his work would always come first. But she also knew that none of that mattered—because Montgomery was a man who reached for the stars, and his invitation to share that dizzying vault made all other considerations pointless. But she could not say that to Billy, partly because Billy stood in Montgomery's shadow, but also because he could never understand the cold, chiseled beauty of that uncompromising drive which set Montgomery apart. And Maggie could. For better or for worse she could never settle for less than what Montgomery had to offer.

So she answered him with a smile. "I don't know. Maybe questions like that shouldn't have to be answered until after the show closes."

Billy frowned, possibly realizing that she had not spoken

her true feelings, but let it go at that. He'd wished her the best and promised to be there if she ever needed him.

And now she needed him. Desperately.

In the early evening she returned to the beach. She packed and then, while she waited for Billy to come and take her away, she sat down at her desk. She wrote Montgomery a long letter, explaining what she knew about Sheila and Jimmy Knowland, and then notifying him of her plans. She started to write of her love for him, but thought better of it. He would, she knew, understand the logic of her course of action if it were stated clearly and simply. But he would never grasp the depth of her conflicting emotions. What she had to say to him was best said objectively and irrefutably. She was weeping again by the time she folded the letter into an envelope.

Nevertheless he would, she knew, react violently to what she was doing. But by the time he received the letter she would be in Mexico.

And she and Billy would be married.

CHAPTER 6

Maggie was determined not to be found by Ben Montgomery, and so she and Billy spent a month aimlessly wandering the byways of Mexico.

At Guaymas, on the coast of the Gulf of California, they were married by a rumpled city magistrate, who spoke the ceremony in broken English. Maggie's voice sounded hollow and disembodied in her own ears as she repeated the familiar vows. Afterwards the magistrate directed them to a hotel of ancient vintage located on the corner of a street which gave onto the harbor. The smell of rotting fish was heavy on the sullen landward breeze. Billy took one look at the two boys butchering a giant sea turtle on the stone steps of the courtyard and grunted, "We're not staying here."

So they drove all night and most of the next day over rutted roads in a hired Studebaker to reach Mexico City. During the drive Billy spoke little, fueling his isolation from her with fifths of local raw tequila. And Maggie was uncertain how to attack the issue which she knew would have to be resolved between them sooner or later.

In the capital Maggie collapsed into an exhausted and troubled sleep in the bridal suite of the venerable Hotel Majestic, on the broad, bustling Zocalo. When, in the early hours of the morning, she awoke in the breezy, high-ceilinged room that looked out on the square, Billy was gone.

She found him in the nearly deserted bar, roaring drunk, and throwing back shots of tequila with a dissolute-looking American journalist who, it developed, worked for the United Press. The Mexican bartender was half dozing on a stool behind the bar beneath an enormous mural of Montezuma's execution by Cortez.

Billy greeted her with a bellow. "Maggie, come over here and say hello to a friend of mine. Powell, meet Mrs. William Reiter, my blushing bride."

Powell, the journalist, stared at her. "I didn't believe it."

Maggie frowned. "What didn't you believe?"

"Him." He jabbed a thumb at Billy. "When he said Margaret Marshall ran away with him last night to get married."

Billy snorted. "Just for that, you lousy hack, you may not kiss the bride. Anywhere but on the lips, that is. The rest of her is spoken for. In various quarters."

Maggie knew he was trying to be cruel to dull his own pain. But in spite of her knowledge, she felt herself flinch inwardly.

But Powell missed the sarcasm; suddenly he seemed to come alive. "Jesus, I've got to get this on the wire!"

He rushed off. Billy called after him, "You can quote the bride as saying she believes in large families, and intends to bear Mr. Reiter many strapping sons and buxom daughters."

When Powell was gone Billy abruptly collapsed into a chair. Fighting back tears she searched for something to say. Glaring at her, he seemed somewhat sobered.

"I could whip his ass, you know."

Maggie knew he was talking about Montgomery. She also remembered the scar under Montgomery's ribs. But she said nothing.

After a moment Billy chuckled to himself. "I *think* I could whip his ass." Maggie smiled.

After another thoughtful moment he sighed and shook his head wearily. "Pretty stinking way to handle it, I guess."

"It's all right."

She sat down opposite him. She felt the deep hurt to his pride. "It's only until he's born, Billy. I meant it. I won't ask you for any more than that."

Billy glanced up at her. " 'He'? Are you sure about that?" She nodded. She *was* sure. Billy smiled. "Well now, you didn't mention that." He shook his head in some dismay. "A boy . . ."

She sensed that the propsect of having a son, even if in name only, intrigued him. His face softened. Maggie, watching him, was filled with a sudden tenderness, knowing that he would never abandon her. And for the first time she faced squarely the fact that the part of her life that had included Montgomery was over, and something else had begun. She reached across the table to touch his hand. "Why don't you come to bed now?"

He stared at her. "You don't have to, you know."

"I know. But I want you."

But he continued to study her. "Maggie, what happens when we go back? He won't have disappeared."

She shook her head. "I won't hurt you that way. I promise."

Finally he nodded. "Fair enough."

Beyond the balcony dawn was softly tinting the forbidding grey stone of the great cathedral across the square as Maggie took Billy into the oversized bed of the bridal suite. Her body remembered his affectionately, and his confident, experienced hands explored her in new ways, helping bring her to a leisurely climax that surprised her with its intensity. It was as though he needed to prove by this physical mastery that she had sacrificed little in turning her back on Ben Montgomery. But she knew quite well what she had sacrificed, and no amount of passion would erase that knowledge.

Afterwards, exhausted, she drifted toward deep sleep, conscious of Billy's gentle fingers tracing the new, gentle swell of her belly.

The wire service story revealing Maggie's elopement broke that morning and she and Billy were forced to flee the Majestic. The hotel concierge slipped them quietly out a service entrance and into a waiting car to avoid the horde of Mexican newspaper writers who had taken over the lobby. The concierge said the hotel switchboard had been overwhelmed by incoming calls from the States, among them repeated, urgent calls from a Mr. Montgomery of American Universal Pictures. By the time it became known that Mr. and Mrs. William Reiter had left the hotel, the honeymooning couple was aboard a train and on their way to Oaxaca and the tropical south of Mexico.

Three weeks later Maggie picked up a telephone in a Matamoros hotel room. She and Billy planned to cross back into the States the following day. She was more than ready. The squalid little border town disgusted her; only a few dusty streets away barefoot prostitutes ogled drunken American tourists from shanty doorways.

When he answered she said simply, "I'm coming back tomorrow."

Montgomery said nothing for a long moment, and Maggie thought he might hang up. When he did speak his voice sounded infinitely weary. "You did the right thing. I won't try to see you."

Unable to speak, she placed the telephone gently back into its cradle. In the bathroom she spent a long time applying her makeup. When she was finished she went downstairs to join Billy for lunch.

On their return to Los Angeles, while Billy began preparing a Lupe Velez picture for Jack Warner, Maggie set about putting her own career back in order. So that there would be only one version of the elopement she invited an AUP publicist out to the beach for a late breakfast and an exclusive interview.

Letty Barnes was a shrewd, persistent young woman of twenty-five or so with ambitions of launching a gossip column of her own. She chain-smoked her way through smoked salmon and toast, eyeing Maggie through her plastic-rimmed glasses and occasionally pushing back an unruly, dishwater colored bang. Maggie answered her questions cautiously; it was common knowledge that Letty peddled inside information that she couldn't use in her studio press releases to outside columnists. But it was just such connections which made her good at her job, and quite valuable to Maggie just now. Maggie knew that her version of the story would receive widespread coverage.

When Maggie finished, Letty put down her pencil to scan her notes. "Let me see if I've got this right. The country's number one leading lady and number three ticket draw, who could almost have her pick of Hollywood's most available bachelors, was swept off her feet in a secret, whirlwind courtship by a middle-aged, journeyman director who—everybody says—has already made his best pictures."

"That's more or less it," Maggie smiled. "Of course, if

you write it that way, Letty, I can promise you'll be out of work before the ink dries on the morning editions."

Letty shrugged. "I don't plan to write it that way. It's all going to sound as dashing and romantic as the Arabian Nights. But, Maggie, that's how its going to read to anybody who knows anything at all in this town."

Maggie shrugged. "Those aren't the people I'm worried about."

Letty chuckled. "I know. You're worried about your box office. And believe me, I admire a girl who knows how to take care of her own interests." She took off her glasses, measuring Maggie. "But off the record, how did Ben Montgomery take it?"

Maggie held the other woman's eyes firmly. "He was delighted, of course. In the first place, Ben's an old friend. But he also believes the public wants its matinee favorites' private lives to reflect conventional values."

Maggie knew that there had been rumors of her affair with Ben Montgomery, but they had been discreet enough so that nothing appeared in print. But Letty seemed to be boring after the truth. Maggie wondered if Sam Lendt knew that one of his publicists was breakfasting with Margaret Marshall today.

It was as if Maggie's thoughts about Lendt triggered a similar thought in Letty's mind. She smiled. "Sam Lendt might be spouting that kind of bullshit, the hypocritical old bastard. But it didn't cost him a bedwarmer."

Maggie suppressed her fury; in fact, she almost had a grudging admiration for the girl whose instincts invariably drove her toward her adversary's throat. But she realized it was time to end the interview.

"My advice to you, Letty," Maggie said mildly, "is to remember who you're working for. And that's Ben Montgomery."

Letty sighed. "True. Well, you can't blame a girl for trying to get ahead."

Maggie accompanied Letty to her car. The publicist smiled as they shook hands in parting. "Say, Maggie . . . you aren't putting on a few pounds, are you?"

The question startled Maggie, and she felt her composure slip in spite of herself. She knew her pregnancy wasn't showing yet. And then suddenly she realized that Letty had taken a shot in the dark, and that it had worked. There was only one way to handle it. "Yes, I am. And I may have another announcement for you in a month or so. Of course, it's too early to tell yet."

There was a triumphant gleam in Letty's eyes. "Yes, of course," she said wryly. Then she arranged herself behind the wheel of her car and drove away.

With a vague sense of alarm Maggie watched the car until it crossed the wooden bridge and disappeared beyond a bluff. Overhead gulls screamed, balancing precariously on the breeze against a brilliant blue sky. Abruptly she turned and went back inside the house. But then something caught her eye and she stopped to stare up the beach toward the familiar green bluffs. After a moment she walked out along the water's edge for a couple of hundred yards. Sea spray stung her cheeks and brought tears to her eyes. Through the tears she could see that the windows of the white villa with the bright red tile roof were boarded over, and drifts of sand from the beach were already piling up on the sills and at the doors, leaving Montgomery's house looking abandoned and desolate.

Montgomery kept his promise not to try to see Maggie, and she put him out of her mind as far as possible as she set about putting together a life for herself and Billy and her unborn child.

She learned from Lyla, who was embarking on an Alaskan expedition with Wilkening in the spring, that Montgomery had fired Jimmy Knowland early in the week following her elopement. Jimmy had apparently taken it badly, and the one time he tried to see Sheila afterwards a private detective intercepted him outside the gate of the Doheny mansion and sent him on his way.

Maggie was visiting the Brentwood mansion that Wilkening maintained for Lyla at staggering expense. He'd just sent over a selection of heavy fur parkas for her to choose from. Lyla plunged into one, then turned to show it off for Maggie. "What do you think?"

"I think you look like an Eskimo," Maggie answered truthfully.

Lyla sighed. "If you like Eskimos."

"You don't sound very excited about going."

"I'm not." Lyla shrugged out of the parka and heaved it atop the pile of others on the sofa. "But at least up there he won't be worried about me going for a romp behind his back. Although I must say the thought has crossed my mind a few times lately. My God, I'm waiting for him to send over a chastity belt."

Maggie knew that Wilkening's fierce possessiveness was beginning to chafe Lyla's spirit. She was not, Maggie well knew the kind of girl a man could lock in a tower and expect not to dangle a rope out the window.

But Lyla's thoughts went back to Jimmy. "You know, for some reason he thinks you're the reason he got fired. That day you made him take you over to Sheila's—he's made some kind of connection." She looked at Maggie intently. "You didn't tell Montgomery what was going on, did you?"

Maggie wanted to tell Lyla the truth, but suddenly the letter she'd written Montgomery seemed a little bit tawdry. She did not doubt that she'd done the right thing, but perhaps she should have warned Jimmy that his world was about to cave in. They were friends, after all. But her own concerns that day had outweighed any other considerations.

Instead she answered Lyla evasively. "You know why I went over there. It wasn't to spy."

Lyla nodded. "I know. That's what I told him."

Maggie felt a sudden, icy foreboding. "What did you tell him?"

"Just that it was important for you to see how Sheila was doing." She glanced up. "He came over here right after it happened. He was in pretty bad shape, yelling and screaming around. I tried to calm him down. I told him it was between you and Sheila and Ben Montgomery and it didn't have anything to do with him."

"Do you think he guessed?" Her feeling of dread was feeding on itself, becoming a ball of nausea in her stomach.

"Who knows?" Lyla said. "Does it matter now?"

"Did he believe you?" Maggie insisted.

"I'm not sure he even heard me. It was like he had the staggers, but I could tell he hadn't been drinking." She shook her head. "There's something wrong with him. He was raving around calling himself Satan's child and claiming he could put curses on people. I don't know what's going on but I don't like him to come around any more."

Maggie left Lyla's soon after, feeling a desperate need to carry herself and her unborn baby back to the safety of Malibu.

Jimmy's hysterical ranting about a curse that Lyla had

described did not frighten her: Maggie was not superstitious. But secret knowledge in the wrong minds did frighten her. She felt instinctively that somehow, at some recent time, events had been set in motion which were building toward a destructive climax. But the form of that resolution eluded her.

By April it was obvious to the world that Maggie was pregnant. She forwarded a brief note to Ben Montgomery that she was canceling all of her professional commitments for the next few months. She received a rather formal acknowledgement back from him assuring her that her substantial salary would continue uninterrupted during her confinement, and wishing her well. And then, on her last day at the studio before retiring to the beach for the rest of her pregnancy, as she was removing a few items from her dressing room, much to her surprise she received a visit from Samuel Lendt.

Lendt materialized in the doorway without warning, smiling thinly and studying her with cold eyes. "I hope I'm not interrupting anything."

Startled by the intrusion, Maggie stared at him blankly. For a moment she was the terrified girl of five years earlier who had trembled under his eyes in his office in the Ivory Tower. But it was not five years earlier and Maggie was no longer a girl. She smiled. "Of course not. What can I do for you?"

Uninvited he crossed into the dressing room to perch casually on the arm of a sofa. "I heard you were pregnant. I came by to congratulate you."

"How thoughtful of you."

He was watching her with cool detachment. The few times Maggie had seen him closely during the past few years his eyes had been guarded in deference to the power that she and Montgomery wielded over him. But there was none of that now, and the glittering triumph that flashed in his eyes frightened her. "When is the blessed event scheduled to come off?"

"My baby is due in late October." It would be early September, but Maggie was beginning to suspect that Lendt already knew that.

"And the proud father? How is he holding up?"

"Billy is as excited as I am." Lendt was obviously intent

on continuing the charade of civility, and Maggie had no choice but to go along with it.

"Oh yes, Billy." Lendt smiled enigmatically. "I expect this whole thing came as quite a surprise to him. Although I wasn't so much younger than Billy when I had Jack."

Maggie frowned. "What are you driving at?"

Lendt ignored her question. "You do remember Jack? He's away. Far away. Not in distance, of course. But that place has taken its toll on him."

Maggie pulled herself up to meet his eye. "I remember your son very well. In fact, I remember everything. I don't know why you're here, but I think you'd better keep that in mind."

Lendt snapped harshly, "My dear, I haven't had much else on my mind for five years." He rose abruptly. "And the reason I came here is to let you know that I plan on taking a personal interest in that child of yours. Just the way you took such an interest in mine."

He paused at the door of the dressing room. "And you might pass that along to the father as well."

That night Maggie sat before the fire, concentrating with all her might on the ripe swell of her belly, where her hands rested lightly. After a few moments there was a slight movement, then a stronger one, lifting up her light cotton smock as if it had been pushed by a tiny finger. She didn't hear Billy enter.

"Looks like there's somebody in there, all right." She glanced up to find him smiling down at her. Her eyes drifted back to her stomach.

"I'm frightened for him, Billy."

Billy joined her on the sofa, sheltering her closely under his arm. "Of course you are. It's a cold world out there."

She considered telling Billy about Sam Lendt's visit to her dressing room, but he was leaving the following day for location shooting in Tucson and would be away for five weeks. She didn't want to worry him and so she said nothing. But she was convinced that Samuel Lendt meant harm for her, harm as devastating as that which she and Montgomery had done him. And that night, for the first time in many months, the dead face of the prostitute, Ellie Wade, floated in her dreams.

* * *

Maggie's eight-pound, four-ounce son was born in a Santa Monica hospital on September 6, 1927, after a short labor. She named the boy Michael William Reiter. She learned later that a tall, elegantly dressed man had appeared at the hospital in the early hours of September 7 and had handsomely bribed a night nurse to allow him a few moments in the nursery viewing area. Maggie knew that Montgomery had come to see his son.

A month later a Warner Brothers picture, *The Jazz Singer* starring Al Jolson, opened in New York and changed the business of movie-making forever. It was the first time an actor had delivered spoken dialogue from the screen. By then Maggie had returned to the beach with her new baby. One day a gangly young man wearing a sweater and a woolen scarf around his throat appeared at her door.

"Miss Marshall?"

"That's right." There was only a cool breeze gusting, but the young man seemed deathly afraid of catching a chill.

"I'm Aaron Spruance. Mr. Montgomery sent me."

He was a voice coach. Maggie smiled; motherhood notwithstanding, Montgomery wasn't taking any chances with his number one leading lady.

Billy, who was more in touch with industry developments, told her that Montgomery had pressed Sam Lendt to finance a full sound development program a year earlier, when rumors first began to circulate that the Warners were about to take an all-or-nothing plunge in that direction. Lendt had balked, willing only to risk short money, as was Bill Fox, on developing synchronized sound scores for AUP's silent film releases. But Montgomery rejected the idea, rightly concluding that either the Warners' gambit would fail, or the industry would be hurled headlong into talkies. And whatever the outcome any half-way measure would be a waste of money.

It was a perilous time for many in the industry. Scores of foreign actors and actresses, realizing their rough command of the language would turn away fans, caught the first boat home when microphones appeared on the sets. And among the native American stars, many could not make the transition; John Gilbert faded into obscurity and the careers of Mary Pickford and Douglas Fairbanks began to dim.

At AUP Montgomery shut down production for thirteen weeks. Maggie heard that he was working eighteen and twenty hours a day, and both he and Lendt were spending months at a time in New York. Montgomery devoted his time there to pirating the legitimate theater for dramatists and actors who had made their living for years writing and speaking dramatic literature, while Lendt squeezed the studio's financing sources for ever-increasing sums to invest in the new technology and to re-equip the studio's nationwide American Lux chain of theaters to screen sound film.

But as frantic as those months were for others, they were a welcome respite for Maggie. The baby occupied much of her time, and compared to her devotion to him the tempest in the film community seemed almost trivial. But nevertheless she devoted what free time she had to learning the demanding new craft of delivering spoken dialogue. Fortunately young Spruance proved to be a proficient teacher and she worked hard to learn the techniques of projection, articulation, and emotional emphasis. Her voice was naturally full and somewhat throaty, and consequently her fans were not disappointed with her sound debut the following summer in a period romance, *The King's Lady,* opposite Adolphe Menjou.

Besides her own success, sound had proven a boon to Billy Reiter's career. Letty Barnes, the studio publicist, had been right when she suggested that some of the energy had gone out of his recent work. But Maggie knew that that was because Billy believed silent film had evolved as far as it could. Now that a new world was opening up, Billy was excited and eager to explore its potentials. After his first Vitaphone short for Warners in the wake of *The Jazz Singer,* Billy was turning down offers, a luxury he hadn't been able to afford for some years.

In all, Maggie could hardly have chosen a happier scenario if she'd been given the opportunity.

One morning, as Christmas of 1928 approached, Lyla hurried into Maggie's dressing room. Lyla had been in remarkably good spirits since her return from Alaska, observing pointedly that after six weeks in the Yukon anyplace was heaven where the only ice she had to confront was floating in a double shot of gin. But this morning Maggie knew instantly that something was wrong.

"It's Sheila Montgomery," Lyla confided tentatively.

Maggie turned to face her, trying not to show her alarm. "What about her?"

"They took her to the hospital last night. She had a baby."

Maggie turned slowly back to stare numbly into her dresser mirror. It was as though a door had slammed firmly closed in her mind, shutting out the barely acknowledged flicker of hope that somehow, in some distant time, the events that had thrust her and Montgomery apart would be turned about and they might be reunited.

Lyla gave her a comforting hug. "I'm sorry, Maggie. As far as I can tell nobody had any idea she was pregnant."

After a moment, Maggie frowned. "Was it a boy?"

Lyla nodded.

In a strange way Maggie was relieved. She knew that forfeiting their son to Billy had hurt Montgomery deeply. However, since the night after her labor when he had secretly visited the hospital, he had done nothing to indicate in any way that he knew the child was alive. Another man capable of caring as deeply as Montgomery might not have been able to resist the temptation to send toys around, or otherwise maintain some feeble contact with his son. But Montgomery had told Maggie that she made the right decision, and she knew that once a decision was made Montgomery could never allow himself to compromise it. She hoped that this son by Sheila would help fill the void she knew existed in his life, in the same way her son Michael had filled a void in hers.

She forced a smile for Lyla's benefit. "Well, then I guess that's that."

That night, over supper, she told Billy about Montgomery's child. He glanced up with a frown. "How do you feel about it, Maggie?"

"I'm happy for him."

Billy nodded. "Good."

It ended there. Billy was in preparation on a film which would introduce a new ingenue, a pert, round-eyed brunette by the name of Claudette Colbert. He showed Maggie the girl's studio photo with obvious enthusiasm, and during the rest of the meal they discussed the problems he faced on the picture.

After supper Maggie quietly slipped into the nursery and watched her young son sleeping in his crib for a long time. Time was merciless; already the boy seemed well launched toward maturity. And despite her own success in the film industry, new faces were moving to the fore. But it was not the fear of eclipse that saddened her; she would undoubtedly enjoy a few more years of supremacy in what Billy called the toughest crapshoot in the neighborhood. It was the prospect of change. Her son would continue to grow older and apart and Billy, with his career rejuvenated, was already moving inevitably, as men will, into his own orbit. She felt the old loneliness beginning to settle over her, the loneliness that she had only truly shared with one man, because his capacity for isolation was uniquely equal to her own.

When the feeling threatened to overwhelm her, she quietly left the nursery. In the living room Billy was on the phone, bellowing at Jack Warner that he would walk off the picture if the shooting schedule wasn't extended. Maggie smiled, and then went to bed alone.

The following morning after Maggie changed Michael and took him into the kitchen for breakfast, she glanced out the window and saw the man on the beach. He was sitting on the sand perhaps a hundred yards or so distant, staring back at the house. There was something disturbingly familiar about his figure, and when Maggie finished making coffee and put the baby's oatmeal on a burner, the man was still there. She glanced at Michael, who was busily tearing up a piece of toast. Billy was still asleep. She stepped out onto the deck.

The day was bright and crisp, but there was a low, impenetrable wall of fog lying offshore a couple of miles; were it to move landward the day would become cold and damp in a matter of minutes. The man on the beach saw her; he rose to his feet and started to walk toward the house, the breeze tugging at his loose sweater and wispy blonde hair. Maggie recognized him: it was Jimmy Knowland.

He was smiling as he trotted up the steps from the sand to join her. But Maggie could see that he was unshaven and his eyes were red-rimmed and dilated. She took his hand. "Jimmy. What a surprise! Why didn't you come to the house?"

His clothes looked rumpled and damp and there were particles of sand in his sweater. It occurred to her, with some alarm, that he might have slept on the beach. But if he was derelict, she realized, looking into the darkly hollowed eyes, it was a dereliction of the spirit.

"I thought I'd better wait until somebody was up and around. I didn't want to get anybody out of bed."

She had little choice but to invite him in for coffee, and immediately regretted it. Jimmy's eyes instantly fastened on Michael, who was playing with the last sodden remains of his toast. Michael strongly resembled Maggie, but his blue, penetrating eyes could have come from none other than his father.

"So that's him," Jimmy said. "Well, he's the one I really came to see."

"Oh, is that so?" She was smiling, trying to cover the unease building within her. "I'm not sure I like that at all."

But he ignored her banter. He pulled out a chair from the kitchen table and straddled it, studying the baby closely. "Some little dickens, all right. You know, if a person were willing to stretch a point, you could even say I was responsible for him being here."

"That would be quite a stretch." Maggie was not smiling now.

"Not really," Jimmy said. "After all, who was it that took you to that party at Wally Gordon's? And if I'm not mistaken, that's where you met Ben Montgomery for the first time."

"Which has nothing to do with Michael." She set a cup of coffee in front of him. "Except, of course, it was through Ben that I met Billy."

Jimmy smiled up at her noncomittally. "Sure."

She tried to re-direct the conversation. "It's been a long time, Jimmy. What have you been doing with yourself?" It had been a long time. Neither Maggie nor Lyla had heard from him since the tirade Lyla had described to her on the night after Montgomery fired him.

"Nothing. Everything . . . I have friends. They've been helping me sort things out. So much to think about, you know." He seemed to be rambling. But suddenly he said abruptly: "Sheila had a baby too. Did you hear about that?"

Maggie nodded. Suddenly she was afraid. She waited.

Jimmy chuckled. "It didn't surprise me. He has so many ways of controlling her. She's helpless against him without me there."

As he spoke his eyes became terrifyingly empty and remote, and Maggie knew he had no business in her house, or near her baby. The oatmeal was boiling on the stove behind her. Suddenly she had to fight back an overwhelming impulse to grab Michael and flee from the room. Instead she said carefully, "Michael's breakfast is ready. Maybe if you come back some other time we'll have more of a chance to talk."

Jimmy smiled blandly. "Why don't we talk while you feed him, Maggie?"

She stood in the middle of the floor with the pan of hot oatmeal in her hand, ready if he made the slightest move toward Michael to hurl it at him. Her voice was a whisper: "Jimmy, what do you want here?"

"I told you," he said guilelessly, "I came to see the baby."

"You've seen him. I want you to go now."

The chilling emptiness returned to his eyes. "Yes. I have seen him. And if I were you, Maggie, I wouldn't let him in the same room with Ben Montgomery. People might get the wrong idea."

Maggie stood rooted, facing the dread realization that Jimmy knew who had fathered her child. Panic rose in her, and she knew that she would scream for Billy. She didn't have to.

"Get out of here."

Billy was standing in the kitchen doorway, dressed only in his trousers, his eyes blazing.

Unalarmed, Jimmy turned to face him. "Hello. I'm not sure we've met." There was mockery in his voice. "I've been admiring the baby. I was just telling Maggie how much he resembles his father."

An instant before Billy moved Maggie saw it coming; dropping the pan of oatmeal, she snatched Michael from his highchair. In the blink of an eye Billy crossed the room and lifted Jimmy from his chair, sending a fist smashing into his face. Maggie screamed. She knew his temper; Billy was quite capable of killing Jimmy if he allowed himself.

But he didn't. The blow dropped Jimmy to his knees and he was laughing hysterically through his bloody, smashed mouth. Billy stood over him, sobered, staring down at the younger man. "My God," he whispered.

He turned to Maggie. "Take the baby out of here. I won't hurt Jimmy any more."

Maggie did as she was told. When Billy returned an hour later he assured her that Jimmy would pose no more problems for them. Maggie tried to believe that he was right. But in the days following she often found herself scanning the beach warily as she passed a window, feeling secure only if it was empty. And she rarely let Michael out of her sight.

CHAPTER 7

But 1928 ended quietly.

In the second week of January Maggie had to be in New York for an opening. With Wilkening in Seattle, where he was negotiating the purchase of another newspaper, Lyla joined her for the trip and, at the last moment, Maggie decided to take Michael as well. The baby was thirteen months old now and had rarely been away from Malibu. Besides, Billy was deeply involved in script revisions on the Warner picture, and was working out of the beach house. Maggie knew that Michael and his nurse would only be underfoot.

The train journey was uneventful, and the studio installed them in Maggie's usual suite at the Sherry Netherland, overlooking Central Park. The opening of *Manhattan Carousel*, a romantic romp in which she shared the female lead with Norma Shearer, was rather disappointing. A wet snow storm kept attendance down and Maggie herself was not pleased with some editing which had been done since she'd screened the finished work print. Besides, she'd never been convinced comedy was her forte. But the entertainment press turned out in force and the next day her picture, smiling out from an ermine cape and hood as she stepped from the limousine in front of the Radio City Music Hall, was displayed prominently on the front page of an inside section of the *Times*.

The next day dawned bright and crisp, lifting her spirits.

The hotel had located a bona fide English nanny to care for Michael, and Maggie and Lyla set out along Fifth Avenue fully prepared to devote the entire final two days of their stay to shopping. Maggie did not particularly like New York. She always associated the city with the smell of stale sauerkraut and ceaseless bustle. But she loved the smart shops and the theater. On their last night she and Lyla attended the Broadway production of O'Casey's *Juno and the Paycock,* which was enjoying a lengthy run.

During the intermission she lost track of Lyla. Eventually she found her engaged in animated conversation with a brawny, shaggy-haired young man with an infectious, Irish sense of humor and a hip flask full of cognac. His name was Richard Flynn and he was a playwright. His first play had recently opened off Broadway to enthusiastic reviews, and he was radiating an appealingly arrogant first flush of success. In fact, his magnetism was almost tangible, and Maggie could see with some alarm that already he and Lyla could hardly keep their hands off each other. It was a good thing, she thought wryly, that Anson Wilkening was no closer than Seattle.

After the play Flynn joined them at an intimate 52nd Street restaurant for a light supper. Lyla watched him with dancing eyes and an expression that Maggie hadn't seen for some time. The conversation turned to matters of trade.

"The movies . . ." Flynn mused condescendingly. "Now I've thought about the movies some. They lack flesh and blood. That's the worst of them."

Maggie smiled. "Oh? Lyla and I show up on the screen now and again. We aren't flesh and blood?"

"Sitting here, lovely as the two of you are, sure. And I'll floor any man who says different." He gave Lyla a squeeze. "But up there on the bloody great screen, it's pictures, that's all. Slick and easy and frothy as cotton candy. But hard to make a meal of."

"Not everybody is looking for a meal." Maggie didn't particularly enjoy these kinds of discussions, but there was a quality about the young playwright that could not be easily dismissed.

Flynn chuckled. "Sure they are. They just don't know it all the time." Abruptly he leaned across the table intently. "Listen, Maggie Marshall, or whatever the bloody hell your name is, let me put you on a stage. You'll work harder than you've ever worked in your life. You'll bleed for your audience. But they'll love it because they can see the blood. And they'll kiss your feet for what you're giving them. Now tell me what the movies have got compared to that?"

Across the intimately candle-lit table his intensity was almost overwhelming. It disturbed her. The movies had given direction to her life, and a son, and made her wealthy for life. But they had never given her satisfaction. Flynn was right; the moves were too easy, made too few demands on either their makers or their audience. She realized that the young man had laid down a challenge she would have to consider. But not just then.

Fortunately Lyla broke the spell. "You want to know what the movies have got, you crazy Irishman? They've got glamour, liquor, sex, oceans of money, and good old California sunshine. That's what."

Flynn roared with laughter. "Well, why didn't you say so, for God's sake. Now you've got me half convinced." He pulled Lyla into a lusty hug. "Come here, you Protestant."

A few minutes later Maggie excused herself and caught a cab back to the hotel. When Lyla showed up the next morning she spoke little of Flynn. But Maggie could tell that he was much in her thoughts during the trip back to the Coast.

The train pulled into Los Angeles in early evening and Maggie was surprised that Billy was not at Central Station to meet them, and had not made other arrangements for them to be picked up. She called the beach house, but there was no answer. Suddenly, despite Lyla's reassurances, she was convinced there was something wrong. They hired a cab to take them to Brentwood, and then bundled into Lyla's new maroon Packard for the drive out to Malibu. Maggie's nerves were taut. She tried to tell herself that Billy was tied up casting or location scouting, and had forgotten about their arrival. But in her heart she knew he would not have forgotten. Her tension seemed to affect the baby, who became cranky and difficult to manage in the close confines of the car. The familiar drive along the ghostly, moonlit seashore seemed endless.

As they crossed the wooden bridge over the inlet she could see the house was blazing with light, and as they pulled into the driveway she saw that the front door was standing ajar and a flap of curtain was being whipped by the breeze through a broken window. Maggie's vague sense of dread was shaping into a chilling certainty. Lyla gave her an alarmed look as she brought the car to a halt. Maggie thrust the baby into her arms. "Wait here. Don't let anything happen to him." Maggie slammed the door on Lyla's protest and hurried toward the open front door.

Her home had been wantonly, mindlessly destroyed. The marauders had axed her precious rosewood desk and the rest of the furniture to pieces, and taken a poker to her crystal and china. Obscenities and bizarre symbols had been scrawled in charcoal on the walls. In the kitchen they had demolished her pantry and icebox, and food was strewn all over the floor. In the bedroom they had gutted the closets and shredded the bedclothes, and defecated on the bare mattress. But she found no trace of Billy.

He was on the patio. They had bound his hands behind his back, and then knotted them to his ankles. And then they had put a bullet in the base of his skull. He had fallen face forward onto the rough wood deck. Numbly Maggie lowered herself to kneel at his side, and reached out to touch his cheek with her fingers. The stubble of his beard rasped her fingertips, but his flesh was cold and still.

She heard an inarticulate whimper behind her. Lyla was standing in the doorway, holding the baby's face tightly to her breast. She looked as though her knees would give way any moment.

From the instant Maggie entered the house she had refused to acknowledge the panic building within her, knowing that if she did it would overwhelm her. Now she extended that rigid control to include her sickening sense of loss and livid rage. She said quietly, "Take him away from here, Lyla. Find a phone and call the police."

Lyla stared at her. "What are you going to do?"

Maggie's eyes returned to Billy's still figure. "I don't know."

But she did know. She'd known the moment she'd found Billy dead. For six years the happenings of one night, in which she had participated only as an observer, had thrown a shadow over her life, planting seeds of destruction that had come to fruition on this night. In her desire to have Montgomery and her career, and to protect her baby, she had knowingly acquiesced to the thrust of events, and by having done so was now party to Billy's murder. But she was through with passive submission. This was an ending of it. She would make sure of that. Or she would die.

When she heard Lyla's car racing away from the house she went back into the kitchen. The marauders had overlooked the utility closet off the pantry where Billy had secreted a .32 automatic. Even before their marriage he'd insisted Maggie learn how to use the weapon for those times she was alone at the beach. The cold steel felt heavy in her hand as she walked down the steps and out onto the sand. In the moonlight she could see the two sets of footprints headed up the beach toward the bluffs. She knew where she would find them. Maggie kicked off her shoes and set off across the packed sand at the water's edge toward Montgomery's bungalow.

As she walked she thought about Jimmy and Sheila. Why had she turned her back on her own baby and gone with him? It was generally believed that Sheila and Montgomery had reconciled. They had even attended an opening together. It was the first time Sheila had been seen publicly in years, and in the newspaper photographs she'd been smiling and radiant. There could be only one reason, Maggie thought: Jimmy had revealed to her that Montgomery had fathered Michael. And Maggie realized then that her last-minute decision to take her baby with her to New York had saved his life. Behind her, far off up the strand, she could hear the faint sound of phonograph music coming from Ingram's house, her nearest neighbor. Even circumstances had conspired to aid Jimmy's design. No one could possibly have heard the shot.

They had pried away some of the boards over the dining room French doors and broken the glass to gain entry. The electricity had long since been shut off, but within she could see dim, flickering light beyond the entryway to the parquet-floored living room. But, except for the muted crash of the surf, all was silent. Maggie eased the safety clasp of the pistol to the firing position, and stepped inside the house.

They had come prepared. An incense burner gave off a sweetly acrid odor, tainting the chill, stale air of the living room. The thick candles ringing the bodies lying on the Persian carpet, which Maggie had selected for Montgomery, were sputtering low. Jimmy and Sheila were nude, their clothes scattered close by, and Maggie could see for the first time that Jimmy's pale legs, arms, and torso were covered with tattoos: bizarre etchings of sun symbols, horned demons and other figures, often graphically phallic.

The bodies were facing each other, locked in an embrace, limbs entwined. Jimmy clutched a heavy revolver in his right fist, his knuckles white on the grip. There was a black, puckered hole in Sheila's left temple, and a similar wound behind Jimmy's right ear. In death Jimmy's expression was shocked, almost frightened. Perhaps in that final instant, Maggie thought, he had discovered that there was not the poetry in death that he had envisioned. She hoped so. She was beyond pitying him now. But for the rest of her life she would remember the faint trace of a smile that death had frozen on Sheila Montgomery's lips.

She walked slowly from the bungalow, back out on the beach, where she stood for a long time letting the night breeze cool her face. After a while she became aware again of the pistol she held in her hand. She remembered why she had brought it with her. And then she hurled it with all her might into the sea.

The sheriff's homicide detectives were mercifully brief in their questioning of her. Drained of any emotion whatsoever, Maggie answered their questions quietly and lucidly. She sensed that they were adopting the theory that Billy had had the misfortune to get in the way of a pair of suicide-crazed psychotics, and Maggie did not burden them with any other than the immediate facts. Reporters were settling on the beach in swarms for what promised to be one of the most lurid stories of the new year, but were kept at bay by a cordon of officers as Maggie hurried from her door to Lyla's car, averting her head from the battery of popping flashbulbs. A patrol car escorted them as far as Lyla's Brentwood flat where the studio had already posted security guards.

Because things moved so quickly, she was not there when Montgomery arrived at the beach. But she learned later that he displayed no emotion as he viewed the bodies and made a curt, formal identification of his wife. Afterwards he took the homicide captain outside for a private conversation. But as he was leaving, when an alert photographer darted into his path to snap a picture, he grabbed the camera away and smashed it on the front steps of the bungalow.

Maggie remained in seclusion for the next few days, allowing Lyla to make the necessary arrangements for Billy's funeral. The press had a field day, but a well-orchestrated one. The official homicide report threw Jimmy's carcass to the wolves. It pictured a warped personality, a known narcotics peddler and user, an occultist, who had brutally kidnaped Sheila Moreno and then gone to the beach with the intent of also abducting Margaret Marshall. Thrown into a psychotic rage when he learned she wasn't home, he coldbloodedly executed her husband, then raped and murdered Montgomery's wife. Despite the obvious holes in the story the press loved it and clamored for more. And once the dead had been carrioned, the writers devoted their efforts to making a heroine out of Maggie, picturing her as the victim of brutal circumstances, left alone to raise her young son. All of it sickened her and she refused all requests for interviews. One day before Billy's funeral Letty Barnes called her at Lyla's.

"Maggie, I know how you feel, believe me. But you really ought to say *something*."

Maggie knew with absolute certainty that Letty Barnes had no idea how she felt about anything. "No. They have no right to pry their way into my life that way."

"Darling, they have *every* right. You gave it to them when you let Sam and Ben make a star out of you. I realize it's dreadful at a time like this but you still have to play the game."

"I said no, Letty."

"Now look, I know a couple of half-sanitary fellows, one from *Life* and the other from the A.P. Pictures and text in one shot. Can't you give them just *five* minutes?"

"No. And I don't want you to call me here again."

Letty sighed. "Sam is definitely not going to like this."

Maggie hung up.

The next day *Variety* carried verbatim quotes from her, released through the studio, saying that she was satisfied with the police investigation, and that she hoped God would forgive the tormented soul who had perpetrated the tragedy. Maggie sighed; Letty would not be silenced.

Stories idolizing what was described as her martyrdom continued unabated for another week. And, of course, her popularity shot up accordingly all across the country.

During this period Montgomery had not called her, nor had she expected him to. But he was there for Billy's funeral, a modest, graveside service at Forest Lawn attended by only a few close friends. Afterwards they stood for a moment by the limousine. She could see how the past few days had affected him. Heavy lines of exhaustion were etched in his face and his suit hung loosely from his frame. As usual he went directly to the point: "I would have called, but I thought Billy deserved better than that."

Through her dark silk veil she looked into the piercing blue eyes. "He did."

But his eyes held hers. "How long, do you think?"

"I don't know."

He nodded, then closed the door after her when she stepped into the car.

Maggie mourned Billy Reiter honestly and with devotion for many months. And in the fall she married Ben Montgomery in a modest church ceremony in Santa Monica, with Lyla acting as matron of honor. Her second husband brought his own child, Brendan, then ten months old, to live with them, and began immediate proceedings to adopt Billy Reiter's two-year-old son, Michael William.

CHAPTER 8

In 1935 Ben Montgomery became obsessed with *Britain*, the first film of his proposed epic, *Trilogy*, which would trace Anglo-American history to its roots. In scope and budget the project was unprecedented in the industry. He was violently opposed by Samuel Lendt and the Eastern money interests that controlled American Universal finances. As the bitterness intensified, Maggie began to feel a growing uneasiness, as though once more events were escaping her control.

The intervening years had been the most content of Maggie's life. After completely remodeling the Malibu house, she and Montgomery and the two boys had returned to the beach to live. And while the work on her house was in progress Montgomery had ordered his own small villa razed to the sand, so there was not a trace left to indicate it had ever stood on the spot. An RKO producer snapped up the lot and almost immediately started construction on a sprawling Cape Cod-style retreat. When Maggie once again took up residence at Malibu, there was little remaining to remind her of the nightmare that had been played out there.

The years seemed to fly by. There was a Wall Street crash, and the country plunged into Depression. But Maggie had put her money in real estate, much of it in the vicinity of the University of California campus at Westwood, and was therefore little affected by the economic plummet. And, perversely, the movies were one of the few industries that thrived during those otherwise bleak years.

"The movies and prophylactics," Lyla observed wryly one spring Sunday in 1932. She and Anson Wilkening had come out to Malibu for the day, and the men were on the patio deeply involved in a conversation about events in Europe. Wilkening had acquired a small Massachusetts pharmaceutical company that specialized in contraceptives and apparently was returning large dividends. Lyla laughed. "The Depression is the best thing that ever happened to us. Every night half the country's parked in a movie house making you and Ben richer, and the other half is at home in bed making Anson another fortune."

Maggie was somewhat surprised at the relationship that quickly developed between Montgomery and Wilkening, although she realized that it was not so much friendship as a mutual respect between two strong-willed individualists who valued each other's opinions. And, ultimately, it was Wilkening's influence that inspired Montgomery's plunge into *Trilogy*. Sitting atop an influential publishing empire which had survived the crash virtually intact, the militant Wilkening now surveyed the world scene with alarm. Mussolini was on the march in Ethiopia while Hitler's rearmed Germany had occupied the Rhineland. Japan was making incursions into China, while Jews were fleeing Europe by the thousands. By 1935 Wilkening could see war on the horizon, war which would pit the English-speaking peoples and their allies against the world, and daily his papers sounded the alarm. Finally he brought Montgomery around to share the same point of view.

From such discussions with Wilkening, Montgomery forged *Trilogy*, with the grand scheme of emotionally bonding the United States with the British Empire in the face of the building storm. Maggie was excited by the individual concepts. *Britain* would deal with medieval times, focusing on King Arthur uniting the Britons. She knew Arthurian legend was rife with romantic violence and chivalry, and would undoubtedly make good box office. *Empire* would tell the story of Drake's conquest of the Spanish armada, and the rise to world supremacy of the British sea lords. It would be yet another simple yarn of high adventure and romance which could reasonably expect to have widespread public appeal. Finally, *America* would chronicle an American pioneer family, whose roots sprang from characters featured in the two earlier stories. This family would prevail over deprivation and hardship by employing such Anglo-American virtues as individuality, tenacity, and objective justice.

Any one of the three films could stand alone, Maggie believed. But she felt instinctively that Montgomery was courting disaster by demanding that they be bonded together and marketed as *Trilogy*.

She told him so one summer evening after supper. The boys were in bed and they had thrown open the doors which gave onto the beach to enjoy the mild breeze and soft crash of the surf. Montgomery had already begun to encounter resistance from Lendt and the studio financiers, and was snappish.

"You told me a long time ago to beware of the big statement," she said. "Remember?"

"Of course I do," he said impatiently. "But there's no point in telling any one of these stories by itself. The cumulative meaning is embodied in all of them."

She smiled and quoted The Book According To Montgomery. "People don't go to the movies for a dose of cumulative meaning. They go to the movies to be entertained."

"They will be. You said yourself they're all full of romance and adventure."

"And that ought to be enough," she insisted.

"You don't understand," he snapped. "I'm not diagramming these stories so that I'll get a statement out of them. It's already there, in the events and characters. It's good, sound movie-making."

Maggie still had doubts, but she let it go at that. The truth of the matter was that *Trilogy* would be made, for better or for worse, because Montgomery had willed it so. And she knew that not even the combined opposition of Samuel Lendt and Chase-Manhattan and all the rest could keep it from being made. For more than a decade Montgomery had almost single-handedly kept American Universal atop the cut-throat film industry. Now he would have his way or they would lose him. And Maggie knew they would not risk that.

Montgomery poured himself a cognac and chuckled. "What if I let you play Guenevere, Queen Elizabeth, and the settler's wife who gets raped by the Indians?"

She knew he was trying to make peace. "I'd have to have a look at the Indians," she smiled.

"You won't have to wait long," he said. "I've already found my writer."

When he told her who his writer was, Maggie realized that her sense of foreboding about *Trilogy* had not been unjustified. Two days later Lyla called her at the beach to announce ecstatically that she had just heard from Richard Flynn in New York. The playwright, with whom Lyla had been having a discreet, very intermittent affair since she and Maggie had met him six years earlier, would be flying out to the Coast in a week for an extended stay.

Montgomery decided that Flynn should stay at the beach for the frst couple of weeks while the two of them plunged into conceptual discussions of the project. When the studio car deposited him at her door one August afternoon Maggie could see that he was little changed. The years had added to his stature as a dramatist, and had somewhat mellowed the youthful arrogance that had both charmed and exasperated Maggie when they first met. But he could still be impossible.

"What on earth are you doing out here, Dick?" Maggie chided him good-naturedly. "As I recall you were of the opinion that the movies lacked flesh and blood. 'Just pictures,' I think you said."

"And I stand by my words, Maggie my love," he said with a grin, giving her a hug. "And as fate would have it, I've been appointed to drag the filthy business out of the gutter and elevate it to the sublime."

Maggie was amused. "Good luck. But you have to tell me, why is an Irish Catholic suddenly in the business of glorifying the British Empire?"

"I think seventy-five thousand dollars an episode might have something to do with it," Montgomery observed wryly.

Flynn sighed. "It's true. This devil of a man has gone and corrupted an innocent immigrant." Then he gave her a wink. "Which only proves what I've been saying about the movies all along. It's no life for a serious man at all. Now where's the whiskey? Or have I fallen into a nest of bloody teetotalers?"

But she enjoyed Flynn's company, as did Montgomery. Flynn seemed to have an indestructible constitution, working with Montgomery until all hours of the morning, and then rising at dawn to bawl Irish ballads in the shower. Later he would pace the beach in a turtleneck sweater with a morning brandy in hand, waiting for Montgomery and Michael to finish their ritual morning swim beyond the surf. He wasn't quite sure what to make of Montgomery. He confided to Maggie, "The man's bloody inhuman, you must realize. Out there every morning, rain or shine, with the water cold enough to freeze the balls off a brass monkey. And dragging the boy along too. And then off to town to flog people about all day without the mercy of a Jesuit. He's either a genius or a monster, for sure."

Aside from his company, Maggie was relieved Flynn was staying with them, for Lyla's sake. Wilkening was living out of the Brentwood flat these days, and the situation made it difficult for Lyla and Flynn to launch a full-blown affair, although she knew they occasionally met for afternoon trysts. In all, she felt the situation was as close to being contained as possible.

But when she told Montgomery about the romance, he was troubled. Wilkening was solidly behind *Trilogy* and had committed his papers to giving it widespread coverage, even before the studio's massive advertising buildup was launched. Montgomery was not about to let an indiscreet love affair jeopardize those plans. Maggie tried to tell him there wasn't much he could do about it, but Montgomery insisted on having a talk with Flynn before he moved into a suite at the Beverly Hills Hotel, where he would begin the actual writing of the massive script. Somehow he convinced Flynn not to see Lyla again until after the shooting drafts were complete and he was officially through with *Trilogy*. Again Maggie marveled at her husband's powers of persuasion.

Lyla, however, fumed when she was notified of the new status of her romance. "Maggie, if you'd ever been to bed with him you might have some idea what Ben is asking."

Maggie gave her a look. "Really?"

Lyla shrugged philosophically. "Oh well, I suppose it's for a good cause. God, I almost feel patriotic."

Maggie knew that Lyla's cynical veneer covered a deeper unhappiness. "Lyla, have you ever thought about breaking off with Anson?"

Lyla shook her head miserably. "I know. I should . . . it's not fair." She glanced up at Maggie, her round blue eyes seeking understanding. "But I do love Anson, in my own way. And I take care of him. You don't really understand how much he needs me. Anyway, I wouldn't know how to leave him, even if . . ."

"If what?"

"If Dick wanted to marry me." She laughed. "Which he doeesn't, the rotten Irish bastard. That much I'm sure of."

Maggie understood why the alternative of leaving Wilkening without the promise of Richard Flynn would never occur to Lyla. In many ways she justified her existence through the attention of men. Solitude, or the prospect of it, held terror for her, and Maggie hoped she would never have to endure it.

In all, 1935 ended on a productive, happy note of anticipation. Flynn's first draft script of *Britain* was a delight, capturing all of the magically light and tragically melancholy qualities of Arthurian legend, yet leavening them with historical purpose. Montgomery suggested only minor revisions, which Flynn endorsed, and immediately set in motion the awesome machinery which would start the cameras rolling six months hence. Flynn moved on to attack the *Empire* scenario with renewed enthusiasm. Samuel Lendt fought the project to the bitter end, but was finally silenced by his Wall Street backers when, as Maggie predicted, Montgomery threatened to leave American Universal if *Trilogy* were not financed for production.

Only one aspect of Maggie's life gave her cause for unease during this period. Brendan, Montgomery's son by Sheila Moreno, was a delicately structured boy, both in frame and temperament. While Michael, her own son with Montgomery, had inherited his father's sturdy build and direct sense of purpose, Brendan was by nature introspective and tentative. To complicate matters Montgomery openly favored Michael and the boy thrived on his father's attention and approval. When he was only seven, much to Maggie's alarm, Michael had started joining his father for the morning swim beyond the surf. That summer Brendon would stay indoors and watch the two of them through the kitchen window as Maggie prepared breakfast.

The following summer, in Brendan's seventh year, Montgomery decided that Brendan should also take part. He'd had swimming lessons, and enjoyed wading in the shallows along the beach, but Maggie sensed he was frightened of the crashing surf. Montgomery's enthusiasm, however, was contagious, and she saw Brendan's eyes fill with anticipation of the rare chance to gain his father's approval.

Maggie remembered that overcast June morning clearly. The expedition had begun playfully enough, with the three of them donning swimming trunks, and Brendan bubbling with excitement about finally joining the morning routine. But when the boy balked at the water's edge, Montgomery's temper flared. Brendan became frightened and began to cry. Suddenly Montgomery picked the boy up bodily and carried him into the surf, until the first wave broke over them. Now completely terrified, Brendan clawed his way out of his father's grasp and ran screaming up the beach to the house. Hysterically sobbing, he hurled himself face down on his bed, and it took Maggie an hour to calm him.

Afterward, when Montgomery announced that he intended to take Brendan into the ocean each morning until he conquered the boy's fear, Maggie flew into a rage.

"You're not! You're going to leave him alone! Why do you want to make him hate you?"

"I don't," he said icily. "And I don't want him to end up like his mother. I don't think that's entirely unreasonable."

Maggie stared at him, knowing that he would not be convinced otherwise. But for the sake of both father and son she knew she had to protect Brendan. "He'll learn," Maggie said with finality. "In his own time. I promise."

For a moment Maggie thought he would try to override her. But then he nodded and walked out of the room.

It required all of Maggie's patience for the remainder of that summer and the next to give Brendan the confidence he needed to overcome his fear of the sea. She worked with him each afternoon, and finally the boy became a good, if never a strong, ocean swimmer. One day shortly before Flynn's arrival, she told Montgomery that Brendan was ready to demonstrate his new ability.

The three of them walked out on the beach; Brendan plunged fearlessly into the surf, and then struck off beyond the breakers. When he came in, his frail body mottled with cold and his face eagerly expectant, Montgomery nodded his approval: "That's fine, Brendan."

But there was not the hearty approval in his voice that came so naturally in his dealings with Michael. As Montgomery started up toward the house, Brendan's eyes remained fixed on his father's back. And as Maggie wrapped a thick towel around the boy's body and began to chafe him, she was chilled by what she saw in those eyes: *if he were able, right now he would kill him.*

After that day Brendan rarely went into the ocean, and never indicated any interest in joining Montgomery and his half-brother in the morning swim.

Flynn saw what was happening with Brendan immediately. "It's cruel, the loneliness in that boy." He and Maggie were watching Brendan playing by himself on the strand, prodding at a beached jellyfish with a piece of driftwood. "You'd think the man would see it."

He was talking about Montgomery, she knew. "He can't let himself see."

Flynn glared at her. "Well, he bloody well ought to," he snapped. Abruptly he went to join Brendan with the jellyfish, and soon the boy was listening raptly to one of the marvelous yarns Flynn seemed able to spin at the drop of a hat.

Maggie was pleased that Flynn spent so much time with Brendan, and in the three weeks he stayed with them the boy came to idolize the whimsical Irishman, following him about like a puppy. Brendan was heartbroken when Flynn left to begin the writing of *Trilogy*.

Michael was her own blood and her first love, so quick and strong with his father's piercing blue eyes and driving intelligence, so determined to seize his manhood at the earliest possible moment. But Brendan's vulnerability wrenched at her heart, and she gave of herself to him in ways that Michael would never require. But she knew that as much as she gave him, it would never be enough. There was only one human being in the world who could feed the hunger in the boy's eyes, and nature and circumstance had placed an unbridgeable gulf between Brendan Montgomery and his father.

On her thirty-first birthday Maggie made a decision to retire. Her popularity was beginning to wane, as she knew that it inevitably would. In 1932 she had placed behind Garbo and Crawford in the running for the top five box office stars, and the decline had been continuous, if not dramatic in the following three years. She was well aware that the public constantly demanded new faces, and hers had been a fixture for a decade. She did not want to fade away, slowly slipping in stature from leading woman down the ladder into oblivion, as she had watched so many others do. And, more importantly, she did not want to compromise Montgomery's judgment with any pressure to keep her career alive beyond its natural demise. Her withdrawal from the film world would be as abrupt and total as her dramatic entry.

Besides, she was bored. She wanted to test herself against new obstacles while her youth and vitality were undiminished. She remembered her first conversation with Flynn, when she realized that her professional life had not provided her with a sense of fulfillment. Contrary to Flynn's judgment, she knew she was not a stage actress. She was, for better or for worse, unalterably who she was, and the motion picture camera had stripped away the trappings to present that person in virtually every picture she had ever appeared in, whether she had portrayed a Southern belle or a World War I nurse. The stage would require that she take on other personas, and she knew she did not have that talent.

But she was independently wealthy, and she did love the theater. Gradually the notion of buying and operating a small theater came to excite her. As her plans took shape, she began to envision an intimate little house which would become a demanding West Coast showcase for new talent. It would carry the stamp of her energies from top to bottom. And it would give her, for the first time in some years, a professional sphere completely separate and apart from that of her husband. She firmly refused, in her retirement, to become merely Ben Montgomery's wife.

She told Montgomery of her plans. To her surprise she learned that he had been seriously considering her for the multiple female leads in *Trilogy*. It was then Maggie knew that her decision to retire was the right one; already their intimacy was beginning to affect Montgomery's judgment. *Trilogy* would be a grueling test of the medium, and the three pictures ought to be cast from the first rank of talent and box office draw, a Garbo or Gaynor to play opposite a Gable or Powell. Still, she was pleased that he had not overlooked her.

Montgomery finally accepted her decision to retire. But he was so deeply involved in the preparation for *Britain* that he could generate little genuine enthusiasm for her theater project. That suited Maggie just fine. Were it to catch his fancy she knew she would have to fight him tooth and nail to keep it her own. The following day Montgomery notified the studio that Maggie would not renew her contract when it expired, and ordered Letty Barnes, now chief of American Universal publicity, to make a suitably extravagant production of the announcement when the time came.

And it was, ostensibly, her decision to retire that prompted Samuel Lendt to pay her another call. He showed up on the sound stage one morning during the final stages of shooting on what would be Maggie's last picture, a new adaption of *Madame Bovary* by the talented writing team of Ben Hecht and Charles MacArthur. He found her off the set in makeup. The hairdresser discreetly melted away when Lendt joined them. He studied her for a moment. "So, you're quitting."

Maggie watched him warily out of the corner of her eye as she touched up her face. In 1931 his son, Jack Lendt, had died of a malignant brain tumor in the mental hospital from which he'd never been released. Doctors had theorized that pressure from the tumor might have accounted for his earlier psychopathic behavior. Maggie had hoped at the time that the discovery might temper Lendt's hatred for herself and Montgomery. But Lendt had given no indication that such had been the case.

"That's right," she said.

Lendt nodded. "I've always liked the way you handled yourself, Maggie. Another year and I would have vetoed renewing your contract. You beat me to the punch."

She turned to face him squarely. "If that's all you had to tell me, Sam, you could have put it in a memo."

He chuckled, as though he hadn't heard her. "You don't kid yourself. That's another thing I like about you. And you're lucky. You and Montgomery both. I could always whip brains and talent when I had to. But luck . . . that's something else again."

Maggie frowned. "What are you talking about?"

"That boy of yours. If you hadn't taken him to New York for *Manhattan Carousel*, he'd be dead now," Lendt said simply. "That boy you had with Montgomery."

Maggie stared at him, her mind rigid with protest of her growing realization of the truth. "Billy Reiter was Michael's father," she said slowly. "Now I want you to get out of here."

Lendt smiled. "Sure." He turned to go, and then

paused. "You win, Maggie. The two of you. And you don't have to worry any more. An opportunity like Sheila doesn't come along very often." His smile drained away. "I just wanted you to know how close I came."

She watched him numbly as he strolled away toward the set, pausing to have a word with von Stroheim, the director. *It was Lendt,* she realized. Suddenly the whole sequence of events of those far-off, tortured days that led to Billy's murder fell into place with irrefutable logic. Lendt was the one who had somehow gotten word to Sheila that Montgomery had fathered Michael. She could imagine Sheila's reaction; all of the repressed paranoia must have come raging once again to the surface. And with Montgomery spending long hours at the studio supervising the conversion to sound, and convinced besides that his wife had recovered, Sheila had time to plan carefully. She had sought out Jimmy Knowland and sent him to the beach that terrifying morning to confirm what Lendt had told her. And it was Sheila who led Jimmy to his death, not the other way around. She should have known. Poor Jimmy; despite his play-acting, he would never have had the courage.

Maggie left the studio without offering any excuses, throwing von Stroheim into one of his patented rages. At the beach she spent a long time holding Michael tightly in her arms, until the boy became impatient and squirmed free to go adventuring among the dunes. When Montgomery called to find out why she walked off the set, Maggie told him only that she'd had a dizzy spell and come home to rest. And then she tried to put Samuel Lendt's words out of her mind.

By the middle of May *Britain* was cast. From the beginning John Ford had been Montgomery's choice to direct, and he'd finally wangled a trade-off with Metro to secure his services. Crawford and the young Tyrone Power would star, picking up leads in *Empire* and *America* as soon as *Britain* was in the can. American Universal had budgeted a staggering eleven million dollars for the epic, and it was already going over budget. "Montgomery's madness" had been the talk of Hollywood for months. Shooting was to begin in the first week of June on location in Wales, where a full-scale replica of Camelot had been constructed.

Montgomery had never been in better spirits. It was as

though he had waited all his life for a challenge equal to his enormous energy and drive. He'd spent the better part of April in Wales, supervising the completion of set construction on *Britain*, and when he returned Flynn handed him a completed draft of *Empire*. Montgomery read the script through the same evening, despite the fact that Maggie hadn't seen him for almost a month, and the next day launched pre-production on the second film of *Trilogy*. He was working until after midnight six days a week at the studio, and during those few times he was home at the beach the phone never quit ringing. Montgomery was thriving on the furious pace, but finally Maggie had had enough.

One Sunday morning, after a quiet breakfast, he fidgeted around for a while, then finally picked up the telephone. He frowned. "There's something wrong with the phone."

"No there's not," she said. "I had it disconnected."

He stared at her blankly, as though the enormity of what she'd done was too much for him to grasp. "You *what*?"

It turned out to be one of the most miserable days of their marriage. It was as though he'd had some psychic umbilical cord severed, and he wandered around the house in a black mood until late afternoon. Then he vanished for an hour or so, and when he returned he was in decidedly improved spirits. "I went over to see if Ingram wanted to come to the party," he said, by way of an excuse.

Maggie sighed; she knew he'd gone over to borrow Ingram's phone. She threw in the towel, and the next day had the phone re-connected.

The party Montgomery referred to was being thrown by Wilkening aboard his yacht, anchored off Newport, for the cast and crew of *Britain* on the eve of their departure for Europe. It was a glittering event on a mild, moonlit evening. Maggie and Montgomery were late because she had to drag him away from the studio, and by the time they arrived the party was well under way. Somehow Wilkening had managed to secure Benny Goodman's orchestra for the occasion, and swinging saxophone and trumpet sounds floated over the water. The press was excluded, but Letty Barnes had a brace of studio photographers ranging among the guests, ensuring that an entirely decorous account of the event would reach the gossips and the trades in time for deadline. The atmosphere aboard the spanking clean, spotless white vessel was intoxicating. The music was fast, the men handsome and elegantly dressed, the women glamourous in gowns that displayed daring expanses of lower back and bosom.

But surprisingly enough, the host of the party was nowhere in sight. Lyla, already half tipsy, told Maggie that Wilkening was tied up at his Los Angeles headquarters on business, and might not make an appearance at all. She grinned wickedly. "I'm sure I haven't the faintest idea how I'll ever survive the evening." It was then, with some alarm, that Maggie saw Richard Flynn at the bar. He was drinking Glenlivet neat and, with his tie discarded and the diamond studs of his ruffled shirt unfastened, there was a decidedly rakish air about him as he flashed Maggie a grin from across the deck.

But she submerged her anxiety as the evening wore on and Wilkening did not show up. Montgomery had cornered Ford, his director, and Maggie knew he would probably keep the poor man on the ropes for most of the evening. She danced with Tyrone Power, whom she had not met before, and found him possessed of a boyish charm. She could understand his delicious reputation, and decided not to mention to Montgomery an invitation the actor whispered in her ear as they waltzed beneath the candy-striped canopy over the stern.

But by midnight she was ready to leave. Champagne had made her sleepy, and besides, Michael was in bed with a cold and she was anxious to get home to him. Montgomery, however, had vanished. She found him in a stateroom below, closeted with Flynn and John Ford, going through the shooting draft of *Empire* for the umpteenth time.

Flynn grinned. "I told you, Maggie. The man's a monster. If his bloody pockets weren't stuffed so full of all that money I'd have nothing to do with him."

She glared at Montgomery. "This is supposed to be a party. You might quit hounding these people for *one* night, anyway."

He glanced up, checking his watch. "I know. You're right. Listen, we're about through here. Why don't you have the driver take you home and I'll catch a ride out with Ingram a little later."

She shook her head in exasperation, kissed him good night and left him to his work.

Maggie was slipping into bed when the phone rang. It was Letty Barnes. Her voice was quavering with near hysteria.

"My God, Maggie, I don't know how to tell you . . ."

But Maggie, her heart suddenly filled with dread, knew. "What happened to Ben?"

"He's been shot," Letty said. "He's dead, Maggie."

Maggie sat frozen on the edge of the bed. When she spoke the forced calm of her voice was a mockery of the screaming protest in her mind. "Are you sure?"

Letty rushed on, almost incoherently. "There was some trouble when Mr. Wilkening came aboard. I don't know what happened. But Ben was trying to stop it—"

Abruptly the connection was terminated at Letty's end. But Maggie barely noticed. Slowly she replaced the telephone. She remained in the same position for a long time, listening to the rhythmic crash of the surf beyond the screened windows of the sleeping porch. Bit by bit she forced her mind to accept the truth. She could guess what had happened on the yacht when Wilkening had returned, and she also knew it was the inevitable ending of a scenario that had begun fourteen years earlier with a shooting at a mansion high in the Hollywood Hills. Among those participants, there was only herself left now. And Samuel Lendt. The shadow had fallen across Wally Gordon, and Jack Lendt, and Jimmy Knowland. And now Montgomery.

Finally she rose to dress and make the long trip into the city.

But another nightmare had just begun for Maggie. In the early morning hours she found the yacht club anchorage deserted, and Wilkening's steam cruiser gone. She stepped from her car and walked slowly out on the pier. There were only a few sodden streamers floating against the pilings under the pier to indicate that a party had taken place. Her mind rebelled. *It couldn't be,* she thought. The police would have cordoned off the whole anchorage, and there would have been dozens of party-goers to question. Above all, they would never have allowed Wilkening to leave the harbor. She stared at the empty mooring. *If they'd called the police.* Suddenly, realizing the truth, Maggie felt utterly alone and helpless.

When she turned she discovered a car had pulled out of the shadows of the yacht club restaurant at the end of the pier. A man stepped out of the car and stood by the door.

She walked slowly to where he awaited her. It was Gerrard, the studio detective.

"What have you done with him?" she demanded.

"He's been taken care of. I was told to take you to the mortuary."

"He was shot," she said. "Where are the police?"

Gerrard shook his head. "There was no shooting," he said blandly. "The doctors said it was a massive coronary. That's what they put on the death certificate."

She stared at him. Then she stepped into his car.

At the mortuary, which was located near the studio, she was allowed to view Montgomery's body, which was draped in a frayed white cotton smock. She held herself rigidly, fighting back the waves of vertigo, and approached the tall metal gurney more closely. The chrome railings gleamed beneath the harsh, overhead lights. When she reached over to raise the smock, Gerrard caught her hand.

"I wouldn't," he said.

Abruptly two attendants wheeled the body away.

A grey dawn was breaking under overcast skies when she stepped numbly out on the street. "It's better this way," Gerrard said, lighting a cigarette. "Say he was shot. You've got a couple of boys at home. It would always be over them. A thing like that always is. Sometimes a thing like that can make a kid go the wrong way."

She said nothing.

"It was an accident," Gerrard said flatly. "He got in the way of something."

"I know," she nodded.

He frowned. "I've got to tell Mr. Lendt something. Are you going to let it alone?"

She looked at him. "What can I do?"

"Nothing." He seemed satisfied. "I'll take you home now."

She left him there, walking quickly away up the empty sidewalk.

She found an all-night coffee shop open on Santa Monica Boulevard. There was a pay phone, and she searched her address book until she found the number she was seeking. Letty Barnes was a long time in answering. Maggie heard a sharp intake of breath when Letty recognized her caller.

"Maggie . . ."

"You told me he was shot."

Letty hesitated. When she spoke there was fear in her

voice. "I didn't. I don't know what you're talking about."

Maggie's voice began to rise in spite of herself. "*Four hours ago you told me he was shot!*"

"I haven't talked to you all night," Letty sobbed. And then she hung up.

A cab carried Maggie quickly across Beverly Hills to the sprawling salmon-pink hotel on Sunset Boulevard. The desk clerk, recognizing Margaret Marshall and used to such liaisons as he assumed this one to be, smiled knowingly as he dialed to announce her.

Surprised, he covered the receiver. "Mr. Flynn says he can't see you just now, Miss Marshall."

"Tell him if he doesn't, I'm going directly to the police."

The desk clerk frowned, but relayed the message.

She could see that Flynn was a wreck when he opened the door to let her into his bungalow. His silk shirt was rumpled and soiled, and his haggard eyes had lost their light. There was a whiskey bottle almost empty on his writing table, among scattered new pages of *Trilogy*.

"Tell me what happened," she demanded.

He stared at her. "All right. I will." He poured himself what was left of the whiskey.

It had played out as Maggie imagined it. After she left the party, and once Montgomery's impromptu story conference had broken up, Flynn carried Lyla below to an empty stateroom. Soon after Wilkening arrived at the party, someone told him that Lyla was entertaining a lover. Flynn had just undressed Lyla when they heard a commotion outside the door, and then a shot. When he threw open the door Montgomery was lying dead on the floor and crewmembers were wrestling a revolver from Wilkening's hand.

Flynn stared out the window with empty eyes. "I suppose Ben was trying to keep the madman from breaking in on us."

At last she had the truth. "And after that? Why didn't they call the police?"

"It was Sam Lendt's notion," Flynn said wearily. "And you'll have to ask him the why of that. For the good of the studio, I suppose. He stepped in and took over everything."

Despite her anguish, Maggie felt a cold surge of satisfaction: the man who had tried to murder her son had made himself an accomplice to murder.

"I'm going to call the police now," she said.

Flynn shook his head. "It'll do no good. I won't say what I told you."

She grabbed his arm to spin him around. "You have to," she said furiously.

But she knew when she saw the fear in his eyes that it was hopeless. "I said I can't!" He wrenched his arm from her grasp. "Don't you understand, it would be the end of me."

She stared at him helplessly. "Dick, I know you," she said carefully. "If you don't do this, it will be the end of you anyway."

He turned away. "You'd better go now, Maggie."

It was still early when Maggie arrived at American Universal, but she knew she would find Lendt in his office. She was quite sure he was planning a very busy day. At the gate the guard peered into the back seat of the cab, then nodded them through. A remote part of her mind realized that this was the last time she would ever return to American Universal. As it had the first time she'd ever come here, the car dropped her off in front of the tall white office building known as the Ivory Tower.

She would not have come back this morning, but for the one last thing she could do for her husband. She told the cab driver to wait.

Lendt's secretaries had not arrived and the outer office was empty. Across the room the door to the spacious inner office was ajar. Lendt was on the phone. He glanced up with an annoyed frown as Maggie entered. He abruptly ended the conversation and placed the receiver in its cradle, his eyes never leaving her. He smiled bleakly. "My condolences."

Maggie had no intention of wasting words. "What are you going to do with *Trilogy*?"

"I'm going to scrap it. What'd you think I'd do?"

"You're three million into it and committed for at least two more, even if you pull the plug this morning."

He nodded. "About that. It won't be the first beating I've taken. And this one will give me a lot of personal satisfaction."

She crossed to the window and looked out over the lot. She remembered the morning Montgomery had stood at this same window, silhouetted in blazing light as he ordered her to tell Lendt that his son was a murderer. She sighed;

the scenario was repeating itself. The actors had only changed roles, that was all. But there was no doubt in her mind that new inevitabilities had been seeded and would one day bear new and destructive fruit. She could smash the play to bits with her knowledge of the events aboard Wilkening's yacht. But she was unutterably tired with her grief and the knowledge that the vital part of her life was over. However, her voice betrayed none of this resignation.

"You're going to finish it," she said clearly.

He chuckled. "In a pig's eye, I am."

"If you don't, I'm going to the police."

He stared at her. "Gerrard said you wouldn't."

"I lied to Gerrard. I imagine a lot of people lie to him."

Lendt wet his lips. "It won't do you any good, you know. The authorities are satisfied it was a natural death. I saw to that."

"Then I'll go to the newspapers. And I'll hire the best lawyers money can buy, Sam. And I promise you, I'll never quit."

He stared at her, rigid with hatred. Finally he spread his hands flat on the desktop. "All right. I'll go forward with *Trilogy*. But I'm going to do it my way."

She turned to face him. "I thought you would."

She walked out of his office and left the building. She told the cab driver to take her to Malibu, and when they passed out the gate Maggie didn't look back. It was almost over. But before she could finally surrender to her grief, Montgomery's sons must be told their father was dead.

Maggie's Epilogue

Trilogy was never finished, and the money and misjudgment that went into its failure put American Universal Studios into a decline that led to eventual bankruptcy. Maggie was disappointed, but she had done all that was in her power to do.

Her life settled into a somnolent routine of looking after her sons and watching the catastrophic events unfold that plunged the world into war. Montgomery's name became a legend in the film industry, but Maggie's own fame evaporated quickly as new faces and talents claimed the spotlight. She no longer possessed the vitality that had inspired her plans to launch a theater, and she gradually abandoned the idea. She never saw Lyla again, and made no attempt to seek her out. If there were men in her life, they were dealt with discreetly. It was as though a rushing tide of events had swept her up, broken over her, and then left her in the shallows. She was a spectator once more, and content to remain one.

She returned to Fresno only once, in 1939, impelled by a restless curiosity and a feeling of rootlessness. She barely remembered those years of her life before she arrived in Hollywood. As her car crossed the tracks and turned onto Calaveras Street, she saw immediately that the rooming house was no longer standing. She ordered the driver to stop, and stepped out on the sidewalk. There was only a weed-choked vacant lot where the rooming house had stood, with some broken foundation stone and scattered, weathered timbers. She could hazard no guess as to what might have happened to the place. There might have been a fire; and if there had, her mother might have died in it. But it was only an idle speculation; she had not come seeking her mother, she had come to invigorate her sense of identity. But the empty lot only heightened her feeling of suspension; her life, which had begun on a reckless night in 1922 and ended on the morning of Montgomery's death, seemed encapsulated in a bubble. She stepped back into the car and ordered the driver to return to Malibu.

On another day in the same week she sat on the beach watching Michael and Brendan play catch with a football. Michael was twelve now, sun-bronzed and sturdy, charged with a contagious energy which had already made him a leader among his schoolmates. Brendan, at eleven, was slim and delicately complected. Maggie had always to be wary that he did not take too much sun. But despite his slight build, she knew there was surprising strength in the lithe muscles of his arms and legs. As with Michael, Brendan's eyes were his remarkable feature; in his case a clear, brooding blue, one moment rebelliously questing, the next guarded and inward seeking. The boys were as yet unaware that they shared a common natural father. She and Montgomery had agreed that both Michael and Brendan would have to be told one day, but not until they had gained maturity. There were moments in which Maggie had questioned the wisdom of that decision, suspecting that if the boys knew the truth it might serve to bring them closer. But the boys had grown closer since Montgomery's death, with Brendan leaning on Michael's strength and purpose, and Michael assuming the role of pathfinder and guardian, often protecting Brendan from the cruelties of older boys. So Maggie waited.

The feeling of suspension had not left her. Watching the boys at play, she tried to put her life in perspective. She closed her eyes. What would have been the shape of her existence had she not done Montgomery's bidding on the night of Wally Gordon's party? For a moment an answer seemed to glimmer just beyond her mind's reach. Finally she gave up. It was an irrelevant exercise.

There had never been any possibility, once Montgomery

crossed her path, that she would not have moved heaven and earth to have him in her arms. And she knew that the price which had been exacted for that brief passion was nothing compared to its glory.

PART II

Michael and Brendan—Love and Hate

1953-1954

PART II

Prologue—Brendan

The sanitarium was in the Catskills, upstate. Brendan hired a cab to take him out from the depot in a cold, misty rain.

One look at the shrunken figure in the hospital bed and he knew Richard Flynn really was dying. Look at his face, he thought. Wrinkled up, with that awful damp, dead, yellow look to it. And his eyes. God, what it did to those wonderful eyes. He knows it too. I know he's dying and he knows he's dying. And in a place like this, with those stale-smelling priests and nuns wandering around like empty shells. And that dirty rain on the window.

Brendan searched for something to say.

"Shit."

The dry lips parted with the hint of a smile.

"Aye. Shit. You said it."

Even his voice sounds that way too, Brendan thought. Like old leaves. He forced himself to return the smile.

"Did you get the telegram?"

"Congratulations."

He shrugged. "What the hell. It had to happen. You always said so yourself."

Flynn's smile evaporated. "So you're flying out next week?"

"That's right. Back home."

"Then that's it, for sure."

This isn't like him, Brendan thought. Not when he's

sober, which he is at last. A maudlin leave-taking? Bad drama. And he must have known this is how it would be.

"I wouldn't have dragged you out here, Brendan, but I've been giving things some thought. Your father. He's what it's all about."

The mention of his father summoned memories. With an effort, he suppressed them. But the familiar throbbing began at his temples.

"I don't want to hear it. You know how I feel about that."

"Don't be an idiot, lad. It's a dragon you'll have to slay sooner or later. And anyway, this is important. So you'll understand the reason I always tried to look after you. More than just the way a friend would. I want you to know."

Brendan waited tensely, wishing he'd ignored Flynn's summons. The old man seemed to be gathering some crucial reserve of energy.

"The reason is, I owed it to him. He saved me one time."

Brendan frowned. Placed next to all of his father's other accomplishments that people still talked about, the fact that he saved Richard Flynn along the way hardly amounted to a major revelation.

"It was the night he died. Aboard that bloody yacht. The true story's never been told about that night, Brendan, and I've been thinking you've a right to know what I can tell you. It was never his heart. He was shot, Brendan. . . ."

CHAPTER 9

On October 3, 1953, a brushfire was scorching the Palisades, fanned by hot Santa Ana winds. Visible in the night as far up the coast as Malibu Colony, the fire had leveled at least nine expensive homes on the ridges overlooking the Riviera Country Club and was threatening to break out along Sunset Boulevard. Elsewhere in the world Joseph Stalin was recently dead, Dwight Eisenhower occupied the White House, and only that summer had an armistice been signed ending the United Nations police action in Korea. A feeling of aftermath was pervasive in the country; a pause as new currents formed and gathered a momentum which would, in a few short years, rush the world into the torrents of the next series of great events.

That evening, in the offices of United Press International on the fifth floor of the Edison Building downtown, Michael Montgomery was pounding out an updated night lead on the Palisades fire when Sayers's phone rang. All around him the teletype machines sent up a ceaseless, hammering din, charging the atmosphere with frenetic urgency.

Michael was night cycle manager and in line for a bureau chief's job. He was twenty-six years old. Korea was behind him, and the black period of his life following Korea. The deaths of his parents, as well as his experiences in the war, had instructed him well in the precariousness of life. As a consequence, he was in a hurry to get where he was going.

Sayers, at the desk opposite Michael, glanced up. "They want you, Mike."

Michael snatched up the telephone. "Montgomery, UPI." He listened for a moment. Sayers, who was preparing the radio file for the upcoming local split, cocked an ear in his direction as Michael began firing questions at the caller.

"You got something?" he asked as Michael hung up.

"It looks like somebody shotgunned Nicky Momasso at Penny Booth's place in the Colony."

Sayers stared at him blankly. "Holy Christ. Can we run with it?"

"Not yet. I'm going out there. As soon as I've got it confirmed I'll phone in a lead. Tell Farrel to pull the file on Momasso and the girl and get the backgrounder punched."

Sayers looked doubtful. "It's twenty miles out there. We could get beat."

Michael was shrugging into his coat. He grinned. "We won't get beat. Trust me."

Sayers shook his head. "Some neighbors you got."

Michael grabbed his cane and headed for the door.

A few minutes later he was racing out along the coast highway, under the bluffs of the Palisades. The ocean lay calm under the stars in the summery night. The surf was only a playful tumble, indicating clear skies far out to sea. Fire wardens had blockaded the canyon roads, but beyond the barricades, high up on the ridges, Michael could see ominous red halos silhouetting the crests, scarred by occasional tongues of flame. With the cool, damp ocean breeze becalmed the firefighters would be in for a long night and an even longer day tomorrow. As he drove, Michael scanned the radio channels. Briggs had told him that the sheriff's investigators were sitting on the Momasso shooting, and he hoped the old man knew what he was talking about. He satisfied himself that the news hadn't reached the radio wires, which meant he was safely ahead of the opposition. He enjoyed the wire service because of the head-to-head competition. There were only two outfits in the game, UPI and the Associated Press. You placed either first or second. And Michael had quickly developed a reputation for placing first.

It was his reputation that had led to the Murrow offer. That would have to be dealt with very shortly. On the Coast to film an edition of *See It Now,* Edward R. Murrow had personally telephoned Michael the week before at the office to ask him to lunch the following day. They met at Musso's where Murrow ordered steaks for both of them and then left his half eaten, seeming to prefer keeping a cigarette lit between nicotine-stained fingers. Michael sat opposite him, awed to near silence by the heavily lined face and stentorious voice. It was that voice which had held Michael riveted to the radio in the dark, early years of the war as Murrow described the blitz of London, broadcasting from atop the BBC building as searchlights swept the skies amid the *thump* of anti-aircraft batteries, and German bombs smashed into the city.

From his briefcase Murrow removed a file of yellowed teletype printouts which carried Michael's by-line. He grinned. "As you can see, I've been following your career. In fact, I'm quite a fan of yours."

Murrow proceeded to sound Michael out about his politics. There was a storm on the horizon, he said. Joe McCarthy, the Red-baiting senator from Wisconsin, was hell-bent on destroying the country, and had directly challenged Murrow's loyalty.

Murrow grinned. "Which leaves me no choice but to take him on every chance I get. What do you think of the man?"

"I think he's a dangerous psychopath," Michael said.

Murrow chuckled, and offered him a staff job with CBS news. He gave Michael two weeks to make up his mind.

Michael had hesitated for one reason only. It would mean moving to New York. And Brendan was in New York.

He hurtled through the intersection at Sunset Boulevard, his speedometer needle leaning against the seventy miles per hour peg, and a California Highway Patrol unit, its lights blazing and siren screaming, shot past him as if he were standing still. Michael nodded grimly; something was definitely going on at Malibu.

But he instinctively slowed as he approached the intersection with Topanga Canyon road. It was there, in 1940, that his mother had died in an automobile accident. Michael had been twelve years old then, and he remembered the utter desolation and sense of abandonment he'd experienced in the weeks and months following the funeral. Again thoughts of Brendan surfaced in his mind; he'd held himself together for Brendan's sake. His mother's death had been a shattering experience for him, and had hardened his spirit prematurely. But he had recovered. He had only recently begun to realize how completely Margaret Marshall's death had destroyed the emotional foundations of Brendan Montgomery's life.

As he crossed the bridge over the inlet, Michael could see that there was a roadblock across the Colony access road, and a half-dozen patrol units converged at Penny Booth's modern tri-level a few doors removed from the rambling old house his mother had built in 1926. As he approached the roadblock he removed the press tag from his windshield. A young deputy scanned his face with a flashlight. "I'm sorry, sir. We're not allowing any visitors through tonight."

"I'm not a visitor. I have a house out here."

The deputy eyed Michael's vintage Oldsmobile skeptically. "Your name?"

"Michael Montgomery."

He nodded. "All right, sir. Go ahead."

The Montgomery place, Michael knew, was something of a legend; partly because it was the first house built on the strand, and partly because his father, a film industry legend himself, had lived there. Michael used it rarely these days, preferring to live out of an apartment closer to the office. His mother's estate, which he and Brendan would divide when they each reached thirty years of age, maintained the house and paid the taxes. His last extended stay had been in the summer of 1951, when he was recovering from the work done on his hip, and the other, deeper wounds Korea had dealt him.

He nodded in the direction of the Booth bungalow. "What's going on? Has there been some trouble?"

"I'm not at liberty to say. We're advising residents to stay away from the vicinity of the investigation."

A few yards beyond the roadblock he stopped at the gatehouse for a word with Briggs. He'd come to know the old man well during his summer at the beach. Briggs had lost an arm in World War I and seemed to understand Michael's occasional need for quiet company in the deepest hours of the night. They also shared a mild, unspoken contempt for most of the people who lived within the rarefied confines of the Colony, the doings of whom, however secret, rarely escaped Briggs. It was the old man who had called Michael earlier.

"Any idea why they're trying to keep a lid on it?"

Briggs gave a disgusted grunt. "Just the way they get sometimes. Makes 'em feel important."

Michael frowned. "I don't think so. What about Penny? Did she come back?"

He nodded. "About the time I phoned you."

A limousine pulled away from the Booth house, turned the corner and glided past the gate. There was an American Universal Pictures logo on the door. There was a man in the back seat. For a moment Michael was plunged back into his childhood, when other big, gleaming cars, stamped with the same logo, would arrive at the beach for his mother.

"Who was that?"

"Jason Lendt. He was out here a couple of times to visit with the hoodlum."

Jason Lendt *was* American Universal Pictures these days, having brought the studio back from receivership after the war. Suddenly Michael's instincts told him that he'd better find out just why the chief of a major studio was visiting the scene of a gangland murder.

He parked at his mother's house, then hiked back the quarter of a mile to Penny Booth's house. The walking sent fierce, stabbing pains into the core of his repaired hip. But at least he could walk.

According to Briggs's account, the old man had heard what sounded like a shotgun blast and run to investigate. He found the glass doors of Penny Booth's patio shattered and "the hoodlum" lying on the floor with half his face shot away. Michael knew that Penny Booth, a pixyish, dimpled blonde who specialized in playing fresh-faced, wholesome teenagers, had been sleeping with Dominick Momasso, a gangster with a Las Vegas gambling license and reputed sado-masochistic sexual preferences. Briggs had told him of some of the bedroom goings on between Momasso and filmdom's girl-next-door. Michael, who grew up in the movie business, was only surprised that people would go to such lengths when they could get approximately the same results by stepping into a grain thresher.

As he approached Penny Booth's gate the two uniformed deputies posted there stiffened like setters on point. One of them, obviously sensing trouble, moved his bulk in a vaguely belligerent way across Michael's path. "I'm sorry, sir. No one's allowed on the premises."

Michael ignored him. "Who's in charge here, deputy? I'd like to have a word with him. I'm Mike Montgomery, United Press."

The man's face fell, as though a carefully laid plan had suddenly gone sour. Which it had, Michael thought wryly.

"You're not supposed to be here," the man said. He glanced uncomfortably at his partner.

"But I am. And I know Momasso's dead. I know he was shot. I know it happened in Penny Booth's living room. And I know American Universal's mixed up in it. Tell your boss if that's what he wants to see on the wire, I'll be happy to oblige."

The deputy gave Michael a murderous look, then finally nodded. "You wait here."

A few minutes later a captain of homicide named Hedges was showing Michael into Penny Booth's house. Hedges was a stout, jowly, affable man whose job at the moment seemed to be to convince Michael there was nothing amiss in Malibu, with the modest exception of a good portion of Dominick Momasso's face.

Momasso was lying face down in a stale pool of his own blood on the expensive, imported tile floor of the living room. Homicide investigators were combing the patio, and beyond them portable floodlights had been set up on the beach and more investigators moved carefully about in the eerie, improbable illumination. Hedges was explaining that the gunmen had likely anchored a fast cruiser some distance offshore and come in on a raft. They had waited on the patio until Momasso passed near the doors and then emptied both barrels of a twelve-gauge shotgun through the glass. Momasso was wearing the vest and trousers of an expensive black silk suit, and a holster harness across his shoulders. There were heavy shards of broken glass everywhere.

"See," Hedges chuckled, "I figure they got a little nervous when they saw Momasso was carrying his piece, which is why they didn't barge in." The policeman's voice had become almost proprietary, as though he were conducting a tour. "So they didn't take any chances. They let him have it from outside. He didn't know what hit him."

"Where was Miss Booth?"

"Perino's. A dinner party. Don't get the wrong idea."

Michael made a mental note that the room looked as if it had been hastily and unprofessionally searched. Hedges watched him for a moment with a frown, then lowered his voice conspiratorially: "But I'll tell you something else off the record, Montgomery. You should've seen the stuff we found up in the bedroom. Leather manacles on the bedposts. These cute little crotch gizmos. The whole show. Listen, you want to have a look, I can get you up there."

Hedges was being more cooperative than any cop in history. Michael suspected he knew the reason, and he wondered how long it was going to take Hedges to get to it.

"I'll take a rain check on the bedroom," he said. "But I need to use the phone. How about it?"

Hedges nodded. "Sure. There's one in the kitchen."

The detective followed Michael into the kitchen. When he picked up the phone, Hedges put his finger on the contacts. "Oh, by the way. You probably want to know why Lendt was out here, right?"

It's about time, Michael thought. "I meant to ask about that. I saw the car pulling out."

"Right. Well the kid, Penny, was all broken up. And this Lendt is an old friend. So he came out to give her a shoulder to cry on. As a favor he asked us not to mention it to you press guys."

"You didn't. I picked it up on my own."

Hedges's jaw tightened, but he kept his smile in place. "Still it was a pretty decent gesture. I hate to see a guy get sucked into this kind of shit just for trying to be a buddy."

Mike nodded. "Okay, I'll tell you what. I'll forget I saw Lendt if you get me a word with Penny Booth. What do you think?"

Hedges sighed. "You got a deal."

Michael dialed the bureau and, as the detective listened, dictated a 200-word first lead on the Momasso killing to be bulletined out on the A-wire. He made no mention of American Universal Pictures and Hedges seemed satisfied. He wouldn't have used the Lendt connection anyway, even if Hedges had refused to set up the interview with Penny Booth. He was the only newsman in town who knew of it and he wasn't about to tip his hand. He hung up the phone with a keen sense of anticipation. Thanks to Hedges, he knew that an even bigger story, yet to be uncovered, had sped out of the colony in an American Universal limousine.

Hedges deposited Michael in an upstairs study and went to fetch Penny Booth. Michael glanced around. This room looked as though it had been gone through as well. The green-eyed, auburn-haired young woman who appeared in the doorway a few minutes later definitely wasn't Penny.

"You press people," she said in a clipped English accent, "you're absolutely impossible, aren't you?"

Her voice vibrated with cold anger, but there was an elegant quality about her that appealed to Michael. He grinned. "Not absolutely. But we try. Who are you?"

"I'm a friend of Miss Booth's. On her behalf I've come to ask you to go away. I'm sure you can understand how upset she is."

Michael studied her. "You don't look like you'd be a friend of Penny Booth."

She looked annoyed. "What on earth makes you say that?"

"For one thing you don't look like a pimp or a dope peddler or a hired killer. Judging from the guy laid out on the floor down there, those are the kinds of people Penny brings home with her."

She glared at him in cold fury. But before she could make a response, Hedges joined them with Penny Booth in tow. The actress's dimpled cheeks were ashen; her dilated eyes scanned Michael vaguely, then drifted away. "There really isn't much I can tell you, I'm afraid," she said almost absently as she floated past Michael into the study to settle into a stuffed chair opposite the desk. The girl in the doorway shifted her glare from Michael to Hedges, who shrugged apologetically.

"Look, Miss Hampton, the way I figure it, the sooner we get this over with the sooner Miss Booth can get out of here. In another fifteen minutes there's going to be reporters crawling out of the woodwork."

Michael made a mental note that Miss Hampton had flinched involuntarily when Hedges mentioned her name. Now she snapped, "Very well," then turned on her heel and left the room.

Michael frowned. "Who was that?"

"Off the record?" Hedges asked warily. Michael nodded. "Lendt's personal secretary. Hampton. Laura Hampton, I think she said her name was. He left her here to see after Miss Booth."

Michael glanced at Penny Booth. She was trying to light

a cigarette, but couldn't seem to make the lighted match connect with the end of the Pall Mall. When the flame burned her fingers she dropped the match on the carpet. Penny was obviously bombed into another world. Michael walked over to crush the match underfoot.

He found Laura Hampton downstairs in the kitchen. She was on the phone. As he came in she hung up. Now she looked tired, and perhaps frightened.

"Did you get what you were after, then?" Her attitude toward him had shifted; he assumed it was on orders from Jason Lendt.

"No. You were right. She was in no condition to talk."

"I was going to come looking for you. I was rude earlier. You were only doing your job. God knows, we all have our jobs to do." Michael waited. Beyond her, through the kitchen window, the ghostly figures were still plying the beach with sieves under the floodlights. "Anyway," she said, "I thought I might give you lunch tomorrow at the studio by way of apology."

"You don't suppose Jason Lendt might drop by the table, do you?"

Her mouth tightened. "He might. Would that ruin your appetite?"

Michael smiled, not wanting to alienate her. "It would depend on what he had to say. Or not say."

Her eyes, showing some surprise, went from his smile to his cane and then back to his face again. "Yes, I can see how it might," she said. She was lovely, and something more. For him, something dangerously more. In her proximity he should, he knew, move warily.

"Well, will you?" she insisted, but now genuinely interested.

"Sure," Michael said.

Michael spent the night at the beach, in his old room. His sleep was troubled by images from his childhood, predominantly that of Brendan, who seemed always to be reaching for him, filling him with a sense of peril.

Floating always in the background was the serene beauty of his mother's face, before Montgomery's death. He called to her in desperation born of the nameless fear Brendan inspired. But she seemed not to hear.

He awoke on a bright, still morning that seemed timeless; he glanced out the window across the sand drifts to the sea, sparkling under the morning sun. He half expected to hear Ben Montgomery's voice booming through the house, and feel his strong hands dragging him from bed for their morning swim.

The warm memory of his stepfather triggered an impulse. He rummaged through the bureau until he found some old swimming trunks, and then limped out on the beach. He plunged into the surf, and the cold, stinging brine exhilarated him, shocking his sleep-sluggish body into full awareness. During the recuperative summer he had spent at the beach house after the war, fighting despair much of the time and living as a recluse, resuming of the old routine had been out of the question. The only swimming he did then was in the therapy pools at the Veteran's Hospital in West Los Angeles. Now he discovered that although his right leg was almost no help at all, he could still cut through the water almost as swiftly as before. His strength in the sea had always been in his powerful arms and shoulders anyway. He remembered with affection Montgomery endlessly lecturing him on developing a proper kick, which had led to the frog-suit episode.

One morning as the two of them were towelling down after a swim, Montgomery had started it. "Listen, Mike, if you ever get a chance, stop and look at a frog's hind legs. A frog's got big, strong hind legs to push with."

"And webbed feet. I should have webbed feet too, I guess."

"The point is, young man, you've got to develop your legs. That's why you can't keep up."

His stepfather had dwelt so tiresomely on the frog analogy that one morning Michael came clumping out on the beach dressed in a frog suit he'd wheedled out of Montgomery's wardrobe master on a trip to the studio the day before. Montgomery collapsed on the sand, roaring with laughter, and thereafter never mentioned frogs again. Montgomery kept the frog suit around the house until his death. Afterwards Michael was never able to locate it.

There was that kind of camaraderie between them, a closeness from which, Michael came to realize, Brendan had been completely excluded.

As he drove into Santa Monica along the coast he could see a heavy, still layer of black smoke lying over the Palisades bluffs. The morning news on the radio said the fire had destroyed a half-dozen more homes and was still to be contained. The Santa Anas were already gusting at the palms lining Oceanfront Park and the prospects for checking the fire were bleak. Michael, however, was in a good mood. He stopped for breakfast at Zucky's on Wilshire and scanned the morning papers. The street edition of the *Times* put him in even a better mood. The paper had, of course, bannered the Palisades blaze, but it carried his lead on the Momasso murder under a 24-point head atop the fold in second position. To go with his by-line over that of their own staffers was an acknowledgement by the editors of how badly he'd beaten the field on the story. And, he thought, if his instincts were right, they hadn't seen the half of it. He ordered eggs and onions and crisp bacon. His plunge into the ocean had left him with an appetite.

When he finished breakfast he drove across Westwood to drop in on Letty Barnes. Although she worked for the *Trib*, she operated out of her hilltop, Tudor-style house in Bel Air, adjacent to Beverly Hills. The Los Angeles *Tribune* was a Wilkening-chain paper, and press club rumor had it that Letty somehow had negotiated a lifetime sinecure there. It was generally assumed that she'd managed to turn up some scandal about the old man himself and was holding it over his head like a sword.

Whatever the truth of the matter, Letty Barnes was good at what she did and had an encyclopedic knowledge of Hollywood goings-on dating from the pre-talkie period. Michael wanted to tap that knowledge before he turned up for lunch with Laura Hampton at American Universal.

It was not the first time Michael had visited the Bel Air house. For her own reasons, which she never explained quite to Michael's complete satisfaction, Letty had taken an interest in his career. She said initially that she'd been a friend of his mother's, but Michael didn't remember her ever having visited the beach house while Maggie was alive. At any rate, after his graduation from Stanford, Letty was instrumental in securing his assignment to Los Angeles when UPI's first inclination was to install him in a radio bureau in Billings, Montana.

The housekeeper recognized Michael and showed him directly into Letty's study, a sunny room overlooking a magnificent garden and pool. Letty waved him cheerfully into a wicker chair while she finished a telephone conversation. There wasn't a typewriter in the room. Letty filed her daily column into the dictaphone on her desk, sitting next to an enormous ashtray overflowing with lipstick-smeared cigarette butts, and then dispatched the discs to the *Trib* city room by messenger where a secretary transcribed them. She called the daily run the "Bitch Express." It was a high-handed style of operation that only the dowager queen of Hollywood gossips, syndicated in more than three hundred newspapers across the country, could get away with.

She was in her early fifties, a tiny woman with streaks of grey in her wispy hair. Her eyes shone with a hard, skeptical intelligence, and there was a cynical flatness in her rather over-projected voice. But she had a true newsman's sense of humor. Michael remembered her observation when Bugsy Siegal was gunned down in Beverly Hills in a murder not dissimilar to the Momasso killing. "Bugsy's problem wasn't that he had so many enemies," Letty said. "It was that all of his friends hated his guts."

She hung up the telephone and turned to give Michael her attention, lodging her reading glasses on her forehead. "You don't have to tell me why you're here. I saw the *Times*. And congratulations on that, by the way. You must have whipped them a country mile."

"I got lucky. A tip from a friend of mine out there."

She nodded. "And now you want to know about Penny and Little Mo." Little Mo was the late Dominick Momasso; Big Mo was his father, Tony, who operated on the East Coast.

"What's to know about Penny?"

"Nothing. She screwed her way up the ladder and it looks like she's about to screw her way down again." Letty chuckled with relish. "She traveled on her back all the way."

"That's what I figured. What do you know about Momasso that I don't?"

She shrugged. "Not much, I imagine. His turf was Vegas. And before that, Jersey. He stayed pretty quiet when he was in town. Although I heard he put a couple of hundred thousand into a little club on the Strip."

"What club is that?"

"The Jester's. It's a Rat Pack hangout, run by an old buddy of Momasso's by the name of Willie Pozo. From the Bronx originally. He's got a loft upstairs for special members. Blackjack, baccarat, and dice. And, I must say, probably the sharpest stable of girls in town."

"You don't say."

She glared at him. "Stay away from there, my boy. In the first place you can't afford it, at least not until you come into your money. And in the second, I've heard some rumbles that the police are getting annoyed with Mr. Pozo."

Michael filed the information. He was after bigger game than a bootleg gambler. "I'll remember that. But what I really want is for you to fill me in on Jason Lendt and American Universal Pictures."

For a moment Letty seemed to freeze, and the hard confidence in her eyes evaporated. Her reaction surprised Michael.

"Why?"

"As I recall everybody was calling him a boy genius when he brought the studio out of receivership after the war."

"Yes. But what's that got to do with anything?"

"Nothing. Unless he did it with syndicate money."

Letty dismissed the suggestion with a wave. "That's ridiculous. I happen to know for a fact that he got his financing overseas."

"From who?"

"German banks, I believe."

"Come on, Letty. The Germans were broke."

"Not all Germans, my boy. And particularly not after Marshall Plan money started pouring in." She gave him an annoyed shake of her head. "Now will you quit badgering me? You're barking up the wrong tree."

She was holding back. Michael decided to let her have it all. "I saw Jason Lendt leaving Penny Booth's place last night after the shooting."

She stared at him, jolted. "You couldn't have."

"No mistake, Letty. In fact, the way it looks to me, sheriff's homicide sat on the killing for an hour and a half to give him a chance to get there and get out."

Letty had regained her composure. She smiled. "I doubt it, Mike. I really do. If what you say is true then he was probably headed out there anyway. He just signed Penny to a three-picture deal, you know."

"No, I didn't."

She laughed nervously. "Shame on you. I thought you read my column religiously."

Michael produced a smile for her benefit. "I only missed one."

"Then that explains it," she said conclusively.

Michael made small talk for a few minutes, and then left. He knew that Letty could not, or would not, tell him what he needed to know.

Michael had not been on the lot at American Universal for sixteen years, but it had changed little. He remembered the route among the towering, hangar-like sound stages to the commissary, opposite a small, grassy square on the fringes of a Western street. On the way he passed his mother's old dressing room suite on a little drive named Galaxy Way, and at the end of another street he could see the tall, white granite administration building where his stepfather's offices were. Since their deaths he had put the studio out of his mind. He had no particular interest in the film business, perhaps because he was so intimately acquainted with it. But the years when his parents were both working at this studio were the happiest time of his life. And, he discovered as he drove among the stages, American Universal symbolized that period in his mind. He felt a surge of unreasonable resentment that other people had usurped the place that once Ben Montgomery and Margaret Marshall had called their own.

The commissary was packed with costumed extras, bit players, camera crews, and the like. As he remembered, off to one side was the executive dining room where high-echelon executives plotted and stars were courted. He had lunched there countless times with his mother and Montgomery. He finally spotted Laura Hampton sitting at a table at the rear of the room. Somehow, even at a distance, she looked less in command of herself than she had the night before.

He smiled as he joined her. "I hope I didn't keep you waiting."

"Not at all. I was watching the inmates. If I'm not mistaken I just saw Marilyn Monroe go in there." She indicated the executive dining room. "I must say you American men seem to have an appetite for brassy women."

He could see something was needling her. She drummed her fingers impatiently on the tablecloth, and her green eyes seemed to stab at him.

"It doesn't sound like you're much of a fan of American men."

"Not at all. In fact my family has a tradition of treating American men extremely well. My mother, for instance. She entertained any number of American officers while Papa was off in Burma slaughtering the Japanese. She even bagged a general or two."

For some reason of her own she was trying to make him uncomfortable. He picked up the menu and began to scan it. "Well, it was for a good cause."

She glared at him. The waiter appeared and took their orders. When he was gone she leaned across the table. "Look here, I have instructions to be very charming and congenial with you. But I don't feel quite up to it just now. So why don't we get down to business? Jason would prefer you not nosing about in his affairs."

Michael nodded. "I suppose he's willing to make it worth my while not to?"

"He's ready to put you to work. You're a writer. Writers at American Universal start at two thousand a week. I suspect you don't earn anywhere near that kind of money."

"I'm flattered," Michael said.

"Then you'll take it?" she said with a wry smile.

"No. But I'm flattered."

She glared at him. "You're being difficult. He's really done nothing wrong, you know."

Michael chuckled. "He's certainly behaving like he didn't."

She sighed. "If you must know, the studio isn't in the best of shape right now. It would be a bad moment for any hint of scandal. That's why Jason is concerned about any sort of investigation into any connection with Nicky, even though he has nothing to hide."

"Of course not."

She looked away. "I knew this was absurd," she said with exasperation. "I could tell last night you weren't the sort of man who could be reasoned with." She turned back to meet his eyes. "Listen, would you like to go to bed with me?"

"Is that part of your assignment?" She made no answer. He knew, of course, that it had been, and it explained her tense mood. She was not the kind of girl, he suspected, who took being coerced into offering her body lightly. "Of course I would," he said. "Under different circumstances." It was not entirely a lie.

"So there's no way to reach you then?" she said.

He shook his head. "Look, I'm sure you realize I could have implicated Lendt last night if I'd wanted to. But I didn't. I didn't because American Universal is a private corporation and, professionally, I have to respect that until I have good reason not to." That was definitely a lie. But it was in Michael's interests not to put Lendt on the alert.

She studied him for a moment. "I see," she said. "I wish you'd mentioned that earlier." She was furious with him for having strung her along. Also, he sensed, she didn't believe that he was going to drop the investigation. He'd won the first round, but he suspected there would be others.

It was then that Jason Lendt joined them. He was about thirty-seven years old and wore a polo shirt and loose corduroy trousers. He had a light, plaid sweater draped over his shoulders, knotted casually around his neck by the sleeves.

"I'll introduce myself," he said, offering his hand as he took a chair. "Jason Lendt. I run this place."

Lendt had a firm grip and his eyes were direct. His dark hair, greying at the temples, was curly and cropped close. His smile appeared to be natural and his build athletic. It occurred to Michael that Lendt might be easily mistaken for a golf pro. Michael had always loathed golf, even before his hip was shot away. Michael shook his hand.

"Mike Montgomery. My stepfather used to run this place."

Laura stared at him in surprise. Lendt also was startled.

"Another Montgomery? Well, I'll be damned," Lendt said softly.

Michael frowned. "*Another* Montgomery?"

"You mean you don't know? About Brendan, I mean." Lendt was staring at him. "Your brother."

Michael could sense Laura watching him closely and knew he was reacting visibly. "No," he said. "I hadn't heard. What about Brendan?"

Lendt smiled. "I'm bringing him out for a picture. And if you want my opinion, your brother is going to become a very big name in the business."

"When did this all come about?"

"We nailed the deal together last week. I'm surprised you didn't know."

Brendan coming out to the Coast again. He desperately needed time to sort out his emotions. Since his recovery he'd come around to the belief that he hadn't been fair with Brendan that ugly morning when he'd finally located him in the walk-down flat in the Village. But his own sense of revulsion was still overpowering. He knew he wouldn't even know how to go about greeting his brother after what had happened. And the Murrow offer . . . And beneath it all lingered the old impulse to protect and guide Brendan. If what he suspected about American Universal were true, what would it mean for his brother? Danger, perhaps . . .

Lendt exchanged a puzzled look with Laura Hampton. Michael had been sitting wordlessly for a full minute. "Well, anyway," Lendt chuckled, "it ought to be a terrific opportunity for him." He changed tack abruptly. "Look, Mike, I hope you're not confused about what I was doing at the beach last night."

Michael shook his head. "Forget it. As I was telling Miss Hampton, American Universal is a private corporation. I have to respect that."

In a few moments he made his excuses and left the studio.

Brendan drove the gleaming black Porsche Speedster off the showroom floor, and turned left into the heavy traffic on Sepulveda Boulevard. The American Airlines Lockheed had deposited him in Los Angeles in late morning and it was now approaching 3 P.M. He drove for almost an hour. When he reached San Marino he stopped only long enough to make a phone call from a booth at a service station, and then slammed the little roadster into gear again.

The big house sat on a large expanse of rolling lawn behind high walls. Tall eucalyptus trees lined the drive and a small, fragrant citrus grove, heavy with bright orange and yellow fruit, had been cultivated along one side of the house. She greeted him at the door, an aged, diminished replica of the woman Brendan vaguely remembered. She looked frightened.

"Brendan. It's been such a long time."

Lyla Moran showed him into the enormous, formal living room. Tall arched windows looked out on the grounds through which late afternoon sunlight slanted in, holding motes of dust in suspension. The heavy furniture seemed planted like statues. He had never experienced such aridity between four walls, such desert-like lifelessness.

She smiled uncertainly. "Perhaps when you go you can take some oranges with you. I have scads of them. More than I can ever use."

"Dick Flynn talked to me before he died."

She seemed to shrink into herself even further. "I know he's dead," she said vaguely. "I read about it in the papers . . ."

"He told me that Wilkening shot my father when he tried to keep him from breaking in on the two of you."

"He shouldn't have said anything!" The anger flared abruptly, and equally abruptly died away. Her eyes pleaded with him. "I was hoping you'd come for a nice visit. Because you remembered . . ."

"He told me something else. He said there were rumors about my father and mother. That they slept together a long time before they were married."

She forced a deprecating smile. "Of course they did. For heaven's sake, Brendan. It was Hollywood. Everything raced along so in those days. They were in love—"

"Even before Michael was born. Dick said you know the truth, if anyone does."

When she spoke her voice sounded as fragile as tissue paper. "Why must you know? Isn't it enough, everything that's happened?"

Brendan felt the pressure building inside of him, in that place which should be strong and secure, yet somehow was shattered and empty. "Because he belonged to me. Through it all, I owned that one thing. I was his only son."

Her eyes studied him for a moment longer. "You know the truth already, don't you. All you want from me is . . ." Her eyes drifted aimlessly away, taking on a distant look.

"No, you weren't his only son, Brendan," she said.

CHAPTER 10

Michael drafted a letter courteously declining Murrow's offer to go to work for CBS News, and posted it in the morning mail. Afterwards he made a phone call, and then drove into Beverly Hills, parking in the lot opposite the law offices of Frankovitch, Ware, and Bohlen on Cañon Drive. The firm was the trustee of his mother's estate, which in worth exceeded three-and-a-half million dollars. He was quickly shown in to see the senior partner, Nolan Frankovitch.

"Brendan's going to be living out here, at least for a while," Michael said without preliminaries. "I'm worried about the people he's mixed up with."

Frankovitch had been a close friend of his mother's. Forever imperturbable, he removed his glasses and stared at Michael through owl eyes.

"All right. Why don't you tell me about it?"

Michael did. Frankovitch jotted occasional notes, his expression unchanging. When Michael finished, he glanced up. "And what do you want me to do?"

Michael told him in detail. The old man listened, then nodded. "I'll see what I can do. It will take some time, unless you want me to force the issue. If they refuse, I could file a suit."

"No. It needs to be handled discreetly."

Frankovitch frowned. "Have you seen Brendan?"

"Not for a few years."

The old man sighed. "That's a pity."

Michael left the office, satisfied that the corporate shield of Lendt's company would soon be pierced. Frankovitch would get him the information he needed. Included in the holdings of the Margaret Marshall estate was seventy-five hundred shares of American Universal Pictures, originally issued to Ben Montgomery and passed on to his wife at the time of his death.

The following day Laura Hampton called him at the office. "I didn't quite know what to make of you the other day. I'm not used to men walking out on a luncheon."

"I'm sorry. It was rude."

"Perhaps we ought to try again. I'd like to see you tonight." There was no mistaking the intention in her voice. "Jason has nothing to do with it."

"Why?"

"Because you weren't awed by him. Most people are. Terribly."

"I don't get out of here till eleven," he said after a moment.

She chuckled. "I thought so. You don't see much of women, do you?" She allowed a note of mockery to slip into her voice. "I assure you there's nothing at all to be afraid of."

He felt the old, helpless rage building in him. He knew that he ought to hang up. But she'd trapped him. "Where do you want to meet?"

"Do you know Jack's on the pier?"

The restaurant was in Santa Monica. He knew it. "Eleven-thirty?"

The seafood house was busy when Michael arrived. Through the windows of the lounge he could see the ferris wheel at Pacific Ocean Park, and the crowded lights of the midway. Laura Hampton was sitting at the bar with a young man in a camel-colored jacket and open-collared shirt. They were laughing at something she'd said when he joined them. Laura glanced up with a smile; her auburn hair was thickly curled and loose and her green eyes were dancing. What he saw in her smile told him all he needed to know about her relationship with this man.

"Oh, Mike, this is Brian King." It was a game, her way of getting even for his having outwitted her at the studio. "He's in our legal department. He was kind enough to give me a ride out. Brian, Michael Montgomery."

King offered his hand, eyeing Michael's cane rudely. "Pleased to meet you."

Michael ignored the offered hand. He turned to leave.

"Really," Laura said. "You could at least say hello."

Michael stopped. King, slightly drunk, returned to his drink. "Not in much of a mood. Well, I get that way myself sometimes."

Against his better judgment, Michael hesitated. There were no rules in this game she was playing with him, the simple object of which was to humiliate him. He watched Laura raise her drink to her lovely, shining lips. "Well," she said. "Can't you?" Brian King was only a pawn, but he wondered if Laura realized just what she'd let the man in for. He allowed the black fury, which he'd so far suppressed, to take command.

"Sure." He smiled, turning. "Hello, Brian." Then, pivoting off his good leg, he slammed the heavy end of his cane into the vulnerable region just below the man's ribs. It was an ugly, cruel blow, powered by a depth of frustration and a sense of inadequacy he had not acknowledged since his worst days after the war. Laura Hampton gasped as King dropped to the floor, writhing in agony. Michael was vaguely aware of a cocktail waitress screaming and the bar erupting into a confusion of shouts and jockeying bodies. He pushed away from the bar and out into the cool night air.

He sat behind the wheel of his car with the window lowered. What he'd done to King had brought a superficial release, but the other remained intact. He felt hot tears stinging his eyes.

A few minutes later he saw Laura Hampton emerge from the bar alone and walk toward him on clicking heels. His keys were still in the ignition. He knew he should be gone. She stood next to the car.

"Shall I come with you?" she asked.

"You're not likely to get what you're after."

"And what is it you think I'm after?"

"An exotic fuck."

She expelled a deep breath, glancing back up toward the restaurant. "Well, we'll just have to see what turns up." She opened the door on the passenger's side and got in.

As they drove out along the coast she seemed thoughtful. "I really am very bad about that sort of thing, aren't I?" She looked at him. "I'm sorry. I really am."

153

She moved closer to him, and the instrument panel cast a dim glow over the full curve of her breasts, exposed in the deep slash of her dress. The moment was electric. A force he could not identify had prevented him from driving away from the restaurant. And now the same force guided his arm around her and slipped his hand inside her dress to cup her breast, his fingers gently massaging the nipple. He felt her sharp intake of breath, and then, after a moment, her breathing became heavier. She put her face into his shoulder. "I'm very bad about that sort of thing too," she said in a low voice. He was only vaguely aware of the highway slipping by under the headlights. The moments seemed to last forever as he waited.

Then, with pain and pleasure intermingled, he felt his penis beginning to thicken. The pain was stabbing, as though atrophied muscles were beginning to feel the first rush of blood after long dormancy. He pulled off the highway. He felt her fingers unfastening his trousers. Soon they encircled him and began to exert a skilled, exquisite pressure. "It's so nice," she sighed. "So very nice." Her fingernails lightly traced the contours of his testicles, and then resumed their knowing exploration of the shaft. His penis was straining rigid. His mind was rigid as well, rebelling against the feeling of helplessness which had seized him from the moment he had surrendered to her. "Don't come," she whispered. "Not yet."

She broke away long enough to raise her skirt and slide her garter belt along her hips. Then she guided his hand between her legs and held it there, covered with her own. He explored the lips of her vagina with his fingers, and then began to massage her clitoris between his thumb and forefinger. Her breath was coming in shudders and, as she molded herself against him, her fingers found his sex again and she resumed what she'd begun, except urgently now.

Suddenly she gasped, "Please!" Her back arched and he was dimly aware of her teeth sinking into his shoulder, through the fabric of his jacket.

He stepped from the car. On a bluff overhead the steep walls of the Getty mansion, lamps burning in the broad, seaward windows, towered against the sky. On the cloudless horizon he could see the lights of an outward-bound freighter. A part of him that had remained broken was now, somehow, healed. But there was still the other.

Laura Hampton got out of the car and put her arms

around his waist. "I thought that was a lovely beginning. And we're only halfway to Malibu."

"We're going back."

She glanced up at him. "Your habit of running out in the middle of things is maddening. You must realize that."

"I don't think there's any way you could understand."

"Oh, I'm not so sure. Before whatever happened to your leg I imagine you were quite a lover. Now you're convinced women will be revolted by you. That deduction hardly requires an Einstein."

After a moment he said, "That was the first time I've been able since Korea."

She stared at him. "Oh my. I had no idea." She frowned. "You really are something, to opt out of the game entirely that way."

He shook his head. "It wasn't my idea."

"Oh yes it was. Of course it was." She looked up at him. "And I'll tell you another thing: for your own sake you'd better take me out to this beach house of yours and make love to me while you've got the chance."

"I hate a woman who plays hard to get," he said, managing a smile.

She sighed, touching his cheek gently. "It's true, you know. Now that you've got a man's equipment between your legs again, you'll have no peace. And unless you've got the will power of a saint, you'll find yourself creeping along back streets and slinking into bordellos. And that, I assure you, is where you'll find all of the humiliation you're so deathly afraid of."

She was right, of course. And to be driven beyond self-control that way would destroy him. He tried to look into her eyes, but in the darkness he could see nothing, neither mockery nor reassurance. *Why must it be this woman?* he thought. Her complexity frightened him. She could be as cold as ice or infinitely tender, and he had no idea what forces within her impelled her in either direction. It was dangerous to put himself in her hands. But he knew that ultimately, if he were to survive, he had no choice.

It was after midnight when they arrived at the house. Laura Hampton would have begun with the lights out, but he insisted on leaving a bedside lamp burning. The lights, he knew, would have to come on sometime. The fifty-caliber bullet had ripped into his right hip, shattering bone and destroying muscle as well as certain vessels and arteries which could not be repaired in the crowded field hospital. His right leg had atrophied, becoming a grotesquely crooked, mottled stick that all of the physical therapy in the world could not right. Then the mechanical rebuilding of the joint, after his discharge, had left it a scarred mass of twisted muscle.

He stretched tensely in the bed next to her naked body. Her eyes roamed over him and she smiled. "My, they did make a bloody awful mess of it, didn't they." She gently ran her fingers over the scarred flesh. He closed his eyes, and as he did so she moved lower in the bed and her lips seemed to leave a burning path across the healed surface of the wound. But he was unaroused. Her fingers lightly teased the sensitive underside of his penis, and her lips took him in. But still he made no response. He lay back against the pillows, his eyes clenched tightly closed, fighting down the panic, knowing that only three years earlier the light brush of her tumbling auburn hair against his testicles would have been enough in itself to drive him rigid with desire and urgent to enter her.

"Stop it," he said.

She looked up at him. "Not bloody likely."

She took him again, her tongue expertly caressing his glans, and this time her fingers explored beneath his scrotum, suddenly penetrating. Startled, he entwined his fingers roughly in her thick hair. But she had succeeded in breaking the dam; blood was rushing into his groin and he felt the hard muscles of his belly tighten. Suddenly raging with desire, he held her face fiercely against him. Then, as he felt orgasm approaching, he pulled her roughly beneath his body. She opened her legs joyously for him and he plunged into her. She held him fiercely, her nails clawing his flesh and her ankles crossed over his back, whispering into his ear, "You can do it. Isn't it lovely?"

They lay together all night, making love intermittently. He told her what happened in Korea. He was a second lieutenant in Ridgeway's Eighth Army, 200,000 men, half South Korean, spread thinly across the peninsula on the 38th parallel. His own company was part of the force plugging Wonju Gap, a gateway to Seoul, at which the Communists hurled 400,000 troops in sub-zero weather on New Year's Eve, 1950.

Michael began the war as an eager reserve officer enlistee. But by the time his unit was shipped to the front the war had already settled into a political and military stalemate. His winter war, until the New Year's offensive, had been a dreary military routine of missed actions and futile attempts to preserve body heat in the numbing cold. Then it happened. He remembered huddling in an icy dugout, listening to Patti Page singing "The Tennessee Waltz" on Armed Forces Radio, when the night sky lit up with flares and the big guns in the north began to rumble.

The full force of the Chinese attack hit Michael's sector, and the line buckled. In the confused, bloody retreat from Wonju, across the frozen wastes, a Chinese half-track had caught Michael's company crossing a moonlit plain and opened up with heavy machine-gun fire.

He woke up in a field hospital where, despite the fact that his leg was attached to his hip only by bloody ligaments, he was not considered a priority case. Michael saw, during those nightmarish days, what *were* considered priority cases and he had no complaints. Eventually he was evacuated to Inchon, and from there home to California. He read in the newspapers that the Chinese attack had been blunted, and then turned back with Seoul retaken. But by then he'd learned the full injury to his hip and its likely consequences, and no longer cared about the war.

"You're really very lucky to be here at all, you know. That's another way of looking at it," she said when he was finished.

He trapped one of her nipples between his lips for a moment. "I've felt a little luckier lately," he said.

He questioned her, but she seemed reluctant to speak of herself. He learned she had met Jason Lendt in London, and he asked her to come to Hollywood and go to work for him.

"Are you sleeping with him?"

She frowned. "Would it matter?"

"Why should it?" It was a defensive response, and he regretted it immediately. He would have taken it back, but then he remembered the way Lendt looked sitting at lunch, and didn't quite know how.

So she responded in kind. "Every so often. Whenever he can fit me into his schedule."

It ended on that restless, vaguely hostile note as dawn was breaking over the Santa Monica peaks. They dressed and he drove her home. She lived in a small, two-story cottage on a small lane off Laurel Canyon, a decidedly high-rent district. In the morning light, even without makeup, the lines of her face were finely drawn, with high cheekbones and naturally arched eyebrows. She was thoughtful, distant. The barrier had come down between them again.

But before she left him she leaned across the seat to kiss him lightly on the lips. "You really mustn't worry about your leg," she smiled. "I can personally assure you that it isn't the first thing a woman sees when she looks at you."

Then she got out of the car and walked quickly toward her front door, searching in her handbag for her keys. She'd indicated no interest in seeing him again.

He drove back to his apartment, trying without success to put her out of his mind. When he reached his apartment it seemed empty and stale. He tried to shake off the feeling by busying himself. He made a pot of coffee, and then sat down to scan the morning papers.

When Michael put aside the papers he picked up his telephone and called his answering service. There was only one message.

Brendan had called.

The hammering inside his head had grown steadily more urgent. Lyla Moran was right; he only sought her out to confirm a truth he'd been unable to face for all the years since he first realized that his father and stepbrother looked at him out of the same penetrating blue eyes.

During those years he violently repressed the tiny voice which, if it were allowed, would have whispered the truth into his mind's ear. But now there was no more repressing it, and the voice swelled within him with anger and resentment. Given a choice, it would have lashed out at his father, to make him understand somehow the outrage he had perpetrated. But his father was dead, and now there was only Michael.

"Destroy him," the voice demanded. "You can do it. You've already done it once. Remember?"

Brendan remembered. It was evening at the beach and his father had been buried that morning. He remembered following Michael's example at the funeral, passing near the bronze casket gleaming dully in the sun and tossing a small handful of sod into the grave as his stepmother, in mourning black, looked on. Brave little men, sober-faced in immaculate double-breasted suits, paying their last re-

spects to their father; that was the picture which appeared in the newspapers. But Brendan knew there were four people in the photo; he was two, not one. The camera captured the boy of eight, ashen-faced with shock and grief, but not the other boy within. That other boy was gleeful that the idol who had rejected him was dead, and exultant with the knowledge that his rival, who walked ahead of him, would never occupy the favored position again. It was that other boy who would come to suspect the truth, because Brendan would never allow himself to.

At Malibu there was a small wake, but he slipped away up into the attic as the solemn-faced adults below continued to speak in hushed tones. He located what he was after in a closet smelling of mothballs. He gathered the thick flannel up into an awkward bundle of green webbed feet and grinning reptilian mouth folded under the bulbous, staring yellow eyes. Outside, behind the house, he filled the incinerator with newspaper and stuffed the frogsuit in. He continued to feed paper into the burner until he was sure the last trace of the thing was gone.

Brendan found the address he was seeking, a modern apartment house just off Normandie. It was utterly lacking in character, its blind stucco balconies rising tier upon tier. Brendan was surprised. He would not have expected Michael to live in a place like this. He wanted to turn away, but the voice within him drove him on.

The door was on the third floor. After a moment it opened and he faced his stepbrother for the first time in seven years.

"Hello, Brendan."

My God, Brendan thought. *He's a cripple.*

CHAPTER 11

Michael saw in Brendan's eyes his stepbrother's recovery from his momentary surprise, and the sudden gleam of triumph.

"Jesus Christ," he said. "What happened to you?"

Beyond the familiar blue eyes and cleft chin, Michael saw that Brendan had changed remarkably: where before there was only frail vulnerability, now there was a new confidence and a restless energy waiting to be focused. Physically and spiritually he had filled out during the intervening years. There were dark circles under his eyes, but Michael, knowing that he must have arrived from New York only recently, ascribed them to travel. Michael was surprised to discover that he felt painfully awkward and uncertain. He had never felt that way with Brendan before.

"Come in. I'll tell you about it."

He took Brendan into the kitchen. With a conscious effort he managed to use his cane as little as possible. He could feel his stepbrother's eyes watching him. "Have a chair," he said. "Coffee?"

Brendan nodded, then straddled a chair at the table in the kitchenette, folding his arms over the chair back and planting his chin atop them. He studied Michael as he poured coffee for the two of them. "Well," he said. "What happened?"

"First I want to say something." Michael knew that they had to dispose of the spectre that had entered the room with Brendan. "About what happened in New York." He turned to meet Brendan's eyes directly. "I wasn't using my head. It wasn't any of my business and I shouldn't have behaved the way I did."

The brooding eyes continued to watch him with disquieting intensity. "Is that all?"

Is that all? Michael contained an almost irresistible urge to drag Brendan to his feet and slam him against the wall. It had taken all of his will power to speak the words of apology. Images of the scene he'd come upon in Brendan's Greenwich Village flat flashed unbidden before his eyes.

Michael had just come from Flynn's midtown apartment where the aging Irishman had reluctantly given him Brendan's address. At his knock a garish face had appeared in the doorway, thick with layers of pancake, rouge, and mascara, with a smeared slash of red lipstick across the mouth. "Yes, darling," the face had smiled in some mockery of seductiveness. The thin, nude body partially revealed in the doorway was breastless and male.

Even then Michael realized he should take it no further. But his stepfather had instilled in him an awareness of Brendan's inadequacy and his conviction that the two of them were responsible for keeping him out of trouble. And now there was only Michael; he could not walk away from the door because to do so would be to fail Ben Montgomery. Suddenly Brendan threw the door open wide, wearing nothing but a towel knotted around his hips. He glared at Michael, his eighteen-year-old eyes smouldering with adolescent rebellion.

"What do you want?" There were lipstick smears around his navel, disappearing beneath the upper fold of the towel.

Michael only vaguely remembered pushing into the basement room, shoving Brendan violently aside. The harridan shrieked and lunged at him with clawing, carmine fingernails. Michael grabbed a pitifully thin wrist and twisted it until he felt it snap, just as the instructor at Pershing had taught him. The grotesquely painted eyes went wide and the face drained to deathly white beneath the layers of cosmetic; isolated by pain, they were the features of a boy even younger than Brendan. Michael relaxed his grip and the boy dropped into a small heap on the dirty, linoleum floor.

He turned to face Brendan, but his stepbrother was staring at him with such loathing that he stood rooted to the floor. Michael, disconcerted, tried to muster some authority in his voice. "Get dressed. I'm going to take you back with me."

Brendan ignored him. His mouth formed a cruel smile. "Screw you. I can be a fairy in Malibu just like I'm a fairy in New York. You wouldn't want word to get around that your brother's a queer, would you?" For a moment Michael's resolution wavered, and Brendan's smile broadened. "No, I didn't think you would."

The boy on the floor regained consciousness, curling up into a small ball around his fractured wrist and whimpering. Confused and sickened, Michael retreated a step toward the door.

Brendan followed him. "Don't leave now, Mike. And don't feel bad about Jaime. He likes it rough. The rougher the better. In fact, if we bandage him up he might even give you a little reward." Brendan's eyes were glowing with a manic light.

"Brendan—"

Michael's voice seemed to extinguish the light and Brendan's smile abruptly vanished. He leaned against the doorframe. "Go away, Mike. You belong in a cartoon somewhere, for God's sake." His voice was empty. "Can't you just go away somewhere and leave me alone?"

Michael left the apartment, closing the door on Brendan. He stood there for a moment, a sense of failure washing over him, knowing he was helpless. The downtown Manhattan traffic was loud with delivery trucks and horn-jamming cab drivers. But above the din he heard the mindless scream from behind the door, riveting him with its unarticulated rage and loathing. When it died away to helpless sobbing, Michael turned and mounted the steps up to the street.

But now, seven years later, Michael set Brendan's cup carefully on the formica-topped table before him and then turned away. "Yeah, that's all."

Brendan's brow furrowed thoughtfully. "I wondered what you'd say."

Watching him from the kitchenette window, Michael suddenly realized that there was something deeply compelling about his stepbrother. Every change of expression in the lean, angular face triggered in him a desire to know what thoughts were passing behind the intensely brooding eyes. But Brendan radiated aloofness; who, he wondered, might ever penetrate that aloofness? It was then that Michael realized that Brendan had developed a presence which was not artifice; it was genuine and powerful. And he knew enough about his stepfather's business to realize that if the motion picture camera projected that presence accurately, Jason Lendt was not far wrong when he predicted that Brendan would become a very big name in the film industry.

"Maybe we ought to try to forget about it," Michael said after an uncomfortable moment. The offer sounded banal in his own ears, and faintly appeasing, as though he feared Brendan had the upper hand.

But his stepbrother seemed to brighten, a prismatic shift of mood that drained the tension from the room. "Sure," he said. "Let's do that."

Relieved, Michael sat down opposite him. There were so many things to talk about bottled up behind the dikes of their divergent experiences, but the words with which to begin breaching those dikes eluded him.

"You still haven't told me how you came by that cane," Brendan reminded him.

So Michael started at the beginning, recounting his years at Stanford and officer reserve, then his activation in 1950. He dwelt at some length on the action that had led to his wound; Brendan sat there nodding and sipping his coffee, but Michael couldn't tell whether he was listening or pretending to. Almost defensively Michael threw in an account of the Murrow offer.

Brendan chuckled. "That's my big brother for you. Straight to the top."

Michael didn't mention that he'd turned the offer down. Talking was easier now, and he decided to plunge into the other thing. "I never did understand why you ran away from Pershing."

Pershing was the military school where both boys had been enrolled following their mother's death. While the attorney, Frankovitch, had been named their formal guardian, their mother had stipulated a private school. Frankovitch had sent his own son to Pershing, an exclusive preparatory campus near the Huntington Library in Pasadena, and did not hesitate to dispatch Michael and Brendan there when they were of age.

Brandan glanced up at him with surprise. "You mean you don't know?"

"I said I didn't."

Brendan studied him a moment longer, as though to certify for himself Michael's candor. Then he shrugged. "Not much to explain. I could take all the hazing and the rah-rah-rah. And the combat drills and detention. But when I got raped, I said to myself, 'Brendan, m'lad, it's for sairten all you'll ever be around this circus is a ripe bum. It's fair past time you were off.' "

Brendan's voice had taken on an uncanny likeness to Flynn's Irish lilt, but Michael sensed the pain underneath. He was stunned.

"My God, why didn't you tell me?"

Brendan regarded him mildly. "I tried to. But you weren't in any condition to do anything but vomit."

Suddenly Michael remembered. It was the night before the morning he was called into the commandant's office to learn that Brendan had run away. He remembered faces . . .

He glanced up at Brendan. "It was Breck, wasn't it?" Brendan nodded.

It was Breck's idea to visit a couple of girls in South Pasadena who had a reputation for putting out to any and all cadets who could lay their hands on a couple of bottles of Bacardi rum. Breck, whose father owned a chain of expensive restaurants in the San Fernando Valley, and who always had a couple of bottles of liquor stashed away somewhere in his duffle when he came back to campus after home leave. Stout, hairy-backed Breck whose idea of fun was to "air" his penis out a third-floor dorm window in view of traffic passing below on Huntington Drive, and who more than once had forced underclassmen into his room after lights out. But Michael knew that Breck wouldn't have dared to touch Brendan; none of the upperclassmen would have. Because Michael had made it clear that any of them who did would answer to him.

All of which hadn't, he knew, made life at Pershing any more bearable for Brendan. Shattered by their mother's death, Brendan had withdrawn into himself. By nature noncombative and unathletic, he'd quickly become an outcast at the military school, rejected as unmanly by the cadre of retired officers who made up the faculty, and despised by his schoolmates. Without Michael's protection he would have been driven from the school long before his third year.

Michael would not normally have joined an outing led by Breck, but he'd not been near a girl since the previous summer when he lost his virginity to Frankovitch's niece, a Berkeley sophomore who vacationed with them at Arrowhead. And Breck insisted that the two girls were pushovers. Finally Michael agreed. Breck made a phone call, and then after lights-out four of them slipped out of the dorm, leaving the laundry door wedged open, and over the fence beyond the darkened athletic field, carrying two fifths of rum. The girls met them in a new Buick belonging to one of their parents. One of them was a thin, freckled redhead, with tiny, pointed breasts. She immediately took possession of Michael and climbed into the back seat on his lap, surrendering the wheel to Breck. Breck pulled away on squealing tires, pounding the horn and bellowing out the open window, "Clear the road for General Pershing's staff car! Clear the road, I say!" They had scarcely gotten rolling when the redhead, whose name was Phyllis, reached into Michael's fatigues and began to fondle him. The other girl, a stout, giggling blonde named Coleen, divided her attentions between the other two cadets, pulling at a bottle of rum as they freed her fleshy breasts and draped her spread legs over the back of the front seat. By then Phyllis had gotten down to business; skillfully she hoisted her skirt, dropped her panties, and settled with a satisfied grunt atop Michael's penis. From then on Michael remembered little of the outing, except an incredible tangle of naked, groping arms, legs, and organs thrashing about in the back seat, accompanied by feminine moans and the slap of sweaty flesh. And Breck pouring rum down him during intermissions.

The girls dropped them off after midnight. By then Michael's head was spinning, and Breck had to give him a boost over the fence. He remembered noting at the time that Breck seemed very much in control of himself, and that the leader of the expedition had been with neither of the girls. They finished the last bottle before slipping into the laundry room where Michael was violently ill.

He looked up at Brendan. "You didn't have to run away. I would have handled it."

Brendan shook his head. "No. It wasn't just Breck. It was the whole place." He pushed his empty coffee cup away, and Michael sensed an undercurrent of resentment in his voice. "Anyway, I needed to be on my own. It was the best thing for me."

Maybe he was right, Michael thought. "Why New York?"

Brendan chuckled. "It was about as far away from Pershing as I could get. And I kept in touch with Dick Flynn. I told him in one letter I thought I wanted to be an actor, and he was for me coming out when I finished school anyway. So I just moved things up a little bit." He frowned. "Dick's dead. Maybe you knew that."

Michael nodded. "It was on the wire."

"I owed him a lot," Brendan said. "He fixed it with Frankovitch not to send me back to Pershing. He was in pretty bad shape when I landed on his doorstep. He hadn't had anything produced in years, but he was still writing. It wasn't until a couple of years ago the booze really caught up with him." Brendan's eyes drifted; memories of Flynn seemed to loosen him up. "Anyway, he still knew a lot of people in the theater and he made kind of a special project out of me. He put me in acting school in the morning and every afternoon we'd go charging across Manhattan pounding on doors. He stayed cold sober for six months, until he hounded Tennessee Williams into giving me a walk-on in *Streetcar*. Everything started to happen after that." Brendan's eyes shadowed. "Then after I was on my way he went back to the bottle."

The memories had obviously become painful for Brendan. Michael decided it was time to deal with present-day matters. "How did you get tied up with Jason Lendt?"

Brendan gave him a sharp look. "Why? Don't you approve?"

Michael recognized the old hostility in his stepbrother's voice. It wasn't the time, after all. Maybe after they were used to each other again, when the footing of their new relationship was less tenuous. "Sorry. You're right. It's none of my business. It's just that you know how Dad felt about his old man."

Brendan shrugged. "That's ancient history." He glanced at Michael, and for the first time since he walked in the door his voice betrayed some uncertainty. "I thought I'd hang out at the beach. You know, until I get a place of my own."

"Sure. It's half yours. And I don't get out there very

much any more, anyway." But despite his words he felt a tug of resentment. There was something casually arrogant about Brendan showing up out of the blue this way and setting up shop in the Malibu house. "I've got a key around here somewhere."

He showed Brendan to the door. "Let's stay in touch." He put a hand on his stepbrother's shoulder. "I mean it. We're both different now."

Brendan nodded. "Sure, Mike. I want to." But Brendan's eyes were cloudy, and Michael didn't quite know how to take his words.

Abruptly Brendan smiled. "By the way, there's something you ought to know."

"What's that?"

Brendan's eyes were dancing. "I like women too. I really do."

Brendan's mind was in a turmoil as he drove from Michael's apartment along Olympic toward American Universal. The raging voice inside of him had been stilled by the completely unexpected shock of finding his brother maimed. Somehow the tables were turned; for the first time in his life he, Brendan, held the upper hand over Michael. But, holding it, he wasn't quite sure what to do with it.

He hadn't even told Michael the real reason why he'd fled Pershing, knowing that the truth would heap even more self-recrimination on him. True, Breck had violated him. Three upperclassmen had dragged him kicking and biting from his room into the latrine. While two of them bent him over a latrine and held him there, Breck had pulled down Brendan's pajama bottoms and dropped his own trousers, spitting saliva into his hand for a lubricant. When Breck was finished he pulled Brendan to his feet.

"Go ahead and tell your brother," he grinned. "It'll be three against one." They left him in the stall, sobbing into his clenched fists. Finally he stumbled out into the corridor with only one thought in mind: find Michael. Mike would take care of them, one against three or one against ten.

He finally found his brother in the laundry room lying in a bin of soiled sheets, full of the stench of his own vomit. Brendan had to shake him a long time before he woke up. Sobbing incoherently, he tried to make Michael understand what had happened, that Breck had hurt him and used him. But suddenly Michael pushed him away. "Get out of here!" he shouted. "Can't you take care of yourself for once in your life!" He staggered to his feet, shoving Brendan violently toward the door. "Get out and leave me alone! I'm sick of you!" He pushed Brendan out into the corridor and slammed the door. Fighting panic, Brendan made his way back to his room. If Michael had abandoned him then there was nothing standing between him and the hostile forces he felt surrounding him at Pershing. They would destroy him. There was only one person left. . . .

So he ran away to New York, where Dick Flynn had taken him in. He realized now that Michael's outburst that night, his complete rejection, had been the best thing that ever happened to him. And Michael didn't even remember.

He identified himself to the guard at the American Universal main gate, and was cleared to the administration building for the meeting with Jason Lendt. He remembered the lot from his childhood, and he drove across it almost absently, his mind still occupied by his meeting with Michael. The rage of all the years had ebbed; he still felt the old resentment that had its origins with his father's rejection of him in favor of Michael, but it had lost its sting. Even the knowledge that Montgomery had fathered both of them seemed to have lost its potency. He would wait and see, he thought.

Brendan was shown into Lendt's office, an expanse of plush carpet overlooking the lot. Brendan had intentionally donned what he called his "who gives a damn?" uniform: old Levis and loafers, a canvas windbreaker over his white t-shirt with the collar turned up. That was the image they were buying, he knew, and they had a right to look it over. Besides, the uniform accurately reflected his attitude. If they didn't like it he would be more than happy to point the Porsche back toward New York.

When Lendt rose to greet him, Brendan smiled inwardly. It was as though the studio chief were trying to out-casual him. He was in tennis togs and sneakers, and he came around the big desk behind an outstretched hand and a broad, healthy smile, looking tanned and fit and Hollywood. "Brendan," he said. "I can't tell you how pleased I am you're going to join my team."

But Brendan's eyes were on the woman. She sat opposite

Lendt's desk looking back at him with green, interested eyes and a faint smile, her auburn hair tied neatly back.

Brendan left Lendt standing in the middle of the floor and planted himself in front of her.

"Hello," he said. "I'm Brendan Montgomery."

CHAPTER 12

Early the following week Michael received a call from Frankovitch, summoning him to the Beverly Hills office. Earlier, Brendan had called to tell him that his picture was to begin shooting interiors on American Universal sound stages the following day and to invite Michael to drop by. Michael's first inclination was to decline the invitation, a gesture he thought might indicate to Brendan his earnest intent not to meddle in his life. But he'd not heard from Laura Hampton. He accepted Brendan's invitation for the ulterior reason, and didn't like himself very much for it.

Frankovitch leaned back in his swivel chair, twining his fingers over the vest of his suit. Michael recognized it as a pose the old man always struck when he was about to deliver news his listener didn't want to hear. "I'm afraid there's nothing irregular about the financing of American Universal Pictures, Michael," he began. "Unusual, yes. But not irregular."

"Unusual?"

"It is a bit surprising that a German financial house is involved. But apart from that, for all practical and legal purposes, Mr. Lendt's house appears to be in order."

Michael frowned. "Why Germany?"

"I had the same question. But the answer is simple. Sy Abrams—he's been in their legal department since the Stone Age—tells me that Jason was a captain in the Third

Army when Patton was running the country just after the war. He seems to have made some influential connections while he was over there. Jason is a lawyer himself, you know. Majored in business law at USC."

"I didn't know."

Frankovitch nodded. "At any rate, after the banks were re-chartered over there in '47, Jason seems to have been among the first in line at the Rhineland Trust in Frankfurt. It gets more complicated than that, but there's the nut of it."

"How do you mean, more complicated?"

Frankovitch sighed. "Well, Sy seems to think that the four-and-a-half million in German marks advanced to AUP didn't come out of the Germans' pockets. After all, they were facing the process of rebuilding their own country. They were in the business of importing capital, not exporting it."

Michael's instincts were beginning to prod him. "Where did it come from, then?"

Frankovitch shrugged. "It could have come from anywhere, once Rhineland was plugged back into the international banking community."

"Switzerland, for instance?" Michael hazarded. "Or South America?"

"Or even this country, for that matter. Sy is reasonably sure that Rhineland was only serving as a conduit." Frankovitch was watching Michael closely. "I know what you're thinking, young man. You're thinking that Jason located the money, but it needed washing. And he found a laundromat during his tour in Germany. That's speculation. There's no way of proving it."

Michael grinned. "I don't know. We haven't tried yet."

Frankovitch glared at him. Then he began to drum his fingers against his vest musingly. "It is an intriguing puzzle, I must admit. It would mean hiring a European investigator. Very expensive. And it might take months . . ."

"I have plenty of time," Michael said.

The next morning, in a cold, misty rain, Michael drove to American Universal Studios. Brendan's picture was a film adaptation of *Rain in the Morning*, a best-selling first novel by a rural Oklahoma housewife about a woman caught in an ill-starred love triangle. Michael had read the novel the year before and dismissed it. But he realized that the role of the young, alienated drifter who seduces the heroine away from her husband, only to be hunted down and destroyed by the town, couldn't have suited Brendan more perfectly.

Michael had been on dozens of sets in his childhood, and the sound stage held no surprises for him. Brendan was working when he arrived. In the cavernous center of the sound stage a farmhouse had been constructed, and Brendan and the female lead, Leslie Martin, were playing a dialogue scene in the kitchen. The director called "Action!" as Michael approached, and he was surprised to see that the crew-members, bundled against the draft, were unusually attentive to the scene.

They were watching Brendan.

He was sitting at an oilcoth-covered kitchen table in faded Levis and a work shirt playing solitaire as Leslie, in a thin housedress, was doing dishes at the sink. The dialogue was nothing short of banal, Michael realized, but what Brendan was doing with it was brilliant. He'd adopted a slow, perfectly timed Southwestern drawl and was using it to weave a web of seduction that drew the woman inexorably toward him. His eyes rarely left the game of cards, and never looked at the actress, but by the end of the scene the sexual tension between the players was electric. *My God,* Michael thought. *His closeups will be too hot for the camera.*

"Print it," the director ordered, breaking the spell, then crossed to pump Brendan's hand. Leslie had thrown her arms around him.

"I knew it," a voice breathed exultantly behind him.

Michael turned. It was Jason Lendt. But he was alone. Laura Hampton was nowhere in sight. Lendt appeared not to recognize Michael, brushing past him to rush onto the set and embrace Brendan. The crew was breaking down the set, getting ready to move in for closeups. Brendan spotted Michael and walked over to join him, with Lendt trailing.

"What'd you think?" He seemed genuinely concerned.

Michael grinned. "Fantastic. But how many takes?"

Brendan shook his head, chuckling. That had always been their father's question when a director or actor came to him inordinately pleased with his own work.

Lendt stepped forward. "Mike. Didn't see you there. How have you been?"

Brendan frowned, surprised that Lendt was on speaking terms with Michael. But he said nothing.

The three of them chatted for a while, then Michael and Brendan went to his dressing room. It didn't compare with their mother's dressing room at the end of her career, but was nevertheless spacious and expensively furnished. Brendan grabbed a beer from the icebox. "Help yourself," he said.

Michael shook his head. "Too early." Then, fearing Brendan might take it as a reprimand, he shrugged. "What the hell. I think we've got something to celebrate. I meant it when I said you were fantastic." He took a beer from the refrigerator and began to sip it.

Brendan dropped into a chair. "How do you know him?" he asked, obviously referring to Lendt.

There was no sense in trying to conjure up a lie. "The job," he said. He went on to tell Brendan about the Momasso killing, and having seen Lendt leaving Penny Booth's beach house. "I thought there might have been something more to it. Lendt went to some pains to assure me that there wasn't. His story is that he was just visiting." Michael didn't mention his ongoing investigation through Frankovich's office.

Brendan frowned. "Do you believe him?"

"Why not?"

"Because he's a lying prick."

Michael grinned. "Do you always go to work for people you think so highly of?"

Brendan shrugged. "They all are." He looked up at Michael. "You ought to know that."

Michael knew that it was an oblique reference to Ben Montgomery, possibly meant to needle him. But he had no idea what had triggered it. He didn't pursue the issue.

When Brendan was called back to the set, Michael left the studio. He was relieved that Laura Hampton had not shown up with Lendt. It would have made a painful scene. She'd known where to find him; if she'd been interested she would have called. It was the first time he forced himself to face the blunt truth, and it left him feeling helpless and angry. For her to have torn down the barricades he'd so painstakingly erected, and then leave him to flounder . . . But there was nothing he could do about it.

The feeling stayed with him through the evening, making him snappish and irritable as he edited the night wire file and directed the flow of news originating in the Los Angeles Basin onto the various wires. Tonight the hammering teletypes penetrated his consciousness, setting his nerves on edge, and images of Laura Hampton fractured his concentration. He became desperate to banish her from his mind, realizing that rejection of her was his only weapon against what she'd done. But he didn't know how. As the end of his shift approached his rage became inward-directed. He began to feel a reckless urge to hurl himself at some obstacle.

After work he passed up the usual nightcap with Sayers and the rest of the nightside staff in the bar of the Biltmore. He sat in his car for a long time, alone in the empty, darkened parking lot. Then he started the engine and pulled away.

He drove west on Sunset. The Jester's occupied a knoll atop La Cienega. A lit marquee promoted Frankie Laine as a coming attraction. The current act was a girl whose name Michael didn't know. But it was early in the week.

It was a private club and Michael wasn't surprised when he was stopped inside the door. The foyer walls were hung with framed, autographed photos of prominent saloon singers and other celebrities. From within he could hear a piano and a girl's soprano singing "Three Coins in the Fountain."

"Is Pozo around?" he asked the slim, sleekly dressed young man with dark, volatile eyes who confronted him.

The young man studied him for a moment, then disappeared. Michael's eyes drifted from Frank Sinatra around the foyer to Sammy Davis Jr., and back again. The hatcheck girl ignored him. Then Pozo appeared, a stubby little man in a tuxedo with slightly bulging eyes and a heavy gold ring on his little finger. He looked at Michael. "I don't know you. What do you want?"

"Nicky Momasso told me to drop in when I got up this way. I got up this way."

"Nick's dead."

"I know. I was there. I've got a place out at the beach. That's where I met him."

"Maybe you're full of shit, too." But Michael knew he was interested.

"I was there when Jason Lendt was there."

Now Pozo was very interested. His eyes seemed to bulge even further. "Yeah? I don't know any Lendt. But come on in."

Pozo set him up at the bar. Michael thanked him for the drink. "Nicky said I could get some action here."

"Maybe," Pozo said. "What's your name?"

"Mike. Mike Montgomery."

Pozo nodded, then disappeared. Michael sipped his drink and listened to the girl, a slim brunette with full red lips and large, melancholy eyes. The piano sat in the middle of a sunken stage in the center of the floor, isolated in a pool of light from above. All around him the bar was crowded with expensively dressed people who carried around a lot of cash and liked to display it. The women wore low-cut gowns and looked bored. Michael knew he should leave. He never should have come. He'd learned all he would ever learn from Pozo, that the saloon-keeper was aware of a connection between Momasso and Lendt. Which proved nothing. His eyes returned to the girl; she appealed to him, isolated in her sterile pool of brilliance, her sad eyes unaware of her plight. He stayed.

The girl finished her set, disappeared backstage, and the house lights rose somewhat. When the girl came out again she joined him at the bar.

"Hi, Mike," she said. "I'm Cheryl."

"Hi, Cheryl," he said.

"Mr. Pozo asked me to keep you company."

"That was nice of him."

She nodded to the bartender and in a moment he set a drink in front of her. Michael paid for it. "I work here during the week," she said. "You know, one of the regular girls. But on Mondays Mr. Pozo lets me sing. He's a terrific guy to work for."

They drank together until her next set. By closing time the bar had emptied and he took her out to his car.

"It's a hundred and fifty for all night," she said, snuggling against him. "What happened to your leg?"

Her apartment was only a few blocks away, off Fairfax. It was two rooms and a kitchen in the rear, fated to dreariness except for a few earnest homey touches the girl had manufactured. She gave him a squeeze, then deposited him in a chair. She turned on the record player, and as an Ella Fitzgerald blues number drifted out over the room she began to undress, swaying to the music. It was a well-rehearsed act by a girl who was not very bright and not very talented. Her body was lean; her breasts were small and hard with large brown nipples, and her narrow hips cradled a thick brush of pubic hair. She undulated her hips toward him, parting her legs. "Come on, Mike," she urged. "Don't you want it?"

He'd known from the moment she opened her door he would feel nothing. He sat in the chair watching her, leaden, incapable of passion, or rage or despair, or even of moving. She abandoned her dance and slipped into his lap. Kissing him, she thrust her tongue into his mouth and placed his hand between her legs. He felt her bristly pubic hair against his palm, and the warm, moist lips of her vagina.

After a moment she pulled indignantly away, looking at him with innocent dark eyes. "Hey, it takes two, you know."

He left her. He descended numbly to the street by an inside stairwell. When he stepped out into the night air he saw the two men leaning against his car where it was parked in the lot behind the apartments. He expelled a deep breath, then started toward them, taking a firm grip on the shaft of his cane. *Hardly any point in trying to run,* he thought grimly.

Anyway, this was what he'd gone to The Jester's for in the first place.

For a moment Brendan was troubled by an irrational conviction that Laura Hampton was familiar with the house. It was the direct way in which she walked through the foyer into the living room, shrugging out of her coat and hardly glancing about. He knew that most women entering a man's house for the first time would glance about for traces of another woman's touch. At the fireplace Laura turned with a radiant smile. "I'd love to be naked in front of a fire."

He smiled. "I guess I'll have to build one then." And he put the notion of her having been there before out of his mind.

Brendan's desire to return to the Colony house had initially been a perverse one. Intuitively he knew that he was traveling a road that would lead to remarkable success. The knowledge flooded him with new feelings of power. He tried to keep these feelings well concealed, a hidden coat of mail. But he could not resist testing that armor against the place where he'd experienced little but failure and the consequent urges toward self-abasement.

It occurred to him that perhaps he'd come to slay the dragons in the combat Flynn had predicted. But as the days passed he realized the dragons required no slaying. Michael, whom at one time he'd revered almost as much as his father, was struggling. Desperately struggling; he'd sensed that in the short time they'd spent together.

His father's memory was another, more pressing matter. Brendan was convinced he would experience an overwhelming sense of Ben Montgomery's presence in the old house. He didn't. And the more diligently he searched for a manifestation of that presence, studying the old photograph albums, running his hands over the faded corduroy jacket still hanging in the foyer closet, or examining the voluminous files of correspondence which had been carted out from the studio after his father's death, the further the perilous memories receded. Those memories were replaced by a growing understanding of the man—a man who, he began to realize, had lived most of his life in terrible isolation, as well as fear of those impenetrable currents of human behavior, beyond his control, that had driven Brendan's mother to suicide.

So that he was surprised to discover that instead of staging a confrontation with his past here, he was rediscovering the peace and sense of release of the place, which lay secreted in the long afternoon walks along the strand and in the night rhythms of the wind and the muted surf. It was an elemental response which he had shared with his stepmother before her death. He also began to realize how much she had protected him, matching his father's rejection with tenderness and understanding. The memory of their intimacy was the one firmly planted stanchion in his life. And it was her soothing presence he found manifested in the rich woods and spacious rooms of the house that had been indisputably hers. It was as though he'd survived a long and perilous journey, precisely as she'd expected him to, and her spirit was there to welcome him home. For the first time in his life he felt whole and strong.

But it came time to begin filming and Brendan's idyll ended.

He hadn't been surprised when Laura Hampton turned up in his dressing room doorway after the first day's shooting. In the few times he'd seen her since their initial meeting in Lendt's office, the current between them had been unmistakable. She smiled at him. "Jason has no idea where I am."

Brendan smiled to himself. If the days of solitude had quieted his inner turmoil, his body was still healthy and yearning.

"Why would I care?" He closed the door behind her. "And for that matter, are you sure he cares where you are?"

"Of course he does. What an honestly bitchy thing to say," she said mildly.

Brendan shrugged. "An honest bitch gets honestly bitchy messages. How about a beer?"

Amused, she nodded. She dropped her sweater over the back of a chair. She was wearing a high-necked beige dress that hinted at the curves of her body. He handed her a can of beer. "Cheers," he said.

She sipped the beer, eyeing him over the rim. "We heard rumors you were fey."

"And you came to find out for yourself?" She smiled. He put down his beer and put his arms around her, unzipping her dress in one smooth motion. He held her eyes confidently with his own. "Well," she said. He gathered her skirt up around her waist and slipped his hands under her panties, forcing them down around her upper thighs. At his touch of her flesh her breathing had become heavier. She was looking for a particular kind of treatment, he knew, and he intended to give it to her. His fingers searched beneath her buttocks, between her thighs, then abruptly entered her.

Suddenly she moved to free herself from his grasp, but only succeeded in trapping herself against the back of a sofa. She glared at him. "I think that's enough for now. You've proved your point."

He smiled. "I don't think I have.". .

"I don't have time. And besides, these clothes are impossible." But her cheeks were burning and her breath was ragged.

He held her firmly as he opened his Levis, freeing his erect sex. He put her hand around the shaft. "Now behave," he said. "And let me worry about your clothes." He held her hand around him until she shuddered, and then began to take up the motion of her own accord, her face buried against him. He reached under her dress and began to massage her clitoris from the front and she lunged against his hand.

After a moment he turned her forcefully around, keeping her skirt gathered around her naked hips. When she saw he intended to bend her over the back of the sofa, she protested. "No. Not that way."

Brendan chuckled. "Oh yes, that way. Your clothes, remember?"

She stared at him. "My God," she gasped. And then she presented him with the position he desired.

Now, only hours later, he lay with Laura Hampton again, stretched out on the thick shag rug in front of the fireplace. The fire cast red shadows over their nude bodies. The second coupling had been a more prolonged, satisfying event, leaving them languid. She traced the lean furrows of his rib cage with light fingers, looking up at his face with amused green eyes.

"Brendan?"

"Sure."

"Are you really?"

He glanced at her, equally amused. "A fairy?" She nodded, still smiling. "It comes and goes," he said. "And you?"

"No. I'm only conventionally decadent."

"Which means you're only conventionally imaginative."

She frowned. "Oh, I don't know about that." The humor had gone out of her eyes.

The sound of a key in the door brought them both to their feet with alarm. Brendan sprang across the living room with the vague intention of intercepting the intruder, but he was not at all sure what he would do when he did.

But it was Michael who appeared in the living room entry. He lurched toward Brendan, slowly dragging his bad leg. His face was puffy and caked with blood, and dried blood stained his torn white shirt. His cane was gone.

Brendan moved quickly to his side. "Mike—"

"I didn't know where to go . . ." His split lips formed the words haltingly.

Then his eyes traveled beyond Brendan to the living room. Brendan could see that he was staring at Laura Hampton. She was looking back at him tensely, clutching her dress in front of her nude body. Abruptly the force of will that had sustained Michael buckled, and Brendan caught him as he collapsed.

"I think," Laura Hampton said, *"I'd better go."*

CHAPTER 13

By the summer of 1954 Brendan Montgomery had not become a movie star, he had become a cultural phenomenon, idolized by American youth and loathed and feared by parents across the land. His performance in *Rain in the Morning* had done more for the film industry, enfeebled by post-war stagnation and the burgeoning of television, than any film since *Gone with the Wind*. Michael kept track of his brother's career in the newspapers, but had hardly spoken with him since the night at Malibu when he'd found Brendan with Laura Hampton. Michael had gone through another bad period after that, but finally, realizing how close he'd come to destroying himself, had pulled out of it. He savagely banished the woman's presence from his consciousness and picked up his life again, more or less intact. So that when the phone at the bureau rang one evening in late June he was startled to hear Laura Hampton's voice, ragged with fear, asking him for help.

He'd seen her only once, at a party at the studio after a screening of *Rain in the Morning*. Michael had gone to the party reluctantly. Since the crucial night at the Colony house he'd remained aloof from Brendan, never going to Malibu and discouraging his stepbrother's visits to his apartment. Brendan seemed hurt by this treatment, but Michael didn't know whether he was reading his expression accurately. There were moments when he was sure he saw mockery in Brendan's veiled eyes and was convinced that

Laura Hampton had told him all that had passed between them. But Brendan had insisted that he come to the party, and rather than risk a confrontation with him, Michael agreed.

Brendan picked him up in his Porsche, which he handled with the reckless authority that had become a subtle part of his personality. Michael, who was not easily alarmed, occasionally held his breath as they wove in and out of traffic along Sunset. "Are we winning or losing?" he said finally.

Brendan grinned. "Sorry. I'm trying to drive by the RPMs and I don't pay much attention to the speed. I'm going to do some racing."

Michael glanced at him, surprised. If Brendan had brought any vestige of his old unaggressiveness out to California with him, it was definitely gone now.

"Driving relaxes me," Brendan said, as though that explained it.

It was the first public screening of *Rain in the Morning*, for select guests of the studio, and halfway through the first reel Michael was convinced his stepbrother was going to make film history. His performance was a brilliant exercise in understatement until the final sequence, a gut-wrenching catharsis in which the drifter/anti-hero was dragged to his death behind a pickup truck. When the lights went up the audience, Michael among them, sat in stunned silence for a moment, then broke into wild applause. But Brendan sat moodily staring at the blank screen.

"What's the problem?" Michael asked him. "It's got to be the best American film in years."

Brendan nodded. "And you want to know how I feel right now? I feel like everything's over, just when it should be starting. I'll never be that good again."

Michael couldn't penetrate Brendan's expression, and before he could make a response his stepbrother was overwhelmed with admirers.

There was a party afterwards, on a sound stage near the screening room. Laura Hampton had not made an appearance, much to Michael's relief, but Lendt was there. Michael made a point of avoiding him. He knew about Lendt now, and the prospect of making small talk with him was unpleasant. He had a couple of drinks and then told Brendan he was going to call a cab.

Brendan broke off a conversation with a group of admirers to take him aside. "Why don't you stay around for a while?"

"I don't go in much for parties."

"I wish you would," he said. "I'm asking you to."

Michael shook his head. "Not tonight."

Brendan shook his head. "Yeah. Suit yourself."

As Michael's cab started to pull away from the sound stage, a limousine cut in front of them. The cab was forced to stop and Michael watched as Laura Hampton stepped out of the back seat of the other car. She was escorted by a man in his early sixties. The man turned to give his surroundings a proprietary survey, and Michael saw piercing dark eyes beneath flaring brows and stern lines in the face.

The cabdriver leaned his head out the window to bellow, "Hey, watch where you're going, why dontcha!"

"Forget it," Michael said, watching Laura and the man disappear into the party.

Now, on the telephone, she was telling him that she must see him. "I know this is awkward," she said.

He had been scanning the night-cycle budget of stories that would be updated throughout the evening. But now the words blurred before his eyes.

"I can't. I'm sorry," he said.

She hesitated, then, with a haggard laugh, said: "I know how wretched this is, believe me. It wasn't easy for me to pick up the wire."

"I can imagine," he said. Sayers, passing his desk, gave him a concerned look.

Stung, some spirit returned to her voice. "I'm not begging. I think we might be useful to one another just now. It's about the murder."

It was Michael's turn to hesitate. Finally he said, "All right. Where are you?"

They arranged to meet at a restaurant, midway for both of them. Michael arrived first. When Laura Hampton entered a few minutes later the attention of the men at the bar swung toward her as though following a weathervane. Michael could not suppress a surge of pride as she walked directly to him. He could see that she looked tired and her carriage was subdued. But she met his eyes directly.

"Hello," she said. "I think we ought to take a booth."

A waitress set martinis before them. Michael waited. She sipped her drink. "It's about Jason," she began abruptly. "I've learned some things about him."

Michael was not surprised. He remembered his conversation with Frankovitch only a couple of weeks before the *Rain in the Morning* screening. The old lawyer had summoned him to report on the European investigation of American Universal which they had commissioned a few months earlier.

"Jason began his post-war career as an investigator for the War Crimes Commission at the time it was preparing prosecutions for the Nuremburg Trials," Frankovitch told him. The old man sighed. Michael knew he'd had family in the Warsaw ghetto. "There was a man, Gerd Breunn, a banker in civilian life. His name appeared early on in the investigation as a middle-level SS functionary who allegedly helped supervise the internment of Hungarian Jews. According to the investigators, the charges against Breunn were dropped somewhere along the way and his files were destroyed, or at least could no longer be located. There's no visible connection between this man and Jason, of course, but it might interest you to know that Breunn is now a director of the Rhineland Trust."

"You think Jason Lendt arranged all of that."

Frankovitch shrugged. "Circumstances point in that direction. Again, there's no proof."

Michael frowned. "But you said the money didn't originate in Germany. He had to locate the money on his own."

"It would seem so," Frankovitch agreed. "And in that connection I was interested to learn that Jason's research staff included a young lieutenant by the name of D. Momasso."

"It's all documented?"

Frankovitch drummed his fingers on the thick file before him. "Superbly."

Michael weighed the package in his mind for a moment. Then he nodded. "I could crucify him." It was true; the case was circumstantial in its present form, but nevertheless damning. A public juxtaposition of the men with the events would make a pariah out of Jason Lendt overnight.

Frankovitch shoved the file across the desk. "I believe you could, young man. Are you going to?"

Michael picked up the folder, thinking of Brendan. "I don't know."

Now, in the darkened lounge, he asked Laura Hampton, "What was it you learned?"

"I'm afraid Jason knew that Nicky Momasso was going to be killed. Even before it happened."

Michael stared at her in surprise. "Are you telling me Lendt is implicated in a murder?" he asked, making it explicit.

She nodded, averting her eyes. "He let it happen."

"Why? What did he have to gain? I thought he and Momasso were friends. From after the war."

She glanced up at him, obviously startled that he had that information. He wanted to startle her so that she would think twice about telling half a story. "They were," she said. "Nicky had arranged major financing for Jason. He was the one who made it possible for Jason to bring American Universal out of receivership."

"What went wrong?"

She told him. The first few years after the war had been disastrous ones for the film industry. American Universal had gone deeper and deeper into debt each year, requiring larger and more frequent infusions of capital. Finally, shortly before Momasso's murder, his backers had said enough. They demanded the return of their money with interest.

"At the time," she said, "Nicky was having a fine time out here in Hollywood. Jason was his patron and his mystique as a gangland figure guaranteed him a following. Besides, his own money was safely invested in Las Vegas. And since his family was influential in those circles, he ignored the demands. But I take it his father was among those who'd had enough of Nicky's gadding about. At any rate, he stood aside."

"Why didn't they kill Jason too?"

"Because he was their only hope of getting the money back. By then it amounted to almost five million. So they sent some people out to the coast to have a talk with Jason. They told him to pay attention to what happened to Nicky because it could happen to him as well. They gave him a year to clear the debt. And the following night it happened to Nicky."

Michael recalled the scene at Penny Booth's place in the Colony, and his first meeting with Laura Hampton.

"Jason's year is about up," he said.

"True," she nodded. "And he's well on his way to paying back the money."

Michael knew from experience the staggering profits a successful film could return. "*Rain in the Morning?*"

"Yes." She shook her head. "He's incredibly lucky, you know. Finding Brendan undoubtedly saved his life."

He studied her. Despite her composed exterior, recounting the story had increased the strain she was feeling, deepening the lines of exhaustion in her face. But he felt no compassion for her. "It all must have been glamorous and exciting as hell for you. What turned things around?"

She looked at him. "I didn't know about Jason until recently. I swear it. And when I found out, I told him I was leaving him. But then . . ."

He could tell by her expression that they were approaching the real reason why she'd called him. "But then what?"

"The men who put up the money behind Nicky . . . one of them is named Joe Donato. Jason asked me to entertain him when he was in town. It started a few months back. He's the one I learned it all from."

Michael frowned. "Why would he tell you?" But he was thinking about Donato. He'd seen his picture on the wirephoto file a couple of years earlier during an income tax evasion trial in which he'd been acquitted. It was the same man who had escorted Laura to the screening party.

"He didn't tell me," she said. "I picked it up from bits and pieces of conversation over the months." She closed her eyes for a moment, as though trying fiercely to maintain her composure. "So you see, I thought I was out of it. I even made arrangements to go back to London. But then Joe showed up again." She laughed shakily. "It seems he wants me to return east with him."

She looked as though she was approaching a breaking point, but Michael was unmoved. His anger surfaced again. "Tell me something: what do you expect me to do? Spread it all over the wire? You think that would take Donato's mind off you? And on whose authority would I do that? Who are you anyway? Let me tell you how it would read: 'A company whore for American Universal Pictures revealed today, etc.' You're not exactly what most people would take as a reliable source."

She shook her head, her eyes averted. "No, I suppose I'm not." She took a deep breath, blinking back tears. "Actually, I had nothing at all like that in mind. It's just that you're the only one I could think of who isn't part of it. I thought if I explained it all to you, you might tell me what to do. You see, I haven't been home for days because Joe threatened to send people after me. I've been living out of hotels. I'm afraid I'm rather at my wits' end . . ."

She was telling the truth, and by doing so had placed herself completely at his mercy. His anger subsided. "Why didn't you go home like you planned?"

She shook her head. "If I'd thought it were far enough I would have."

The bar crowd was thinning out. The cocktail waitress was at the jukebox again, punching buttons. Michael felt weighted down. He owed her nothing. Considerably less than nothing, in fact. And now he could have the satisfaction of leaving her on her knees. But he knew that in weeks to come he would torment himself with feelings of impotence at having failed her. Furthermore, he knew she wouldn't stay on her knees for long. She would finally go to Donato because she wasn't strong enough to do otherwise. Then she would be gone. And he realized, when he faced the truth, that despite everything he did not want that.

But there was one more thing. "Did you tell Brendan we went to bed?"

She looked at him. "No," she said. "No, I didn't."

He nodded. "All right. Where can I find Donato?"

"I can't let you do that." There was genuine alarm in her voice.

"Then don't tell me where I can find him."

After a moment she looked away. "He's at the Beverly Wilshire," she said, barely audible.

Michael went to the back of the bar and placed a phone call. It took some time. When he returned to the booth he said to Laura, "Tomorrow. We'll see what happens."

The bar was closing and it was time to leave. She looked at him. "Let me come with you. I don't want to be alone."

"I don't think so." He knew what she was asking for, if she didn't.

But her eyes told him she did know, and she went back to his apartment with him, walking in front of him silently into the bedroom. She slowly began unbuttoning her dress, still facing away from him. He watched as she allowed the dress to fall slowly from her bare shoulders. He remembered the last time they had been this way, and what had followed, and the rage he knew he would be unable to control began to swell within him. Abruptly he spun her around to face him. "Why?" he demanded. "Tell me that."

But she only waited, watching him half expectantly. Her bra was awry, exposing one breast. He slapped her; the blow snapped her head around and left a raging blush on her cheek. But she stood before him with her eyes closed, fighting back tears. "It's all right," she said haltingly.

Then she slowly began to slip the other bra strap off her shoulder. The utter submissiveness of the gesture only fueled his rage, but now, suddenly, passion was driving him as well. His mind was enflamed with an obsession to violate her in ways that would make her understand the despair to which she'd driven him. He slapped her again, and this time the blow sent her stumbling across the bed. She lay looking up at him, waiting for whatever he was going to do. Her bra was gathered beneath her breasts; he reached under her hips to pull her garter belt down around her ankles, exposing the rust-colored mound of pubic hair. Abruptly he fell between her legs, tongueing and biting her violently, the woman odor of her filling his head. She moaned and arched against him, her fingers entwining in his hair pulling him fiercely against her sex, her body vibrating instantly with orgasm. Then he rose between her legs, his sex exposed and rigid, and drove himself into her. And into her he poured spasm after spasm of the rage and pain he'd suffered at her hands, until he was empty.

Later, as they lay together, she turned to him. "Do you really want to know why I didn't come back to you?"

He nodded, knowing he probably wouldn't like the explanation very much.

"I was going to," she said. "I almost called you a dozen times." She glanced at him. "I know you don't believe that, but it's true."

"Why?"

"Because I need someone like you. Someone who seems to know what he's about. I don't, you know. It's really quite frightening at times."

"What kept you from calling all those dozens of times?"

She sighed. "It seemed like too much to take on. One of the reasons I need someone like you, I suppose, is that I'm not very good at taking things on."

"Like handicapped veterans."

She looked at him with annoyance, then nodded. "Yes, if it must be laid out so goddamned explicitly. It was that. And knowing how much I might hurt you. Even more than I already have."

She told him about herself then, and he began to understand what she meant. There were some ways in which she would likely never change, for reasons that went deep into her past. She told him about London during the war, the terror of the German Blitz; her dreams were still full of the crashing bombs and the city in flames around her. And through this holocaust of a memory marched her father, the colonel, sure and commanding, a pillar of strength in whose strong arms she felt safe and protected. Until he'd gone off to Burma with Mountbatten to be blown up by a Japanese mine in the later stages of the war. And floating through all of this was also the image of her alluring mother, adrift in the absence of her father, finding her own solace among the American officer corps. Until Laura Hampton's signals for love and security were hopelessly entangled and left her vulnerable in the hands of powerfully willed men. But it was a double-edged sword; once taken by these men, she felt compelled to destroy them.

She told him about some of these men, including Jason Lendt. He had found her working as a production assistant for the BBC in 1950.

"He was the epitome of the victorious, energetic American determined to set the world aright despite all. Whoever said, 'The British behave like they rule the world, which is bad enough, but the Americans behave like they don't care who rules it,' drew a perfect picture of Jason. We were in bed in a flash."

He apparently had fallen for her, although not rashly enough to propose marriage. He brought her back to the United States. It was then that she discovered he was in trouble.

"I didn't know what it was all about, and there were enough distractions so that I didn't trouble myself with it. I must give him credit; he never outwardly revealed it. But in private he was almost constantly in a state of panic. And, of course, it wasn't long before I began to take lovers.

"It came to a head the night Nicky was killed. Jason was impossible. I'll never forget the ride out to the beach. He was beyond reason. It was insane, but he believed he had to make sure there was nothing on the body or in the house that connected the two of them. But he was so terrified he could hardly speak.

"That's where you came in." She glanced at him. "For

the first time I was truly frightened. And I suppose that's the reason I reached out to you."

Her look became reproachful. "If you'd called me I would have come to you. Gratefully." She glanced away. "When you didn't, I . . . I drifted."

She was offering herself. And if he accepted her offer and it destroyed him he couldn't claim there had been any pretense. But the question was not whether she would destroy him. It was whether he would destroy himself without her. He rested his head on her breast, remembering the night he'd gone to the Jester's, and she held him close.

The crowd surged around the limousine, young faces pressed against the glass of the rear windows, their eyes beseeching him, their fingers trying to claw their way inside. Brendan fought down the terror and ordered Chuck to hurry.

It had been a sneak preview of Brendan's second film, Sax, detailing the life of a young jazz musician who is destroyed by his rise to fame. It wasn't as good as Rain, but Brendan had a following which, Jason Lendt assured him, would pay to watch him read the telephone book.

Chuck tried to pull away, but the crowd in front of the theater surged and heaved, making headway almost impossible. Goddam Jason, Brendan thought. I warned him. Not again like this. Finally the limousine broke clear and, as the last adolescent was left lunging after it, Brendan's fear subsided.

He knew he should be used to the adoring crowds by now. They should have filled him with feelings of power and success. That's how it should work. But it didn't. The sense of strength and confidence he'd experienced early on had evaporated as the pressures on him mounted: pressures to promote his career with whirlwind, cross-country tours that left him reeling for days, pressures from his agents to commit to future scripts, pressures from ever-increasing hordes of young people like those they'd just left behind to give something of himself to them when he had no idea what he had to give. What they adored about him, and what the screen magnified and the scripts glamorized, were the defenses he'd erected over the years as an umbrella over the void within him. He understood that; it seemed inconceivable to him that his worshippers did not.

And Michael, to whom he'd finally reached out after all

the years of alienation, had rejected him. He didn't know why; he thought that he and his brother might finally have found a common ground of mutual need. But now, when he needed Michael as much as he'd needed him that night when Breck had dragged him into the latrine at Pershing, Michael had turned away again.

Chuck Brodin, the driver, an aspiring young actor whom Brendan had met at Googie's on the Strip in the quiet period before the opening of Rain, *glanced at him in the rear view mirror with concern. "Take it easy, Bren," he said. Chuck reached over his shoulder to open the glass partition. "See. I've got you covered."*

Brendan took the little yellow pills Chuck offered. More and more it was the rushing surge they gave him that was all he could rely on to obliterate the raging fear within him. The pills, and sometimes Chuck himself.

CHAPTER 14

Michael met with Joe Donato in Jason Lendt's office at American Universal Studios. Lendt was irritated by the intrusion, and impatient. But Donato watched him with calculating eyes. Michael assessed him as a man rarely likely to underestimate an adversary. He was a large man, trim and muscular for his years, and he shook Michael's hand firmly. "So. Jason told me you work for the United Press. I always try to get along with reporters. It's a tough job."

Lendt remained seated behind his desk; a boy in the same posture would be described as sulking. He snapped: "I don't have a lot of time this morning, Mike. So whatever you've got, let's have it. Frankly I think you're in way over your head."

Michael had told Donato enough over the phone to guarantee Lendt had received a thorough reaming. But his tone tempted Michael to turn around and walk out. It wouldn't take him long to demonstrate to Jason just who was in over his head.

Donato sensed his mood, giving Lendt a sharp look. "Hey. Remember what we're here for. We're going to listen."

Lendt subsided. Michael laid out the case against Jason Lendt that he and Frankovitch had unearthed, complete with photostat copies of the European material. Donato sat apart, smoking a cigarette and listening without change of expression. Lendt, however, grew more livid as Michael continued.

At one point he snapped, "You can't prove any of that. And if you print it, I'll have you for libel." But the words had a hollow sound, and Michael could see the uncertainty and fear in his eyes.

"I haven't tried to detail it yet," he said, "because I wasn't going to use it. I didn't want any of it to rub off on Brendan. But even you must realize I've got enough here to get the Army and the FBI interested." He gave Donato a look. "And maybe Treasury too."

Donato seemed to sigh. He waited patiently until Michael had finished, then asked, "You said you weren't going to use it. What changed your mind?"

"Laura Hampton," Michael said.

Donato's eyes barely wavered. "How so?"

"She doesn't want to go home with you. I don't want her to either."

Donato nodded. "I see. And if she does go, then you intend to bring Jason's house crashing down around his ears."

"And yours," Michael assured him. "If the money gets chased far enough. I think it might. I'm not sure how Jason would stand up under oath."

Donato frowned, and his eyes drifted to Lendt. Lendt spoke up. "If you go ahead, it's still going to splash mud on Brendan."

Michael nodded. "I know."

"But this is more important?" Lendt was studying him.

Michael had said his piece and it was time to go. He rose to leave. "Don't talk to her again. Either one of you."

Donato sighed, then nodded. "You made your point, Montgomery."

But Lendt rose. "Just a second." He unlocked a drawer in his desk and then crossed the room to hand Michael a manila envelope. "I want you to have those," he said. "There's one in there you should put in your scrapbook." He nodded. "Think about them if you're ever tempted to try to ruin me."

The envelope obviously contained photographs, and Michael suspected that he knew of whom. He held the packet between his hands for a long moment, resisting the impulse to rip it to shreds. Then he turned and left Lendt's office.

When he reached his car he sat behind the wheel for a

long while before opening the envelope. There were almost a dozen high-quality black and white photographs of Brendan and a young man in various positions of homosexual union. And, as he anticipated, there was one photo of Brendan with a woman. She was Laura Hampton.

Michael had not been to the Colony house in some months. He didn't want to go now, but he had no choice. For his own safety Brendan needed to know what Lendt was holding over his head. The day was hampered by the early summer overcast, and the ocean lay grey and sullen under the overcast. When he reached the Colony he found a number of cars parked at the house.

Brendan opened the door. He was shirtless and barefoot, and his eyes looked haggard. He surveyed Michael with dull eyes. "What an unexpected surprise."

The dilated pupils and mild slur told Michael that Brendan was slightly drunk, but underneath the drunkenness he could sense the old hostility. He had not been pleased when Brendan had made no move to move out of the house and find a place of his own. Now he feared that staying might have had a destructive effect on him. "We need to talk," he said.

Brendan nodded, then opened the door wide.

The house was a shambles. It looked as though a party had been going on for some days. Everywhere there were empty wine and cognac bottles, all bearing expensive labels. Spilled food and drink stained the carpets and the ashtrays were full to overflowing. A half-dozen people, young men and women in various stages of dress and undress, milled about. The record player in the drawing room was filling the house with Mozart, lending a surreal effect to the scene. Michael caught a faint, residual odor of weed.

"I'd introduce you," Brendan said, "but everybody's about half messed up."

Michael swallowed his resentment at the condition of the house. "Let's go out on the patio," he said. One of the young men hovered near Brendan, eyeing Michael with hostility, and he recognized the boy as Brendan's partner in the photographs. A silent signal that escaped Michael passed between them and the young man melted away.

Michael was abruptly seized by an impulse to flee, to go away and leave Brendan to his life, whatever that life was. But the old urge to shelter him from harm, whatever the cost, was strong and he followed him out onto the patio.

When they were alone, without preliminaries he handed Brendan the envelope. "Jason Lendt gave those to me. I thought you ought to know. He still has the negatives."

Brendan removed the photographs and scanned them one by one, his face registering no apparent surprise or concern. Michael had torn up the photograph that included Laura Hampton. When Brendan finished he tossed the photos onto the glass-topped table.

He looked directly at Michael. "So what?"

The accusing look in Brendan's eyes made Michael uncomfortable. "If he leaked those somewhere you wouldn't have much of a career left."

Brendan laughed. "Sure. I can see him doing that. Sinking his meal ticket. Jason isn't about to leak anything. Anyway, what if he does?"

Michael stared at him, alarmed by the ragged edge on his voice. Brendan moved toward him. "Hey, big brother, look at me. What do you see? *I don't give a damn!* that's what I am; what you see is all there is!" He laughed again, almost hysterically. "In fact I may send them to *Confidential* myself. It's time that creeping scum out there knew what it was getting." He began to stride up and down the patio, declaiming, "It's past time, in fact. Hey, wouldn't it be a laugh if it turned them all into queens. You could write a story about it: 'In 1954, Brendan Montgomery single-handedly turned America into Fairyland.'"

The young man in the photographs appeared in the doorway, watching Brendan with some alarm. Michael felt helpless in face of Brendan's demented performance, blaming himself for somehow triggering it. "You need some help, Bren?" the young man asked warily.

Brendan yelped with manic delight, grabbing Michael by the arm and pointing at the young man. "Look, there's one already. It's already started! Look out, America. You better break his arm, Mike. Or his whang. Or something. You've got to stamp out this shit in the bud."

Michael could think of nothing to say, and there was nothing for him to do. "I'm sorry I came, Brendan," he said quietly. "I'll go now."

He walked back through the house and out the front door. As he was getting into his car Brendan appeared in the doorway.

"I know what you wanted," he called. "You didn't fool me."

"Tell me what I wanted."

Brendan grinned slyly. "You wanted to rub my face in it. But it didn't work."

Michael shook his head. "No," he agreed. "It didn't work."

Brendan raced for the first time the following weekend in an amateur event at Pomona. He won, driving a $25,000 modified Mercedes gull-wing coupe which, he complained afterwards, handled like a tugboat. The newspapers hailed his victory as a daring exhibition of driving skill and courage. His studio bosses were horrified that he was risking his priceless life behind the wheel of a racing car, but were secretly gratified at what the daredevil image did for his already skyrocketing popularity. But the other drivers cursed him. Some of them swore they would never run on the same track with him again. He drove, they claimed, as though he was trying to kill himself.

CHAPTER 15

Michael and Laura Hampton were married in August, 1954. They did not invite Brendan to the wedding, but Michael later wrote him a note mentioning it. He had tried to contact Brendan a number of times, but the tide of their relationship had turned again and Brendan remained steadfastly apart. In November Michael was given the Atlanta bureau of United Press International, the important hub of the Southern states network, and was to report there at the first of the year. He was not unhappy to be leaving Los Angeles, and that night he took Laura out to celebrate at Braddock's, a downtown pub that catered to newsmen. There she told him that she wanted to have a baby.

Laura, looking exciting in a shimmering green gown with low cleavage, was greatly and vocally admired by Michael's friends who were congregated at the bar. The evening had been an animated one and Michael was in good spirits; the best, in fact, he'd experienced since before going away to war.

Their wedding had been a subdued celebration, a private affair before a justice of the peace. They were both wary of the tenuous nature of their relationship, and agreed that in the beginning they would judge the marriage on a day-to-day basis. It was not the most romantic of matings, but it was one they could both live with.

But each day seemed to justify their pairing. Laura's dry sense of humor tempered Michael's passion for issues and order. In return he was satisfied that he gave focus and security to her life. She trusted him, he knew. And she'd trusted few men in her life.

And they never spoke of Brendan.

Now she'd surprised him. He hadn't thought about children.

"Are you sure?"

She smiled encouragingly, her lovely cheeks flushed by the whiskey. "I'm quite sure. I'm really a very different girl these days."

"We're not rushing things a bit, are we?" He was jockeying for time, trying to make his own judgment on the matter.

She frowned. "I need a baby, I think. I think I've needed one for some time."

Suddenly the prospect of having a son appealed to Michael immensely. Possibly, he reminded himself, because he was slightly drunk. "All right," he said. "It's settled. We're going down to Dixie and have a baby. A big, strapping boy."

She laughed. "Absolutely. Out comes the governor this very night." "The governor" was what she called her diaphragm.

They toasted one another with new intimacy, and when they returned home, both a bit tipsy, she took him to bed with a surprisingly violent and profoundly satisfying passion.

Michael's note telling Brendan of the wedding took him by surprise. He found it hard to imagine Michael and Laura together.

His own affair with Laura Hampton had ultimately become a savage game of cat and mouse. He understood her nature instinctively; she was easily manipulated as long as one kept the knives out of her reach. Fortunately, in the game they were playing, he had outclassed her. He knew no boundaries, sexual or otherwise. And Laura depended on men who placed limits on themselves, so that she could drive them beyond those limits. Because he left no quarter vulnerable to attack, he'd held an almost hypnotic power over her. When he finally wearied of the game, he quit returning her phone calls.

But he couldn't help wondering how Michael would fare with her. He suspected she was easily capable of destroying him if he put the weapon in her hands. The question was, would he?

Brendan himself was having bad periods. There were days when he could not bring himself to leave the Colony house; shutting himself in to while away the time drinking cognac and smoking the marijuana that Chuck brought back from the Venice coffeehouses where the Beats hung out. When the irate calls from the studio began to bore him, he would drop the receiver into the toilet.

It amused him to keep Chuck around. He knew that Chuck had sold out to Lendt, providing him with the photographs and a dossier of Brendan's personal life. Brendan played perverse games with him; one of his favorites was to sit at the table with a big ashtray and a stack of twenty-dollar bills in front of him. He would burn the currency piece by piece, slowly tilting and turning the bill in the air to control the flame, while Chuck watched him, tight-lipped with fury. Chuck was very greedy.

He played that game with Chuck on the evening after Michael's letter reached the Colony house. He had been smoking weed all day. He lit another twenty-dollar bill carefully, absently enjoying Chuck's writhing, mute frustration. But his thoughts were of Michael and Laura. Finally he said musingly, "I think I'm going to see her again."

Chuck frowned. "What are you talking about? Who?"

Brendan rose. As he passed Chuck he dropped the burning currency into his lap, then watched with interest as Chuck tried to thrash out the flames before they completely consumed the bill.

"My brother's wife," he said.

The next evening he drove into the city to Michael's apartment. He knew his brother worked late hours. Laura opened the door. She was wearing pedal-pushers and a sweater, with a bandana tying up her auburn hair. She stared at him in surprise. "Brendan—"

"My God," he said. "You even look like a housewife."

She watched him warily. "I'm afraid Michael's at work."

"Good." He moved past her into the apartment. She hesitated a moment, then closed the door.

"What is it you want?"

He shrugged. "I started thinking about you. So I thought I'd come over and see you, that's all."

She wet her lips. "I do wish you'd go." But he detected a

tremor in her voice. He put his arms around her, but she held herself rigid. "I'll go when I'm ready," he said.

He slipped his hands under her sweater and deftly unsnapped her bra. She tried to pull away, but he held her firmly. "I'm going to call Michael," she said.

"You can call him later."

She stood trembling as his hands moved under her sweater to begin kneading her breasts. In a few moments he opened his Levis and guided her hand to his swollen sex. Her face was buried against his shoulder. "I can't," she gasped. She wrenched away violently, this time freeing herself from his grasp.

He lunged after her. She fought him silently, with incredible fury. But he was stronger than she, and when he finally pinned her wrists behind her back and wrenched her capris and panties down around her knees, she lay gasping, subdued. He turned her over and plunged into her from behind. After a moment she began to moan and lunge against him, and he let go of her wrists. Her scarlet nails dug into the sofa cushions as she shuddered, sobbing, into a climax.

Afterwards she lay on the sofa watching him, her expression clouded. Her eyes followed him closely as he went about putting on his clothes.

"You're staring," he said, irritated.

"Do you really hate him so much?"

He pulled his t-shirt over his head. "Come off it, okay?"

"That's really what you're all about, isn't it? Some dreadful, tangled-up thing with Michael." She shook her head. "What an idiot I am. I always thought it was so much more complex."

"Listen, I wanted you and you wanted me. Don't blow it up. It's got nothing to do with him." But the words didn't sound right, even in his own ears.

She smiled. "We are a pair, aren't we? Puppets, really. You pull my strings, Michael pulls yours. Except, of course, he doesn't realize it." Her eyes still followed him, but now there was a triumphant gleam in them. "And the problem for you, Brendan, is that you're not half the man he is. You'll never be able to break the strings. In fact, you'll more than likely strangle on them."

He fought back his rage, forcing a smile. "I'll tell you what, Laura. I'll call the next time before I come over. Then you'll have time to look up some more metaphors."

Still smiling, she rose from the sofa, making no effort to cover her nakedness. She kissed him lightly. "There won't be a next time, Brendan. I know all about you now."

He slammed the Mercedes onto the Santa Monica Freeway, winding third gear out to sixty-five hundred RPMs and watching the speedometer needle quiver past the ninety-five mile an hour peg. It was 10 P.M. and coast-bound traffic was light. There was a misty rain falling and the concrete glistened under his headlights, but his raging mind needed an outlet. He'd made a mistake in going to see Laura. He wanted to put a weapon in her hand to use against Michael. And he did. But she used it against him. Not half the man he was, she'd said. Confused images of his father and Michael and Flynn and the commandant at Pershing filled his mind. And other images too, confused montages of Chuck and Laura and Lendt and the screaming hordes of people reaching out for him. . . . It was almost a relief when the red lights appeared in his rear view mirror, blurred through the misty rear window. Here was an object to pit himself against; the Mercedes might corner like a barge but there was nothing on wheels that could touch it flat out. He slammed it into fourth gear, the engine howling in his ears.

CHAPTER 16

By the time Michael approached the scene of the accident traffic had choked to a standstill. People had abandoned their cars in the middle of the freeway, and hundreds of them were surging forward on the divider and between cars, ignoring the dozens of police trying to maintain order. Word that Brendan Montgomery was dead in an automobile accident on the Santa Monica Freeway had spread like the wind. Michael abandoned his own car and hurried forward as best he was able, pushing and shoving his way to the nearest policeman. He identified himself and was escorted to the immediate scene of the crash.

The area had been cordoned off under big, portable floodlights. Patrol units, fire trucks, and ambulances surrounded the wreckage, and crews were still in the process of cutting the body out of the smashed Mercedes. Michael could see at a glance that the car had spun out of control at high speed, overturning, and shearing a light standard before coming to rest on its roof, mangled and fearfully compressed.

The big floodlights cast an eerie pallor over the scene, making it seem like an old film running on a derelict projector. The crowd was surging against the cordon, with young women sobbing and screaming and young men shouting taunts at the police. Michael was escorted closer to the wreckage and a workman, cutting torch in hand, lifted his goggles and stood back. Michael crouched to look into the car. There was no doubt at all that the driver was Brendan, and that he was dead. Michael rose and stepped away, nodding to the officer in charge.

Another patrol unit arrived from the opposite direction. Jason Lendt stepped out of the back seat and a couple of officers escorted him to the wreckage. He wore a grim expression, conscious of his position and the eyes of the crowd following him. He passed near Michael, but either didn't see him or ignored him. It was just as well, Michael thought. They had nothing to say to each other now.

He watched as Lendt by his very presence seemed to take over the operation. Michael watched him, not entirely unimpressed. It was a quality you needed to run a studio. He knew that from experience, from having known Ben Montgomery. He watched a moment longer, then, satisfied that Brendan was now in the hands of those who would inevitably have received him anyway—the image-maker Lendt and the adoring crowd—began to make his way back to his car.

Michael's Epilogue

A wet dawn was breaking over the U.S. Marine Corps base at Khe Sanh in the central highlands of Vietnam. It was the beginning of February, 1968, the second week of what was beginning to be called the Tet offensive in the dispatches. Michael Montgomery, special correspondent for United Press International, in stale fatigues, sat in the back of a wrecked deuce-and-a-half writing his daughter a letter while he waited for the Charlie ambush to come in. The North Vietnamese owned the mountains after dark, and it was members of these marine ambush squads, who went out to meet the NVA in the deepest of the jungle and the night, who often gave Michael the intimate accounts of small, vicious engagements which made the horror of fighting in Vietnam come most alive.

This dawn, he knew, was a poor time to try to write to Shannon, who was thirteen. The big Russian and Chinese guns dug in beyond the Laotian border had pounded Khe Sanh all night and he was numbed by sleeplessness and aching, dull fear. And he was confused. The world was changing in ways that did not sit well with him. This war was bad, even worse than his own, which had crippled him. And it had ripped his country apart. Michael had no business being here, not at forty-one, with a useless leg and a family at home. But he'd watched the disruption accelerate for four years and finally decided he had to go and see for himself if there was any sane reason why the war should be pursued. He'd concluded early that there was not, and the Tet offensive was only serving to strengthen that conviction.

But the damage on the home front was already done, and was irreparable. He saw institutional and ethical chaos on the horizon, and the words of Yeats's poem echoed in his mind:

> *The blood-dimmed tide is loosed, and everywhere*
> *The ceremony of innocence is drowned;*
> *The best lack all conviction, while the worst*
> *Are full of passionate intensity.*

On this morning he felt an urgency to explain his feelings of apprehension to Shannon, to somehow give her an anchor that would hold fast against the tide. But there was so much to be explained. What words could he use to tell her that she was not his daughter, but Brendan's? And having surmounted that awful obstacle, how to explain Brendan to her so that she would not hate him? So that she would understand that all of their lives, hers, Brendan's, his own, had been shaped by the events and personalities of an even earlier generation? The small, stained notepad on his knee suddenly seemed hugely inadequate for the task he'd set himself to.

Given time with Shannon, at home, he knew that he could make her understand all of these things. She was an intelligent, if somewhat subdued girl, and very much like him in many ways. Michael and Shannon were close, much closer than the girl was with her mother. Laura, perhaps unfairly, had been prevented from drawing close to her daughter by Michael's devotion to Shannon. He realized that he had created a presence in the girl's life that left no room for any other loyalty. But he'd been driven by a conviction that he'd failed Brendan, and in doing so had failed his own father, who had assigned him the role of Brendan's protector. He would not allow himself to fail with Shannon.

But, he realized, the years had not been easy ones for Laura. It had begun with the decision that she would bear Brendan's child. She had told him of the rape on the night of Brendan's death. When it became clear that Laura had conceived, Michael's immediate impulse was to seek out an abortionist. But Laura resisted. At first he was angry, but finally he began to understand. She'd told him that she needed a child to add stability to her life, and an abortion might leave her sterile. And when she spoke of the bleak reality of the act, he realized that he too was repelled by the prospect of destroying the child. And so they went ahead.

Michael's relationship with his wife might have improved in following years if he'd been able to father children himself. But he was not. Doctors told him that his sperm count had been affected by his wound. Again he felt diminished, buffeted by the old feelings of inadequacy. But he endured. So his life with Laura settled into an uneasy routine, with Brendan's presence never quite banished from between them.

When he glanced up he saw the ragged file of Marines appear at the end of a bamboo hedgerow a couple of hundred yards beyond the barbed-wire perimeter, hurrying, as best they were able in a shuffling, exhausted gait, through the ground mist up the slope toward him. It was a dangerous stretch of ground where returning patrols often took fire.

Michael scribbled a hurried note to Shannon on his pad. Then, on impulse, he removed the yellowed, creased letter from his billfold, the letter that he'd received from his father so many years before. In one sense the letter from Montgomery summed up many of the feelings that had been troubling him. He quickly buttoned the note and the old letter into a shirt pocket, then climbed down from the troop carrier to meet the returning Marines.

The first troops were crossing the perimeter when Michael heard the chilling, remote whistle of incoming mortar fire. The rounds would fall close, he realized, horribly close. He hurled himself to the ground and, as the high whine seemed to fill his mind, for an eternal moment the vague sense of urgency that had been with him since early morning welled up within him, until it took the shape of the unalterable knowledge of his own end.

PART III

Shannon—Survival

1976–1979

Shannon's Prologue

Every May in Malibu the fog drifts in from the sea, climbing the chaparral-covered foothills, a stubborn reminder of winter just before the sun-drenched summer. Early on a misty May morning in 1976, when the ocean was grey, the sky leaden, and the rising mountains in the distance a dusky purple, a lone rider galloped with breathtaking abandon up a narrow trail leading to the top of a bluff overlooking Santa Monica Bay.

The rider, Shannon Montgomery, leaned forward, urging on the palomino gelding, her auburn hair streaming behind her. Her brilliant blue eyes were wet and shining from the cold, stinging wind and there was excitement and anticipation on her fresh-scrubbed face. At that moment, an onlooker might have thought she was a healthy, well-to-do young woman, perhaps freshly graduated and home for a holiday before embarking on the serious adventure of life.

Shannon Montgomery was all of that. And more.

At the top of the bluff she dismounted, letting the reins drop, resting her forehead briefly against the gelding's steaming, heaving flank. Then she surveyed the view below her. She could see the entire curve of the bay, from Point Dume, a hulking, massive promontory jutting out into the ocean, to the tall white buildings of Santa Monica, and beyond them the gradual slope of the Palos Verdes Peninsula. Immediately below her was the Colony, with its wide, smooth stretch of beach and magnificent beach houses. At the far end of the Colony, slightly apart from the other houses, and much older than most, was Shannon's home, the house built by Maggie Montgomery, a long, low wooden structure with broad windows facing the ocean. There was something timeless and classic about it. Unlike the other houses there, it seemed somehow to be a part of the surroundings, not an intrusion on them.

Shannon knew very little of the history of the house, other than the fact that it had been built by her grandmother fifty years earlier. But she loved it, as she loved all of Malibu, from the glistening white beach to the rugged crags with their gently rolling hills, tree-lined canyons, and shady valleys, all framed by a towering background of tall, stark mountains. She loved Malibu in January when the "grasshopper" rain, as the original Mexican settlers called it, came, followed by the warm spring sun that sweated the eggs deposited on the bushes, bringing out thousands of grasshoppers. And she loved it in August, when the green of the towering sycamores turned to russet, falling leaves blanketing the ground.

But in the late fall, when the Santa Anas blow, Shannon felt estranged from the place. It was on such a day that word had come that her father had been killed in Vietnam, covering the war for U.P.I. Since that time, the hot winds made her uneasy. She could almost imagine that in the high, keening wind she could hear a veiled warning of coming tragedy.

The death of her father caused a profound change in Shannon. By nature an inward-directed personality, she became even more withdrawn, although not from timidity but from defiance. Her taste in music began to change as well, from the classical jazz her father had encouraged to the driving, primitive rhythms of the Rolling Stones, Janis Joplin, and others. The waves of raw sound were uniquely able to absorb all of her unarticulated anger and despair and give form to the bleak vision left by her father's death.

But whenever the music failed her, she committed herself to intense physical activity, swimming dangerously far out into the ocean, or riding recklessly along the rugged paths in the hills. Today, her first morning in Malibu after a long absence, she purposefully took the familiar path to her favorite viewpoint. From there she could survey the land where she was born and raised.

As she stood, silently taking in the mountains, beach, and ocean, she thought, *I've come home. For better or for worse, I've come home.*

CHAPTER 17

"Good morning, Miss Montgomery. Nice to have you back," the guard, Walter, said as he raised the gate for Shannon to pass through into the Colony. Middle-aged and balding, Walter had worked there longer than any of the other guards, since shortly after the gates were first put up to keep the Colony private and safe. It was this security, and the beautiful environment, that brought rock stars like Cher and Gene Simmons of Kiss, Kris Kristofferson and Rita Coolidge, Linda Ronstadt, and others, to live there. Shannon knew that Walter didn't like the newcomers, dismissing them as flashy and often ill-mannered. But her family, the Montgomerys, were different, he assured her. Briggs, his predecessor, had told him that they went back to the beginning of the Colony. Of course, Briggs was gone now, but Walter himself remembered when Michael and Laura were first married, when Briggs was still alive, and he had watched Shannon grow up to be the image of her beautiful mother.

As Shannon turned onto Malibu Colony Road, suddenly a metallic white Rolls Royce Silver Cloud with black windows came out of nowhere, the earthy rhythm and blues rock of a Rolling Stones album blaring out from a tape player. The Rolls bounced off a curb, ran a stop sign, then slammed into the side of Shannon's ten-year-old Mercedes convertible. She didn't even have time to turn her head before she was thrown forward, then sideways by the force of the impact, barely restraining herself from being thrown through the windshield. After spinning around in a complete circle, the Mercedes came to a stop in the middle of the road.

The black-windowed Rolls spun crazily off into a vacant lot. Steam poured out from the broken radiator, the front of the car was badly dented, and the chassis was twisted, but the tape was still screaming out, "Can't Always Get What You Want."

Stunned, Shannon sat absolutely unmoving for a long moment. The whole thing had happened so quickly that she not only had no time to avoid it, but no time to be frightened. Now, sitting there, she felt a sickening sense of fear welling up inside her, as her hands gripped the steering wheel so strongly that her knuckles were white. Then, before the fear could take hold, she came to her senses. The Mercedes's motor was still running, and she quickly turned it off. Looking at the other car, she saw that the driver was slumped over the steering wheel, while a passenger was slowly getting out. Desperately Shannon tried to open her door, but it was bashed in and wouldn't move. Sliding across the seat, she got out through the passenger door and ran to the Rolls.

The passenger, a youngish man with shoulder-length hair, was just stumbling around to the driver's side of the car. The driver, a young woman whose forehead was leaning against the steering wheel, was perfectly still as Shannon, her heart racing, ran up to her.

"Are you all right?" Shannon asked, nearly shouting with fear.

Slowly, the woman lifted her head and Shannon sucked in her breath at the sight of the ugly gash just above her right eye. Blood was streaming down her face, but instead of becoming hysterical, she was utterly quiet, as if oblivious to the pain. And with the shock of recognition Shannon thought, *it's Tina Tobias*!

The lovely heart-shaped face framed by a mass of wildly uninhibited blonde curls was unmistakable even through the blood and the curious lassitude. The pale hazel eyes stared confusedly, lacking the fire that lit them on her last album cover. Though Shannon had shied away from drugs herself, she had been around enough to recognize a stoner when she saw one. And Tina Tobias, considered the preeminent female rock singer of the '70s, whose last album had gone platinum before its release, was stoned out of her head.

The young man still seemed dazed. Shannon looked around desperately; no help would be forthcoming soon from behind the high walls that surrounded the Colony homes. Pulling herself together, she ripped off the cotton scarf around her neck, then wrapped it around Tina's head, stemming the flow of blood. Shannon's gentle touch seemed to awaken something in Tina, who moaned softly, then smiled shyly, like a very young child who knows she's done something wrong but egotistically assumes that she won't be punished too severely. Shannon was touched, though she wasn't sure why. She knew she should be furious at Tina, who might easily have killed them all, but she couldn't bring herself to feel angry toward her.

"I'll take care of her," the young man said roughly, suddenly coming to his senses and pushing Shannon aside. "Come on, Tina, we've got to get out of here." He pulled Tina out of the car.

"But she's hurt! We should take her to the hospital."

"Jesus, are you for real?" the young man muttered, trying to prop Tina upright against the fender.

"We can take my car," Shannon persisted. "It's still running."

Exasperated, the young man turned on her. "Who are you, for Chrissake? The Red Cross? Look, she lives right over there," he snapped, indicating a large redwood house only a few yards away. "She's going to be fine." Then, digging in his pocket, he pulled out a wad of hundred-dollar bills and shoved them into Shannon's hand. "This should take care of your car. If you really want to help Tina, you'll just forget about this. Understand?"

Shannon understood. As wasted as she was, Tina would almost certainly be arrested. She nodded silently, then watched the young man help a very shaky Tina walk away. She turned to look at her car and sighed. If it had been anyone but Tina Tobias she would have called the police. But she loved her music and didn't want to go down in history as the fink who got Tina busted. Shannon got back in her crumpled car and slowly drove home.

As Shannon pulled her car into the garage, she was surprised to see a magnificent black Bentley S3 parked there. She knew only one person in Los Angeles who drove such a car, and she frowned as she walked into the house.

They were sitting together on the sofa in the living room. A fire crackled in the brick fireplace, and an elegant silver tea service sat on the coffee table. It looked like an English country house drawing room, an impression that Laura Montgomery, Shannon's mother, had carefully fostered. Laura was laughing like a schoolgirl at something Sir Charles, her fiancé, had said. Laura was forty-four, but could easily pass for a woman ten years younger. Her rich, auburn hair tumbled about her shoulders, her complexion was fresh, and she'd kept her figure slender and firm.

Sir Charles was a stout, blunt widower. Although a brilliant financier who had built a small currency exchange into an international empire based on Spring Street in Los Angeles, he was not an imaginative sort and appreciated the rather overbearingly tweedy atmosphere that Laura had created with him in mind. But it was all a farce; walking into her grandmother's house was like stepping through the looking glass into a scene out of a Wodehouse novel. And the brittleness in her mother's laughter . . . Shannon knew how tenuous was her mother's grip on her composure, having watched it slip more than a few times in the months immediately following her father's death.

Those months had been the darkest period of Shannon's life. Nor had her mother borne up well, although that had not surprised her. Michael, she knew, believed Laura not to be strong, needing his guidance and support. And beyond that, there had never been complete intimacy between her father and mother: a hostility that was never quite consummated in open warfare prevailed, and Shannon had sensed from her earliest childhood that she was at its focus. And, since she and her father had been so close, drawn together both by temperament and Michael's will that it be so, Shannon had come to level all of the blame for the rift, which isolated all of them, on her mother.

Had Laura, at the time of Michael's death, offered herself as a source of comfort and reassurance, Shannon was convinced things might have worked out differently. But she hadn't. Emotionally shattered, Laura withdrew into herself, abdicating her role as head of the household and, in effect, reversing roles with her daughter. Shannon coped as best she could because she knew that Michael would have expected that she do so. But her own nights were filled with loneliness and terror of the unknown. When, a few months later, Laura began seeing a young actor who had a house on Trancas Road, Shannon rebelled. After a violent scene with Laura, she packed a bag and ran away from the Colony house.

She was returned, after an aimless, nightmarish forty-eight hours on buses which finally deposited her in Tacoma when her money ran out. Laura seemed sobered by the experience. Her mother decided they would return to London, where she had family, for a period of adjustment. But there was no adjustment; the wounds merely scarred over, leaving Shannon with a deep mistrust of her mother. Two years later, when Shannon joined the Royal Academy, Laura returned to Malibu and began to cultivate the expatriate community of British well-to-do.

Specifically Sir Charles. Shannon wasn't quite sure what her vivacious mother saw in Sir Charles, but she had certainly laid her traps with care and was rewarded by the magnificent diamond that blazed on her ring finger. They had not set a date but Shannon hoped it would be shortly. The sooner they were off making a home of their own, the sooner Shannon would have the Colony house to herself.

"Oh, Shannon, you're finally back," Laura said lightly, for her fiancé's benefit.

"Hello, Sir Charles," Shannon said. She neither liked nor disliked Sir Charles. He was infinitely ignorable.

He arranged his bluff features into a smile. "Hello, Shannon. Nice to see you again. I was just telling your mother that I have tickets to the Russian ballet tonight. Would you like to come with us?"

"No thank you. Maybe some other time."

"I should warn you that Shannon prefers rock, Charles," Laura said. "In fact, she wants a career as a singer."

"Oh really," Sir Charles said blankly. "Rock and roll, is that it? Well, maybe we can hear you some evening." He didn't sound terribly enthused.

"Maybe," Shannon smiled. "Some evening." She excused herself to change out of her riding clothes.

In her room, Shannon lay on her bed, staring at a framed photograph on her dresser. It was a picture of her and Michael, taken in 1967 just before he left to cover the war in Vietnam. Shannon was twelve, awkward and skinny, but already showing signs of developing into a real beauty. Michael's arm was around her shoulder, and they were both grinning, two pairs of brilliant blue eyes staring into the camera.

Shannon could remember that time so clearly, as if the intervening years had never happened. It was summer and Michael was home, working on a book. Early each morning he and Shannon would go for a swim, while Laura was still asleep, just the two of them alone on the beach. Shannon loved those early morning hours when she had her handsome, dashing father all to herself. They talked about every conceivable subject, from the famous people Michael had known to the bewildering changes Shannon could sense taking place within her body. Always he treated her as an intelligent equal, never talking down to her as her friends' parents invariably did.

It was that summer that Michael gave Shannon a guitar, a beat-up, ancient instrument that was a holdover from his own childhood. Recognizing her natural musical talent and wanting to encourage it, he taught her the few chords he still remembered, then turned her over to a teacher. Shannon never became a very good guitarist. Her fingers were too short to allow for great proficiency. But Michael listened avidly to each new song she learned, always encouraging her.

It was while playing the guitar that Shannon first began to sing. She had never thought much about her voice, but now, as she sang the songs she played on the guitar, she discovered that she loved to sing. Her voice was as clear as the summer sky; a vibrant, strong soprano, edged with a startling purity. The emotion that filled it seemed to well up from somewhere deep within her, from a part of her that she didn't understand. She only knew that when she sang she revealed something of herself that otherwise lay hidden.

"Shannon . . ."

Shannon looked up to find her mother standing in the doorway, looking rather uncomfortable. "I'd like to have a word with you."

"All right." The almost clandestine formality that was the mark of their relationship when they were alone resurfaced now. Laura entered the room and sat down in the chair near Shannon's bed. She stared out the window at the ocean for a moment, collecting her thoughts.

"I thought you should know that Sir Charles and I will be married on the seventh," she said.

Shannon smiled. "I think that's wonderful, if it's what you want."

Laura glanced at her with genuine surprise. "Do you really?" she said eagerly, then frowned. "I'm sorry, darling. Of course you do. It's just that I never seem to be quite sure what you're feeling. You're much like Michael in that way."

The mention of her father, the eternal point of unacknowledged conflict between them, added an uncomfortable dimension to the conversation. Laura seemed to realize she'd made a mistake and moved on hurriedly.

"But that's not what I wanted to speak with you about." She smiled. "The marriage was only a question of time. First of all, Sir Charles and I will be returning to London to live, at least for a while. He's looking for a swing to the Conservatives, and hopes to help form the new government when it comes."

It was Shannon's turn to smile. "I can imagine Sir Charles in the Exchequer."

Laura nodded. "Yes." She looked at Shannon uncertainly. "Darling, we were hoping you would come and live with us."

"Mother—" Shannon knew from her mother's expression that she didn't want to hear what was going to be said.

"Please," Laura said quickly. "I must finish." She continued in a halting voice. "Shannon, I've felt for the past few years that you and I have grown needlessly apart. I know that I behaved poorly when Michael was killed. I'm sorry for that. I should have reached out to you then, but I didn't know how. I honestly didn't. But I think I might be able to now. And I deeply want to have a moment of time with you before it's too late."

Shannon turned away, feeling the old hostility rising in her. Inevitably on those few times Laura had tried, however awkwardly, to communicate with her Shannon pulled away, rejecting the effort as an attempt to come between her and the memory of her father.

Laura swallowed. "So, if you would consent to come with us, if only for a few months . . ."

"I'm sorry. I couldn't," Shannon said.

For a moment Laura's face became haggard. "Shannon, there's so much you must be told. Michael would have found a way . . ." Her voice trailed off. Then she seemed to force herself to finish the thought. "But I need time with you. I must have time with you, Shannon."

Memories of the months after her father's death came

flooding back to Shannon on a wave of angry resentment; memories of that period when she'd been so unutterably alone and frightened, and Laura had not been there to help her through it. And now, suddenly, her mother had come around to the notion that they must have time together, that all of the bitterness and pain could be wiped away with a gesture. It was too late. Far too late. Shannon forced herself to face Laura with complete control. "Mother, I honestly think marrying Sir Charles and going to London is the wisest thing for you to do. But I'm going to stay here, in Dad's house." Then she unleashed the cruelty. "You see, I don't think you ever quite belonged here. At least I never felt that you did all the time I was growing up. I don't even think that you really belonged with Dad."

Laura's face had gone ashen as Shannon continued. After a moment she said in a hushed voice: "You're terribly ignorant, Shannon. You have no way of knowing how ignorant. But I assure you, without me your father would have destroyed himself."

"I don't believe that." Shannon met her mother's eyes coldly. "If anything, he propped you up. And when he wasn't there any more you fell apart. Now I think you'd better go."

Laura's eyes wavered, then fell away. The anger seemed to drain out of her, to be replaced by something like weary resignation. "Yes, I suppose I ought," she said, almost to herself. "Because if I stay I'll harm you, Shannon. I will harm you terribly."

Shannon watched her mother rise slowly and and leave the room, closing the door behind her. But her vision was blurred and there was a terrible hammering at her temples; she'd said it, the dreadful thing that had burned inside her for so many years. And she knew how deeply Laura had been hurt by her words. But Shannon did not feel the exultant surge of triumph she'd expected. Instead she felt only a growing emptiness and a new sense of loss. Confused, she threw herself across her bed and gave way to aching sobs, which were akin to those she'd cried for the loss of her father.

Shannon returned to the beach late that night, with the specific intention of avoiding Sir Charles and her mother. She'd spent the evening at a small West Los Angeles club listening to a band that tried to sound like the Doors, but that never managed to surmount a strident amateurism that was almost embarrassing. She left when the lead singer sat down at her table before the last set and invited her out to the group's bus for a snort.

But Sir Charles's Bentley was still parked at the Colony house, although all was dark within. Frowning, Shannon stepped from her car and crossed angrily to the patio gate. She expected that Laura and Sir Charles were sleeping together, but not in her father's house. And not when she was home.

"Shannon?"

It was Sir Charles, sitting by himself in a chaise on the darkened patio. In the moonlight Shannon could make out his shadowy figure behind the glowing coal of his cigar. Shannon approached him uncertainly. "Where's Mother?"

His bluff features were obscured, but his voice sounded thoughtful. "Laura? She's turned in, I'd guess. She was rather upset this evening. We let the ballet go."

"Oh? That's too bad," she said warily.

"Mmm," he nodded. "Really quite upset, actually. I took it upon myself to wait up so I might have a word with you."

Shannon tried not to allow her angry resentment to filter into her voice. "Sir Charles, I have nothing against you. In fact, I don't have any feelings about you one way or the other."

"Mmm. Flattery, eh?" he chuckled.

"But I hope you understand," Shannon continued tersely, "that what goes on between my mother and myself is none of your business."

She saw him nod. "I agree entirely, my dear. Up to the point that Laura's well-being is affected. Then, I'm afraid, I can't sit idly by."

"Good night, Sir Charles," Shannon said abruptly, turning toward the glass patio doors opening into the house.

"Sit down for a moment, young woman," he snapped. "I'm not finished."

Shannon stared at him. He hadn't moved. But the surprising tone of his voice had effectively placed a barrier between herself and the patio doors. Rather surprised at her own acquiescence, she took a seat somewhat apart from him.

His voice resumed its mild tone. "I have no intention of

lecturing you, Shannon. I merely want to say one or two things on behalf of your mother. Things she can't bring herself to say to you herself. At least, not just now."

Shannon frowned. "She asked you to talk to me?"

"No, of course not. I'm sure she'd be appalled. But I'm aware of what is troubling her." He sighed, shifting in his chair. There was a pause. "This sort of thing really isn't my forte, if you must know."

Shannon was amused, in spite of herself. "I never would have guessed."

"Laura really does care for you, Shannon," he began. "She cares for you greatly. And she realizes that you've slipped through her fingers. She blames herself a great deal for the way things have worked out. But I assure you she doesn't bear all of the responsibility."

"What do you mean by that?" Shannon said grimly.

Sir Charles abruptly changed tack. "Shannon, I'm going to ask you to take what I say next in the spirit it is intended. Not to condemn, or exonerate, even. But perhaps to shed some light on some of the forces that have influenced your life.

"Your father was, by all accounts, a very exceptional man. A good, well-intentioned man. He must have been to have inspired such devotion from both you and your mother. But, I'm afraid, he may have done you a disservice."

Shannon stared at him in near disbelief, trying to penetrate the shadows that shrouded his expression. She was barely able to control her voice. "Sir Charles, I don't think it would be wise, or in particularly good taste, for you to discuss my father."

He shrugged. "Perhaps not. But since I've already begun, I intend to finish." He paused, drawing on his cigar, awaiting some further protest from Shannon. She made none, intrigued by either the audacity or the blunt insensitivity at work in the man.

"As I was saying," he resumed, "with the best of intentions and concern for you, your father appears to have created an insular little world peopled exclusively by the two of you. A world in which there was no room for your mother. There are complex reasons why this came about, reasons which I have no intention of going into, but I believe if you will study your memory objectively you will recognize the truth of what I've said."

Shannon laughed humorlessly. "I think your sources of information might have been biased, Sir Charles."

"Oh yes. Laura. But since the engagement I've made something of a study of your family, Shannon. Others have said the same thing. Men and women who respected Michael Montgomery greatly."

"Is that all you have to say?"

"Not quite," he said matter-of-factly. He puffed thoughtfully for a moment. "I've watched you these past few days, Shannon, since your return. You're not a happy young woman. I personally believe that you're headed into a difficult period in your life, and I think you're trying to sustain yourself with rejection. That's very dangerous, my girl. Very dangerous indeed."

Shannon rose. "Good night, Sir Charles. You'll see yourself out?"

He nodded. She crossed to the patio doors.

"Shannon."

She stopped, glancing back at him.

"You had a right to a mother, Shannon." The cigar end glowed. "You still do."

A week after the accident, impelled by curiosity as much as anything else. Shannon walked down Malibu Colony Road to Tina Tobias's large modern house. A moment after she rang the bell on the electrically controlled gate, a female voice, remote and suspicious, came through the speaker against a background of pounding electric organ.

"Who is it?"

"It's Shannon Montgomery." There was a long silence and Shannon realized with a start that this person didn't know her from Adam. "I live down the road. I'm returning some money that was given to me to pay for damage done to my car."

There was a pause before the voice came through the speaker again: "Okay, come on in."

Immediately a buzzer sounded and the gate swung open. As soon as Shannon walked through, the buzzer sounded again and the gate closed tight, shutting out the world. Tina Tobias, superstar, was well protected from anyone who might want to invade her expensive isolation.

The house was striking, architecturally bold and intriguing, filled with expensive modern art and odd-shaped, custom-designed furniture. Shannon mentally priced the whole thing at well over a million dollars, but the figure didn't impress her. Spectacular as the house was, she didn't like it. There was no warmth in it, no feeling that it was a *home*. Above all, there was no sense that it belonged to a particular individual. Anyone could live here and it would make no impression on the house itself; whereas in the Montgomery house, old and relatively small as it was, there was a definite, almost overwhelming sense of history. The people who lived there had left something of themselves in the house. Here, the electronic organ music reverberated through the high rooms as though through desolate canyons.

"All right, what do you want?"

It was the young man who had given Shannon the money after the accident. He looked less stunned, more in control now. And he was clearly hostile. It belatedly occurred to Shannon that he might think she was here to blackmail Tina. From elsewhere in the house, the organ music died away.

"You gave me too much money," she said. "This was left over after my car was repaired." She handed him two hundred dollars.

He was clearly surprised and unsure how to respond. *He probably throws money around a lot*, Shannon thought, *and very few people ever throw it back*.

"I don't believe it."

The voice was unmistakable. Shannon turned to find Tina Tobias standing in a doorway nearby. She was dressed simply in faded tight jeans and a loose cotton blouse, looking more like a college student than a superstar. Her eyes were clear and alert today, and despite the mocking tone in her voice, there was something friendly and likable about her.

Smiling, Shannon responded, "It's an old car. There wasn't an awful lot they could do for it. At least now it has a new paint job."

Tina glanced at the young man. "Why don't you split, Carl. I've got company."

"Just where the hell am I supposed to go?" he asked petulantly.

Tina's eyes were dancing. "Anywhere, sugar. I'm a little tired of looking at you just now. Why don't you try scoring some grass? The way it disappears around here you'd think I was keeping half the town high for free."

He nodded sullenly, then left, giving Shannon one last disapproving look.

"Considering his personality rates zero on a scale of one to ten, I don't know why the hell I keep him around. Except he's hung like a horse."

Tina was watching Shannon out of the corner of an eye, and Shannon suspected that she was measuring the shock value of her estimate of Carl.

"Come on in and sit down."

As they went into the living room, a high-ceilinged room with huge windows overlooking a redwood deck and beyond it the ocean, Tina explained, "Don't mind Carl. He's a paranoid. He was convinced you're gonna make trouble. I didn't figure it that way myself. In fact, I was gonna call you and say thanks, except nobody knew who you were. We were calling you the Phantom among ourselves."

For a moment Shannon was too busy staring at a naked man and woman sunbathing on the deck to respond. Finally, pulling her eyes away, she said, "I'm Shannon Montgomery."

"Pleased to meet you. Hey, you sound kind of English."

"I lived in London for the past few years."

Tina grinned. "Yeah? I thought you were just trying to be sophisticated or something. In my business I run into a lot of people who are trying to be something they're not. I'll tell you something, it's a relief to meet someone who's not hustling."

Shannon laughed. "I guess I'd better not ask you for your autograph then. I was going to, you know."

"In your case, I'm flattered," Tina responded, smiling. "So what do you do, Shannon Montgomery, besides run around rescuing crazy people?"

Shannon hesitated, intensely embarrassed. How could she say to someone like Tina Tobias that she, too, was a singer? And three years at RADA had merely convinced her that there were a lot of people in the world who were much more talented than she.

"I, uh, I've been studying singing."

"Uh, oh." Tina's hazel eyes lit up with amusement. "Everyone I meet is either a singer or songwriter. At least they *think* they are. So, are you any good?"

"Is that for me to say?"

"Sing something and I'll tell you what I think."

"You mean right now?"

"Sure. I've gotta hire some back-up singers for my new album, and if you're good enough I'll give you a job. I owe you one. But I won't lie to you. If you're not good enough, I'll say so. I may mess up my head, but not my music. Not for anybody."

Shannon knew Tina was being ruthlessly honest. Later Shannon would learn that Tina's refusal to compromise, despite intense pressure from managers, record company executives, and producers, was bought at a high price. But the bottom line was music as honest and totally devoid of artifice as her personal life was entangled.

Already feeling a tight knot of nervous tension building in her stomach, Shannon asked, "Do you have a guitar?"

"Sure."

Tina opened a nearby cupboard and took out a beautiful, expensive instrument. Shannon strummed it experimentally for a few seconds, then chose a song that she herself had written, "Superstar," a ballad that gradually increased in tempo and intensity. By the time she was well into it, she was no longer concerned about Tina's presence. Lovingly, her voice sang, "Superstar, secret lover, I close my eyes and we're together . . ." By the last line, the plaintive "It's better than any real love could be," her shyness was gone and she was left, as always, with a feeling of sweet release.

Reluctantly she turned to face Tina, feeling like a defendant facing a jury.

For a long moment Tina said nothing, her expression noncommittal.

"You're not gonna be a back-up singer for me or for anyone else," she finally said bluntly. Then, while Shannon felt herself crumble inside, Tina continued, "You don't know the first thing about singing. You'd be all right in a high school choir, but that's about it."

Shannon began to feel angry. It was one thing to be honest but . . . She stood up abruptly, intending to leave, but Tina stopped her.

"Wait a minute before you get all pushed out of shape. Let me explain what I mean. You don't know enough to be a good back-up singer. And even if you did, it still wouldn't work. Because your voice is too damn good."

"I don't understand." Shannon was confused and irritated.

Tina looked at her closely, a smile playing about her mouth. "Look, you've got a voice that would stand out in the Mormon Tabernacle Choir. It has that unique quality. Baez has it. Maybe I have it. It's that human quality, that lets people inside you. People would be listening for you instead of the lead singer."

"Then why did you say that I don't know the first thing about singing?"

"Because you don't. That might have been a decent little song you wrote, but I can't tell because you have no idea how to sing it from the heart, with feeling."

"But I *was* feeling the song."

"*No*. If there are two things I know, they're how to tell good dope from bad and how to sing. You may have thought you were really in touch with your feelings in that song, but you were just scratching the surface. You have to bring total physical and emotional commitment to a song. You have to sing the *truth*. But to do that you have to know what the truth is. And I don't think you do. You're afraid to look honestly at yourself because of what you might find."

"And what do you find when you look at yourself?"

Tina leaned back in the corner of the huge, overstuffed sofa, and for a moment her eyes seemed to retreat deep within herself. Shannon immediately regretted the question.

"I know what you're getting at. Well, I find a lady who's getting it all while she can because she's never going to see thirty." Then, tonelessly, "And she doesn't care." Pausing, she looked directly at Shannon. "And that's what I give the people who listen to my songs."

Shannon realized that Tina had articulated her own response to Tina's music. It celebrated the explosive moment, trading off the future for the present. It was urgent and incandescent, full of the knowledge that it would blaze only briefly. Shannon felt excitement building in her. Tina flirted daily with chaos and death, and now Shannon was beginning to understand the thrilling defiance of her way of life.

Fractions of colored light from the stained glass windows spilled on the carpet, charging the atmosphere with an almost religious quality. Tina had done her best, Shannon realized, to share with her a basic tenet of her life, in telling her that Shannon Montgomery was not the person she thought she was. Sir Charles had said much the same thing, that she was a creation of her father, exclusive of her mother.

But Michael's creation was a sturdy one, which had a solid foundation and clearly defined horizons. However, her father was gone now, and Tina was offering a world where the best didn't skate on thin ice, they danced. And Shannon was in a mood to dance.

"How would I begin?" she asked slowly.

"I'll teach you what I know. I'm gonna be here for the next few months cutting an album." Then, "I know what you're thinking. This place is a zoo. People drop in and out all the time. My back-up guys, my road manager, my business manager, friends. But I like having people around. Half the musicians on the West Coast have crashed here at one time or another when they were broke or splitting up with someone. Keeps the place lively, y'know."

"What about privacy? And when can you write?" To Shannon, Tina's lifestyle sounded unbearable.

"Privacy is as overrated as virginity. And I write when it hits me. On a plane. In the can. Anywhere." Looking away, she continued, "Besides, I tend to go a little crazy when there's no one else around." She laughed nervously. "Listen," Tina went on, "the only thing you should be worried about is whether or not you really want to do this. I think you've got a shot or I wouldn't waste my time. But it's up to you."

"I *know* I want to sing."

"Sure. But that isn't all there is to it. I was terminally innocent myself once, a wide-eyed kid from Utah who thought dope meant grass. But then I got a crash course in reality—five years on the road, where it's just another town, another high, another lay. No future, no past. No *place*. It messes up your mind after a while. And that was *before* I hit. When you hit every dream you've ever had becomes reality. But you can't understand why it isn't the way you thought it would be."

Suddenly she stopped, staring hard at Shannon. "You have no idea what I'm talking about, do you? Oh, to hell with it." Then, "I meant it, though. The offer still stands. Come back any time."

Shannon rose to leave. "I'll see you," she said uncertainly.

CHAPTER 18

On a warm June day, when the ocean was perfectly still and the sky was clear and pale blue, Laura Hampton Montgomery married Sir Charles York. The wedding ceremony was held at the beach house, with only a handful of close friends attending. All of the bride's family, as well as the groom's, were in England.

Shannon served as her mother's only attendant. As she watched her mother standing proudly next to Sir Charles, Shannon thought how lovely she looked in her wedding gown, a short, simply cut dress of beige Alençon lace.

After the brief reception, when the bride and groom were preparing to leave for the airport, where they would board Sir Charles's private jet for the flight to England, Laura turned to Shannon for one final word.

"You won't change your mind?"

Shannon shook her head. Laura nodded, her eyes glistening. They embraced and then Laura was gone.

Later, when everyone had gone, Shannon walked around the silent, empty house, lovingly passing her fingers over the gleaming wood and faded chintz of the furniture, her eyes lingering on the beautiful watercolors that her grandmother had collected. Like a cat searching for the warmest, most comfortable shelter on a rainy night, she finally came to rest in her father's old leather chair in the small, book-lined den. She was comforted somehow by the thought that this was the house he had grown up in. When she finally went to bed that night, she felt no fear or loneliness, for she was surrounded by his memory.

Time passed quickly. Malibu came alive in the summer, invaded by thousands of people who were drawn to the beaches and the waterfront restaurants. On weekends especially, Pacific Coast Highway was one long, narrow traffic jam. But the Colony itself remained quiet, a peaceful enclave shielded from the crowds and the noise. However, even the Colony couldn't escape the smog, at its worst then, lying along the horizon like a dirty yellow ribbon above the azure ocean.

Shannon spent her time working on her songs, swimming in the ocean when it wasn't too crowded, and occasionally going out with the few friends she'd kept in contact with while traveling back and forth between Los Angeles and London. She corresponded with her mother, but it was a rather arid exchange of trivialities that left more unsaid than expressed. More often than not, Shannon simply stayed at home, waiting for Tina's return from the tour she was on.

Shannon felt that she was poised on the brink of a tremendous adventure and she was eager for it to begin.

Finally the summer was gone, and with it the hordes of people. For the most part, only full-time residents remained at the Colony.

One night in October the Santa Anas began to blow. In only a few hours, the entire Los Angeles basin was crystal clear, the smog whisked away as though by a giant broom. From Point Dume to the Palos Verdes Peninsula, the entire curve of the bay was a sparkling clear, brightly lit arc. Known as the "queen's necklace" view, it looked exactly like a fabulous, glittering diamond necklace.

Through the huge window in the living room, Shannon could see the blinking lights of planes taking off and landing at Los Angeles International Airport just beyond Santa Monica. The wind brought with it the familiar, vague anxieties connected with the death of her father. So, in defiance she played the guitar and sang, trying to drown out the insistent, threatening whine of the wind.

By midnight the wind had died down and Shannon, not ready for sleep, decided to go for a walk along the beach. The night was mild. The frothy tips of the gentle waves were white in the moonlight, contrasting with the black of the ocean. Barefooted, Shannon walked slowly along the water's edge, her hands thrust in the pockets of her jeans, thinking about the lyrics to a song she was writing.

Momentarily she paused, surprised to hear music coming from Tina's house. The sound of the Who was blasting through a door opening onto the beach. With a surge of excitement, Shannon realized that Tina must be back. Then suddenly she heard it, a desperate, low moan, like a wounded animal in the throes of death.

Racing up to the open door, Shannon stopped suddenly and peered reluctantly inside.

A TV flickered with the sound turned off, as music screamed from big monitor speakers. Incense burned in little holders, and the room was lit only by a few scattered candles. As Shannon's eyes grew accustomed to the darkness, she finally made out a form in a chair in the corner. Despite the filthy, bedraggled hair, and a face horribly contorted with pain, Shannon recognized Tina.

She was slumped in the chair with a syringe hanging from her arm, barely conscious, moaning and whimpering like a baby. As Shannon ran up to her, Tina looked up at her helplessly and said softly, "My left side is paralyzed. The smack was bad. The dealer . . . cut it with strychnine." Laughing weakly, she finished, "Rat poison . . . he got it from rat poison . . ."

"Don't try to talk," Shannon cautioned, trying to control the feeling of nausea sweeping over her. "I'll call the paramedics."

But as she rose to look for the phone, Tina lifted her head and insisted desperately, "No, you can't do that, they'll put me away!"

Her eyes were wide with terror. Shannon was swayed by the fear in her voice, but nevertheless she responded matter-of-factly, "You're very ill, you need help."

"*You* can help me." Tina was crying now, and Shannon felt tears stinging her own eyes.

"I don't know what to do."

"I do! Listen, first take the needle out of my arm." At Shannon's look of hesitation, Tina repeated the instruction slowly, "Take the needle out." As Shannon did so, revolted by the mere touch of the instrument, Tina continued, "Get me some coke. It's in that little wooden box on the mantel."

"No," Shannon nearly shouted.

"Listen, I have to get my heart going or it will stop! The coke will do that. *Please*."

Slowly, reluctantly, Shannon picked up the box and handed it to Tina, who quickly stuffed some of the white powder into a tiny gold tube on a chain around her neck, then snorted it deeply. All the while, Shannon was massaging her left arm, trying to bring feeling back to it.

"Get me some brandy," Tina ordered, her eyes watering from the immediate effect of the cocaine.

Shannon, hoping that Tina really did know what she was doing, poured some brandy from a decanter in a portable bar. Tina drank it down as if it were water.

"My leg's coming round now. Help me up, I've got to walk on it."

Fortunately Tina was short and slight, her head barely brushing Shannon's shoulder. Hooking an arm under Tina's paralyzed left shoulder, Shannon helped her up, then walked up and down with her. The odd treatment—coke, brandy, endless walking back and forth in the darkened room—lasted until dawn. To Shannon it was a baptism by fire. She learned more about the look and feel and effect of drugs during those few hours than she had in her entire life. By the time Tina was out of danger, and Shannon's arm ached horribly from supporting her, there was only one question in Shannon's mind—*why?*

The sun was up and Tina was lying on the sofa, wearing a clean nightgown and covered with a warm blanket. Shannon had just given her some strong, hot tea. The room was quiet now, the stereo turned off and the candles and incense extinguished. With her face washed clean, devoid of makeup, and her hair pulled back, Tina looked young and innocent and vulnerable. She didn't look like a heroin addict who had nearly suffered a painful, sordid death only hours before.

"Why did you do it?" Shannon asked softly.

"I wasn't trying to kill myself, for God's sake," Tina answered defensively, her words coming a bit too quickly. "So quit looking at me like that."

Then, "We got in from Oakland last night. I was dropping quaaludes. I was really spaced so the guys brought me here and split for a party. When I got myself together I looked around and I was alone. I got a little spooked, I guess."

"But heroin . . ."

Tina leaned back against the pillow, looking away from Shannon, her eyes seeming to focus on an oil tanker on the horizon. "The dealer I was scoring coke and stuff from would only sell it to me if I bought smack as well. I gave it away at first, or just put it in a drawer. I didn't want to get started on it. Then one day a guy I was living with left and I needed something. I was out of coke but the smack was there so I took some. And it was nice . . . real nice. After that . . ." Tina shrugged.

Shannon, deeply shaken, stared at her. "But it nearly *killed* you."

"Oh, Shan, you just don't understand," Tina sighed. "Eric Clapton said it best. Musicians live on a very intense plane of emotional necessity—and heroin is the strongest pain killer we can get."

Shannon leaned back in the chair, the same one in which she'd found Tina hours earlier. Tina was right—she didn't understand.

Tina continued fervently, "When I'm on stage, performing, I feel all this energy coming from the audience. It's like they need something really bad and they're looking to me to give it to them." Her hazel eyes shone with a feverish intensity so that she looked like the fired-up girl on her album covers.

She went on, struggling for the right words. "I don't feel like the same person, even, when I'm up there. It's like I'm seducing the audience, it's definitely a sexual thing, the most intimate experience of all . . ."

She stopped, sighing deeply and shaking her head. "It's no use. I can't make you feel it. It's like I was trying to explain to you when we first met. Being a singer isn't what you think it is, none of it, the performing, the lifestyle. It's like you're a motor that's constantly revved up to the highest rpm. You need something to bring you down, whether it's dope or people . . . just *something* to slow down for a while."

Shannon looked away. Her earlier notions of the glamour and defiance of Tina's speeding assault on life were severely mauled in this bleak dawn by the horror of the preceding night. But despite all, something still beckoned her into the world Tina offered. It frightened her, but she knew she was stronger than Tina. She wouldn't let the forces that had propelled Tina to the brink of death overtake her.

Abruptly Tina reached out and took Shannon's hand, looking into her eyes with utter, almost childish candor. "You saved my life, Shan. We're sisters now. There's nothing of mine that isn't yours, and there's nothing I won't do for you."

Shannon visited Tina often after that, and began to learn from her. She'd been genuinely moved by Tina's declaration of sisterhood, and if Shannon had possessed any last-minute doubts about the wisdom of her course of action, they were washed away. But she suspected that Tina looked upon her as something of a curiosity. One afternoon Tina broke off the "lesson" to observe: "You're completely different from all of the other people I have to deal with, Shan. It's hard for me to accept the idea that there's somebody in this old world who doesn't want anything from me. And you're not stupid. Most of the people in this business are either unaware there's anything else going on in the world or they're just plain stupid." Then, firmly, like a mother admonishing a very young and vulnerable child, "Don't ever get caught up in the bullshit. Stay apart from it. Don't let the people get a hold on you. They'll eat you alive."

Shannon sensed that Tina was really talking to herself. But for her the warning was too late.

Gradually Shannon began to understand what Tina was trying to teach her, and her singing improved dramatically. Her voice no longer sounded merely sweet, but acquired a rich, deep fullness that was the difference between the singing of an inexperienced girl and a woman who has seen something of the dark side of life. Tina was a surprisingly hard teacher, gruff and insensitive at times, but very effective, and always encouraging. The longer Shannon worked with her, the better she became.

But all the while Shannon was being drawn deeper and deeper into the vortex of Tina's life. Sometimes she would arrive at the big redwood house to find Tina out cold from a combination of sleeping pills and brandy. Shannon would put her to bed then, sitting nearby, watching to make sure she was all right. But more often than not she would find Tina "wired," a fidgeting mass of nervous, paranoid energy from "speed." When it wasn't amphetamines or brandy, it was marijuana or coke or opium. Her near-death had convinced her to give up straight heroin for a while, replacing it with "speedballs," mixtures of tiny amounts of cocaine and heroin which produce the euphoria of heroin without the drug's tendency to make one unconscious, then sick.

And always there were the people—young men like Carl, who shared Tina's bed and scored dope for her, disappearing when she grew bored with them, young women who served as secretaries and housekeepers, and every variety of manager—road managers, band managers, personal managers, financial managers. The people were there during the day and the night because, as always, Tina was terrified of being alone.

Early one morning Shannon came to Tina's from along the beach, entering through the door on the deck that was nearly always left unlocked. The house was surprisingly quiet and Shannon thought of leaving. But Tina had asked her to come, and was usually waiting eagerly for her. Worried that something might be wrong, Shannon hurried into Tina's bedroom.

There were three couples, all naked, all heaped on top of one another on Tina's huge, outsized bed. One of the men was snoring in blissful, drugged unawareness, while the others slept quietly, soundly, faces pressed against feet, arms and legs entwined.

Shannon turned to leave, concluding wryly that little in the way of music instruction would likely be conducted today.

She was walking out onto the deck when she saw the man coming up from the beach, dripping wet from his early swim. He was toweling himself briskly as he walked up to the house, and when he saw Shannon, he stopped and smiled rakishly. He was short, barely as tall as Shannon, and slight. But there was *something* about him, an aura of raw sexual magnetism in the sardonic, don't-give-a-damn look in his heavy-lidded grey eyes, and on the sensuous, cruel mouth. He surveyed Shannon haughtily, as if she were a slave girl on the auction block, and she felt herself blush under his frank, intent gaze.

"I don't remember seeing *you* here last night. And you're not someone I'd overlook."

When she heard the voice, husky and tinged with a touch of a New York accent, she suddenly realized who he was. Andrew Clark. Second only to Mick Jagger in terms of his reputation as an almost violently hypnotic singer. They called him "superstud" because he went through singers, actresses, models, and groupies as if they were so much wheat before a reaper. But Shannon found his music unexceptional. Now, with his eyes on her, she began to understand his appeal.

He was standing only inches from her now and she was disturbingly aware of the too-tight swim trunks that outlined his large penis. Suddenly something began to happen within her. It was as if a part of her that had lain long dormant was finally coming alive, being violently aroused for the first time. Looking at Clark, she was overwhelmed by a reaction she had never thought herself capable of—pure animal lust.

"My name's Shannon Montgomery. I'm a friend of Tina's," she managed finally, forcing herself to sound normal. She added, as if to validate her presence there further, "I live down the beach."

"Shannon . . . even your name is pretty," he responded, still staring at her intently. Then, "Come on inside. Tina should be getting up pretty soon. You might as well wait."

He took her arm, and she allowed him to lead her back into the house which only moments earlier she had been determined to leave as quickly as possible.

That day passed in a blur for Shannon. Tina and the others woke up shortly and joined Shannon and Clark. Tina insisted that Shannon spend the day there, joining in the extended party, and Shannon agreed readily. Clark hardly spoke to Shannon, but she was intensely aware of him at all times, her mind reeling from an onslaught of emotions over which she had no control.

In the afternoon she went for a swim to try to take her mind off Clark. But it didn't work, and when she returned to the house, she found that she still couldn't take her eyes off him.

"You like him?" Tina asked softly, coming over to the deck chair Shannon was sitting in unhappily.

"Is it that obvious?"

"It's just that I've never seen you react to a guy like this before. It's like you've never seen a man until now." Then, concerned, "Be careful, Shan."

"I know where babies come from, Tina," Shannon laughed.

"That isn't what I meant. Look, the world of rock musicians is about as chauvinistic as you'll ever find. Women are treated like not very valuable possessions, dropped, handed around, swapped, and laid, with no regard for anybody's feelings. Why do you think I'm so rough on the guys I take up with? Because I've been on the other end of it for too long.

"Andy's no different from the other guys. He just gets around more than most." She finished bluntly, "I'm just trying to tell you not to expect him to be around for the orange juice the next morning because he'll probably be long gone."

Shannon accepted what Tina was saying. She had seen enough of Tina's lifestyle, and heard enough about Andy Clark, to understand the reality of the situation. But it didn't matter. Relatively inexperienced for a twenty-one-year-old, she had enjoyed only one love affair, with a fellow actor at RADA. It lasted for over two years and was very pleasant, but it hadn't affected her the way this did. Compared to the raging desire that Clark unleashed in her, the other affair had been purely platonic.

"Well, maybe you should give me something to help me relax, then. If you're right, I'm going to wind up either rejected or frustrated," Shannon suggested, only half joking.

Tina looked at her soberly for a moment before responding with forced casualness, "Forget it, you're not cut out to be a doper. Have a joint instead."

Shannon couldn't help being amused at the irony of Tina's attitude. Tina lived most of her life on one kind of drug or another. It had taken a close brush with death to get her off heroin, though she still took speedballs, like a kid playing with fire. Yet she never offered drugs, other than marijuana, to Shannon. It was as if Shannon had assumed the role in her life of someone she could always count on to be straight, the one unwavering, dependable element in a hectic, unhappy life that more often than not seemed like a headlong rush toward oblivion.

Shannon had no idea what devil drove Tina. But whatever it was, Shannon sensed that she herself was getting closer to it. In introspective moments like this she wondered where it would all lead.

"I think I'll take a shower and go home," Shannon suddenly announced. She was depressed and irritable, convinced that Andrew Clark was totally uninterested in her.

Tina's bathroom was huge, a poor girl's fantasy of a rich

girl's most intimate room. In the center was a tiled sunken tub surrounded by plants grown dark green and lush from the moisture in the air. The entire room was carpeted with thick plush carpet in a deep forest green, adding to the impression of being in a forest glade instead of a house. One wall consisted of floor-to-ceiling tinted windows that overlooked the ocean.

Shannon took off the wet top of her bikini, then bent down to turn on the water in the tub.

"Well . . ."

The voice was low, husky, unmistakable. Shannon whirled around to find Andrew Clark standing in the doorway, watching her appreciatively. She had forgotten to lock the door. She stood there, her breasts bare, only a tiny fraction of her body covered by the tiny triangle that was her bikini bottom. And yet she felt no embarrassment, just a rising excitement.

He locked the door behind him, then walked over to her. His grey eyes held hers as he reached to pull down the bottom half of her bikini slowly until it fell to the floor.

"That's interesting. Your hair's red all over."

His fingers played with the coarse curling tendrils, teasing her. One hand moved lightly across the outline of her jaw, down her neck to her breasts, stopping to pinch her nipples roughly. She gasped, and he said coolly, through a devastating smile, "A little pain makes it more exciting."

All this time Shannon had said nothing, offering no protest or resistance as he made it clear he was going to take her, in whatever manner he chose. At that moment she was his to do with as he pleased.

"I think we'll play slave. Unbuckle my belt," he ordered curtly.

Without hesitation she obeyed.

"Now the zipper."

She unzipped his jeans slowly, feeling her excitement rise unbearably as the zipper slid past his pubic hair.

"Take it out."

Her fingers trembled as she gently pulled out his penis, already stiff and full.

"On your knees, slave."

She knelt down and took him in her mouth as he stood, watching her.

When he was ready he shoved her down on the carpet and took her quickly, roughly, holding her hands above her head so that she was completely vulnerable; unable to resist him, she arched to meet his thrust. She came immediately, as he did, in a rush of violent waves of pleasure.

Afterwards he dressed and left, pausing only long enough to kiss her lightly on the lips. She took a long bath, reluctant somehow to join the others outside. It was the first time she'd allowed herself to partake of the sexual carnival that Tina operated almost nonstop. The wave of delicious, reckless sensuality was followed by a fierce resentment at having been arrogantly and rudely used. But she realized that she would do it all over again; that she was eager for him, in fact. She'd looked into his eyes as he entered her, and what she saw there was dark and bottomless, and it was that thrilling abyss her thighs had embraced. For some reason Tina's words of the previous summer echoed in her mind: "I find a lady who will never see thirty . . ."

Shannon rose from her bath and towelled herself. She wondered what she would feel when she saw him again.

She needn't have worried. When she went downstairs he was gone. Tina, aware of what had happened, told Shannon that Andy was leaving that night for a month-long tour of Europe. Shannon stared at her in complete dismay.

"Sorry, Shan. That's what I was trying to tell you." She gave Shannon a sympathetic hug. "The orange juice is in the fridge."

CHAPTER 19

"I'm giving a party Saturday night," Tina announced one day, "to celebrate finishing the album. And I want you to come."

Shannon hesitated, but Tina wasn't about to let her get out of it. "I know what's bothering you, you feel like it just isn't your scene. But it isn't going to be only singers. There'll be a lot of industry people, record company executives and managers. You gotta get out and boogie with these guys if you expect to get anywhere."

"I'm not a hermit, Tina," Shannon smiled. "I may not get around as much as you do, but then very few people do."

"So what's the problem?" Tina persisted. "Hey, Andy won't be here, if that's worrying you."

"It isn't that. Look, I know you're trying to get me started, and I'm not sure I'm ready."

"You're ready. You're just scared. Don't worry, everyone is at first. But you've gotta get over it."

"Okay," Shannon gave in reluctantly.

"Go to Holly's Harp and get something that'll really knock their eyes out," Tina suggested encouragingly. "Put it on my account."

Shannon laughed. "I've got money of my own. Not as much as you, granted, but a lot."

"I'm just trying to be helpful. With that sexy but innocent look of yours you've got a lot going for you up front.

All the guys will be living out their Little Red Riding Hood fantasies. Half of them will want to protect you and the other half will want to screw you."

"Thanks."

"Don't mention it."

And that was the end of the argument.

On Saturday evening Shannon stood in front of the full-length mirror in her bedroom, scrutinizing herself carefully. Though she was not normally a vain person she had to admit she thought she looked pretty good. Her auburn hair tumbled past her shoulders in soft, glossy waves, and her blue eyes needed only a touch of mascara to bring out their brilliance. She had inherited a sense of understatement in fashion from her mother, and it gave her a much classier look than most Southern California women possessed. Tall, nearly five feet, eight inches in her bare feet, she had full, firm breasts that added a womanly touch to an otherwise slender, girlish figure. Her long legs were strong and firm from years of riding and swimming.

She had taken Tina's advice and shopped at Holly's Harp for her gown. It was long and white and deceptively simple. Most people wouldn't notice it particularly, except that they would be aware that Shannon looked exceptionally good in it. The only jewelry she wore with it was a gold chain. On it was a heart-shaped locket Michael had given her for her twelfth birthday. She wore it constantly, despite the fact that she had other, much more expensive jewelry given to her by Sir Charles for various birthdays and Christmases.

After procrastinating as long as possible, Shannon finally left, walking the few hundred yards to Tina's house.

The party was in full swing by the time Shannon arrived. The street in front of Tina's house was packed with every kind of expensive car. Shannon could hear the music and laughter and talking before she even entered the house. Inside, every room was packed with people, a bazaar of people dressed in everything from tuxedos and long gowns to leather trousers and jeans. The odor of grass hung heavy on the air, and liquor flowed from the three bars situated at strategic points.

Tina had arranged it so that every room had a different atmosphere. Acid rock blasted from the huge speakers in the living room and people were dancing on the redwood deck. The dining room was set up with long narrow tables piled with food, an expensive array of lobster, prime rib, quiche lorraine, and countless varieties of hors d'oeuvres. People were packed three deep against the tables, gorging themselves on the free feast. In the bedrooms, candles flickered and incense burned, as people used the quiet and relative privacy to smoke joints and snort coke.

For a few minutes Shannon simply stood in a corner of the living room, watching the beautiful people stroll by. A young woman garishly dressed in a jade-green satin gown studded with rhinestones plopped down in a chair next to her, observing casually, "Great party, huh? My boyfriend says Tina really knows how to do it right, plenty of food and coke. There's even some heroin around somewhere. The real stuff, pink, straight from Thailand. You score yet?"

"No," Shannon answered absentmindedly, digesting this news uneasily. If heroin was being dished out somewhere, it was doubtful Tina was turning it down.

Shannon wandered around for an hour, wondering where Tina was, growing more and more worried about her. Several men came up to her, offering everything from simple conversation to any drug she could name to quick sex in the bathroom, their car, the nearby motel (if they were married) or their apartment (if they weren't). Shannon was too preoccupied with Tina to consider any of the offers seriously.

Finally, long after midnight, when most of the guests were beginning to leave, Tina turned up, walking through the door between the deck and the living room, her hair disheveled and sand clinging to her dress. With her, his arm around her possessively, was a handsome young man Shannon hadn't seen before.

So that was it. Tina had simply found another playmate. Shannon breathed a huge sigh of relief.

"Hey, Shan, you look terrific, kiddo," Tina said happily, walking over to her and ignoring the other guests.

Shannon looked at Tina carefully and was relieved to see that her hazel eyes were clear and sparkling, her expression calm and satisfied. She was neither drunk nor high, just basking in the warm afterglow of sex.

"You've managed to miss most of your own party, Tina."

"I know, I meant to. Now that the freeloaders are gone, we can *really* have a good time."

Tina knew what she was talking about. The party had settled down to a small group of people, some of them record company executives and personal managers, others rock music superstars, among the biggest names in the business. Tina dragged Shannon into the group, introduced her, then let her sit back quietly, listening to the conversation.

Tina unwrapped some marijuana from a silver foil package, rolled it into a joint, then passed the bulging cigarette around. Shannon listened to the conversation, puffing on the joint when it was handed to her. As usual, she found the slightly herbal taste unpleasant. But shortly she began to pick up the familiar buzz, and soon began to feel more a part of the circle.

The talk revolved around deals and contracts, which records were making it and which weren't.

"When McCartney jumped to CBS they threw in a music publishing company. I hear the catalogue of songs makes a million bucks a year."

"Yeah, the ultimate in deferred income."

"His lawyer knew what he was doing."

The talk went on and on until finally someone suggested that Tina do some numbers from the album she had just wrapped up. She pulled out her guitar and sang some of the softer numbers. But even on those she opened herself up fully, singing in a flat-out, nothing-held-back style. Shannon marvelled again at the raw talent, the sheer genius really, that Tina possessed, and wondered for the hundredth time why it brought self-destruction instead of self-fulfillment.

After that, some of the others sang, and Shannon immensely enjoyed the impromptu, personal concert. These were people who normally would never perform together because their egos were too big to allow them to share a stage.

Finally, when it was near dawn and the party seemed about to break up, Tina announced casually, "I've got something I want you to hear. Shannon here is a pretty good songwriter and a damn fine singer."

The mellow feeling that had come from the grass disappeared. Shannon froze, as a tight ball of nervousness filled the pit of her stomach. She couldn't do it, not now, not in front of these people. She just wasn't in their league.

But Tina was handing her the guitar and smiling encouragingly. "Knock 'em dead, Shan," she whispered, then leaned back on one of the huge cushions that were spread around the room.

I'll just do it and get it over with and leave, Shannon told herself. *Anyway, they're all so tired and so high, maybe they won't even pay any attention.*

Quickly, without prelude, she went into the opening bars of "Superstar," her favorite of all the songs she had written.

Immediately, almost in spite of herself, she became caught up in the words, and she found herself singing not perfunctorily but with feeling. This song, more than any other, expressed the side of her that she normally kept hidden, the Shannon Montgomery who was passionately curious about life and all of the experiences she'd never had.

When she finished, looking up reluctantly, feeling the sense of embarrassment return, she was surprised to find everyone staring at her with interest, not boredom.

There were scattered comments of "Not bad," "Damn good," and "Where'd you find this girl, Tina?" One singer, an established star who'd managed to slide from the '60s to the '70s, changing style but keeping her devoted audience, said quickly, "That's some song. Is it for sale?"

Before Shannon could answer, a young man sitting in the shadows in the corner said coolly, "You could never do it the way she just did. Forget it, Linda."

Clearly angry, the singer rose, clutching her purse. "You're just a *lawyer*, Mark, *not* an artist. You don't know anything outside of contracts, and you'd better not forget that."

She left, and the others soon followed. But the man named Mark remained behind. Shannon could only barely remember having seen him earlier during the party. Dressed in a simple brown sweater and slacks, he didn't stand out in any way. Though as she looked at him now, she realized there was something about his eyes . . . it went beyond confidence, she decided. There was real arrogance there, and something else, a disturbing quality that Shannon couldn't quite grasp. For no apparent reason, she found him vaguely intimidating.

"You really pissed off Linda, Mark," Tina began casually, amusement in her voice.

"It doesn't matter, I don't need her," he responded matter-of-factly. "Her concerts still make money, but she hasn't had a hit in years. All I'm interested in is records."

"Then it's true—you *are* taking over White Horse Records."

"Well, I put together the deal when they went with American Universal. I know their situation better than anyone."

Shannon didn't understand the record industry well enough to catch all of the meaning of this conversation. But she did understand that this abrasive young man named Mark was taking over one of the most successful of the new record companies that had sprung up in the '70s. And her legendary grandfather, Ben Montgomery, had steered AUP to its first ascendancy so many decades before. She listened more closely.

"And the fact that you have special connections at AUP had nothing to do with the merger," Tina commented wryly.

"I'm a good businessman," he responded succinctly. Then, turning to Shannon, "I'll give you a lift home."

It wasn't an offer but an order.

"I only live a short way down the road," she began, resisting somehow the idea of being alone with him.

"Then I'll walk you home," he responded firmly.

Shannon turned to Tina, but she was merely smiling in amusement.

A few minutes later Mark and Shannon were walking down Malibu Colony Road, deserted now in the cold early light of dawn. Shannon was waiting for him to make a pass at her. But Mark had much more than sex on his mind.

"The announcement won't be made until next week that I'm taking over White Horse. But I'm already making some decisions. I want to sign you. Who's your agent?"

"I don't have one," Shannon managed to answer, stunned.

"Okay," he frowned. "I'll tell Jerry Annenberg to get in touch with you. He's a member of the firm I was with and he knows enough about entertainment law so that you won't need a manager. We'll get together some material for an album—"

"An album?" Shannon was having trouble keeping up with him.

He nodded. "That's what I said. I think the single will

probably be that song you did tonight. When the mix is done on the album, we'll shoot for a date at the Troubadour. That'll be just before we release the single, so the publicity will help it."

They arrived at her house. She leaned against the gate, studying him. He made her feel uneasy; perhaps it was his calculating, unemotional drive. Whatever it was, it did not remotely approach the primal nihilism of Andy Clark, the mere memory of which violently aroused her. But nevertheless, she suspected, she oughtn't to underestimate Mark. "I take it," she said wryly, "you'll hand over the key to this fantasyland just as soon as I take you to bed."

He looked at her without expression. "Are we going to bed?"

"No."

"The offer still stands."

She frowned. "Why shouldn't I shop around?"

He shrugged. "Go ahead. But you won't find anybody in the business who will take you as far and as fast as I will. And I'm ready to gamble with you tonight. I may not be tomorrow."

She lingered with him. The remoteness of him, the feeling that he was dangling her future before her like an amulet, roused in Shannon an impulsive urge to jolt him out of his complacency. She felt suffused by a thrilling anticipation. But he broke the spell.

"By the way, I didn't catch your last name when Tina introduced you."

"It's Montgomery. Shannon Montgomery."

He looked puzzled for a moment, as if the name was familiar but he couldn't quite remember where he'd heard it. "Montgomery? How long have you lived here at the Colony?"

"All of my life. My grandmother built this house back in the '20s." Shannon wondered why he asked that particular question, as if it had some significance.

His brown eyes narrowed in concentration. Suddenly he looked hard at her and said quietly, "Your father was Michael Montgomery. And your mother was Laura Hampton."

Shannon didn't understand why he was staring at her as if she were a prize specimen of a species thought to be extinct. "Yes. Why, do you know my mother?"

"Not really," he answered, smiling strangely. Then, "She

worked for my father once, back in the fifties. And I believe that your father's father was my grandfather's partner at American Universal Pictures."

"Oh, what's your name?"

"Lendt. Mark Lendt."

CHAPTER 20

"So, did you end up in bed with Mark last night?" Tina asked bluntly the next morning.

Shannon had come by to ask Tina about Mark. She smiled. "We wound up talking about genealogy."

"What?"

"Well, it seems our families have known each other in the dim past. My grandfather was his grandfather's partner at AUP. I vaguely remember my father talking about it when I was growing up, but I had forgotten about it until Mark mentioned it. Also, it seems that my mother worked for his father at the studio at one time. Which came as a surprise to me, since she never mentioned it."

"Mark's old man still runs AUP. Everybody assumes that it was that connection that really made the deal between AUP and White Horse work out. Not that the little bastard wasn't successful on his own. He would probably have gotten control of White Horse or some other company eventually. His father just made it happen a little sooner."

"That's what I wanted to ask you about, Tina. Who is Mark Lendt, anyway?"

Tina poured herself another Bloody Mary, and explained between long sips, "I guess if you weren't in the business you would never have heard of him. But believe me, in the business he's big. *Very* big. He started out as an associate in a big firm specializing in entertainment law, then went out on his own."

"But why is he so important?"

Tina leaned forward in the chair, ignoring her drink for a moment. "He's really powerful because he controls some of the top talent. And the guy who controls the talent controls the business. This is something you'd better understand now, Shan, because it's important if you don't want to get ripped off. You can work your ass off and end up with nothing because nobody has any idea where all the money went. Hell, accountants are still trying to figure out what happened to all the money the Beatles made."

"Okay, so what has that got to do with Mark?"

"Lawyers run this business now. They put together the deals. They see to it that you're not ripped off. Or they're supposed to, anyway. Mark is one of the few guys the heads of record companies *always* call back. It started when he put together White Horse a few years ago, and he's just gotten more juice every year."

Tina laughed. "A lot of people hate his guts because he's got a way of cutting through the bullshit that leaves a lot of bodies in his path. I've heard it said that he lights up a room by leaving it. But that has nothing to do with the fact that he can make your career, if he wants to. And fortunately for you, he wants to."

"Then you think I ought to sign?"

Tina shrugged. "You could do a hell of a lot worse."

Suddenly she looked away from Shannon, pretending to be engrossed in watching the fishing boat that passed the Colony each morning on its way to Paradise Cove. Her voice grew thoughtful as she continued, "He is a cold son of a bitch though. The kind of guy who'll get a little slappy with a girl if she gives him a chance. A real put-down artist."

Shannon knew, as clearly as if she had been told, that Tina and Mark had been lovers once. And for Tina it had been a bad experience.

Shannon smiled. "Well, you said he could give me a career."

"That's the problem with being a woman in this business. We need people like that. And they always turn out to be guys."

When Mark called that afternoon to set up an appointment with Shannon and the attorney, Jerry Annenberg, she agreed. That night she wrote to her mother, bringing her up to date on developments. In the letter she carefully explained who Mark Lendt was and what he could do for her. She finished by asking her mother if she remembered working for Mark's father.

The call came through at midnight, waking Shannon from a fitful sleep. When the phone rang, she was dreaming that she was running from a terrifying monster, but her legs moved slowly, as if weighed down by something, while the monster came faster and faster. Somehow the monster was connected with Mark, though Shannon didn't understand how . . .

Groping for the phone, Shannon finally found it and answered sleepily, "Hello."

"Shannon?"

"Oh, Charles . . . yes, what is it?" She was so sleepy that it didn't register that only very bad news would prompt such a late call. It was 9:00 A.M. in London, but Charles would know that it was midnight in Los Angeles.

"I'm sorry to wake you so late, dear. I know it must be around midnight there."

His voice was hesitant, awkward, unbelievably weary. By now Shannon was awake enough to sense that something was terribly wrong.

"I'm afraid I've some very bad news. I don't know quite . . . that is . . . I'm sorry if I seem to be babbling but I've been up all night and my mind's rather foggy. I'd best begin at the beginning, I suppose. Your mother received your letter yesterday afternoon and it upset her terribly for some reason. She seemed very preoccupied and worried and when I asked her what was wrong, she said she was rather concerned about you. She didn't explain exactly what the problem was, and I, of course, didn't ask."

Shannon felt herself growing anxious as Charles talked on and on. "Yes, Charles, could you please just tell me what's happened?" she asked irritably.

"I'm sorry, dear, I'll do that. Your mother wrote you quite a long letter and went out to mail it herself because she was very anxious that it go out in the next post. We've had some problems here with the I.R.A. placing bombs in mailboxes and . . ." He stopped and Shannon could feel the effect of will it required for him to go on. By now her hand was clutching the telephone tightly.

"There was a bomb in the mailbox and it went off just as your mother opened it. She was taken to the hospital, along with about six other people who were nearby. I'm sorry, Shannon, but she died early this morning without regaining consciousness."

Shannon listened numbly to Charles.

"I'll wait until you can come before making the—the arrangements."

"Yes." She hung up.

She sat on the edge of the bed for a long moment, trying to confront her utter aloneness in the world. Despite all of their trials, Shannon had unconsciously relied on her mother's existence as a buffer against the darkness that had swallowed up her father. The truth came crashing down on her now, almost overwhelming her—she had never realized how much she loved her mother, and now it was too late to ever tell her.

There was only one place for Shannon to go. Fighting down panic, she threw on a robe over her nightgown but didn't bother putting slippers on her bare feet. She ran out of the house and down the beach to Tina's house. The lights were out and Shannon had to pound on the door for several long seconds before a light came on in Tina's bedroom window upstairs. A moment later Tina came to the door, wearing a man-size t-shirt that hung to her knees on her short, slight frame. She was rubbing her eyes and muttering sleepily to herself.

"Who the hell is it?" Then, "Oh, Shan, it's you . . ."

She unlocked the door but Shannon just stood there, suddenly unable to move or speak.

"Shan, what is it? Jesus, you look awful."

After a long pause Shannon finally said in the soft, shy voice of a frightened little girl, "My mother's dead." And the tears finally came pouring down as Tina tenderly put her arms around her shoulders.

Shannon stayed in London for several days after the funeral, putting her mother's personal possessions in order, deciding which to keep and which to give to charity. To her surprise, she got along extremely well with Sir Charles, who sublimated his own grief in trying to comfort her. Immediately after the funeral he told her that she was welcome to stay as long as she wished, permanently if she wanted.

"I think you might consider it, Shannon," he said quietly. "That whole rock and roll business is run by a lot of unpleasant people as far as I can make out."

They were sitting in the drawing room in his townhouse not far from Hyde Park. Shannon smiled, amused by his stuffiness but appreciating the genuine concern in his voice. "I'll think about it. Thank you. I mean that, Charles."

Shannon did consider it seriously. Returning to the familiar streets of the enchanting old city that she loved so much, she realized the random, directionless turn her life had now taken. It was November, cold and rainy, and London was a peaceful place. She felt safe here somehow. California was a far-off, vaguely frightening place, where danger, in the form of fame and wealth and the attendant excesses, waited. While shopping in Harrods, bustling with Christmas shoppers, or walking in Hyde Park, Shannon thought constantly of Malibu, trying to decide if she should return.

Her deal with Mark Lendt was still waiting to be finalized, and Tina called every day, urging her to return and get to work. But Shannon continued to delay for one excuse after another, reluctant to cast off her moorings once again.

But as the days passed she began to feel a familiar restlessness, and at night memories of Andy Clark's casual possession of her fired her passions. She'd begun something with Tina and that whole world which was still unfinished, and she began to realize that she'd have no real peace until she explored all of the dimensions of that world—and herself.

One evening she told Charles that she would be returning to Malibu soon.

"I see," he said thoughtfully. "I wish I knew what Laura would have expected of me," he continued hesitantly. But he didn't finish the thought and Shannon thought no more of it.

The final mix of her first album was completed in April, 1977, and in May, only a week before "Superstar" was due to be released as a single, Shannon was booked at the Troubadour in her first professional appearance as a singer.

The Troubadour, an intimate club in West Hollywood, had a respected reputation as a jumping-off place for new talent. In the dressing room, Shannon was waiting to go on when Mark came in, looking, as usual, arrogant and domineering. He took one quick, critical look at her and ordered, "Let your hair down. It looks too formal up."

Shannon took the comb out that was holding up her hair, letting it tumble past her shoulders in a mass of red-gold-brown curls. "Satisfied?" She knew enough about him now to realize that he operated through negative input. He expected resentful, angry feedback which he was expert at manipulating. She kept him constantly baffled by maintaining her composure. It was a game they played. She knew he wanted to make it with her and had expected to have done so before now. But to Tina's delight she kept putting him off. In this case, it was Mark who was the victim of his own anger and resentment.

"That's better. Are you all right?"

"Sure," she lied, trying to convince herself as well as him.

"Are you on anything?"

She shook her head, applying mascara and not looking at him.

He frowned. "Maybe you could use a blast."

"No." The rush of a light hit of coke was dangerously appealing at the moment, but she resisted the temptation. One look at Tina showed her where that road led.

"Andy Clark's in the audience. Don't let it throw you. He's not here to check you out, he's just having a good time with some friends. Anyway, it doesn't matter what he thinks of you. He isn't at the top any more."

She frowned. Andy . . . she hadn't seen him, or heard from him, since that day at Tina's so long ago. Why was he here tonight? Did he come specifically to see her or was he, as Mark assumed, just out having a good time? Just thinking about seeing him again flooded her memory with sensation . . . the feel of his hands, so strong and sure, assuming control of her body as if he owned it, the raging, uncontrollable passion he aroused in her . . .

"What's wrong?" Mark was looking at her intently, as if he could read her mind.

"Nothing. I'll be all right."

He looked as if he didn't believe her. But he continued smoothly, "Be on time at the party afterwards. There'll be some music critics I want you to meet. They're the people who count. They can either plug you or forget you."

"Sure." She continued applying makeup, not looking at

him. Finally, looking as if there was something more he would like to say, he left.

Shannon wondered for the hundredth time why she and Mark were at such odds with each other. It made no sense because it went beyond mere dislike or resentment. If she'd been forced to explain her wariness of him she would have come up with the confusing answer "instinct." Part of it was understandable. He wanted her and she didn't want him. But it went deeper than that. It was the way he would watch her sometimes when she was in the studio. He would stand off to the side, looking at her as if she were somehow more than just another client.

Tina told her that she was crazy and should simply avoid him as much as possible. But Shannon knew that wouldn't solve anything. Deep inside she had the feeling, unarticulated even to herself, that she and Mark were joined together by a tragic inevitability—as if they were fated to resolve a conflict that went as deep as blood itself.

"Hey, Shan, what's happening?"

Tina came in like a breath of fresh air. In the months since Laura's death, Shannon had come to depend on Tina to banish the specters of loneliness and isolation, just as Tina depended on Shannon for some measure of sanity and normalcy in her free-wheeling life.

"I was merely terrified before Mark told me that Andy is in the audience. Now I'm suicidal."

"Don't worry about it. Everybody gets warped before going on, no matter how long they've been doing it. You don't have any idea how much shit I go through before a show. My dressing room looks like a pharmaceutical convention. It's the only way I can make myself get up on stage." She smiled wickedly. "But the reason I came by is that I've got a surprise for you."

"What is it?"

"Can't tell you now. But you'll know soon enough. Listen, it's about time for your set. Now, don't worry. You're damn good and they're gonna love ya."

A moment after Tina walked out, the manager came to tell Shannon that it was time for her to go on. The opening act, a local New Wave band, had just finished, leaving the audience in a happy, receptive mood. As Shannon walked out onto the stage following her brief introduction, the applause was polite and expectant.

The band, a special back-up group that Mark himself

had hand-picked to work with Shannon, led into the opening bars of a rollicking, old-fashioned hard rock song. And before she knew it, she was singing, holding the microphone just a little too tightly, her body swaying to the rhythm of the music, the familiar lyrics coming out in a rush of infectious good feeling. It was the perfect song for her to open up with. She loved it, felt comfortable with it, and her good feelings were communicated to the audience. Halfway through the number they were clapping along with her, and she realized, with that immeasurable sense of relief and joy that every successful performer knows, *they like me!*

She went from one song to the next, pausing only briefly between numbers because she was still too nervous to talk easily to the audience. Toward the end of her set she came to a song that she had actually written for Tina, and that Tina was going to feature on her next album. As the band began to play, suddenly the audience started shouting and clapping happily and when Shannon turned around to see what was causing the commotion she found Tina walking out on stage to join her. They hugged briefly as Tina whispered. "You're a smash, Shan!" Then together they swung into the music.

It was an electric moment as Shannon felt herself come completely alive and uninhibited as an artist for the first time. Inspired by Tina, Shannon sang the song as she had never sung it before. Their enjoyment of the song, their sheer exuberance in singing it together, were felt by the audience, who loved it. When they finished there was a huge burst of enthusiastic applause.

Later, the tiny dressing room was total confusion. Shannon was surrounded by well-wishers. The room was a madhouse as the members of the band, the manager of the Troubadour, Tina, and a handful of music critics were raining compliments on her and thrusting glasses of champagne into her hand. Once, as she looked up at Mark who was standing off to one side, she found him watching her with a strange expression on his face, a mixture of triumph and malice. Quickly, she looked away, chilled by what she had seen, and came face to face with Andy.

He stood in the doorway just long enough for everyone to realize he was there, then came in. As people rushed up to him, he never took his eyes off Shannon. Beneath that intense gaze, Shannon felt herself tremble. Her body grew weak, as she vividly remembered those deliciously erotic minutes they had spent together.

He spoke to Tina first.

"Tina, good to see you again, babe. You were really cookin' tonight."

"Thanks Andy."

Shannon was surprised and relieved to see that Andy was alone. In the audience earlier he had been with a stunning Oriental girl who was now nowhere in sight.

Andy turned to Shannon and said easily, "You've got somethin'. Mark knew what he was doin' when he signed you."

Shannon remembered that Andy, too, was on the White Horse label. "Thanks," she managed to respond casually.

Then he took her hand and said huskily, "It's good to see you again."

The gentle but insistent pressure of his hand awoke the initial passion he'd triggered in her, and she saw in his eyes, in the dark, silent laughter there, that he was aware of his effect on her. She forced a frank smile. "I'm surprised you remembered."

He laughed. "What are you talking about? Red's my favorite color."

Mark joined them, breaking the spell. "We've got to make the party, Shannon."

"You come with me," Andy said. Mark frowned, but made no protest.

The party went by in an almost psychedelic blur, a crazy-quilt scrapbook of imagery; of faces and hands seeking her out to bestow praise and partake of her triumph, of writhing bodies on the strobe-blasted dance floor, of offers, direct and implied, of everything from dope to sex to money. Shannon began to experience the rush of success Tina had described so many times to her: an incomparable high fueled not by the considerable and varied stash being passed around like hors d'oeuvres, but by the outpouring of envy, admiration and lust being rained on her by the glittering crowd, all of it supercharged by anticipation of what would happen with Andy when he took her home. Her senses were alive, nakedly extended, and the delicious tension building in her belly and thighs was unabashedly sexual and demanded release. It was a fever of a kind she'd never experienced before, and she surrendered to it. *So this is what it's like to dance,* she thought.

Tina left early with a handsome, bearded young critic from *Rolling Stone* who had caught her fancy. "Press relations," she winked at Shannon. But before going, she took Shannon aside.

"Hey, what's happening? You're behaving like Andy isn't the same guy who screwed you over once. Don't get me wrong. I think it's high time you found somebody to boogie with. But you don't *need* him now."

Shannon laughed recklessly. "You're right. But I *want* him."

Tina shook her head. "Well, I guess you've graduated. Have fun."

Some time later Andy gave her a look from across the room. She smiled. It was time to go. As they drove along Pacific Coast Highway, sitting in the back seat of his long, elegant Cadillac limousine, neither of them was in a mood to wait until they reached the Colony.

"You're really somethin', you know," Andy began, putting an arm around her and staring at her intently.

"Oh?"

"You look like a real old-fashioned well-bred lady. But when you sing it's like the difference between an angel and the devil—like you're offering yourself to every man in the audience. Five minutes after you started singing tonight, I knew I had to get it on with you again. It drove me crazy waiting for the party to end. Shannon . . . God, you're beautiful!"

His voice, husky and masterful, filled with naked desire, was almost hypnotic. Her eyes were locked with his, as if she were watching a snake swaying back and forth, preparing to strike.

Slowly, provocatively, he began to unlace the ribbon that held together the bodice of her dress.

"The chauffeur," she said worriedly, suddenly remembering that they weren't alone. In the front seat, beyond a glass partition, the black-uniformed young chauffeur drove on silently, his head staring rigidly at the highway in front of them.

"He knows better than to turn around," Andy said, continuing to unlace the ribbon slowly.

As the ribbon was loosened the two halves of the bodice began to pull apart, exposing more and more of Shannon's full, firm breasts. She held her breath as the bodice came totally undone and her breasts spilled out, naked and quivering in the dim light of the car. Nervously Shannon looked up at the chauffeur, but his head was still turned away.

Andy drew an outline lightly with one finger around her breasts, then began massaging them and pinching the nipples until they stood out erect and unbearably sensitive to his touch. Bending his head, he licked the firm pink points until Shannon's breathing became heavy and erratic.

Suddenly, roughly, he pulled down her dress, exposing the entire upper half of her body to her slim hips.

"No . . ." she protested weakly.

But he continued, smiling. "It's all right, babe. He can't hear us and he won't look around."

His mouth and hands were all over her then, squeezing her breasts together, then flicking each nipple lightly with his tongue, while Shannon moaned. He pulled the dress completely off her, and with one hand reached down and tore off her lace panties, ripping them savagely.

Shannon was beyond protesting by now, filled with an unbearable, overriding hunger that stilled any sense of shame or embarrassment. Andy pushed her down in the seat, and she lay there, completely naked, as his mouth and hands explored every inch of her body with excruciating deliberateness.

"Please, please . . ." she begged, as his tongue traveled down between her legs, on the soft insides of her long, slender thighs, moving up inevitably to the downy hair above. She raised her hips to meet him, welcoming him urgently, and when his tongue parted the tender lips of her vagina she thought she would explode as all reason left her.

She turned her head just then and her eyes were met by the frank gaze of the chauffeur who was watching them while the car was stopped at a traffic signal.

"Oh, my God," Shannon thought, shocked, as his eyes travelled over her nude body, taking in her heaving breasts and the hips that she kept pressing urgently against Andy's probing mouth.

But Andy was entering her now, and she was too desperate to stop him or to cover herself as she felt her body tighten like a coiled spring before the sweet release spread through her.

They made love again when they reached the beach

house, and a third time the next morning as dawn was breaking in deep crimson and gold over the ocean. Each time was more erotic, more satisfying than the last.

As Andy dressed to leave, late in the morning, he announced calmly, "I'll be back tonight. That'll give you enough time to tell anyone else you're involved with to get lost. I'm not letting you go this time." Then, kissing her lightly, possessively. "You're mine now, Shannon Montgomery. And I don't share the things I value."

Long after he left, Shannon pulled herself together enough to visit Tina.

Tina shook her head knowingly. "I'm not surprised he's so turned on by you now. He knows you're gonna be real big and that charges him up."

"I don't care what charges him up," Shannon said. "He brings out something in me that I never knew was there. I have absolutely no control where he's concerned."

They were sitting on the deck in the bright morning sunshine, watching a big speedboat cutting the swells beyond the frothy, breaking surf, pulling a water-skier in its wake. Tina frowned thoughtfully. "There's something a little spooky about you, Shan. Like I said, you're going to make it big, bigger than me, maybe. But you're never going to be part of it like me." She reached over to squeeze Shannon's hand. "I'm glad. Because to really groove on it you've got to kind of kiss your ass goodbye. But you've got a different kind of karma working. It's like a part of you bought a ticket for a ride and the other part is just laid back, waiting till it's time to get off."

Shannon smiled. "Both parts got some ride last night."

"I'll bet. But I'm not jiving you, lady. When the time comes to get off, you jump. You hear me?"

Tina's hazel eyes, normally bright with lively humor, were narrowed with concern. Shannon said something to reassure her, full of the exciting knowledge that the time to jump wasn't even on the far horizon.

CHAPTER 21

Superstar was an immediate, massive hit, quickly establishing Shannon as an important artist and propelling her to platinum status. The fact that she was Andy Clark's "lady" only added to her patina of glamour and mystique. In short order they replaced Mick and Bianca Jagger as rock music's version of the First Family. But when Shannon's second album, *Working Girl*, turned into an even bigger hit than *Superstar* she began to eclipse Andy in popularity. His career was beginning to slide and, helpless to turn things around, he began to turn on Shannon.

In the weeks after the release of *Superstar* Shannon's life changed completely into a daily frenzy of phone calls, negotiations, personal appearances, television spots, interviews, and on and on, until the initial rush of success became a ceaseless and grueling test of her nerves and stamina. And her liaison with Andy, which was quickly exploited by White Horse, only added fuel to the fire. "Kris and Rita, eat your hearts out," Tina joked when Shannon and Andy appeared together on the cover of *Rolling Stone* and *People* magazines in the same week. But Andy had been around for some years now and recently his records hadn't managed to crack the top ten, either albums or singles. He became depressed, withdrawing from her. It came to a head the night Mark Lendt threw a party to celebrate *Working Girl's* going triple platinum, selling three million copies in the first six weeks following its release.

Mark's Bel Air mansion was secluded behind heavy gates and an acre of near impenetrable forest. Tonight it was lit up like an arcade and packed with record company executives, performers, and the inevitable cadres of hangers-on. A light stash of reds and downers and good Colombian grass could be had for the asking, but Mark enforced an unwritten rule that no hard drugs would be allowed on the premises. When Shannon and Andy arrived there were already nude bodies frolicking in the hot tubs and pool, and two live bands were dueling in the huge private disco in the basement.

Something had been troubling Andy all evening, and he'd been drinking J & B and dropping pills since early afternoon. Shannon watched as he drifted away, apparently forgetting about her, to flirt openly with several of the beautiful women who were there. She began to understand; this party was for *her*, to honor *her* achievements. For the first time in their relationship he was merely her escort, and it was a change in roles he couldn't handle.

She was immediately swallowed up by the party, but later caught a glimpse of Andy headed out through the drawing room, his arm around a svelte blonde in skin-tight pants and a low-cut blouse. Not long after Mark Lendt broke through the group of friends and well-wishers who surrounded her. He gave her the obligatory hug and kiss, and said, "Let's find someplace we can talk business."

They went to an upstairs study. It was a large expensively paneled room containing a small law library and an inset bank of television monitors. He lit a joint and offered it; she inhaled deeply, to maintain the high she'd begun after Andy wandered off with the blonde.

Mark came quickly to the point. "I think you ought to kiss Andy off. In another year he's going to be a liability to your career. It's tough enough staying on top without sleeping with a loser."

Typically, he was trying to nettle her. Shannon smiled. "I don't think my sex life is any of your business."

"Maybe not. But your business is my business. And you should know that I may not sign him again." He was watching her with wry amusement and, she knew, desire.

But she also knew him well enough to realize that he hadn't brought her upstairs to talk about ending Andy's career. If he'd made an irrevocable decision like that, she was the last person he'd reveal it to. He was playing with her.

"You *may* not?" she said, going along with him.

He smiled. "There is an alternative. You two could cut an album together. That might put some new juice into his act." He crossed to where she was sitting and lifted the hem of her dress, drawing it up to expose her long legs. "At least, I might be persuaded to give it a try."

She sat still, convinced that he'd already made the decision to go ahead with the joint album. All he was doing at the moment was using the issue to take her body. She idly ran a fingernail over the back of his hand, and with the other accepted the joint he offered. But it was a move fraught with consequences. It would be no secret that Andy was riding on her success, and it could only make things more difficult between them. But it was out of her hands, and there was no reason she should submit to Mark. She looked up at him languidly, wanting to savor the moment.

"I suppose that's up to you," she smiled, and then rearranged her skirt. As he stiffened with anger, she rose to leave.

"Just a minute," he said grimly.

She turned as he crossed to his desk and opened a built-in console. He stabbed a button and one of the television monitors came to life. "You might enjoy this, Shannon. I'll even send you a tape if you like."

Shannon stared at the screen. There was Andy, sitting on the edge of a large, opulent bed with his trousers unbuckled. The naked blonde knelt between his knees, her head moving urgently and his fingers entwined in her hair.

"You see," Mark said. "Everybody's doing it."

Shannon turned and hurried from the room.

A month later they were in the studio together, cutting the album. Andy had come back to her, and she'd taken him in. And instead of resenting the prospect of a joint album, he seemed to embrace the idea enthusiastically, perhaps sensing that it might be the one means left to him to reinvigorate his career. Or perhaps, Shannon came to suspect, refusing to acknowledge that it was her name and talent that launched the project. At any rate the album went better than anyone had anticipated. There was a chemistry between them, an electric saint-and-sinner presence, that communicated in the music. And Andy reached for his old enthusiasm. *He's got his old magnetism*, Shannon thought happily, as she listened to the playback of the lead song.

The record, *When Love Dies*, was number one for ten weeks in a row. It was a phenomenon, inspiring t-shirts, discussions by music critics, and comments from everyone from news commentators to politicians. Easily the number one single for 1978, it was still in the top fifty in early 1979 when Shannon and Andy set off on a sixty-day, forty-five-city tour. Andy was excited, confident, aware that he was on the verge of becoming bigger than ever. Shannon was concerned only with the fact that he was hers again. Since the release of their record, Andy was closer to her than he had ever allowed himself to be to any woman. They were living together now in his modernistic Beverly Hills mansion, a huge white edifice filled with expensive erotic art. Shannon could see the envy on the faces of the women they met, and if she felt bothered by a vague sense of unease that somehow her independence had been compromised, that she was becoming less and less her own person, she eased her mind with increasing amounts of marijuana. Andy seemed to have a limitless supply of every kind of drug.

The first time Shannon did coke with him, she watched, fascinated and a little nervous, as Andy carefully made two thin lines of the substance on a mirror. Then he rolled up a dollar bill and vacuumed the powder into his nose. He breathed deeply and his grey eyes watered. Then he handed it to her. At her first attempt she blew the expensive white dust across the table. But at her second attempt it worked, and she felt the cool numbness spreading across her cheeks. She was rather relieved that there was no effect otherwise. Then, as she talked, she became aware of an exceptional sharpness and clearness in her thinking and in her conversation. She was no longer a rather reserved and somewhat insecure novice in the world of rock, but a confident woman at ease in her new environment.

After that she sniffed the white diamanté crystals whenever she felt tired or uncomfortable around Andy's friends. It lifted her up. There was no unpleasant comedown from the stimulation of coke, as there was with other uppers she tried, so she kept snorting more and more.

The adrenaline produced by the rocket-fuel burst of a quick snort of coke was rapidly becoming necessary to get her through the busy days and wild nights with Andy. Only Tina seemed concerned about the change that was taking place in Shannon. At a kick-off party the night Andy and Shannon were due to leave on tour, Tina took Shannon aside.

"What the hell do you think you're doing?" she demanded furiously.

"Come off it, Tina, I'm not using that much," Shannon answered defensively.

"Maybe not now, but you'll keep snorting more and more. It works that way, once it gets a hook in you."

Shannon sighed, irritated. Tina was getting on her nerves.

"Tell me something," Shannon asked bluntly. "When was the last time you were straight for a whole day?"

Tina stepped back, as if Shannon had hit her. Shannon's harsh words weren't like her, and she regretted them. But then, she realized, nothing she did lately was like her.

The next day Shannon and Andy and all of the support personnel for the tour left on a private chartered jet. There was a road manager, personal assistants, roadies to set up the equipment on the stage, a hair stylist and makeup expert for Shannon, a flagrantly gay young man in charge of the wardrobe, and a middle-aged man whose sole job, Shannon later learned, was to score dope for the performers in each city. Aside from Shannon the only women were Shirley and Sheila, blonde twins who giggled a lot and were friendly with everyone. When Shannon asked Andy what the twins' jobs were, he merely smiled and answered cryptically, "They help keep everyone from gettin' too tense, y'know? After a few weeks on the road, everyone starts gettin' a little crazy."

Shortly after the plane took off from Los Angeles International Airport heading for the first stop, Tucson, Shannon found out exactly what service the twins provided.

A member of the band grabbed one of the twins, it was impossible to tell which, and pulled off her tight sweater and jeans. She wore nothing underneath, and giggled as she was being stripped. The other twin, giggling and protesting half-heartedly at the same time, was stripped by one of the roadies, while everyone watched in amusement.

At that point Andy steered Shannon, who was watching in stunned disbelief, into their private compartment in the rear of the plane.

Her first tour had just begun.

They performed in a huge stadium in Tucson before a stoned, demented throng of ten thousand. The smell of grass at some places in the stadium was so strong that it made eyes water. The security guards interfered only when a fan tried to scale the ten-foot-high fence surrounding the stage.

This was the first time that Shannon had seen Andy perform before a live audience, and she was amazed and frightened by the transformation that came over him. She understood the dialogue of energy between the performer and an audience that makes the performer feel differently onstage than off. But with Andy the energy seemed to make him violent, as if he were barely holding in check an overpowering urge to destroy something.

From the moment he came out onto the stage alone, until Shannon joined him halfway through the first number, he had the frenetic, screaming audience springing to its feet like a puppet whose strings he had just pulled. People were standing on their seats, dancing in the aisles. The pulsing energy, the almost uncontrollable hysteria that he elicited from them, affected him immediately. Prancing and posing, moving his body seductively, singing with all of the fervor of an evangelist trying to whip up his audience into an emotional frenzy, Andy went wild.

When Shannon joined him, things calmed down slightly, but she still felt that the building was about to pull apart at the seams. Dozens of kids, most of them barely in their teens, went berserk, thrusting toward the stage, eluding the tired, frustrated security guards. As Shannon watched, horrified, it seemed for a moment that the entire stadium would erupt as the whole audience seemed to be hurtling toward the stage, determined to reach her and Andy. But almost as quickly as it began, the security guards had the riot in check, removing the more determined participants.

Shannon continued to sing with Andy, swept up in the emotion and excitement, matching his energy with her own. But at the back of her mind she was thinking, *This has nothing to do with my music. It's chaos.*

After the concert, when she and Andy were hustled quickly into an armored van for the short trip to their hotel, she sat stunned, like a victim of shell shock.

But Andy was buoyant, alive with vitality, ready to party all night. "We were fantastic together, babe! This tour's gonna be the biggest thing since the last time the Stones came through. I'm gonna call Mark tomorrow and tell him we should do a live album. It's the perfect follow-up to our first one."

But as he talked on and on, Shannon said nothing. She was too dazed to respond, too troubled to think clearly.

That night she refused to make love to him, insisting she was too exhausted. He left angrily and didn't return until they were due to leave the next morning. Shannon didn't ask where he had been.

Mark agreed that a live album would be a good idea; the shows were going well and the reviews by music critics were almost without exception good. By the end of the tour the album was ready to be released, Andy and Shannon were the new reigning king and queen of rock, and Shannon was suffering from nervous exhaustion. For two months she had gone up and down like a yo-yo.

Images of the tour assaulted her. Endless airports and limousine rides, the faceless, hysterical crowds, pulsing like live entities with lust, nameless angers, and an insatiable appetite for more of whatever it was that she and Andy were giving them. And the groupies in every town, willingly performing tricks with wine bottles and each other.

Unable to put it behind her, even with increasing amounts of coke and grass, Shannon realized she was in trouble.

She checked herself into St. John's Hospital in Santa Monica, a respected drying-out spot for Hollywood celebrities. For a week she did nothing but sleep and read and try to gain back the twenty pounds she had lost during the tour. She asked the doctor to inform everyone except Andy and Tina that she wasn't up to having visitors. But it was hardly necessary. Tina was on the road, and Andy only came once, on the first day, insisting that he couldn't stand hospitals.

"I'll see you when you get out, babe," he concluded, leaving her with a huge bouquet of roses.

Spending a great deal of time alone, experiencing once more the luxury of privacy and solitude that she hadn't known for over a year, allowed her to think clearly again. She now realized the danger Andy posed, but she still clung to him sexually. He sought destruction, she knew: hers, the crowds he whipped to a frenzy, ultimately his own. But nevertheless he could do as he pleased with her, and she didn't have the will to resist.

Tina returned a few days before Shannon left the hospital. She looked bad, thin and discolored, but acted mellow and Shannon knew with a sickening feeling that she was mainlining again.

"It's good, Shan. No pain. That's what it's all about. No pain . . ." she said abstractedly.

Shannon could get little out of her. The tour had been a bad one, jinxed by bad weather and some roustings on minor drug charges. And it was complicated by the fact that Tina had turned twenty-nine at the midway point of the tour.

"I want you to come back to the beach with me, Shan," she said, tears suddenly filling her eyes. "You and me, we'll shake off all the bullshit and live out there like sisters, the way we used to."

But Shannon could find no words with which to reply. Andy would expect her to go back to him, at his house. And, more importantly, Tina frightened her now. In her heart she knew she was no longer strong enough to support both of them. "I can't," she said finally.

Tina stared at her with dull, pained eyes. "Oh, yeah. Right. Andy. I forgot about Andy . . ." Then, with a visible effort, she became animated. It was a mockery of the old Tina but Shannon knew what effort of will it required. "Listen," she said. "Don't worry about me. This old ballbuster ain't quit shakin' yet. I'm going to get my shit together and come right back at 'em."

When Tim left, Shannon called Andy to tell him she was worried about Tina and to make sure someone stayed with her. But there was no one home. Desperately she called Mark Lendt and told him of her fears, but he shrugged off her concerns.

"Don't worry about Tina," he said. "She knows what she can handle. Anyway, I've got other things for you to be thinking about."

He told her that with the success of the tour, and with the live album set for release in the summer, he'd decided to make a movie starring Andy and Shannon, tied in with a novelization of the film, to tap their following in a multimedia blitz. The script was already being drafted, based on "When Love Dies," their big hit duet.

"So many people are familiar with the song that the

movie will almost be pre-sold. David Delaney is already working on a half-dozen new songs for the film."

Delaney, Shannon recalled, had written "When Love Dies." It was his first big sale. She had never met him. Rumor had it that he'd stayed in town long enough to sign the contracts, then headed back to his home in the mountains somewhere up north.

"It sounds like you've got everything all set," Shannon observed wryly.

"I didn't want to disturb you while you were under the weather," Mark said with equal wryness. "But I understand from Andy you're about ready to rejoin the world."

"If you can call it that," Shannon said, and hung up.

But Tina remained very much in her thoughts. Few, even in the hyper-paced world of rock, laughed at smack. It had sucked under Jimi Hendrix and Janis Joplin and countless others. It was the fire, bright and beckoning, totally consuming.

Later in the evening Shannon called the beach, but there was no answer at Tina's house. It was incredible that no one was there. Frantically Shannon began to call as many of Tina's friends as she could remember, but was unable to locate her.

Her anxiety was increasing by the moment. She thought about calling the sheriff's department but rejected the idea. The law would welcome a legitimate reason to go through Tina Tobias's house.

She tried Tina's again, and there was still no answer.

Shannon checked herself out of the hospital and left for Malibu in a cab. A thunderstorm, ominous and threatening, was moving into Los Angeles. As the cab turned onto Pacific Coast Highway she saw that the ocean was dark and angry, wind-spawned whitecaps skimming the surface of the heaving water. The sky was a mass of boiling grey and black clouds, and before Shannon was out of Pacific Palisades the rain started, falling in hard sheets. Shannon felt a growing urgency.

When she reached the Colony she went straight to Tina's. The lights were out. There was no answer when she rang the doorbell. Finally she walked around the side of the house to the deck. The door, as usual, was open but the house was dark and quiet.

As Shannon walked inside she could smell and feel the presence of death. She paused, knowing subconsciously what she would find and reluctant to face it. Finally she forced herself to climb the stairs to Tina's bedroom.

Tina's body was hanging over the edge of the bed, her short golden curls just brushing the floor. Blood had dripped from her mouth and lay drying and foul-smelling in a pool below her face. The syringe was still in her arm, empty. Tina—hopelessly self-destructive, eaten up by misery and loneliness, a genius who could never come to terms with her art, who sought solace in pills and booze and any drug that would take her mind off reality for a while—was dead.

Shannon called the nearest sheriff's station, then sat down near the body. For a while, anyway, Tina wouldn't be alone.

CHAPTER 22

As Tina had requested in her will, her funeral service was private and attended by only a few friends. Shannon sang a few of Tina's best compositions without accompaniment, her high, clear voice filling the small Beverly Hills chapel. Then it was over. Tina's remains were to be cremated, and the ashes scattered over the ocean.

In the following days Shannon discovered that Tina's death did not have the effect of reaffirming her decision to change her life; in fact, that resolve seemed to have been extinguished with her friend's life. She was totally alone now, and she clung to Andy because she didn't have anyone else to cling to. But, as the plans for the movie went ahead, she was subdued and remote. Unresisting, she allowed the flow of decisions and events to pick her up and carry her.

Mark seemed to find a special amusement in the situation. One afternoon the three of them were sitting in his office at American Universal. He smiled at Shannon from behind his massive square desk that was bare save for a gold pen in a holder and a short stack of papers arranged neatly. "I'm going to make you a movie star," he said. "Just as my father made your . . ." he hesitated for just a fraction of a second, watching her closely, ". . . *uncle* a star. And long before that your grandmother was working for my grandfather. It seems our families can't keep away from each other. But then I guess you know all about that."

Shannon frowned, not quite sure of his meaning, and not particularly caring. "My parents never talked much about the past."

Mark and Andy began talking about the script and Shannon drifted to the window to look out on the bustling movie lot below where so much of her family's history had played out. Without being able to pinpoint the reason, suddenly she was anxious to leave the place.

Andy was becoming impatient with her moodiness. "You need something to pick you up, take your mind off Tina," he said one night. She had already picked up his habit of routinely using marijuana and coke to boost the day along, and that night he introduced her to opium. Andy invited some friends over and they sat around a table. One of the men took out a polyethylene bag that contained pure opium from Thailand, depositing the thick oil into a pipe on the table. He lit it and each person drew deeply in turn, then lay back. As it came to Shannon's turn she could feel the acrid fumes burning their way into her lungs. She sputtered and coughed; then her head became as light as a balloon and as she lay back she felt that she was floating . . . away from sad memories of Tina . . . away from Andy . . . and away from her fear of Mark. . . .

Shannon and Andy went into the recording studio in March to record the songs for the movie. It was there that she met David Delaney. She was singing a solo number, alone in the spartan, antiseptic room, when she looked up and saw him watching her from the control booth. She didn't know who he was, only that he looked totally different from the other people around her. Wearing a plaid Pendleton shirt and faded jeans, there was something fresh and unspoiled about him. His blue eyes sparkled with a vitality that reminded her of Tina, but without the underlying tension. Though he was barely thirty his face had the tanned, weathered look of a man who spends a great deal of time out of doors. Not strictly handsome, he was quite pleasant looking. His appeal lay in his innate masculinity, his sure sense of his own maleness.

He watched Shannon as she sang, and when she finished he broke into a huge grin. Leaving the control booth, he came down to join her.

"Miss Montgomery, you sang that song just the way I imagined it could be sung," he said with genuine warmth.

There was something decidedly Texan in his voice, but it was not uneducated. "By the way, I'm David Delaney."

"Well . . . thank you, Mr. Delaney."

"You know, I've been waiting for a chance to tell you how much I admired the way you did 'When Love Dies.' For a while there I thought I was never gonna get to meet you. I was laid up with a busted leg when you recorded it, then when I got well you were on tour."

"I'm sorry I missed you," Shannon said sincerely. "I hope your leg's all right now."

He slapped it with a grin. "It'll do. I was skiing. Caught an edge and came down on a rock." He laughed with appealing self-deprecation. "Mama told me I never should have left Lubbock."

He asked her to lunch and she agreed. They found a booth in a crowded coffee shop opposite the studio. David Delaney, she learned, was a variety of conflicting characters: cowboy, songwriter, outdoorsman—and scholar.

"Oxford?"

"Yep," he grinned. "I was a Phi Beta Kappa at Houston and that earned me a Rhodes scholarship." He took a huge bite out of a cheeseburger. "Some little overachiever, I was."

"What did you study?"

"Literature. Poetry mostly. Especially Donne. It was reading him that got me started writing songs. I had a beat-up ol' guitar with me, and one thing led to another . . . Anyway, I dropped out of school and did some time on the road. I kept after the music but nothing happened for a long time. I'll bet you know how that is."

Shannon nodded. She didn't know, but she enjoyed listening to him talk.

"Truth is, when it looked like I wasn't going anywhere I got myself just the least bit strung out. After six months of that I woke up straight one morning and realized I was really in trouble. I looked in the mirror and said, Delaney, son, you're going to have to make a choice here. If you're gonna kill yourself, then get on with it. Don't drag it out. If you're not, then get on with that too. 'Cause this way you're just wasting everybody's time."

"So you kicked it?"

He nodded. "Took me six months to get clean. I just locked myself in a little cabin a friend of mine loaned me and wrote songs night and day to stay busy. But I kicked it." He frowned, "In fact, that's where I wrote 'When Love Dies.' You see, my lady and I were trying to hack it together. And she couldn't. So when she split, I knew I had to get it down on paper."

"What happened to her?" The mention of his hooked girlfriend had given her a cold feeling in the pit of her stomach.

He shook his head. "Couldn't say." He glanced up, shaking off the frown. "Anyway, that cabin I was talking about, I've still got it. Complete with seventeen bushels of unpublished songs. Maybe you could come up and see it some time?" His blue eyes waited for her response unselfconsciously. It was almost amusing; this country boy had just asked one of the country's leading rock artists to run away to the mountains with him. It fell short of humor because she suddenly realized just how tempted she was to accept. But she remembered Andy.

"I don't think that's likely to work out," she said.

"Andy Clark?"

She nodded.

He grinned. "Well, the invitation's open. You remember that. And meanwhile, it looks like I'm going to be spending some time in L.A. Mark says he wants me around while they're setting up the songs."

Shannon detected a note of concern in his voice.

"You don't like L.A.?"

"Not my style," he said. "Not any more."

Suddenly Shannon felt that she would like very much to show David Malibu—not Tina's Malibu of drugs and disillusionment, but *her* Malibu of gentle hills and green glens, clean white beaches and endless expanse of deep blue ocean. She could picture him at the beach house and knew somehow he would fit in there. Something about him stirred a deeply buried memory . . . something her father had said long ago about *his* father, Ben Montgomery . . . something about his special strength and courage that set him above the hustlers and manipulators in Hollywood: "He loved to create for the joy of creating, not for the money or the power."

"Shannon!"

With a start, Shannon came back to the present. Mark was walking up to them, the perennial amused half-smile playing about his lips. Shannon always felt that he was laughing at some secret joke that only he knew the punchline to.

"Yes, Mark?"

"I see you've met David. Good. He's done some good stuff for you and Andy. Between the three of you this movie is going to be the biggest thing since *Saturday Night Fever*." He turned to Delaney. "I'm glad I ran into you, David. I want to add a solo for Andy at the end of the film. Will you excuse us, Shannon?"

She watched David Delaney leave the coffee shop with Mark. At the door he turned and gave her a tip of his hat. She laughed, in a way she hadn't laughed in a long time.

The movie cameras began to roll in April with a budget of eight million dollars and a director, Ryan Bercovicci, whom Shannon loathed on sight. Young, fresh out of the American Film Institute, with only one low-budget but highly successful film to his credit, he was every inch "New Hollywood." He proudly wore his custom-made gold-plated cocaine works, a tiny spoon and tube, on a chain around his neck. And he constantly asked Shannon about Brendan, her uncle who had become something of a cult idol, particularly worshipped by young film school graduates.

"I really don't know anything about him," Shannon insisted firmly, and it was true up to a point. Her parents almost never had mentioned Brendan to her, but on rare occasions, as she was growing up, she heard them arguing about him. As children will, she sensed the most critical thing about Brendan—he must have done something very bad otherwise people would have talked openly about him instead of in angry whispers. Later on she heard stories about Brendan from people in the entertainment industry and learned what the big secret was all about—he was bisexual. Somehow that seemed to add to his mystique.

Ryan kept bringing up the subject of Brendan, comparing Shannon to him.

"You have the same quality he had—an intensity that will keep the audience glued to their seats, watching you. You even look like him."

"No, I *don't*," Shannon responded shortly. Ryan wasn't the first to make such a comment. It inadvertently triggered a deep-seated, almost instinctive resentment in her.

"Well, anyway," Ryan continued doggedly, changing his approach, "it will be great publicity for the movie. Brendan

Montgomery's niece following in his footsteps. Directing you is the closest I'll come to working with him. It was a tragic loss for the art of film when he died so young."

Shannon went to her dressing room, muttering angrily to herself about pretentious directors conceited enough to think that film was art instead of craft.

Surprisingly, in spite of the fact that she thought Ryan was an idiot, Shannon came off extremely well in the movie. At RADA there had been so many immensely talented people around her that Shannon had grown extremely critical of her own acting ability. But on this movie she was working for the most part with people who were hired because they were popular with the young record-buying audience Mark wanted to attract. They weren't brilliant actors, and Shannon quickly stood out as much more talented than the rest of the cast. At one point she found herself thinking, *Maybe I do have some of Brendan's talent*. But the thought made her uncomfortable and she dismissed it.

But it wasn't so easy for Andy to dismiss, she realized. His real talent lay in his ability to interact with a live audience. He could whip up thousands of people to a fever pitch of excitement when he was standing in front of them on a stage. On film he tended to overact and was strangely lacking in charisma.

They were sitting in a small, dark screening room at the studio watching the rushes from the previous day's shooting. Ryan and Mark were sitting together in the top row of seats. Shannon was just below them, and Andy was down in the first row, several feet away, talking to the prop man who did a brisk sideline in hustling drugs for the cast and crew. The first shots were of Andy's first really dramatic scene. Halfway through, Mark said quietly to Ryan, "It doesn't matter that he can't act. People will come to hear his singing and to see if he and Shannon are as hot on-screen as they are off."

Ryan nodded pragmatically. "He's got a definite sexual attraction. Hopefully, people will be too turned on by him to notice that he can't say his own name."

Shannon stiffened. What they said was true, and painfully obvious to everyone in the room. She looked down at Andy who was staring resolutely ahead at the screen, saying nothing, though other people in the room were whispering to each other. When the lights came on a half-hour later and they all walked outside, she saw that Andy was wearing a forced smile. Shannon dreaded the ride home together and the long night ahead of them.

The house was empty for a change; Andy had cut off the constant stream of visitors and hangers-on when the movie began. He was determined to concentrate totally on it. Succeeding as a movie star meant even more to him than succeeding as a singer. Shannon was glad they were alone; this way there would be no one to witness whatever was about to take place.

To her surprise, Andy said nothing. He went straight up to their bedroom, and when he didn't come back down after a few minutes, she went up to join him.

She found him in the bathroom, skin-popping heroin. He had diluted the minuscule heroin jacks, then put them into a syringe to jab into his body. He only needed one-tenth as much heroin that way as he would need if he snorted it. And he could still pretend that he wasn't hooked on the drug that he feared and had managed to avoid throughout his singing career.

"Andy . . ."

"*Don't* say anything. I just need something to bring me down. Just—just a little something."

Shannon knew he was lying. A moment later he was floating gently into unconsciousness, and the next morning he woke up feeling calm and satisfied.

The pattern began. Andy took coke while working on the movie during the day—"for energy" he said—then used heroin to come down at night. The more coke he used, the more "wired," hyperenergetic, and hyperparanoid he became, so that he desperately craved the heroin come-down. He was using so much coke now in a desperate attempt to add excitement to his performance that sometimes he would have to scrape the thick white residue out of his nose with a fingernail. Eventually he burned away his nasal septum and had to have a new plastic partition put in.

Their sexual relationship became a nightmare. He used sex to humiliate and degrade her, forcing her into acts that she hated, then savagely criticizing her performance. He became physically abusive, bruising her breasts and raising welts on her thighs and buttocks. She was torn between a consuming desire to flee him and a paradoxical willingness to submit to his cruelest whims, complicated by her own enervating, growing dependence on cocaine. Their lives were plunging toward disaster at a constantly accelerating pace but she felt powerless to halt the rush. Some mornings she hardly knew who she was. The people she cared about, who might have helped her—her parents, Tina—were dead. She was a planet, spinning out of orbit.

So that she wasn't even surprised one evening when Andy produced a syringe and paraphernalia and began preparing a fix. They were in the back seat of the limousine which was taking them home after the day's shoot. Andy used the purest Thai heroin, as innocent-looking as pink talcum powder. But now skin-popping and sniffing it wasn't enough. He rolled up a sleeve and began pumping up a vein. Shannon looked away.

CHAPTER 23

David came to the set often, but Shannon rarely spoke with him. Andy was nearly always there, which made her feel awkward. David had made it clear from the start that he was attracted to Shannon, and she could hardly encourage him in the presence of the man she was living with. But even when Andy was gone, she felt intensely uncomfortable around David. He was different from the people she was used to now—different from the person she had become.

He would stand on the sidelines, well out of the way of the crew and especially Ryan, whom he clearly disliked. As Shannon went through her scenes, he watched, fascinated, his clear blue eyes looking at her in a way that no one had done in a very long time.

One morning when Shannon finished shooting early he came to her dressing room as she was removing her makeup.

"I checked. You have a whole free day, for a change," he began easily, watching her as she used cream to remove the heavy makeup. "What are you going to do with it?"

"I don't know. I haven't had so much free time since we started shooting. Ryan seems to go by the theory that the leading lady should be on hand all day every day just in case he decides to change the script."

David's eyes were twinkling as he said wryly, "Ryan's a real funny guy. Goes on and on about how much coke he takes. I told him he'd better start usin' the diet stuff if he didn't want to gain weight, and he just looked at me for about a minute. Walked away with a real funny expression on his face."

Shannon burst out laughing. At that moment she knew she was going to spend the day with him.

An hour later they were passing Malibu Civic Center in Shannon's Corvette, under the huge, old-fashioned castle on the bluff that some imaginative entrepreneur had built. With round towers and narrow slits for windows, crowned with turrets, it would have looked like a spectacle out of Arthurian legend if it hadn't overlooked ranks of condominiums, fast-food outlets, and the row of expensive beach-front bungalows on the sand.

"What is *that* supposed to be?" David asked.

"I'm not sure," Shannon smiled. "I know it's crazy, but I like it. I call it Camelot. Sometimes I'm tempted to buy it and lock myself in there. Like Guenevere."

"Guenevere had her own problems," David chuckled. He frowned. "The question is, what do you want to run away from?" She realized it was not a question, but a challenge to open herself up to him. But she was unable to. She was beset by a growing uneasiness: it had nothing to do with his presence, but the presence of a gram and a half of coke in her purse. To take her mind off it, she began to tell him about her family, and the history of the house her grandmother built, which she was taking him to visit.

They arrived at the old house. As Shannon unlocked the door her hand shook slightly. Coming home always affected her this way. She had spent little time at the beach house since moving in with Andy. Somehow the pliant, peaceful qualities of the house were at odds with the person she'd become. She had come to feel that she had betrayed the house and what it represented.

But today was different. David was by her side as she walked in and Shannon, joyfully, was struck by the old sensations. Collectively they amounted to an almost tangible sense of the past, a feeling that people had lived and loved and died here, a reassuring feeling of continuity. David frowned, then seemed to relax, and Shannon knew that he sensed something special about the place too.

Slowly, with great pride, Shannon took David through the house, pointing out the mementos left by her parents and grandparents. In the study he looked carefully at a framed photograph of Maggie and Ben Montgomery on the set of her last movie. Next to it was the letter Maggie had framed—the letter that Ben Montgomery had written to Michael and that Michael had sent to Shannon just before he died. Written in a bold, heavy script, it read:

> Eidyn, Wales
> April 12, 1936

Dear son:

I am sitting before a blazing fire at this small inn where we are lodged, listening to a storm pound the coast. Weather has delayed construction on the Camelot exteriors for two days now, and left all of us sitting on our hands. It is wasteful and frustrating. Still, it has given me time to think.

My thoughts turned to you in particular because of a near tragedy we witnessed here yesterday. The gale broke suddenly, catching the Eidyn fishermen at sea. These Welsh are a sturdy people, brooding and seawise, and I realized something was terribly amiss when I saw the alarm in the faces of the wives and the old men ashore. The innkeeper here told me it would be a race for the boats to reach the breakwater before the seas became too heavy on the incoming tide to safely navigate the inlet. The whole town, we visitors included, climbed to a promontory from which we could see some distance seaward. It was going on evening and I cannot describe the fury of the gale.

To abbreviate the story, all of the boats made it safely to harbor except one. Lagging far behind the others, this captain was confronted by a terrible dilemma: either try to wait out the storm at sea, or attempt to put his boat through the narrow neck between the breakwater and the rocky bluffs at the head of the inlet. For a time he chose to put about, reefing his sails and heading into the wind, hoping that the gale would abate. But the storm only increased in ferocity. The seas became towering, and each time the little boat vanished in the troughs we on the promontory held our breaths.

For two hours the drama continued. Finally, realizing that the gale was far from abating, the captain made the crucial decision: to try to run the channel. He tacked wide to the north, judged his angle, and then bravely came about, putting the full fury of the wind at his stern. Again we held our breaths as the sea lifted the tiny vessel like a leaf on a torrent and brought it hurtling down on the mouth of the narrow channel. The moment of truth passed quickly; the captain had judged rightly and his boat slipped safely between the rocky teeth of the headland and the barrier of the breakwater. We all sent up a cheer.

I recount this adventure to you, Michael, because it seems to me that men and women are often tested in this life; if not always so dramatically as this captain, certainly as profoundly. The captain, whom I met later, is a fine man of strong character, which shows in his face and his manner of speech. And that is the way of things, Michael; those of us who are tested to the limit, and survive with courage and dignity, are fortified and emboldened by the experience. That is what I wanted to say to you while it was fresh in my mind.

The wireless forecasts clear skies tomorrow, and with good weather we will return to our task. Wales is a fine, brooding place, given to producing actors, poets, and other madmen, and I hope you will experience it one day.

With affection, as always,

Your father

"He must have been a very special man," David said quietly.

"Yes. My father always spoke of him as if he were the greatest man who ever lived. I think he spent his life trying to live up to his example."

"Then your father must have been pretty special, too."

"Oh, he *was*," Shannon responded proudly. Abruptly, she fell silent. *What would he think of me now?* she wondered sadly.

David, sensing that something had disturbed Shannon, said quickly, "Hey, what about that swim? I can't go back to the hills and tell people I didn't even set foot in the Pacific Ocean."

"Okay."

A few minutes later they were on the beach. David looked definitely odd in an old pair of Michael's swim trunks that were at least a size too large, but he took Shannon's teasing good-naturedly. And when he came up sputtering a few minutes later after being surprised by a good-sized wave, Shannon, still sitting on the beach, laughingly shouted, "Amateur!"

David, grinning wickedly, came out of the water, ran to Shannon and, picking her up easily, tossed her into the water. They played all afternoon until finally, exhausted and hungry, they went back into the house. While David showered and changed in Shannon's old room, Shannon did the same in her parents' room. While she was alone she began to think about the cocaine stashed in her purse. She stood rigidly for a few seconds, summoning her will, determined not to give in to the urge to rely on the drug. Then she quickly finished dressing.

Together they shopped at the Colony Market for some ribs that David swore he could barbecue "Texas style."

By nightfall they were sitting in the living room in front of a fire expertly built by David, feeling sated and exhausted. Sunset had brought an abrupt drop in temperature and the fire was cozy and pleasant. Shannon was lying on the sofa, watching the dancing flames, while David poured them each another glass of deep red wine.

"This place reminds me of where I live, in a way," he said softly. "There's a kind of peaceful feeling here."

"Where *do* you live, David?"

"The town's called Three Rivers, in the foothills up north. That cabin I was telling you about is up on the middle fork of the Kaweah River. A buddy of mine owned the land and I helped him build it a couple or three years back." He smiled. "It's got a big ol' granite stone fireplace in the living room, and we hauled every one of those rocks up from the river. The Coors people must have made a fortune off of us that year." He nodded with satisfaction. "I'm buying the place this year."

Shannon smiled, picturing David and his friends laughing and working and drinking beer.

"You know, your whole face changes when you smile," he said intently. "It's like a shadow leaves you."

He was sitting close to her now, his face barely inches from hers.

"I'll bet you used to look that way all the time."

She was watching him out of frightened, desperate eyes, unable to move or speak. She had known this moment must come sooner or later, and she had both feared and longed for it. As she lay on the sofa, watching him expectantly, her breath coming fast, he leaned toward her. Pushing back the strand of hair that covered her cheek, his finger touched her lightly and she felt herself shiver at the rough, masculine feel of it.

Bending over her, he kissed her, softly once, then deeper, his hands bringing her face up to meet his. There was barely restrained passion in his touch, but also infinite tenderness, and Shannon felt herself open up as she never had before.

Then, as suddenly as it began, it ended. David pulled away, leaving Shannon shaken, her body and mind in turmoil.

"I won't take you like this," he said roughly, "when you still belong to Andy." He was breathing hard. "Leave him and come with me! He's bad for you, Shannon, and you know it."

"You don't understand," Shannon began hesitantly. But she didn't know how to explain.

"I won't let you go. You can go back to him tonight but I'll be there tomorrow and the day after and the day after that. I love you, Shannon. I've loved you since the first time I heard your voice singing the words I thought I had written to no one. I realized then I had written them to you without even knowing you."

"David . . ."

"You're going to be my wife and have my children and sing my songs forever. I won't let it happen any other way."

Later, as she lay in bed beside Andy, whose sleep was just short of a heroin-induced coma, she remembered David's words, and she cried softly.

The shooting was almost over. Everyone was working so frantically to finish on time and under budget that Shannon had almost no time alone with David. He came to the set every day now, watching Shannon constantly, patiently. She knew he was waiting for her as he promised. Andy was too strung out to notice, but Mark wasn't so blind. Shannon could tell by the way he looked at both her and David that he realized something was happening. She knew he would not approve; a lot of money was tied up in the team of Andy and Shannon. And she also understood dimly that Mark was satisfied that Andy had her if he could not: because he controlled Andy, and through Andy, herself. She realized with some alarm that Mark would not stand idly by, but she didn't know just how far he would go.

She found out dramatically the night the picture finished shooting.

They were at a wrap party at Mark's, everyone connected with the film, including David who tried all evening to get Shannon alone. But Andy always seemed to be around. Finally, when Mark took Andy off for a private conversation, Shannon looked for David. The sound track from the movie was playing loudly over Mark's elaborate stereo system, and people were talking and laughing over the music. The noise and crowded confusion made it difficult for Shannon to find David and when she eventually saw him impatiently answering a journalist's questions in a corner she breathed a deep sigh of relief. She badly needed to talk to him, to be reassured by him.

David looked up, saw her, and started to rise. And just then Andy came up to her.

"We're going." His voice was cold, authoritative. Shannon knew that tone and knew that it was no time to disobey him. *When we get home*, she thought, *I'll tell him that I'm leaving.*

Andy was utterly silent on the ride home, and Shannon wondered what Mark had discussed with him that was bothering him so much.

When they walked into the house, Andy suddenly said quietly, "Let's have some coke, babe."

"Andy, I need to talk to you," Shannon began firmly, as he led her up to their bedroom.

"Okay, but let's have some coke first. Just a little, to make the talkin' easier, y'know."

Taking some powder from a black enamel box in the top drawer of his dresser, he handed it to Shannon along with a small tube. She hesitated. Since the day at the beach she had been forcing herself to taper off.

"C'mon, just a little. Then I'll listen to whatever you have to say."

The white powder was tempting. And if it would make him listen to her . . . "All right."

She snorted the powder. Within seconds she felt a huge bubble of air swelling inside her mind, the room blurred, and she floated gently into unconsciousness.

She came to several minutes later, feeling relaxed and happy, empty of the tension that had been building inside her for so long. Andy was watching her quizzically. As she looked up at him, he asked matter-of-factly, "How'd you like your first taste of smack?"

Heroin. The knowledge penetrated slowly. He'd given her heroin. Tina's words on the last afternoon they'd spent together came floating back to her. *"No pain . . . that's what it's all about."* Now Shannon understood.

But Andy was shouting at her. "Mark told me about you and Delaney. You little bitch, running off to your beach house with him behind my back. Well, I'll bet he can't give you what I just did. And I'll bet he can't give you *this*."

What followed was a nightmare in slow motion. He tore her clothes off, ripping them savagely. The numbness in her mind made his movements seem enlarged, almost burlesque. Instinctively she made a vague effort to resist. He slapped her, his hand seeming to descend on her face like a cloud, then abruptly snapping her head back. He raped her brutally, turning her over to enter her from behind, debasing her in a way she'd never experienced before. The room spun and she heard herself crying out as he lunged into her again and again. When he was through she lay there in dull pain, unable to do more than close her eyes as he prepared a syringe and reached for her arm.

CHAPTER 24

Four days after the wrap party Shannon sent David a short letter telling him she didn't want to see him again. Then she and Andy left for an extended vacation in Mexico. It was easier that way—she didn't have to refuse David's persistent phone calls or risk having him see her. When they returned she learned that he had gone back to his house up north.

Six weeks into the editing of the movie, Mark announced his plans to promote it.

"We'll have a free concert. It hasn't been done, really, since Altamont. Andy, you and Shannon will headline, and the other performers from the movie will appear. I've already talked to them, and it's all arranged. It'll be the biggest event of the '70s."

He could barely control the excitement in his voice, and Shannon, who along with Andy was sitting in his office listening to him, thought he seemed almost obsessed with his idea.

"We'll get film on it and use that to promote the movie as well. A million people will go to the concert and a hundred times that many will go to see the movie that inpired it."

Andy jumped at the suggestion. "Where will it be held?" he asked, excited.

"We'll use the American Universal acreage out near

Palmdale. It will make Woodstock seem like a country fair. And we'll open the movie a week afterwards."

All Shannon could think about as she and Andy drove home was the fact that it meant another live performance in a circus atmosphere. She had been shooting a fourth of a gram of heroin a day, but the thought of the concert drove her up to a third of a gram.

David had called. One of the servants had taken the message and left it on Shannon's desk in her bedroom. The slip had David's name, a Los Angeles phone number, and the simple request, "Call if you've changed your mind. I haven't."

Andy was gone that night, and Shannon paced the house alone, tormented by the knowledge that David was only a phone call away. She stayed up all night, not touching the new, unopened polyethylene bag of heroin that Andy had left for her. Finally, toward morning, when she felt the craving growing more intense, she opened the bag. And as soon as she injected it, she knew something was wrong.

The same thing that happened to Tina, she thought, terrified. Vividly she recalled the way Tina had looked that night, slumped in a chair, the syringe still hanging out of her arm. Bad heroin, mixed with strychnine . . . Shannon knew she would be dead soon if she didn't do something. Suddenly something snapped inside her. For the first time in three months she felt that she wanted to live.

Weakly, her hand shaking almost uncontrollably, she dialed the number. When he answered, his voice tired and thick with sleep, she said desperately, "David, I need you . . ."

Shannon spent two weeks in the hospital, going through withdrawal. Her skin started to crawl, her nose ran, her stomach muscles were constricted by agonizing cramps. Vomiting, fever, and horrible delusions followed. Through it all, the hideous journey back to a sane world, David was with her, holding her, comforting her, never turning away. And in the worst moments it was his voice that pulled her through, whispering, "I've been there, sweetheart. If I can make it, you can."

No one, with the exception of David, was allowed access to her during the withdrawal period, and when it was over he took her to the hills, to his cabin, where she would not be disturbed.

It was everything he had said it was, built on a plateau overlooking a giant river canyon. She paused on the pine-log porch, and the vaulting panorama, the tumbling rapids of the river thousands of feet below, the densely forested chasm, the high, snowcapped peaks of the Great Western Divide, took her breath away. It was a warm spring day and hummingbirds attended feeders suspended from the porch rafters. She felt a deep sense of peace settle over her, a peace that had much in common with the contentment she'd often felt at Malibu, in her grandmother's house.

In the days that followed Shannon did little but sleep and read, listening to the songs David was working on and eating the huge meals he prepared. She was building up her strength, both physically and emotionally, waiting for the moment that she looked forward to nervously—the moment when she would be ready for him.

But there was an ominous presence in the cabin also, one that was acknowledged by neither David nor Shannon. It was a composite presence, made up of elements of her life before: Andy, Mark Lendt, the drugs, all of the plans and issues that remained unresolved. It would have to be dealt with in time, she knew, but for the moment she and David were content to pretend that the idyll they were living had sprung whole from nothing; that there were no perilous tendrils trailing into a past life.

One night, when they had been at the cabin for about a week, David said gently but firmly, "Tell me what happened."

She shook her head. "No, I don't want to talk about it."

But he insisted. "You were going to leave him. Why did you change your mind?"

She stared into the fireplace, the big stone fireplace on which David and his friends had labored so lovingly. She forced herself to remember, and now, looking back objectively, she understood the depth of savagery Andy had surrendered himself to. By the time she finished recalling the events to David, her own behavior had taken on the dimensions of a giant riddle. Why had she submitted to the destructiveness, and not only submitted, actively sought it out? She could not explain it, except that it was akin to walking a precipice and battling the urge to drop into the consuming emptiness. And, staring into the fire, she knew that the demon that had driven her to the edge of the cliff had not yet been vanquished.

David held her closely, and she could feel the rage within him. "They'll never hurt you again, Shannon, I promise you that. The bastards will never hurt you again," he said softly.

And she knew that within his power to prevent it, they would not. But it was not Lendt or Andy who posed the danger. The danger, she realized, lay within herself.

Shannon's health and spirits improved each day. The combination of sturdy food and the crisp, pine-scented mountain air brought her around rapidly. They began to go for long walks in the mornings, which rapidly developed into full-fledged hikes up and down the river canyon and into the heavy timber above, which left her exhausted and ravenously hungry. And one day she knew she was ready.

The problem was how to let David know. Finally, while reading his copy of a book of John Donne's poems, she decided what to do.

David was sitting in the living room, putting the finishing touches on a crackling fire in the fireplace, when Shannon walked in wearing a lacy silk robe that clung to her body, outlining her full breasts and slim hips. It was slit in front, and as she walked it parted to reveal her bare legs up to the middle of her thighs. David looked at her appreciatively, his eyes betraying frank desire.

Shannon sat down on the carpet in front of the fire next to him, and said softly, "I've been reading your copy of Donne. I was wondering if—if you'd read one of his poems aloud to me."

She held out the book, already opened to the correct page, and he took it slowly. When he saw the title, "Elegie 19: To His Mistris Going To Bed," he looked up at her with a mixture of amusement and excitement.

He began reading in a curiously husky voice, "Come, Madam, come, all rest my powers defie," and when he came to the line, "Your gown going off, such beautious state reveals," his hand reached out and began slowly unbuttoning her robe as he read.

"License my roving hands, and let them go,
Before, behind, between, above, below.
O my America! my new-found-land,
My kingdome, safeliest when with one man man'd,

My Myne of precious stones, My Emperie,
How blest am I in this discovering thee!
To enter in these bonds, is to be free;
Then where my hand is set, my seal shall be."

He stopped, laying the book aside. Her robe was open now and his eyes roamed freely over her round, firm breasts, past her hips, to the red-gold hair below. Slowly, carefully, he slipped the robe off her shoulders, leaving her body naked and glowing in the firelight. With hands that were both sure and gentle he began to explore her, running his fingers over the hollows and curves, brushing his lips across her skin lightly, making it tingle. She lay back, putting herself completely in his power, knowing he wouldn't abuse her as Andy had.

With infinite patience and skill he awakened the raw passion in her, the passion that she had viewed before as violent and degrading. But with him it was combined with love, and it became a magical thing that brought them together in the most powerful of unions. This was the final thing she had needed to learn—that it could be both lusty and good, a thing of beauty and not just physical satisfaction.

Sensing that he would bring her to an orgasm shortly, she stopped him, then began undressing him. His blue eyes watched her, pleased at her eagerness and tolerant of her awkwardness. She knew that she had a great deal to learn about the ways a man and woman can bring pleasure to each other, but she also knew that with David she would learn them all.

They were together now, skin against skin, lips touching, exploring, taking possession of each other.

"Where my hand is set, my seal shall be," David repeated softly, running his hands down the full length of her body. She breathed a long sigh of contentment as her body melted under his touch. Gently but possessively he traced the outline of her breasts, waist, and hips, then buried his face in her breasts like a sucking baby. His mouth tasted her hungrily; his tongue, soft and moist and whip-like, explored the mounds and hollows of her body.

When she thought she could bear the waiting no longer, he entered her, and they rode the night together.

* * *

In the morning David had to go into town on business. He asked Shannon to go with him, but she was curiously eager to clean the long-neglected house thoroughly.

"All right, stay here if you really want to," David relented, kissing her forehead as he left. "Use the time to decide if you want to be married here or in Malibu." He grinned at her expression. "Either one's okay with me. I figure the Delaney family will be spending a lot of time in both places."

"David!" Shannon was almost unbearably happy. But before she could say another word he was gone, leaving her open-mouthed and radiant.

An hour or so later, as she was straightening David's work table, she glanced out the window. A long Mercedes limousine was throwing up a trail of dust on the one-lane road that snaked up the canyon. Her mind noted how incongruous the big car looked on the mountain road, but an icy ball of fear had settled in her stomach. It couldn't be Andy; she knew Andy would never be able to handle the kind of scene he would be inviting by coming to David's. Only one person would be able to handle something like that.

She met Mark on the porch, not wanting him inside the cabin. He glanced around. "Where's David?"

"He won't be gone long. What do you want?"

His eyes roamed over the cabin with a wry tolerance. "I see. All quite rustic. But this foolishness has gone on long enough. I've been patient for three weeks—"

"I'm not going back with you, Mark," she said tensely.

He ignored her. "The concert is tonight, Shannon. I've come to take you to it. If you don't come with me, you'll be in breach. And when I finish with you, you won't have any choice about living in a shack. I promise."

"I don't care. I'm not going." She was feeling stronger by the moment. Somehow she had feared he would have carried some spectre with him from that other world, the demon of chaos and lust which had mated once so destructively with her own. But Mark was merely waving lawsuits at her, meaningless threats which even if realized could never touch what she'd found with David.

Mark's brown eyes shadowed. He waved vaguely at the cabin, a dismissing gesture that seemed to take in the surrounding mountains and forest. "Shannon, this isn't for you. It's really not," he said. "I think you realize that you have an unstable core. You really can't help what you are and if you try you're going to bring yourself, and David, a lot of unhappiness."

"I'll take my chances," Shannon said. "Now I want you to leave. We'll see enough of each other in court."

"We're not going to court, Shannon," he said confidently. "I was hoping you'd listen to reason, but I suppose that was quite a lot to expect of Brendan Montgomery's bastard daughter."

The mountains seemed utterly still for a moment. Her heart seemed to go dead. "That's a lie," she said. But there was no confidence in her voice. His words had struck her with all the force of long-suspected truth. The resemblance between herself and her uncle, down to an identical cleft in the chin, her almost fanatical devotion to Michael because somewhere deep inside her was the fear that she would lose him, because he wasn't really hers . . .

"It's not a lie, Shannon. And I think you know that it's not. Your mother became pregnant with you by a psychopathic introvert who generally preferred his own sex."

She recoiled from his words. "How can you know? You can't prove that!" Her breath was coming in gasps as a nameless panic threatened to engulf her.

He shrugged. "Not absolutely. But I think I can make a convincing argument. Come with me."

He led her from the porch to the waiting car. From his briefcase he took a large envelope. "There are photographs in here, Shannon. They date back to the time Laura Hampton was employed by my father. They demonstrate rather conclusively just how attracted your mother was to Brendan. Frankly, I don't think you should look at them. But if you still doubt what I'm telling you . . ."

Shannon stared at the envelope. Mark was playing no game, she could see it in his eyes. She knew what she would find, even before she slowly reached for the envelope. But she had to know. She began to open the flap, her legs barely able to support her.

"I think you'll have to agree now, Shannon," Mark smiled. "You don't really belong with David Delaney."

The lighting men had started erecting the huge scaffolding and setting up the massive stage the night before the concert. Forklifts brought in a powerful 10,000-watt PA system. The generators and arc lights buzzed like giant bees, while wave after wave of people surged into the vast, flat field that normally was grazing land for livestock, some of them having been camped at the gate for days. Mark had promoted the concert well. A quarter of a million people were there by early afternoon, a half-million by nightfall.

And they kept coming, an onrush that exceeded anyone's wildest expectations, or the preparations that had been made for them. By the time Shannon arrived by chartered helicopter from the Palmdale airport, it was beginning to get out of control. Narcotics were circulating freely in the crowd, and sanitary facilities were overrun. Food and drink concessions had been overturned and looted, and the crowd had begun to chant demands for the show to begin, a deafening roar from hundreds of thousands of voices that made the ground tremble. As the helicopter dipped low over the throng, Mark paled at the spectacle. "Jesus Christ," he said softly. "We did it." Shannon stared down numbly; in her mind the crowd took on the proportions of a great, ravenous beast. It would devour her, she knew. And she was ready.

As soon as the helicopter touched down Mark ordered the first acts on stage ahead of schedule to quiet the crowd. But it had the opposite effect; when the first group began performing, the crowd surged forward, only to be beaten back with excessive force by the frightened, understaffed cordon of uniformed security guards. And the violence was contagious. Fights broke out over anything: women, drugs, territory. People lashed out with bottles, knives, rocks, anything they could lay their hands on, the screams and curses swallowed up by the driving rhythms blasting out over the behemoth loudspeakers.

Behind the stage, Andy watched, fascinated, energized by the sea of faces and the violence, waiting impatiently to go on. He barely noticed Shannon, who hadn't said a word since arriving. She stood transfixed, unable to believe what she was seeing. And then it was time for her and Andy to go on. As he pulled her onto the stage with him, she heard the crowd roar and press even closer. This was what they had come for.

Andy began singing, with an intensity and power that Shannon had never seen before, while she stood mutely next to him. And as he teased the audience, consciously working them up into a desperate fever, they began to shed their clothes, crawling toward the stage as if offering themselves as human sacrifices to an insatiable god. The guards beat them back, but the more they were beaten, the more they seemed compelled to return.

Shannon, horrified, didn't notice that a second helicopter was speeding in over the crowd to land somewhere behind the stage. She was too busy staring, hypnotized, at Andy. *He's the devil and they're his disciples*, she thought, terrified. *And it can only end in death.*

Immediately in front of the stage, two young men began to fight, and one pulled a gun. Before the guards could get to them, one young man was dead, his chest a bloody gaping wound. As the guards wrestled with the killer, his gun went off again and a young girl crumpled. She fell to the ground and didn't move. All the while, Andy continued to play to the carnage.

"Shannon!"

The voice came from behind her. She whirled around, brought out of her zombie-like trance by the familiar voice. David was crossing the stage, striding purposefully toward her. She started to run to him but Andy, seeing what was happening, stopped her, holding her arm tightly. At the same time, Mark ordered a guard to stop David. The man came after David with a billy club, swinging it viciously. Quickly, in one smooth movement, David ducked the club, then came up smashing the guard's face with a forearm. Wrenching away from Andy, Shannon ran to David.

"David, oh David!" she sobbed.

He held her tightly for a moment, then started to lead her back to the rear of the stage. Andy seemed torn; he wavered as David led Shannon away. But the crowd was hurling a solid wave of sound toward the stage, a chilling primitive demand that their appetite be fed. Andy turned and screamed into the microphone. For one incredible moment all sound died away.

In that unreal vacuum, Shannon and David came face to face with Mark Lendt, standing between them and the helicopter, which David had left idling behind the stage. The expression on Mark's face was murderous, and Shannon felt her blood run cold as she faced him.

"You can't do this, Delaney," he shouted furiously. "I'll ruin you in this business!"

"You can take your business and shove it," David responded, grabbing him and shoving him against the base of a scaffolding. "And if you ever mess with me or Shannon again, I swear I'll kill you." His voice was cold, forbidding, completely unlike any tone Shannon had heard him use before. She knew that he meant what he said—he would kill Mark. And she could read in Mark's eyes his naked fear of David. *He knows it, too*, she realized. *He's afraid of David. And I don't have to be afraid of Mark any more.*

Suddenly, Andy launched into a number and the crowd roared its approval, the enormous sound becoming a terrible, living thing.

But a moment later Shannon and David were aboard the helicopter and lifting away, higher and higher, dwarfing the monster as they climbed into the night.

EPILOGUE

They were married in the house that Maggie Montgomery had built half a century before, on the sea at Malibu. Shannon now accepted that Brendan was her father, that it was Brendan's blood in her veins. But her spirit belonged to Michael, who had cherished her, reflecting the endless hours he'd spent with her and the lessons he taught her.

Michael, she realized, had been endowed with those same qualities by his own father, Ben Montgomery. She paused in the study a moment to make fresh in her mind Montgomery's words to his son. The formal language of the letter gave her an impression of a reserved, rather stern man whose capacity for expression would never equal the depth of his emotion. She found the line she was searching for: *"And that is the way of things, Michael; those of us who are tested to the limit, and survive with courage and dignity, are fortified and emboldened by the experience."*

As Shannon and David drove away, headed for his cabin in the hills and a long honeymoon, Shannon looked back at the Colony house. Her grandfather had been right, she thought. Events had dictated that three generations of Montgomerys be tested to the limit, each in its own way. By dint of courage and dignity their blood had survived, and she was its product. Somehow she felt as though a journey through a long tunnel was ending, a journey that had begun years and lives before her own. And she was emerging into the light.

Special Preview

THE HOLLYWOOD ZOO

by Jackie Collins

The following is an excerpt edited from the first chapters of THE HOLLYWOOD ZOO,* a high-tension novel about the ordinary and extraordinary people of the movie industry. Jackie Collins, the younger sister of actress Joan Collins, writes with authority, revealing a world she knows from the inside. THE HOLLYWOOD ZOO, published by Pinnacle Books, on sale wherever paperbacks are sold.

**Copyright © 1971 by Jackie Collins*

The woman caressed the man beneath her, and in return his hands stroked her arched naked back.

She was beautiful in an unconventional sense. Long wild hair, framing a tanned, almost animalistic, face. Eyes a mixture of brown and yellow. Mouth wide and sensual.

They lay on a bed with black silk sheets, one sheet covering the woman just below her waist. She had a marvelous body, a combination of long limbs, curves, and fine muscles.

She sighed and bent to kiss the man. He was also naked. A brown hard body with hairs on his chest and the back of his hands.

As they kissed, she reached down to the floor and from under the bed produced a small gun which she stealthily brought up to his head.

Ending the kiss, she whispered, "Goodbye, Mr. Fountain."

In one quick movement he threw her off him and twisted the gun from her hand.

Furious, she crouched on the floor, glaring at him.

He laughed. "Better luck next time, baby, you're not dealing with a Boy Scout."

She brought up her arm to try to strike him, and a voice shouted "Cut."

Sunday Simmons's hands flew to cover herself, and a wardrobe lady appeared and threw a robe around her.

Abe Stein, the director, strolled over. He was fat, and chewing on an ancient, stinking cigar. He spoke to the man lying on the bed. "Sorry, Jack, too much tit."

Jack Milan grinned. He was a well-preserved forty-nine, with jet black hair and a smile that had kept him hot at the box-office for twenty years. "There's never too much tit for me, Abe old boy."

Everyone within earshot laughed, except Sunday, who huddled miserably on the floor, clutching the robe around her.

Why had she ever agreed to do this film? In Italy, in fact, in most European countries, she was regarded as almost a star; and here in Hollywood, she was treated as a nothing.

Abe addressed himself to her. "Look, honey, I know you got a gorgeous pair of boobs there, but just keep them pointed at Mr. Milan, huh?"

"I'm sorry," Sunday said stiffly. "When he throws me to the floor it is very difficult. Perhaps if you let me wear some sort of covering, as I wanted to . . ."

"No, those things look worse than nothing." He was referring to "pasties," which some female stars insisted on wearing in nude scenes. They were round flesh-colored pads which stuck over the nipples. Sunday had asked to wear them, but her contract for the film stipulated that she had to do what the film company wanted, and they wanted no pasties. So here she was, exposed except for a brief pair of panties to the entire unit, which seemed to have doubled itself on this day.

She dreaded having to remove the robe again.

As if reading her thoughts, Abe said, "Get on the bed, let me show you what I mean. Do you mind, Jack? Shall I get your stand-in?"

"Do I mind? Just get me a Scotch and a cigarette and I'll shoot this scene all day!"

More laughter, and Sunday reluctantly took off her robe. She tried not to care, she tried to blank out the grinning faces watching her.

She got on the bed, partly under the sheets, and half lying across Jack Milan.

"Now let's take it in slow motion," Abe said. "Show me how you throw her off you."

Jack's strong arms lifted her slowly and edged her

sideways. Abe's fat arms brushed across her until both men were holding her.

"Try to keep her toward you like this," Abe said. "That's it, marvelous. Now on the floor, dear, when you go to hit him, just make sure your back is to the camera. Like this."

Once more he handled her body, and this time she was sure his fat hands didn't slide across her breasts by accident.

"We'll break for lunch now." He turned to Jack Milan, who climbed out of the bed, wearing orange jockey shorts and matching socks. "Everyone back by two P.M. sharp. Come on, Jack, I'll buy you that Scotch."

Sunday walked slowly to her dressing room. She was close to tears. It was so humiliating to be treated like this. She had thought a Jack Milan film would be a good thing to do, but she had turned out to be just another girl in a multi-girl spy film. She had been so anxious to leave Rome that she had hardly even looked at the script. And she had wanted to see Hollywood; the nearest she had been before was Rio, where she had been born.

Sunday had had a happy childhood. Her father was South American and her mother French, and the two nationalities were very compatible.

By the time she was sixteen, she had decided to be an actress, and she persuaded her parents to send her to a dramatic academy in London. It was the best, and arrangements were made for Sunday to stay in London with her mother's elder sister, Aunt Jasmin. Of course, she was to return to Rio for all vacations, and immediately if she didn't care for England.

It didn't make any difference whether she cared for it or not. Her parents were killed in a car crash two days after she left.

Sunday was heartbroken. She kept on blaming herself, reasoning that if she had been there, it might not have happened.

Her father left hardly any money at all. Generous, he

had lived big, spending and lending in every direction.

After the funeral, Sunday decided to stay in London and continue her studies. She had a few thousand pounds left to her by her mother.

It was a far different life for Sunday to adjust to. A small flat in Kensington, the cold weather, and Aunt Jasmin who thought it a sin to show any affection.

Sunday found this strange and disturbing. She *needed* love and affection, and it seemed there was no one she could turn to.

She threw herself into her work at the academy.

One day after she had been there a year and a half, she met Raf Souza.

Raf was a dynamic young man, currently the most in-demand fashion photographer and very aware of it. He turned up at the school with three thin models, a hairdresser, a battery of equipment, and three huge dogs.

He had permission to use the interior of the academy for a *Vogue* layout with students in the background.

At that time, Sunday wore her fair flattened down and scraped back. She dressed for the cold, wearing at least three sweaters and baggy trousers. She wore no makeup. However, Raf picked her out immediately, made her loosen her hair, and had her kneeling with the dogs looking up at the three model girls.

Sunday was secretly delighted, but to the other students she pretended it was an awful drag.

When Raf left he handed Sunday his card and said, "If you want to see the pictures, drop around tomorrow about six."

Raf's studio was the wrong end of Fulham Road, and it took Sunday ages to find it. He hardly gave her a glance when she arrived, and threw the contact sheets at her.

She studied them intently. How blank her face looked beside the models. How lumpy she appeared in her loads of sweaters.

"How old are you?" Raf asked casually.

"Nearly seventeen. Why?"

"Just wondered. I had an idea you might be good for. You want to try some test shots?"

"Yes, I'd like to."

"If they're any good it will mean a week abroad plus all expenses paid and a hundred quid."

Raf was no fool. He was getting paid a thousand for the job, and if he took a really good professional model it would dig deeper than a hundred. Anyway he saw a great potential in this girl. That fabulous skin would photograph a million dollars in color, and with the right makeup and hairstyle she would be a knockout.

He was fed up with the usual faces; they almost all looked the same. This little lady could be quite a diversion.

Raf, in his short career, had been to bed with many of the top photographic models, lady editors of magazines, and generally any female who could do him some good. He was stocky, untidy, with a little-boy smile that turned women on.

He tried it now on Sunday. "What do you think? Could you make it with no family problems?"

Sunday thought how nice he was. "Yes, I'm sure I could. Term ends tomorrow, and I didn't have any definite plans."

"Great! Let's get started. You'd better get out of all that gear; I'll give you a shirt to put on. Oh, and take your hair down, it looks terrible scruffed back like that."

Sunday had second thoughts. What sort of pictures did he want to take anyway? She hesitated when he threw her a shirt. He noticed her hesitation. "They're going to be fashion shots, darling, beach jazz and harem gear, I've got to see if you've got a body underneath all that. Get changed upstairs if you like." He busied himself with a camera.

Sunday took the shirt and went upstairs.

She put it on over her bra and panties. It looked quite decent. She loosened her hair and padded quietly downstairs.

Christ! Raf thought, he'd picked a winner this time. The girl was magnificent. She had the most incredible long legs, and he imagined the wild shots he could do with her. Her breasts jutted through the shirt, and she had a special kind of walk. Very, very sexy.

He spent an hour taking photographs. She fell into poses naturally. He couldn't wait to get her out of that shirt. Apart from fancying her, she was going to make this assignment really good.

Arrangements were made, and they went to Morocco.

Raf, who used women purely as a convenience, found himself completely fascinated by Sunday.

Because of the situation with her aunt, Sunday found herself spending more and more time with him. On her seventeenth birthday he made love to her, and shortly afterwards she moved into his studio.

Aunt Jasmin accepted the move as she accepted everything else in life, with tight-lipped silence.

"I'll keep in touch," Sunday promised.

Aunt Jasmin just shrugged her disapproval.

Raf was the first person Sunday had been really close to since her parents died.

They lived together for several months, Sunday finishing her last term at the academy, and Raf getting on with his work. Then the pictures of Sunday in Morocco appeared, and the magazine was inundated with calls wanting to know who she was. There were offers for Sunday to do a hair commercial and a toothpaste commercial, and a film company wanted to test her.

Raf withdrew into a black mood. Sunday was thrilled.

The magazine wanted Raf to arrange another session with Sunday immediately. He talked her out of doing the commercials, although the money was excellent. But she insisted that she wanted to do the film test.

Raf took her to Rome, and while they were taking the photographs she fell in love with the city. It reminded her of Rio.

When they got back she did the part in the film she had tested for.

Raf brooded, extremely jealous about having to share Sunday. For the first time since she came to live with him he had other women, got drunk before she came home, and took to insulting and ridiculing her in front of their friends.

She couldn't understand why Raf had become so bitter toward her. What had she done?

But he couldn't explain how he felt about her success, that he was terrified of losing her.

Sunday did a couple of other small parts, and then the first movie appeared and she received an offer to do a film in Rome.

"Take it," Raf said bitterly, "we're about through anyway." And to settle the matter he told her he had found someone else.

Sunday was quite successful in Rome, appearing in a string of movies that usually showed off her more physical charms.

All thoughts of becoming a "serious actress" were pushed to the back of her mind. She enjoyed the excitement and attention she seemed to create wherever she went.

The Italian men chased after her in full force, but Sunday's thoughts still remained with Raf.

He had been her first man and she had loved him. She had *thought* he loved her.

Then Paulo appeared on the scene. Count Paulo Gennerra Rizzo. He was to bring nothing but trouble.

"Miss Simmons." There was a knock on her dressing-room door. "Miss Simmons, you're wanted on the set please."

Automatically, Sunday checked herself in the mirror and vaguely realized she hadn't had any lunch. Oh well, back to the charming Abe Stein and delightful Jack Milan, who hadn't addressed one word to her. What a way to start one's first day's work in Hollywood.

On the set there was much activity. Word had spread

about the nude scene, and little groups of men whom Sunday hadn't noticed before were dotted around the sidelines. She also noticed several men with cameras who hadn't been there before. Neither Jack Milan nor Abe Stein was present.

A makeup man whom she had argued with that morning approached her. It had been a silly argument as far as Sunday was concerned. She had asked to do her own eye makeup, as she always did, and the man had refused. That annoyed her, as she knew her face a lot better than someone who had merely glanced at her for five minutes. She insisted, and the man stamped out of the room in a fury, muttering about "foreign starlets."

Now he approached her with a cake of makeup and a sponge. He said, "Take your robe off. I've got to check your body makeup."

She glared at the man, who had gathered a bunch of friends to watch the fun. "Where is the woman who did it this morning?" she asked.

"On another set. Don't be bashful; everybody's seen your big tits already!"

Sunday felt her face blaze and she turned to leave the set, bumping into Jack Milan and Abe. "Where are you rushing off to, honey?" Abe asked, gripping her arm with his fleshy hand. "Let's get this scene in the can, come on." He pulled her back to the set.

She had a sudden feeling that she wasn't going to be able to take her robe off in front of this whole group. She said to Abe, "In Italy when we shoot such a scene, the set is cleared until only the essential technicians remain. I would like that done here, please."

"Oh would you?" Abe coughed and spat. "This isn't Italy, honey, and all these guys are needed around here."

Sunday, who rarely lost her temper, was burning now. "In that case you can shoot the scene without me. I am not an animal to be stared at; I am an actress."

"Ha!" Abe snorted. "An actress, huh? One that can't even keep her tits out of the camera. Don't get high-hat with me, baby, you've got a contract, remember?"

"Yes, I am well aware of that. However, I cannot work under these conditions. I'm so sorry."

And with that, Sunday walked off the set.

It was the first time anyone had walked off a Jack Milan movie.